ROAD TO ANTIETAM

ROAD TO
ANTIETAM

A NOVEL

TOM E. HICKLIN

Palmetto Publishing Group
Charleston, SC

Road to Antietam
Copyright © 2018 by Tom E. Hicklin
All rights reserved

First Edition

Printed in the United States

ISBN-13: 978-1-64111-118-8
ISBN-10: 1-64111-118-6

CHAPTER ONE

PICKET DUTY

Private Christopher Galloway of the 8th Ohio Volunteer Infantry stood alone in pitch darkness, looking out on what appeared to be an empty field. It was a moonless night, and he couldn't see anything before him but a flat landscape broken up by darker shapes he hoped were trees or large bushes. Behind him, a woodlot thick with second growth trees separated him from the camp.

Fresh out of training, this was their first night in the field. Christopher had the two-to-four shift for picket duty, which was the worst shift because the enemy could sneak up on you, unseen, and kill you before you could react. Or so he'd heard.

The feelings of isolation and fear reminded him of a hunting trip he'd gone on with his father and brother when he was ten. His first time camping, he did not know how easily he could lose his bearings in the woods at night. It had been a moonless night then as well when he woke needing to pee. Careful not to wake his father or Daniel, he got up and left the camp. When he finished, he turned to go back and realized he didn't know how to retrace his steps. He froze, afraid of going the wrong way. The longer he stood still, the harder it was to breathe, and the heavier his legs became—taking a step suddenly seemed impossible.

The trees seemed to lean over him as they swayed in the wind, the sound of their rustling leaves like beasts pawing the earth. In his mind, every tree and bush hid a bear, or wolf, or worse—an Indian. It didn't matter that there hadn't been a hostile Indian in the area for almost fifty years, or that bears and wolves were nearly extinct. He knew they were out there, waiting to pounce. Christopher turned in circles, looking for any recognizable landscape marker or ferocious attacker. He saw neither.

His father, Jack, found him the next morning, curled up in a fetal position with his thumb in his mouth. Jack carried him back to the camp and set him next to the fire. When he tried to move away to put more wood on the fire, Christopher reached out and grabbed his coattail, shaking his head, his eyes wide and mouth open in a silent scream. Jack sat back down, draped his arm over Christopher's shoulders, and squeezed him tight against his side.

Daniel built up the fire, cooked breakfast, and set a plate of flapjacks at Christopher's feet. He sat down next to his brother but didn't touch him or say anything. He just sat there, poking the fire with a stick.

After several minutes, Christopher's hunger got the best of him. He crawled out from under his father's arm, picked up the plate of flapjacks, and wolfed them down.

"There's my boy," Jack said, patting him on the back.

"Want some more?" Daniel asked.

Christopher nodded and looked up at his father. "I'm sorry, Da. I went to pee and didn't know how to get back."

"No harm done, son. You weren't far from camp. You shoulda just hollered—one of us would have come got ya."

"I was afraid," Christopher whispered.

"Bah, there's nothing to fear in these woods, son. In fact, with me and your brother about, you have nothing to fear from anything."

"That's right," Daniel said, looking him in the eye. "Nothing as long as I'm around."

Now, as Christopher stood in the dark field, he knew Daniel was somewhere nearby on the picket line. Their first time in the woods together in years. And, for the first time in years, Christopher remembered what it felt like to be alone and afraid, conjuring up hostiles behind every bush and tree. Only now they weren't wild animals and Indians, but rebel soldiers.

Despite a chill that settled in as the night progressed, Christopher's collar was wet with sweat, and he ran his finger under it to dry his neck. He wiped his hands on his jacket several times, but they still seemed damp and slippery, and he feared dropping his rifle.

A breeze came through the trees and set the landscape in motion. Christopher's grip on his rifle tightened.

The tension combined with the quiet of the night and lack of sleep took their toll and Christopher started to sway, then jerked upright with a start. He tried marching back and forth, but it didn't help.

Sleep filled his every thought—a sweet surrender from the fatigue, fear, and isolation that enveloped him. But if he slept, he might be killed or captured by the enemy or, if caught, shot by his own side. But worst of all, if they were attacked while he slept, he would be responsible for the destruction of his regiment.

Christopher closed his eyes. *Only for a moment.*

He smiled as he recalled the train ride from Camp Dennison. The men drank, sang, and bragged non-stop for two days. It was his first taste of alcohol and, once he got past the burning sensation, he found he liked it. It made him feel confident and in control.

In every town, people came out to line the tracks and cheer them on. In Zanesville, the citizens had even prepared a feast for the regiment. They were heroes, revered by all.

It was in Zanesville where he'd met Susan—who, unfortunately, bore the same name as that harpy Daniel wanted to marry. Though they only had a short time together, it was full of passionate affection that brought a tear to Christopher's eye. When they parted, she'd given him a silk scarf and an apple pie she had baked herself. The last of the pie was consumed with last night's supper, but the scarf was still in his pocket.

He retrieved the kerchief and ran it through his fingers. Its softness made him think of Susan's hands in his as the train whistle blew and the drumbeat called him away. He held the cloth to his nose, closed his eyes, and breathed in her scent.

They parted with promises to write, and Christopher said he would stop and visit her on his way back from the war. Susan. Sweet Susan. Susan…His eyes flew open. He didn't know her last name. How would they correspond if he didn't have her full name? Angrily, he shoved the scarf back in his pocket.

The realization he'd been stupid enough to leave without getting Susan's full name gave Christopher a brief charge. His thoughts flew from berating his forgetfulness to doubting Susan's intentions of ever writing. But soon, even that couldn't keep his eyelids from drooping and his head from falling down on his chest.

He jerked upright. He would not sleep.

He should have listened to Daniel and slept that afternoon instead of wandering the camp with Ezra, taking in the sights and visiting with the soldiers who'd already been in the field and seen action.

Christopher stamped his feet, shook his head and slapped his cheek. Though against regulations, he unbuttoned the top buttons of his shirt and jacket, hoping the cool air would help keep him alert.

"Well, Chris old boy, your first night in the field," he said aloud. "Somewhere out there are men willing to kill you on sight. And all you can think of is sleep."

Then he saw something move. A jolt of electricity shocked his body. All thoughts of sleep disappeared.

What he thought were bushes appeared to be moving. He brought his rifle up to the ready position and leaned forward, squinting to see better. Even after having plenty of time for his eyes to become accustomed to the dark, he still couldn't make out anything specific in the landscape before him.

There it was again! He was sure now that something had moved. The "bushes" were no longer in the same place.

His rifle was loaded with ball and powder, bayonet fixed, so all it needed was a percussion cap to fire. Christopher reached down, unlatched the cap box on his belt, and reached inside with shaking fingers. He pulled out three caps and dropped one. He tried to put the extra cap back in the box but missed and dropped both the remaining two. Cursing, he reached in again and pulled out a single cap. He brought it up to his rifle, then realized that the hammer was down on the nipple. He had to secure the cap between his fingers before he could pull the hammer back to half cock. In doing so, he dropped that percussion cap.

"Dammit!"

Christopher looked up to see if whatever was moving had gotten closer. His breath caught in his throat when he realized it had. Whatever-or whoever-it was, it/they had covered half the distance to him while he was fumbling to cap his rifle.

Christopher made sure the rifle hammer was half cocked before pulling out another cap. He pushed it onto the nipple before he could drop it.

He brought the rifle butt up to the crook of his shoulder and raised the barrel until it pointed at the ground about five yards before him.

"HALT! Who comes there?" he cried. His voice cracked on the word *halt* and he felt his cheeks burn. He sounded like a frightened child.

No response, but now he had no doubt something was out there. The whole landscape appeared to be moving. What he thought were bushes were growing larger as they approached his position.

"HALT!" he repeated. "Who comes—"

They charged. The ground shook and he heard metal clanging. In his minds eye, the shapes became a line of rebel soldiers, their canteens and tin cups beating against their sides as they ran. They let loose a mournful cry—almost as if they regretted having to kill him.

Christopher raised his rifle and fired without aiming. The mournful cry grew louder, and the din of their many feet stamping the earth was like thunder. He turned and ran. "Corporal of the Guard! Post three! Corporal of the Guard! Post three!" he yelled.

Christopher had gone only a few feet when it occurred to him he should reload his rifle. He looked down while he ran, trying to get a cartridge out of the box hanging on his right side, and ran headlong into Lieutenant Sutton. Behind Sutton stood Sergeant G and Corporal Bunce.

Lieutenant Sutton grabbed Christopher's arms before he toppled over and shook him. "Calm down, private. Did you fire?"

Christopher nodded. "They're coming, sir! They're coming."

"Who's coming, private? Slow down and take a breath. Tell me what you saw."

"No time, sir. They were in the field right in front of me. A regiment, at least."

Without taking his eyes off of Christopher, Lieutenant Sutton barked out orders. "Sergeant Reid, head back to camp. Sound the alarm. Bunce, go on ahead and check the other pickets. If necessary, pull them back. You," he said to Christopher, "better be right."

Bunce and Reid disappeared into the night. Lieutenant Sutton pulled out his pistol and had Christopher reload his rifle. "Cap it off, son, and take me to where you saw the enemy."

Christopher led him back to the clearing. Lieutenant Sutton crouched down and pulled Christopher down with him. To Christopher, it seemed they stayed like that forever, but was just a few minutes. All was quiet in the field.

"Well, private. It would appear you single-handedly scared off a whole regiment."

"It could have just been their skirmish line, sir. Maybe they pulled back to join the main body."

"Maybe." Lieutenant Sutton was quiet for a couple minutes while he thought. Finally, he said, "Let's go back. We'll pull back the picket line and send out our own skirmish line to investigate."

They stood and turned to go when they heard the unmistakable lowing of a cow.

Their eyes locked-Lieutenant Sutton's half-lidded and stern, Christopher's wide as saucers.

"That better not be what I think it is."

"S-Sounds like a cow to me, sir," Christopher squeaked.

Lieutenant Sutton grabbed Christopher by the arm. "Come on, private. Time to charge the enemy."

He pulled Christopher out into the field. As they moved through the high grass, the lowing got louder, and Christopher's cheeks burned hotter with each step. His stomach was in full revolt, and he feared he would lose his supper at any moment.

They came upon five cows, shuffling nervously and lowing in distress. Two of them had large bells hanging from chains around their necks that produced a dull clang if they moved suddenly.

"Apparently, they don't like being shot at," Lieutenant Sutton said.

"No, sir," Christopher responded.

"Shut up, private."

Christopher's head dropped. He couldn't remember ever feeling such shame. He thought he would be sick. His stomach churned and his limbs felt limp. It seemed to take all his strength to stand there in front of Lieutenant Sutton and not run off into the darkness.

"Come on, private. Let's go back." Sutton looked at Christopher. "On second thought, you stay here. We can't leave the picket line unmanned." He turned his attention toward camp. "I just have to decide what to tell Major Sawyer and Captain Daggett."

Right after Lieutenant Sutton left, Christopher heard the drums. The long roll. The 8th's first real call to fall in under arms. Only, it wasn't real. They didn't know that though.

He imagined the men spilling out of their tents in various shades of undress, throwing on belts and cartridge boxes and running to line up. They thought they were about to see the elephant. Instead, all they'd see was a cow. And a fool. They'd get a real good look at a fool tomorrow.

Christopher lifted his head and threw his shoulders back. Under the circumstances, anybody would have done the same thing. Something was out there, and it didn't respond to his commands. What was he to do, walk out and say hello? He still felt nauseous and weak, but he'd be damned if he'd let anyone criticize him for doing his duty.

His shoulders slumped. Who was he kidding?

Christopher grunted with disgust and turned to face the field. The drum roll ended, and he could hear the officers shouting commands.

"Damn me for a fool," he mumbled.

CHAPTER TWO
APRIL 1861

The room was dark—dark wood, dark carpet, and dark leather all barely lit by a single lantern. A pall of smoke hung in the air, making it hard to breathe. Daniel Galloway's nose itched, but he didn't dare scratch or crinkle it. Before him sat the father of the woman he loved. Rich and powerful, Benjamin Johnston was the local prosecutor, and made his living at intimidation.

According to Daniel's father, the Johnston family had made their money in agriculture. They were one of the first families to settle in the part of Ohio called the Firelands. (Congress had given the area to men whose homes were burned down by Tories for supporting the Revolution.) Johnston's father was careful with his money, and when a neighbor fell on hard times, he was quick to buy up the land at the cheapest price possible.

Soon, the Johnstons owned most of the county and could afford a good education for their son. After graduating from Harvard, Benjamin Johnston considered going to New York, or Washington City, but instead he came back to Ohio with his eye on local politics. Johnston started out as a Democrat, but changed to the anti-immigrant American Party—the Know Nothings—in the early 1850s.

In contrast, the Galloways came to Norwalk in the late 1830s, fleeing the poverty and famine in Ireland. Penniless and hungry, they did whatever it took to survive, be it taking in laundry or working twelve hours a day during harvest. A cobbler by trade, Jack Galloway saved enough money to start a shoe shop. His work was good, and that quality eventually overcame prejudice and he thrived. As his business grew, so did his family. By the time the fifth child was born, he could afford a nice home on the edge of town.

Johnston sat still, his eyes lidded, staring at the cigar in his hand as he rolled it back and forth between his fingers and thumb.

"Daniel," he said. "I respect your father, and your family." His fingers stopped. "But I can't allow you to marry my daughter."

Daniel pulled his shoulders back and tried to look the older man in the eye. Despite the sting of Johnston's words and a fear that threatened to immobilize him, he knew from talking to Susan that Benjamin Johnston hated weakness and lack of control. If he let either his anger or his fear show, the man would devour him. He wanted to demand an explanation. Instead, he responded, "All I ask is permission to write Susan while I'm gone. We can talk of marriage later." It was not what he came for, but it would have to do.

Johnston looked up into Daniel's eyes, giving him his best courtroom scowl.

Daniel returned the stare and did not flinch.

"I don't see the point. You are an Irish papist, son," he said. "I would rather die than see any descendant of mine raised in the Catholic Church."

Daniel broke eye contact and looked to the floor. He exhaled sharply as if physically struck. Though the room was cool, a single drop of sweat broke loose from his hairline and ran down his forehead, settling on his brow and threatening to drip into his eye. Still, he dared not flinch.

Johnston let a small smile flicker across his lips. Daniel could see the gleam of victory in his eye.

Daniel raised his eyes. "I would allow Susan to raise our children in any religion she saw fit," he said.

Johnston grunted in disgust.

Sensing his answer did not go over well, Daniel tried to explain. "I'm a Catholic, sir. That is true. But, I think the God I love and worship is the same God you love and worship, and to Him there are many paths as long as it is through Christ. I believe that, even if we attended separate churches, my children, my wife, and I will all be together in the Great Hereafter."

"A pious sermon, son." Johnston smirked. "Have you considered joining the clergy?"

Daniel blushed. "No, sir. In my faith that would preclude my getting married."

Johnston let loose a short guffaw before he caught himself and returned to a scowl.

Johnston turned his gaze toward the door, ignoring Daniel.

Daniel knew the man had wanted to send Susan to school back east, but she'd talked him into allowing her to stay in Norwalk and go to school at Oberlin College. All was fine for a while, but then Johnston found out Susan's real reason for wanting to stay in Norwalk was so she could continue to see Daniel and he'd flown into a rage that lasted for days.

Daniel flinched when Johnston's hand flexed and broke his cigar. Whatever thoughts were going through the man's mind, they were dark.

The silence in the room was becoming unbearable. As nonchalantly as possible, Daniel raised his hand and brushed the sweat off his brow. He fidgeted with his hat and tried to think of something to say. "Sir, I love and respect—"

"Enough!" Johnston slammed his palm on the desk. "You've made your feelings clear. I need not hear it again."

Johnston took a deep breath and blew it out slowly. He let his gaze drift back to the door.

Daniel felt on the verge of panic. Was he trying to tell him to leave? He'd gotten nowhere with the older man. How could he make him understand? Soon he'd be off to war, to face death and deprivation. The thought of leaving without some assurance Susan would still be here when he returned made him physically ill. Daniel dreamed of a triumphant return followed by a grand wedding. He saw it so clearly—her in a flowing white gown and him in his finest uniform, his medals and rank proving to himself, his father, and this man before him that Daniel Galloway was a man of courage and honor, deserving of the hand of the most beautiful woman in the county.

He had to find the right thing to say…

Johnston interrupted his thoughts. "So, you are leaving for the army?"

"Yes, sir. If there is to be war, I intend to do my part."

"There will be war, son. This slavery nonsense needs to be settled once and for all—it's getting out of hand. And now, with South Carolina firing on Fort Sumner…there will be war."

Johnston turned his gaze back to Daniel. "War is a terrible thing, son, nothing but death and destruction. But, from the ashes of that destruction can come glory. Men are broken or made by war, depending on how they comport themselves."

Johnston stood and paced the room, his hands behind his back and his head hung low as if he were thinking. "This may be your chance, not just to serve your country, but to serve yourself. You do well and rise to the challenge, maybe then you will prove yourself worthy of my daughter's hand." He stopped and looked Daniel in the eye.

"But, if you shirk your duty, disgrace yourself, or just be content to get by, then you will prove to me, and hopefully to yourself and Susan, that you are undeserving of such a reward. When this war is over, come back here with a hero's rank and insignia, then we will talk further about you taking— seeing my daughter."

Johnston returned to his seat. He picked up and shuffled through some papers, ignoring Daniel.

Daniel stood with his mouth half open, staring. It was as if the man had been reading his thoughts. He would return a hero and—

"Well, is what I said clear?" Johnston snapped.

"Ye-Yes, sir. It is more than clear."

"Good, go now." Benjamin Johnston stood up and came around the desk. "And once the war is over, come back here and show me what you have done."

"Yes, sir, thank you, sir. I will not let you down." Daniel almost skipped as Benjamin Johnston led him through the door and out into the foyer.

Both men stopped. Halfway up the stairs stood Susan Johnston, small and thin-waisted, wearing a dark gray dress. Her golden hair was parted in the middle and draped over her shoulders in tight ringlets. Daniel could smell her perfume over the cigar stench. She stood as if in mid-step, staring at both men with eager curiosity.

"Susan, it's all right——" Daniel began.

"Susan!" her father interrupted. "Go back to your room. I'll be along shortly and we'll discuss this matter, you and I."

For a moment Susan's eyes moved back and forth between the two men. Then, "Yes, Father." Her eyes lingered briefly on Daniel's before she turned and went back up the stairs.

Daniel knew that Johnston had not missed the brief connection. If the older man had had a gun, Daniel would have feared for his life.

Johnston opened the door and stepped aside to let Daniel pass. A cool, damp April breeze blew into the room. "Remember what we discussed, Daniel. This is your chance to prove yourself. Until you have done so, I expect you to keep your distance."

"I had hoped she would see me off——"

"And I had hoped she'd...I had hoped we had an agreement. Do we?"

"Yes, sir. Of course." Daniel stepped through the door and Johnston closed it behind him.

He stood on the front porch of the Johnston home and let the cool breeze dry the sweat on his brow. As he started for home, he couldn't shake the nagging feeling that, while uncomfortable, his encounter with Benjamin Johnston had gone too easily.

—⋙—

Christopher Galloway ran through the streets of Norwalk toward the train station. The plume of smoke that lingered above the station assured him he wasn't too late.

When he arrived, flushed and out of breath, he saw his whole family waiting on the platform. His father was sucking on a pipe, looking deep in thought as he conversed with Franklin Sawyer, the elected captain of their company. His mother was trying to keep the younger girls, Rebecca and Rachel, entertained with games of pat-a-cake and childish conversation. The older daughter, Elizabeth, fourteen and already showing a streak of precocious rebellion, was twirling her umbrella and eyeing the line of young men standing on the platform waiting to board the train. Daniel was pacing back and forth and, seeing Christopher, stopped and threw up his hands.

"Where have you been? We'll be boarding soon."

"Well, you ain't boarded yet," Christopher shot back.

"You *have not* boarded yet, Christopher. You know better," his mother said without missing a beat of the game of pat-a-cake she was playing with Rachel.

"Yes, Ma." Looking at Daniel, Christopher stuck his nose in the air and said, "You have not boarded yet. Therefore, I am not late."

"Galloway, you're late!"

Christopher's smug expression froze at the sound of Sawyer's voice. Daniel cracked a small smile of victory.

Looking at Mr. Sawyer and his father, Christopher tried to approximate what he thought was an attention stance. "Sir?"

"Everyone was to be on the platform at nine a.m. It is after nine-thirty. Where have you been?"

"I thought the train didn't leave until ten o'clock," Christopher said.

"Doesn't matter when the train leaves. Your orders were to be here at nine o'clock and not a minute later. Do you understand?"

Christopher felt his whole being melting away under the glare of his father and Franklin Sawyer.

"I thought…No one woke me," he mumbled, casting a sidelong glance at his mother.

"Bah," his father burst out in disgust.

"And what about tomorrow? Do you think your mommy will be there to wake you every morning? Your brother?" Sawyer asked. "From this day forward, until you are released from service, Daniel is not your brother. He is not responsible for you or your actions. Not even you are responsible for you. The army now owns you. Is that understood?"

"Yes, sir," Christopher mumbled, trying not to slump, or worse, let a tear slip.

"I suggest you two make your goodbyes and join the line," Sawyer said to Christopher and Daniel. Turning to Jack Galloway, he held out a hand and said, "Jack, I'll see you when this war is over."

Jack Galloway shook Franklin Sawyer's hand. "Thank ye, Frank, for watch'er doin'. Look after me boys, and all three of you come home safe and sound, ya hear?"

Sawyer smiled, tipped his hat, and bowed slightly to Mary Galloway. Then turned and walked to the head of the line.

"Come on, girls," Mary said. "Come say goodbye to your brothers. Elizabeth, get over here and make your goodbyes."

The girls lined up by age and height. Elizabeth looked bored, and the other two tried their best to appear coquettish. Daniel approached each girl and handed her a yellow silk ribbon. "Save this until my return," he promised, "and when I get back, I'll turn it into a pretty dress."

Each of the girls curtsied. Rachel and Rebecca hugged their oldest brother and gave him a kiss on the cheek. Elizabeth held out her hand, which Daniel took and gallantly kissed.

Christopher hesitated, realizing he had nothing to give his sisters. His mother stepped up beside him and slipped three pieces of red ribbon into his hand. He gave her a quick smile of thanks and stepped up to the girls.

"Here you go, girls, that'll be two dresses you'll get at the end of the war."

Rachel and Rebecca each gave him a hug and a kiss. Elizabeth stuck out her hand. Instead of lightly grasping the outstretched hand and kissing it as his brother had, Christopher grabbed it in his right hand and pumped it up and down while chucking her on the shoulder with his other hand. "Don't worry, sis, you'll grow out of this homely phase before you know it."

"Oooh, poo!" Elizabeth stamped her foot. "I hate you, Christopher Galloway!"

"And I love you too, darlin'!"

Mary Galloway stepped away from Daniel and approached Christopher. "You are a brat, young man." There was no anger in her voice. Christopher stopped teasing his sister when he saw the tears in his mother's eyes. His own eyes teared up, and he hugged her, thinking it would never be the same.

"I love you, Ma."

"I love you too, son. Please come back to me. Both of you." She took a hand of each of her sons and gave them a squeeze. Then she turned away, unable to hold her tears in check any longer. The girls gathered around their mother and tried to console her.

After swallowing the lump that had formed in his throat, Christopher turned to his father. He stood up straight and threw his shoulders back as he held his hand out. "Da, I promise to make you proud."

Jack Galloway shook his youngest son's hand and said, "Just do as you're told, do nothing stupid, and you'll be all right."

With that, the Galloway brothers picked up their bags and joined the queue that had just begun boarding the train.

CHAPTER THREE
CAMP DENNISON

The train rumbled through the night on its way south to Camp Dennison, near Cincinnati—hundreds of miles away from the only home Daniel and Christopher Galloway had ever known. The night was cold and rainy, and the men were miserable, crammed into cattle cars for the last leg of the journey. Gaps in the walls allowed the rain to come into the cars in the form of a cold mist, soaking the men's clothing. The smell of wet wool mixed with that of wet hay and the lingering odor of the car's previous occupants.

The first few days of army life had been difficult for the young men raised in a small, quiet town known for its maple trees and private institutions of higher learning. But, after two weeks of training at Fort Taylor in Cleveland, they were used to being quartered with hundreds of other men and immune to the odors and noise.

The bone-chilling wet was a new level of discomfort for the boys. As soon as they got used to whatever deprivation the army threw at them, the generals—the "big-bugs"—would just turn it up a notch. There was still hope though. At least they could warm up when they arrived at their destination.

To pass the time, Daniel thought of Susan Johnston. They had had so few opportunities to be together, but on those rare occasions, he'd felt drawn to the soft-spoken, educated young woman with a deep abiding emotion that he knew was love. And she had professed feeling the same.

Most of their visits together were brief assignations on the grounds of Oberlin College between her classes. There they had walked the grounds, talking of the world, their hopes and dreams, and their intimate thoughts and beliefs. Daniel knew they were kindred spirits, destined to be together.

He remembered the last time he saw her, the morning before the Norwalk Company enlistment ceremony. Waking early, he had rushed down to the college green to linger and wait for her to arrive for her first class of the morning. The grass was wet with dew, and the trees budding. The breeze was cold, but the sun promised a fine spring day.

Unlike Susan, most of the girls of Oberlin College were visitors to Norwalk and lived on campus. Proper circumspection dictated that he remain a respectful distance from the dormitories. Instead, he lingered closer to the street—where he would be able to see Susan when she arrived. She usually arrived early every morning so they would have time together before her classes began. But she was late that morning, the morning after his meeting with her father.

Daniel pulled out his pocket watch. Almost eight o'clock, the time her first class started. He put his watch away and rubbed his stomach, trying to ease the cold knot that was forming there. Despite the chill, he was sweating and worried how he would look and smell when Susan finally arrived. He closed his eyes and almost stumbled. He felt lightheaded and had trouble drawing a satisfying breath. He wondered if he'd overstepped his bounds the night before. Had he ruined his chances of them ever being together? He feared the worst and was ready to march to the Johnston home and demand to see her one last time before he marched off to war. It was his right as her almost betrothed.

Then he saw her.

She had been walking slowly, with her head down and shoulders slumped. He went to meet her and, as they got closer to one other, she ran into his arms with such force it knocked him back a step. He felt an instant thrill at so much of her body pressing up against his. Before this, they had only held hands. Now he could feel the shape of her body against his and he flushed with embarrassment. Her cheek, wet with tears, brushed his. He held her for a moment and then stepped back despite an overwhelming desire never to leave her arms.

"My dear, what's the matter?"

Her eyes dropped to the ground, and she shook her head. "Father is sure you will be reckless in your efforts to prove yourself to him and will not survive the war."

"He told you that?" Daniel snapped. He knew with Benjamin Johnston nothing was ever as it seemed, but this was coldhearted even for him.

She shook her head. "Not in so many words, but I know my father. After you left last night, his anger quickly subsided until he was almost in a giddy mood. I heard him in his study, humming no less.

"Then this morning over breakfast, he told me not to pin too much hope on you, that you were an impetuous young man, which made you a poor candidate to be a soldier." She looked up and fixed her eyes on his. "I heard what he said to you last night-about proving yourself worthy of me." He opened his mouth to speak, but she shook her head. "I want you to be brave and true to your country and your fellow soldiers, and I want you to come home a hero. But most of all, I want you to come home."

She laid her head on his chest. "You have nothing to prove to me."

He closed his eyes and breathed in her scent.

"I can't say your father's words had no effect on me. They will be a motivating factor in my efforts to be a good soldier. I would battle the minions of hell itself if it were to win me your hand," he said. He paused, and his cheeks reddened at the use of such overblown theatrics. "But I can't say one way or the other what kind of soldier I will be until I am there and face the elephant."

She smiled at the well-worn phrase. "Since Lincoln's call for volunteers, every man in the town is eager to 'face the elephant.'"

She surprised him again by stepping forward and kissing him on the cheek. Then she pushed herself away from him and ran in short, quick steps toward the main building.

—ᴍ—

A long blast of the train whistle and a change in the sound of the engine told the men they were approaching their destination. Daniel nudged Christopher, and they both stood with their bags in hand, ready to get out of that stinking cattle car as fast as possible. The train slowed and lurched its way to a stop, throwing men into one another. The engine wound down in a symphony of hissing and whistling steam accompanied by the clanks and knocks of cooling metal as the cold rain won its war against the hot fire within.

Up and down the train, over one thousand men now stood pressing against the doors. As they waited, curses that made the Galloway brothers blush and calls to be let out filled the cars. Then the doors opened, and the crowd surged forward.

And stopped.

As bad as the smell and the cramped quarters were, the steady rain and standing water that awaited them outside looked worse. It looked like the train had stopped in the middle of a swamp. They could see the moonlight reflected in the standing water covering the field next to the tracks. Gusts of bitter-cold wind blew the rain sideways and sent ripples through the puddles. Sergeants and officers walked up and down the tracks, yelling at the men to disembark.

"Company A, line up here!"

"Company B, here!"

Slowly, the men exited the cattle cars and moved toward the areas where their companies were assembling.

Daniel and Christopher waited their turn and listened for the call. Upon their assimilation into the Volunteer Army, the Norwalk Light Guard and the other volunteers from Norwalk had become Company D of the 8th Ohio Volunteer Infantry. Despite their new military designation and time spent drilling and training, tonight was to be their first true lesson in what it meant to be soldiers.

The men of the 8th lined up in two lines, as they'd been taught, but no one made any attempt to come to attention. Instead they hunched forward, pulled their collars up, and turned their heads down. They clutched their bags to their chests and looked out into the dark, wet landscape. They had been given no supper, and they were wet and cold and still nauseous from the smell of the cattle cars. On top of all that, there was no relief in sight. There were no warm, dry barracks or tents anywhere in the vicinity. In the distance they could make out the shapes of some log huts and Sibley tents, but from the smoke rising out of the chimneys it was obvious they were already occupied.

The commands rang out, "Attention! Regiment, in ranks of two, left…" Sergeants ran to their guide posts. "…FACE!" The miserable men shuffled and turned to their left. "Guide on the colors, MARCH!" The regiment followed the color guard out into the rain-soaked field.

They marched through the rain until they reached the middle of the water-logged wheat field. Water and mud covered Daniel's feet. He felt it soaking through the leather and wool.

"Regiment, HALT! FRONT!"

Colonel DePuy strode down the line with his staff in tow. He kept his eyes forward and down, never looking at his men. Staff members were informing the company commanders to take command, and company commanders were passing the order on to their junior officers before falling in line behind the colonel. Soon all the officers of the rank of captain or higher were striding off the field and toward the officers' quarters.

"I guess someone gets a dry bed tonight," Daniel mumbled.

The remaining lieutenants took their men to the spots in the field where they would sleep, delegated their commands to sergeants, and hurried after the senior officers. Soon, there were no officers left, only eight-hundred miserable and angry men wondering why they'd been abandoned in this wet field, in pouring rain, with no shelter.

Stacks of firewood were available on the edge of the field, but they weren't covered, and the high winds, steady rain, and wet wood made fires out of the question.

Stacks of lumber and other building supplies also sat at the edge of the field. Some sergeants attempted to form details to build shelters, but the men weren't interested. The sergeants were as disenchanted as the rest of the men and quickly gave up. No one made much of an effort to take charge.

Men wandered in all directions, looking for the best place to settle. As Daniel and Christopher stood wondering what to do, a group of Irishmen from Company B strode by, accompanied by a stranger, laughing as they made their way to the barracks. Others wandered off into the woods. Some just dropped where they stood, resigning themselves to their misery for the rest of the night.

Christopher grabbed Daniel's arm, nodded his head toward the tree line and said, "Let's go sleep in the trees. It's got to be dryer in there." Daniel nodded, and the two headed in that direction.

Soon they were in the trees, stumbling through the wet undergrowth. Any part of their clothing not yet soaked through when they entered the woods was now. The two brothers found a white pine tree whose close-spaced limbs offered minimal protection from the rain. They crawled down next to the trunk where the ground was less wet, brushed aside the pine cones that littered the ground, and lay down to sleep.

Then, they heard leaves rustling. Both boys sat up. Daniel squinted as if that would make it easier to see in the dark.

A familiar voice rang out, "Galloway boys, are you up here?" It was Ezra Rouse. Tall, stocky, greasy-haired, and pimple-faced, Ezra had been a bully in school and Christopher was one of his main targets. Daniel had had to thump Ezra good a couple times, but as far as he was concerned, that was in the past.

Christopher groaned and Daniel nudged him in the ribs. "We're over here," Daniel said.

Ezra crawled under the tree and sat down cross-legged. "You boys left before they passed out rations," he said, pulling a handkerchief out of his coat with three hard crackers wrapped in it. He handed Daniel and Christopher each a cracker and then proceeded to chew on the corner of the third.

"Hardtack," Christopher groaned.

Daniel thumped the cracker with a knuckle. "At least the rain softened it a bit."

While Camp Taylor had a regular mess where the men were served at least two hot meals every day, they had already become too familiar with the rock-hard crackers. Hardtack was ubiquitous. When they were on fatigue duty or drill practice ran over, hardtack was there. When it rained and cooking fires were hard to keep burning, hardtack was there. When they traveled in the cramped cattle cars, hardtack was there. It was hard as steel and just as flavorful. But it did not spoil and kept forever in all kinds of conditions.

"All the officers have dry quarters tonight," Ezra said. "I hear we get to make our quarters tomorrow."

"What about tonight?" Daniel asked.

"This is it. You have a much better setup here than most."

"Well, you are welcome to share it with us," Daniel said, earning a dark frown from Christopher.

"How you holding up, bub?" Ezra asked Christopher.

"Fine." Christopher scowled and crossed his arms.

"You seem to be in a fine pucker, what's got your goat?"

"I said I am fine, thank you very much."

"We're all a little put out by everything that's happened tonight," Daniel said.

"Alrighty. Anyway, I was thinking," Ezra said. "Maybe the three of us could make up a mess. We can pool resources, take turns in the mess line, and share canteen duty."

"I do not—" Christopher began.

"That sounds fine," Daniel interrupted. "We can start tomorrow by putting together our quarters."

Ezra smiled and held out his hand for Daniel to shake. Christopher let out a loud harrumph and lay down with his back to the other two.

"A fine pucker, indeed," Daniel said smiling.

CHAPTER FOUR
BOYS WILL BE BOYS

The next day dawned warm and sunny. After a hot meal of soft bread and salt pork with fresh coffee, the men started building huts to live in. For the sides of the huts, they used rough-hewn boards, already cut and stacked for the task. For roofs, they used tent canvas issued to the men from the quartermaster's office. Each hut housed six to seven men and included a small cook stove. Though, as the weather continued to warm and most of their meals came from the commissary, the men had little use for the stoves. When they cooked something themselves, they did it on open fires in front of their huts.

In the camp were men from all over Ohio. There were Germans and English and Dutch immigrants, and real Irish who spoke with a thick accent like Jack Galloway, and sometimes they even spoke in Gaelic. There was even an officer, Charles DeVillier, who, rumor had it, fought with the French Zouaves in Africa. Whenever he had a free moment, Christopher roamed the camp and tried to talk to them all (except for Colonel DeVillier, who was a stickler for discipline and unapproachable to enlisted men). It proved challenging though, as there was little free time, and many of the immigrants spoke little English.

They had no uniforms or weapons, yet they drilled every day. Each morning started with company drill, where they learned the proper way to march and maneuver as a group. Individually, they learned proper stances, how to salute, and how to hold and load a rifle. Christopher didn't understand why they were so picky about the different rifle positions. If they wanted him to put his rifle on his shoulder, why couldn't he put his rifle on his shoulder and be done with it? And loading? Just load the powder and ball and shoot. He didn't understand why they had to break it down into steps and have everyone do it the same way.

After a midday meal, the 8th drilled as a regiment. Then all the companies had to work together. They would form a battle line that stretched from one end of the field to the other. When they marched, they had to keep that line straight. Sometimes, individual companies received different commands and had to march around one another in intricate patterns that the officers assured them would be critical to perform on the battlefield, though no one seemed to know how or why.

A couple times a week, the 8th joined other regiments to drill as a brigade. Two or three thousand men would be on the field at once, bumping into each other and marching in long, ragged lines. Though Christopher didn't see how, the officers assured the men they would eventually work together as a precise unit.

It seemed simple at first. The men would line up in two ranks; this was the battle line. Each two-man spot in the battle line, front and back, was the file. Once they were lined up, each file would count by twos from right to left. Knowing your file partner and your number was important to many maneuvers. If the order was to turn right into columns, the even-numbered men, the twos, had to step out and up next to the man on their right to form a row of four men across. If the order was to the left, the ones had to step out and up next to the man on their left. The goal was to march out onto the field in battle formation and, at the command, "By the right flank—MARCH!," turn to their right and shift into the four-man column. Then, at the command, "Company—FRONT!," turn left back into their battle line. Then they would repeat the sequence to the left with everything backwards. Once you had the basics and nothing ever changed, it was easy.

Then men began getting sick at an alarming rate, and the lineup would change from day to day. One day Christopher would be front rank two, and the next, rear rank one. He never knew what position in the line he would be in from day to day, and he had to pay close attention. But that was never Christopher's strong suit. He started second-guessing himself and overthinking the maneuvers as he was trying to perform them and always seemed a step behind everyone else. Or worse, he would turn the wrong direction and either bump into his neighbor or march off in the opposite direction as the rest of the company.

By the afternoon—just in time for regimental maneuvers—Christopher would get frustrated and his mind would wander. He would imagine them all in uniform, with real rifles, performing the maneuvers on a battlefield. Then, the officer conducting the drill would issue a command to change front and he'd forget if he was a one or a two or if he should step left or right.

The confusion on the field was worsened by the officers' inexperience. They walked around the men, consulting little pocket manuals, hesitantly calling out commands and then correcting themselves when they realized they got the wording wrong. Discipline was lax, and the men would deride the officers with laughter and catcalls every time they made a mistake.

Everyone was learning at once, trying to figure out his own place in an all-volunteer army. A few regulars helped run the camp, but not enough to train all the new regiments coming in daily from across the state. On the field the men would curse and deride the officers and the officers would shout their commands in loud, almost hysterical tones. The regulars would curse them all and mutter under their breaths and, when it became too much for them, throw up their hands and storm off the field. Every man had to learn how to be a soldier on his own.

Everyone in the regiment echoed Christopher's frustration, and complaining around the campfire soon became the favorite pastime.

—⚏—

After almost a month of drilling every day, the men had a full day off. It was a beautiful spring day and afforded the perfect opportunity to take care of things they hadn't had time to address while training. To his shame and consternation, Christopher had found he was developing a bad case of lice.

At first he tried to remove the pests when he thought no one was looking. But, he soon found out everyone else was doing the same. Lice, it seemed, were as regular a part of army life as marching or uniforms. So, the whole regiment spent the first part of its day off bathing and soaking their clothes in cauldrons of boiling water to rid themselves of the bugs.

Afterward, the men relaxed and took care of their personal business. Daniel was writing a letter to Susan Johnston, and Christopher was poking the remains of the morning fire with a stick when Ezra grabbed another stick and joined him. For several minutes, they both sat staring and poking at the dying fire.

"I know you don't like me much—" Ezra began.

"Forget it," Christopher mumbled.

"It's just, kids do things, you know…"

"Yes, I know."

"Anyhow, we're soldiers now, and men. What happened before is in the past."

Christopher looked at Ezra but didn't respond.

The two sat in silence for a time. Ezra threw his stick in the embers and said, "Let's go exploring a bit."

Christopher again looked at Ezra without speaking. As a child, Ezra had driven him to the point of tears multiple times. No one seemed to take the physical and verbal abuse seriously, saying "boys will be boys." But, it still bothered Christopher. He knew he hated the person across from him, but, if he was to hold on to a childhood grudge now, when everyone had to work together, it might look bad with the brass.

Christopher looked around. The street between the log shelters was full of men who were reading, writing, and smoking. Some were mending cloths, and others had formed into groups and were gambling the soldier's pay they had yet to collect. The constant noise of thousands of men going about their lives in camp was suddenly overwhelming. And the smell was worse—unwashed bodies, smoky cooking fires with a variety of dishes, and the stench of human waste drifting down from the sinks. Christopher realized he was squeezing the stick in his fist as if it were to blame for everything going on around him. He threw the stick into the fire.

"Why not," he said and rose. They set off for the woods in awkward silence.

The boys skirted the parade ground, where another group of recruits struggled to learn the intricacies of regimental drill. Christopher and Ezra had learned enough to look beyond the wide assortment of civilian attire—and the broomstick and wooden dowel rifles—to see that the men were getting the hang of marching in unison. Their feet all moved together and their strides were almost uniform. At the call of "right shoulder shift," in one crisp motion, everyone tucked the end of the sticks they were carrying in the palm of their right hand and raised them straight up until their hands were almost even with their armpits. Several recruits, forgetting just how light their "rifles" were, lost control and sent their sticks flying over their shoulders and onto the heads of the men behind. The four-man column fell apart as some men ducked and scattered and others spun around to grab their errant "rifles."

Christopher and Ezra burst out laughing as officers and sergeants screamed at the hapless recruits. Not wanting the men on the field to see them, the two boys ran for the tree line. Once in the trees, the ground rose and the boys slowed down, but they continued on until they reached the top of the hill. They looked around, trying to get their bearings, but all they could see from their vantage point was more trees.

Ezra pointed in the general direction of Cincinnati. "Ya know, the way they're cutting down trees for building and firewood, by this time next year you'll be able to see all the way to Cincinnati from here."

Christopher shrugged. "We'll be long gone by then. Probably in South Carolina."

Ezra nodded and slapped Christopher on the shoulder. "Those secessionists will rue the day they thought they could leave the Union once we get down there, bub."

Christopher suppressed a flash of irritation at Ezra's familiarity and being called bub. It was bad enough when Daniel called him that. "Rue. Where'd you get such a fancy word?"

"It means they'll be sorry," Ezra said.

"I know what it means. I'm surprised you do. You never seemed much interested in book learning."

Ezra kept looking toward Cincinnati even though all they could see were the trees. "I heard an officer say it."

"So you were just mimicking someone else."

Ezra squirmed and wouldn't meet Christopher's gaze.

"Mimic means doing something you saw someone else do first."

Ezra nodded. "I guess I mimicked then."

He paused for a few minutes and then continued. "My pa used to beat me if I spent too much time with books. He said men were meant to work. And he was bound and determined for me to be a man, no matter my age. But that don't mean I couldn't have learned if I was allowed."

"Is that why you were so mean?" Christopher asked.

Ezra looked at Christopher. "You had two parents that wanted you to get educated, but you just laughed it off as if it were nothin'," Ezra said. His lips continued to move, but the words stopped coming. He choked back a sob and turned it into a cough. He looked away again. "If I sometimes beat you up and stole your lunch money, well...I was just hungry."

The two boys stood in silence for several minutes, staring at the trees as if they'd seen nothing like them before.

Christopher grinned.

"They'll ra-ooo the day, all right," he said with a laugh. He tilted his head back and turned it into a howl. "Ra-ooooo."

Ezra smiled and joined in. "Rawooooo the day!" Soon they were both cupping their hands around their mouths and howling at the treetops. "Ra-wooo! Ra-ra-rawooo!" They took off running through the trees, like two wild animals on the hunt, leaping over logs and stones, dodging trees, howling as they ran.

—⁂—

Later, as they returned to camp, Christopher spotted a garter snake sunning itself on a rock. He looked toward camp to see if Daniel was still writing. He was, and Christopher's mouth spread into a wicked grin.

Back in camp, Ezra went straight to their shack and his canteen while

Christopher sauntered up behind Daniel. "What'cha writing there, brother? Writing your girl?"

"None of your business, bub. Run along and play," Daniel replied without looking up.

Christopher took another step closer and looked over Daniel's shoulder, pretending to read aloud. "Oh, my dearest Susan," he said in a sing-song voice. "How I miss you. Your eyes, your hair, your smile…Even now, as I think of you, I can't help but play with the snake in my lap." With that, Christopher dropped the snake he'd picked up into Daniel's lap.

Daniel shot up, knocking over the writing desk draped across his thighs. Paper flew everywhere, and ink spilt all over the desk and Daniel's pants. The frightened snake lashed out at the nearest thing it could sink its teeth into, which was Daniel's forearm. Daniel cried out in shock and rage, shaking his arm to get the snake to let go.

He shook off the snake and spun on Christopher, who was bent over laughing, holding his sides and trying to catch his breath. "You…you…you miscreant! I'm gonna…!"

Christopher barely managed enough breath to scream through his laughter, "Retreat!" And he took off running down the company street. He looked back and saw Daniel gaining on him, which dampened his laughter and allowed him to gain enough speed to stay ahead.

Soon, they were in unfamiliar territory, surrounded by men they didn't know. Everywhere it seemed, strangers stopped what they were doing to stare at the two brothers as they ran by.

Christopher stole a glance over his shoulder. In doing so, he stepped into a cooking fire, overturning a pot of coffee and a skillet full of sausage and vegetables.

The man tending the skillet jumped up and yelled something that sounded like, "What's zoom?" to Christopher. He jumped up and joined the pursuit along with two of his messmates.

Christopher found himself pursued by an angry brother and several strangers yelling in some foreign language. Now the snake joke didn't seem so funny.

The pursuit came to an abrupt halt when one of the strangers got a handful of Christopher's shirt and pulled him off his feet. Christopher land-ed flat on his back, knocking what little air there was out of his lungs.

Before Christopher could fill his lungs, one of his pursuers kicked him in the ribs. A jolt of pain coursed through his body. He opened his mouth wide and tried to suck in air, but nothing happened. His vision blurred and narrowed to a small dot before him. His head was pulsing and pounding to the point Christopher thought it would explode. Somewhere far away Christopher could hear shouting and the shuffling of feet, but he was pow-erless to move.

As Christopher felt himself about to lose consciousness, his lungs start-ed working again. With a loud gasp, he sucked in as much air as he could and quickly coughed it back out. The coughs caused sharp pains to shoot through his chest. After a couple deep breaths, he took in his surroundings. At first, all he could see were feet moving back and forth as if they were dancing. Then, as he followed the attached legs upward, he saw one pair of feet belonged to Daniel, and the other pair to the big foreigner whose din-ner he'd ruined. *German*, he thought. *That's it, they're German.*

Daniel and the German, who was a good head taller, were pushing each other back and forth. "That's my brother!" Daniel was screaming. "You can't kick him like that." The other man was still speaking German, so Christopher didn't understand what he was saying.

Christopher reached out, grabbed the German's pant leg, and tugged. "I'm sorry I ruined your supper," he croaked. The man kicked his hand away and reared his foot back to kick him again. Christopher flinched and tried to cover both his ribs and face at the same time.

That's when Daniel hit the big German in the jaw with a powerful haymaker. Christopher watched Daniel's whole body rotate into the punch, almost throwing himself off balance. The German's head whipped back, and then forward again, his eyes wide with shock.

"I don't zink you should have done dat," someone said in a thick accent.

Like a freight train, the German's fist came up and back, and sped forward in a large arc toward Daniel. Daniel had plenty of time to get his hands up and block the punch, but it did no good. The ham-sized fist hit Daniel's forearm and drove his own fist into his face. Daniel took two steps back and stared at his opponent with a look Christopher imagined must have been much like the look David gave Goliath when he first stepped out onto the field.

The big German took a step toward Daniel, his fists raised in front of him. By that time, Christopher got his feet under him and pushed up to a wobbly crouch. He sank down as low as he could get and pushed off, straight toward the big man's legs. Daniel saw what his brother was doing and simultaneously threw himself into his opponent's chest. The big German found himself horizontal, three feet off the ground. He hit the ground flat on his back with two wiry Irishmen on top of him.

With a roar, the big man rolled over onto his stomach. The Galloway boys held on—Daniel with his arms wrapped around the big mans face and neck, and Christopher straddling his legs and punching the German in the kidneys with little effect. The German got his arms under him and pushed himself up onto his knees. Daniel held on, but Christopher lost his grip and fell back on his rear.

Slowly, the German leaned backward, pulled down by Daniel's weight. Christopher scrambled to his feet and yelled at the German, as if speaking louder would somehow allow the man to better understand him. "Lay off, pard! It was an accident!"

By that time, a large crowd had gathered, mostly made up of men from Company D and the company to which the German belonged. Arguments were breaking out all around and it was one punch away from turning into a riot. Then the provost guard appeared, actual rifles at the ready position across their chests, led by a mean-looking sergeant with a nasty scar across his right cheek.

"Break it up! Break it up!" the sergeant bellowed. "What's going on here?" The guardsmen pushed the riotous crowd back with their rifles. "Who started this?" All eyes turned to the two brothers and the German, still tangled together on the ground.

"What's this? A couple of mountain-climbing dwarves?" the sergeant spat. Everyone laughed, and the spell broke, riot averted. Most of the potential participants were in high spirits, laughing and making jokes at the expense of the Galloway brothers and the German, thankful for the break in the monotony of camp life.

The combatants untangled themselves and stood up. "Corporal," the sergeant said, not taking his eyes off the three. "Put these men under arrest."

"But," Christopher began, "we need to get back to our company."

The sergeant stepped forward until his face was inches from Christopher's and growled. "You have to do what I tell you to. Or I'll have Jenkins here spear you with his bayonet. Understood?"

"Yes sir, Sergeant." Christopher gulped, wide-eyed.

As the guards led them away, Christopher caught Daniel staring at him. The look in his brother's eyes told him he there was still to be a reckoning. *Dang me for a fool*, Christopher thought. *I should have left that snake alone.*

CHAPTER FIVE
MILITARY DISCIPLINE

Camp Dennison was so new, and growing so fast, they lacked the resources yet to deal with disciplinary issues. So the Galloways and their opponent were returned to their respective companies. As they dropped off the big German at his company headquarters, he spit at the Galloway brothers and said something that sounded like "fiesling."

Daniel's first reaction was to yell something back, but the thought of facing Captain Sawyer sapped all his strength. Sawyer was a prominent attorney in Norwalk, and Daniel was sure he and Mr. Johnston knew each other well. The thought of word getting back to Susan and her father about this incident made Daniel sick to his stomach. He hung his head and went along with the provost guard, all anger and fight drained away.

Then he looked over at his brother.

All his life, his parents expected Daniel to look after Christopher, and all it ever seemed to get him was trouble. Even when they were young children, Daniel was always pulling Christopher out of difficult and sometimes dangerous situations of his own making.

Even the earlier troubles between him and Ezra were as much Christopher's fault as they were Ezra's. Christopher had made fun of Ezra's parents' thick German accent on more than one occasion.

Now, thanks to Christopher, Daniel's future with Susan was in jeopardy. Once word got back to Mr. Johnston that Daniel was a camp troublemaker, the man would never give his blessing to their union. At that thought, Daniel's anger flared back up, but not at the big German—at his brother.

Christopher looked up and caught Daniel's eye. His younger brother opened his mouth as if to say something but stopped and quickly looked down at the ground before his feet.

An image entered Daniel's mind of him hitting Christopher the way he'd hit that German. He saw Christopher's head fly back, blood gushing from his nose. Then he saw an image of his mother, looking at him in hurtful reproach, and he was ashamed. He knew he could never hurt Christopher like that. He just wanted him to keep his mouth shut and stay away until the anger passed. Because it always passed eventually.

Soon they were outside the captain's quarters. The provost sergeant announced himself and a muffled "Enter" came from within. The provost sergeant pulled aside the tarp that served as a door to the crude hut and stepped inside. Daniel and Christopher remained standing in the company street, surrounded by armed guards with fixed bayonets. It seemed the whole company was there.

Daniel glimpsed Ezra holding his writing desk and letter to Susan that he'd scattered when Christopher had dropped the snake in his lap. His first reaction was relief, then a jolt of embarrassment and anger. "You better not be reading that letter, Rouse, or I'll tan your hide!" he yelled.

Ezra shook his head. "Don't worry, Danny boy," he yelled back. "I was just taking your things to the hut." At that, he turned and disappeared into the crowd that had formed around the captain's tent.

"Hey, Galloway," someone hollered. "We're here to fight the secesh—not the Huns!" The men burst into laughter and soon the wisecracks were coming from all sides.

Even their corporal, John G. Reid, was joining in the fun. He paused in his laughter long enough to say, "Boys, maybe you can't tell your left from your right, but you can sure fight."

Captain Sawyer and the provost sergeant stepped out into the street, followed by the company first sergeant, William Hoyt. The laughter and teasing abruptly ceased. The two sergeants stayed back as Captain Sawyer approached the two prisoners.

Sawyer was a stocky man with thick wavy hair, a long goatee, and a piercing gaze that could silence the toughest man in the company. At thirty-six, he was almost a father figure to the young men and teenagers he led.

"Well, I suppose your father will be proud. You two are proving to be quite the soldiers," he stated sardonically. "You've managed on your own to disrupt not one, but two regiments—throwing them into complete disarray. To tell you the truth, I don't know if I should be disappointed or proud for having two such prodigious fighters in my company."

The captain stood staring at the two brothers as if he were actually considering the two options. Daniel and Christopher exchanged fervent glances.

"So what will it be?" the captain finally spoke. "You two want a couple medals?" As he spoke, he stepped forward until his face was inches from Daniels. He got so close, Daniel could smell the coffee on his breath and see the dirt in the pores of his cheek. "A promotion?"

Trying to put on a brave face, Daniel looked Captain Sawyer in the eye and started to speak. "Nnnn-no, s—"

"Eyes front, private! I didn't give you permission to look at me."

Daniel went rigid and shifted his gaze forward. Sawyer's closeness meant he was unable not to look at the captain without turning his head. Not wanting to break his attention stance yet trying to avoid the captain's eyes, Daniel wildly shifted his eyes around without moving his head until they settled on a stray strand of hair curling up above the captain's left ear like an errant wave.

"The fact of the matter is, gentlemen, an army thrives on discipline. Nothing kills an army faster than disrupting that discipline. The only reason you two are not being locked up and facing a court-martial right now is that you, this army, and this camp are all brand new. I suppose they weren't expecting disciplinary problems so soon. I guess they weren't expecting the likes of you two."

Captain Sawyer turned and walked back to where the two sergeants stood. "Sergeant Hoyt," he stated.

"Sir!" Sergeant Hoyt barked, coming to attention.

"Who do we have on picket duty right now?"

"That would be Casper and Miller, sir!"

"Have these two relieve them. They can take the rest of their shift, and the following shift as well."

"Yes, sir!"

Daniel felt the tension leave his shoulders. This wouldn't be so bad. Though three or four hours of picket duty would be dreary and tiring, it could have been much worse.

"But first, Sergeant Hoyt, I want you to find two knapsacks and load them with rocks for our intrepid fighters to wear while they are on picket. If you can't find two knapsacks, march them over to the lumber stack and pick out two sturdy logs for them to carry.

"Have their corporal accompany them. We wouldn't want them shirking their loads while on picket, would we?"

"No, sir!"

"I want you, or someone you assign, to check on them periodically. If you find them without their loads, or shirking picket duty in any manner, hang all three by their thumbs for the rest of the day. These two for not following orders and the corporal for letting them. Is that understood?

"Yes, sir!"

Captain Sawyer turned to the Galloways, who stood with mouths agape as they tried to imagine what it would be like to carry a load of rocks on their backs for several hours. "Do both of you understand my instructions?" he asked.

Unable to speak, the two nodded.

"Sergeant," Captain Sawyer addressed the sergeant of the provost guard. "You and your detail are dismissed. We can take it from here. Once the punishment is complete, I will send a full report to your commanding officer."

The sergeant came to attention. Because he was carrying a rifle at the shoulder arms position, he saluted by bringing his left arm horizontally across his chest, palm down. "Yes, sir! Thank you, sir. Detail—attention!"

The four guards that surrounded the Galloways had relaxed but quickly snapped to attention, their backs straight, eyes front. Their rifle butts were planted firmly on the ground next to their right feet, the barrels nestled in their right hands.

"Shoulder—arms!" With a precision Daniel would have admired under other circumstances the four reached across with their left hands, grasped their rifle barrels, and pulled them straight up. They completed the command by grasping their trigger guards with their right hands and giving their rifles one final adjustment to make sure they were tight against their shoulders. Then, with the same precision, they all brought their left hands back down to their sides at the same time.

"About—face! Forward—march!"

The guard detail marched away, leaving the Galloways standing outside their captain's tent, surrounded by their solemn-faced comrades and company officers. Out of the corner of his eye, Daniel saw John G. Reid no longer laughing. Seeing he had caught Daniel's eye, Reid shook his head and turned his back. What was he so upset about? He would not be the one carrying a bag of rocks around camp for the next several hours.

—⁓—

Picket duty comprised walking back and forth at various locations around camp and challenging anyone who wished to pass. Since they had no rifles yet, and most of the people entering and leaving the area were camp officials, it was purely a training exercise. Monotonous and tiring at the best of times, in bad weather picketing was downright miserable. But, nothing could have prepared the Galloway brothers for the agony they experienced over the next two hours.

The knapsacks were shallow—designed to sit high on the upper back. Once filled with rocks and put on Daniel's back, the weight caused him to stumble until, by leaning forward, he could balance the weight. After only a few minutes in that position, his lower back started to cramp and spasm. When he tried to straighten to ease the pressure on his lower back, he would stumble until he found the position where the knapsack was fairly balanced.

Looking at his brother, Daniel saw Christopher going through the same struggle to remain standing, but for Christopher it seemed much worse. His small frame was not made for this kind of punishment. After a few minutes, they both settled on a system of walking hunched over like old men for five to ten minutes, then straightening up and stumbling around like a couple of drunks for several steps.

The straps dug into Daniel's shoulders so sharply that his arms went numb almost immediately. There was no shift in posture that could ease that. Though if he put his thumbs under the straps and pushed up for a few minutes, he could get some blood flowing back into his arms.

They continued that way for two hours. They were to do a full two-hour shift and complete the remaining thirty minutes of the shift for the men they'd replaced. But, after an hour, Christopher was weeping as he walked, and both boys were falling to their knees regularly. Each time one of them fell, it took longer to get back up, until finally Christopher fell forward and couldn't rise again.

As Christopher struggled to rise, Daniel turned back and stumbled over to his brother, offering words of encouragement until his legs gave out and he too collapsed to the ground. As he lay wheezing a ragged breath and shaking like a palsied old man, Daniel anticipated Corporal Reid's command to rise, but it never came. Instead, the corporal sent a runner to Captain Sawyer to report that the prisoners could not continue their punishment.

After a few minutes, Christopher lay down completely and became unresponsive. Daniel called his name and reached out to shake Christopher awake, but his arm was too weak to extend that far. He looked to Corporal Reid for help, but the corporal was staring off in the direction of Captain Sawyer's tent. Daniel didn't think he had the strength to call Reid's name loud enough to get his attention, so he looked around for someone else to help.

Many members of the company had come out to watch the punishment. Some were quiet, moved by the agony they witnessed. Others treated it as a sport, trading bets on who would last the longest and egging the boys on. But, after the first hour, all but the most zealous gamblers had had enough and returned to their cabins and cook fires. By the time the brothers had collapsed, everyone was gone but Corporal Reid and Ezra, who was watching intently, but too far away to help.

Finally, the runner returned with a message from Captain Sawyer, dismissing the prisoners provided they completed their punishment the next day after drill. Ezra came up after the runner left and helped Corporal Reid remove the knapsacks.

Daniel gasped in pain as the blood flowed back into his arms. He gasped his thanks to Ezra and took a drink from his canteen. Christopher was still unresponsive. Despite his pain, Daniel felt his pulse quicken.

Reid and Ezra picked up Christopher to carry him to his quarters, but Daniel rose to his knees and tried to push the two away. "He's my brother," he gasped. "I'll take care of him."

"Dan, you can barely take care of yourself," Reid responded. "You rest. Once you're able, come on back to camp. We'll take care of Chris."

Still on his knees, Daniel swayed back and forth. "No," he mumbled. "My brother." He lifted his arm to grab Reid's shoulder and gasped in pain. He didn't interfere with the two again as they carried Christopher away. "My brother," he sighed as he closed his eyes and keeled over.

CHAPTER SIX
SICKNESS STRIKES

Though he didn't remember doing it, at some point Daniel must have made his way back to the cabin, because when he woke he was on his cot and it was pitch black. Something had woken him, but he didn't know what. Something different from the constant snoring and farting of six young men with no social graces.

Daniel lay still and listened. There it was again…some kind of chattering noise. A woodpecker? He didn't think so. Daniel was pretty sure woodpeckers were not nocturnal. Also, the wood used to build the cabin walls was fresh cut and not bug infested that he could see. But something was chattering away, like it was beating on the walls with some kind of fine instrument.

Daniel rolled over at the sound of someone striking a match. Every muscle he moved seized and cramped, causing him to gasp in pain. Looking around, he didn't see a light. Then he heard a curse.

"Damn you, lucifer." It was Ezra's voice.

"What's going on?" Daniel asked.

"Don't know." Ezra responded. "Something's wrong with Chris."

"Chris?" Daniel sat up. Sharp pains shot down his back and into his buttocks. He moaned and slid his feet off the cot and rotated until he was sitting upright with his feet on the floor. He had to pause and take in several shallow, hissing breaths until the pain receded. "Chris, answer me. What's going on?"

"He ain't talkin'. Let me get this lucifer lit and we'll find out." Ezra struck the match again. There was a brief flash of light. Then nothing.

"Dammit!"

By then, the others in the shack had woken. Daniel, Christopher, and Ezra shared the cabin with John and Perry Fleharty and Charlie Howe. Perry, the oldest of the group at twenty-three, growled, "Keep it down, people are trying to sleep."

"Something's wrong with Chris," Daniel responded.

"Well, whatever it is, tell him to keep it down."

A bright flash in Ezra's hand and an exclamation from the boy told Daniel they would finally be able to see something. Ezra lit the candle lantern hanging over his bed and removed it from its hook. Daniel rose with a groan, and together they approached Christopher's bunk.

"What is it, bub?" Ezra asked.

They saw the younger boy was shaking violently and drenched in sweat. The noise that had woken Daniel was Christopher's teeth chattering.

Daniel put his hand on his brother's shoulder and gave it a gentle shake. "Chris, it's me. What's wrong?"

As if in response, Christopher groaned and shook his head from side to side.

Daniel took the lantern from Ezra and leaned over his brother's bed to see better. His lower back muscles contracted and sent sharp pains shooting up between his shoulder blades and down his buttocks and legs. He dropped to his knees, and his hand holding the candle trembled as he held it over Christopher's face.

Suddenly, Daniel jerked back. The sudden movement caused his whole body to spasm, and he fell to his side and cried out, dropping the lantern in the process and plunging them back into darkness.

"What is it?" Ezra asked. "What's the matter?"

Daniel shut his eyes and squeezed out the tears that had appeared there. He didn't know if the intense physical pain caused them, or the shock of seeing the small red marks on Christopher's face.

"Smallpox," he whispered.

The darkness came alive with shuffling and banging as everyone was suddenly awake and interested in what was going on. "Smallpox!" someone hissed.

Matches flared and lanterns were lit. Everyone was staring at Daniel in the flickering light.

"I don't know," Daniel said. "Look at his face. Does that look like small-pox to you?" No one moved.

For what seemed like several minutes, but was probably just seconds, the bunkmates were all frozen. Finally, Perry spoke. "Someone needs to go get the surgeon."

At that, everyone moved. There were several hasty pronouncements of, "I'll be right back," followed by a mad rush for the door. Soon, Daniel was alone with his brother in the darkness. He crawled back to his bed to search for his own candle lantern. Once that was lit, he took his blanket and placed it over his still shivering brother. He then sat down to wait for the doctor to arrive.

Two hours later, the door to the hut opened, and Dr. Tappan entered alone, carrying a bag and a much brighter oil lantern. He waved Daniel away from his brother's bunk and kneeled down. "Back to your own cot, young man. Let me have a look."

Daniel lay down and watched the doctor work. He looked at Chris-topher's skin first, then under his eyelids and in his mouth. Using a brass funnel he pulled out of his bag, he listened to Christopher's chest. He then moved the boy's legs, arms, feet, and hands in multiple directions, all the while breathing loudly through his nose.

Finally, the doctor rose and exited the hut without a word or glance to Daniel.

Daniel sat up and exclaimed, "Wait! Is he going to be all right? What is it?" The slamming of the door was his only answer. He got up and followed the doctor out, but was stopped at the door by a provost guard who quickly raised his rifle to the ready position.

Looking around, he saw officers and sergeants and several members of the provost guard filling the company street in front of their shack. Dr. Tappan was speaking to a group that included Captain Sawyer, Colonel

DePuy, and General Cox, the camp commander. Despite being restrained by the provost guard for the second time in twenty-four hours, Daniel was overcome with relief at the words, "…not smallpox." He took in a large breath of air, let it out slowly, and sank to his knees, silently thanking God for not taking his brother.

"But," he heard Dr. Tappan continue, "it may be measles, or maybe just a heat rash from the fever and the day's exertions. I recommend you retrieve the other boys and confine all of them to their living quarters until we know for sure what we're dealing with."

"I wish the hospital was finished, doctor," General Cox said, "but we should have it ready within the week if you find yourself faced with an epidemic."

Dr. Tappan nodded, but it was Colonel DePuy who responded. "Thank you, General. Hopefully, that won't be necessary." Looking to Captain Sawyer, he continued. "Franklin, see to the doctor's recommendations. I'll expect a full report on their condition as soon as you know something definite."

Everyone came to attention as the general and colonel left the area.

Once the officers were gone, Captain Sawyer called out. "Sergeant Hoyt!"

"Here, sir."

"Send a detail to retrieve the other occupants of this barrack. And assign men to guard the door. No one comes in or out of that cabin except for Doctor Tappan."

"Yes, sir." Sergeant Hoyt saluted and, as he walked away, called out, "Corporal Roberts…"

Daniel struggled to rise as Captain Sawyer and Doctor Tappan approached. "Did you hear my report, young man?" Doctor Tappan asked.

"Yes, sir. Thank you, sir."

"I didn't do anything. Bathe your brother's face and neck with a cool wet cloth. I'll send over some laudanum to help him sleep."

"Yes, sir." Daniel nodded.

"Don't try to leave your barracks until we know for sure what we're dealing with," Captain Sawyer said. "I guess you get out of finishing your punishment tomorrow," he added with a small smile.

"Yes, sir. Thank you, sir," Daniel repeated.

"But don't think I have forgotten. I expect better from you."

Daniel winced at the rebuke. "Yes, sir. I won't let you down."

Daniel entered the hut, poured water into a pan, dug out his hand-kerchief, and proceeded to follow the doctor's orders. Within the hour his bunkmates returned, Perry carrying a small bottle of the promised lauda-num and Ezra a slop bucket. "It's gonna get rank, boys," Ezra said as he placed the bucket in the corner.

Daniel gave Christopher a sip of the medicine and continued to bathe his face and neck with the wet cloth. Everyone else settled into their bunks and all turned their backs on the brothers except Ezra. *Maybe we are a couple Jonahs*, Daniel thought. Though not a superstitious person, the thought of bad luck attaching itself to him depressed Daniel more than he thought it should. He imagined Captain Sawyer telling Mr. Johnston over brandy and cigars about the two Jonahs in his company who couldn't go twelve hours without causing some kind of trouble. At the mention of their names, the wicked smile he pictured on Mr. Johnston's face made Daniel groan.

Fortunately, the cooling effect of the wet cloth and the laudanum Daniel got in him gave Christopher the relief he needed to sleep. Daniel crawled back into his bunk and despite—or because of—of the intense emotional Nantucket sleigh ride he'd just been through, he was soon fast asleep.

CHAPTER SEVEN
RE-ENLISTMENT

Christopher woke to a pain he never imagined possible. Every muscle ached, his head pounded like a sledgehammer against an anvil, and his stomach roiled and contracted, threatening to expel its feeble contents. It seemed as if he'd been asleep for days.

He tried to open his eyes, but they were wet and crusty. After wiping them, Christopher looked around and saw everyone was still in the hut. The Fleharty brothers were playing cards with Charlie Howe, Ezra was whittling a stick, and Daniel was reading a book. At the sound of his stirring, they all paused and looked over at Christopher.

Good. It must be early, or everyone would be at drill. "What time is it?" he croaked.

"Well, Lazarus wakes," said Ezra.

"About noon," replied Daniel.

"Noon!" Christopher tried to sit up, causing the pounding in his head to intensify. The room began to spin, and he lay back with a moan. Why wasn't everyone out on the drill field, he wanted to ask, but all he managed was "Why…"

"You're sick, Chris," Daniel replied. "We are confined to quarters until the surgeon determines if it's contagious."

Christopher felt a stab of fear. "Is it serious?"

"Well, it ain't smallpox," Perry Fleharty replied, looking over at Daniel.

Daniel's face flushed, and he refused to make eye contact with Perry. "It's not too bad now, but last night you had red splotches all over your face and neck. I thought you might…" He looked intently at the book in his hands. "It looks like you will be okay."

At that moment, the door opened, and Dr. Tappan entered the hut, accompanied by a hospital steward. Without a word, the doctor approached Christopher, knelt next to his cot, and placed a hand on his forehead.

After a moment, he spoke. "The fever's broke, that's good. Mr. Merrick, bring that lantern."

The hospital steward stepped forward and raised a lantern he'd lit while Dr. Tappan had felt Christopher's forehead.

Dr. Tappan grabbed Christopher's chin and turned his head from side to side. "The redness appears to be clearing." Addressing the room, he said, "It looks like you're all in the clear. Probably a fever brought on by exertion. The red marks were just a heat rash. You gentlemen can return to your duties."

"Bully," Ezra said flatly. "More drill."

Dr. Tappan looked down at Christopher. "You will need to spend a couple more days in bed, but I don't want to move you to a building housing the truly sick for fear you'll catch something worse. Can I trust you to stay in your cot as much as possible the next two days?"

Christopher took a mental assessment of his weak, aching muscles, pounding head, and queasy stomach. He nodded. It seemed like an easy promise to keep.

—∞—

The third day of his convalescence, Christopher imagined the small room was getting smaller. The first day, he didn't leave the room at all—Daniel had brought him his meals and he'd used the slop bucket Ezra had brought in the night before to relieve himself. But that night, his bunkmates revolted at the smell and took the bucket away. So the second morning, he'd made it to the sinks with Daniel's help. Other than that, he'd not left the room.

As Christopher lay staring at the ceiling, imagining it slowly descending toward him like something out of a Poe story, a lieutenant and two corporals Christopher didn't know entered the hut.

"Good afternoon, private. No need to rise, I understand you're under the weather. Nothing serious, I hope."

Christopher was not familiar with the phrase "under the weather," but it seemed a good description of being sick. He shook his head.

The lieutenant looked around, found a three-legged stool, and brought it over next to Christopher's bunk. As he sat, he said, "I'm sure you've been keeping up with our efforts to bring to heel our secessionist brothers down South. Things are not going as well as hoped. As you know, we lost Virginia last month, then Arkansas and North Carolina seceded this month. A stubborn lot, those Southerners." The lieutenant sighed and shook his head.

"In a nutshell," he continued, "it looks like quelling this rebellion will take longer than we thought. Ninety days will not be long enough. We will need at least six months, maybe a year, to do the job right. Are you up to re-enlisting? To continue helping Uncle Sam bring his rebellious children back to the fold?"

A year. What would his mother say? His father, he was sure, would approve. After all, he'd sent him here to become a man and learn responsibility. He still had a ways to go on that score. Events of the last few days proved that. And Daniel...he was sure Daniel would re-enlist, if for no other reason than to impress Susan Johnston.

"It's a lot to take in," the lieutenant said. "I know what you're thinking. But, imagine the adventure. And, when you return, think of the adulation of your community and the admiration of the young ladies thereof." The lieutenant winked and smiled, though with no real emotion, as if he were following a script.

Christopher sat up, stifling a groan. He remembered the crowds that came out in Cleveland and Columbus to cheer them on their way—the banners, the applause, the young ladies waving their handkerchiefs...especially the young ladies. Then, he imagined the thrill of stepping out with his brother and comrades in arms in a battle line, facing down a determined foe. That was an image he'd played over in his mind countless times during drill. It would be a shame to miss it, at least once.

The lieutenant must have seen the emotions playing across Christopher's face. His eyes lit up and he let the ghost of a smile curl the corners of his mouth. Raising his hand, he barked, "Davis!" One of the corporals stepped forward and handed him a piece of paper and a writing board. The other corporal stepped forward and produced a steel-point pen and ink well.

"If you would put your John Hancock on this piece of paper, you can be part of history and the coming glory. It would be a shame to miss it."

It would. Christopher took the writing board and paper and, while looking it over, reached for the pen. Suddenly, he stopped, and his eyes got wide. He looked up at the lieutenant. "This says three years."

Without hesitation, the lieutenant responded, "A mere formality. That's the standard enlistment for the regular army. But, I can assure you, once we quash this rebellion, the army will have no further need of your services and you can return home. One decisive victory, and this whole thing will be over." He leaned forward. "Don't let a mere formality stand in your way, young man. You want to see the elephant before you go home, don't you?"

Still, Christopher hesitated. Three years. Three years in tents and stinking small huts like this one. Three years eating tasteless starches and undercooked meats. Three years taking orders from pompous buffoons like the one before him.

Once again, he imagined the battle line, an angry foe so close before them he could see the whites of their eyes. The crushing sound as they fired, the cheers of him and his comrades as the cowardly enemy turned tail and ran, the huzzah and charge with fixed bayonets.

Christopher looked into the lieutenant's eyes. For a moment, he was reminded of his old dog at feeding time. He'd had that same look.

He took the pen, the tip already wet and dripping ink, and signed.

—⚏—

Later that day, the company returned from drill, and Christopher's bunkmates burst into the hut, talking excitedly. It appeared recruiters had addressed the whole regiment.

"…if we sign up now," Daniel was saying, "we can stay together. If we wait, who knows where we'll end up."

"After the last couple days, Danny, that's not much of an incentive," Perry responded.

Daniel opened his mouth to respond, but closed it and went over to Christopher's bunk. "How you feeling, bub?"

Before Christopher could respond, Daniel continued. "Did you hear? Some recruiters came and spoke to the regiment. The war will take longer than originally thought." He sat down on the three-legged stool by Christopher's bunk without asking how it got there.

"Yeah, three years," John Fleharty said.

"UP to three years," Daniel responded. "More likely just a few more months though."

"Well, I'm not re-enlisting," Charlie Howe said. "My daddy said he'd tan my hide if I wasn't back in time for harvest."

"I don't think you should re-enlist either, Chris," Daniel said. "Ma's worried about you. You should go home."

"What are you going to do, Dan?" Christopher asked.

Daniel sat up straight. "I'm re-enlisting, of course."

"Well, so am I."

"No. I told you. You need to go home."

"I'm with you, Danny boy. All the way."

Daniel clamped his mouth shut. Christopher could see the conflict on his brother's face. Show him a little loyalty and devotion, and he could wrap his brother around his little finger. He could just tell him he'd already signed up, but this was more fun.

"Chrissy, think about Ma and Da? They entrusted me to look out for you, and that's what I'm doing. If the war takes longer than thought, it will also be harder fought. You should go home—where it's safe."

Chrissy? He hated that name, even more than being called bub. "You think I'm a baby that needs coddling? I'm as good as any man in this outfit."

"Yes, you've done as good at drill as any man," Daniel responded. "But, you need to think of our parents. Both of us gone in harm's way for that long would be too much for them. They need you."

"If you're so concerned about Ma and Da, you go home."

Daniel raised his hand as if to hit him. "Bah, you are a baby, always thinking only of yourself."

"That's not true. I'm thinking of our country first and foremost."

"Sure you are. Thinking of girls and glory more like—in that order."

"Well, it's too late, anyway."

Daniel's eyes turned to slits. "What do you mean?"

"A recruiter came to see me, special. Sat right where you're sitting now. I heard my country needed me and I didn't hesitate—signed up right then and there." Christopher lifted his chin, moved by the nobility of his sacrifice. The motion caused a sharp pain to shoot up into the base of his skull, and he winced.

"Haw!" Ezra guffawed. "He's got you there, Danny. It looks like we three are in it for the duration."

Christopher and Daniel both gave Ezra a dirty look. Christopher lay back down on his cot and rubbed his neck. Daniel violently rose to his feet, knocking over the stool, and stormed out of the hut.

CHAPTER EIGHT
JACK GALLOWAY VISITS

Though eager to get out of the hut, Christopher's recovery took longer than he would have liked. It was almost a week before he was able to fall in for drill with the rest of the company, and then for only a few hours at a time. He would try to hold out as long as he could, but when he would sway and stumble and have trouble comprehending basic commands, Captain Sawyer would order him back to his quarters. Christopher looked at the hut he shared with five other soldiers as a prison and found the sight and the smell repulsive. He wanted to be a soldier, living off the land and sleeping under the stars. Not a bed-bound schoolboy with nothing but a Hardee's *Rifle and Light Infantry Tactics* to keep him occupied.

But each day Christopher found himself a little stronger and soon he was performing drill with the rest of the company for the whole day—company drill in the morning, regiment and battalion drill in the afternoon. And, though he would never admit it, the time he spent reading Hardee's manual helped him understand and perform the commands—even when given incorrectly.

One day, while performing a march in line of battle after a heavy rain, most of the company was more interested in avoiding puddles than marching in step with the leading sergeant. At the sight of a puddle or a deep-looking bog, a man would lengthen or shorten his stride to avoid the obstacle. Soon, the entire company was out of step and, as Sergeant Hoyt put it, "hopping around like a bunch of two-bit chorus girls." Captain Sawyer was yelling, "You're out of step! You're out of step! Clean it up!"

Christopher looked at the sergeant leading the line and began muttering, "To-the STEP, to-the STEP…" as his feet did a little jig to get back in rhythm with the sergeant. Several of the boys around him noticed what he was doing and recognized the command—it was a common one in the early days of their drill—and praised him for it afterward. Christopher felt himself swell with pride and lectured those that would listen on the importance of consistent commands. Until he looked over and caught an angry glare from Daniel. Christopher felt himself shrinking inside and shut up.

Not everyone wants to follow a troublemaker, he thought.

As they walked back to the hut, both brothers were quiet. Christopher kept stealing glances at Daniel, wondering what he was thinking. He knew his brother was still mad at him for getting them in so much trouble and for re-enlisting without telling him first. But today Daniel was more quiet and brooding than usual.

As they entered the hut, Christopher saw why. Their father was sitting on his cot.

The claustrophobia that had been building inside Christopher whenever he spent any time in the hut wrapped itself around him like a rope, squeezing the breath out of his lungs. His legs were so weak, he feared they would give out on him and he would collapse in the doorway.

Jack Galloway stood up. "What, no hug for your dear ol' Da?" When neither son responded, he shook his head. "Close your traps boys, you're catching flies."

Daniel was the first to recover, moving forward and giving his father a brief hug. "It's good to see you, Da."

Christopher was sure that Daniel knew their father was coming, and why he was here. But, it was too late. He'd signed a contract with the army.

Unable to display that defiance and self-confidence on the surface, Christopher shuffled up to his father and gave him a hug. He stepped back, thinking it best to get things out in the open right away, but he could not meet his father's gaze as he asked, "What brings you down this way, Da?"

"What, I can't visit me two soldier boys?" the older man replied. "Big doin's going on down here from what your brother writes me, Chrissy boy."

"Well, we've been busy drilling and learning the——"

"And fightin' and carrying on, too, I hear."

"Just the one fight, Da. And that was just a misunderstanding with a German fellow in the regiment next door."

"And re-enlisting?" There it was. The old man appeared calm and re-laxed, but there was a fire in his eyes. "And breakin' your dear mother's heart to boot."

Straight to the point. It seemed to Christopher he'd been breaking his mother's heart since he learned how to walk.

He'd thought of what he would tell his father since signing up for the three-year stint. "Our country needs us, Da. They've spent all this time and money making us soldiers—it would be a waste not to follow through and do our part. Both of us." At that, he looked up and met his father's gaze.

"What would be a waste is if you were to die from some dirty rebel's bullet. That would be a waste. And you being only seventeen makes any-thing you signed worthless."

"Only if you don't back me," Christopher replied. "There are boys in the 8th younger than me." Christopher didn't know if that was true, but neither did his father.

Jack Galloway dismissed that with a wave of his hand. "I don't care about the other boys in the 8th. You're my son. Daniel's my son. You are my only sons. Am I to risk both of you in this coming conflict?"

Christopher's eyes dropped again. He had no argument for that. Then, things took an unexpected turn.

"He's becoming a good soldier, Da," Daniel said.

Jack Galloway's eyebrows shot up. "Is he now?"

Christopher stared at his brother.

"I can't explain it, Da. These last couple weeks, since the illness, Chris has been behaving himself. And he looks right sharp out on the field. You should see him."

Jack Galloway sat back down on the cot. "Your mother..." He looked up at Daniel then. "You talked me into letting him join up by saying it'd do him good. Then you write me a letter saying what a hellion he's been, so I come here to see for myself. Now you're singing a different tune yet again. Which is it, boy?"

Christopher couldn't recall the last time their father had called Daniel "boy."

"I know, Da," Daniel responded. "I'm sorry. But, like I said, just the last couple weeks, Chris has been practically leading the drill. He knows all the commands—some even better than the officers. And when they say boo, he's right there while the rest of us are still scratching our arses and trying to figure out left from right." Daniel took a big breath. "I never thought I'd say this, at least not for a few years yet, but little Chrissy's growing up. I think the army had something to do with that."

"When you boys left that day, it broke your mother's heart. Mine too. And that was only for three months. Now, you're talking three years. I don't know what I could say that would ease your mother's troubled mind thinking of you boys out in harm's way for three long years. Never knowing if you're all right and have what you need, if you're even still alive…" Both boys' jaws dropped at the sight of their father choking on his words.

"Come out to the field tomorrow morning," Daniel said. "Watch us go through our company drills. You'll see for yourself what I'm talking about."

Jack Galloway stood up. "I've got a room at an inn nearby. I think I'll do that." He tugged on his waistcoat and patted his belly. "I don't know what you boys had planned for supper, but I have a package somewhere around here from your mother with a few treats you probably aren't getting on a regular basis. Ah, here it is." He made a big show of reaching down at the foot of the cot and lifting a large basket. "Canned meats and vegetables for a stew, and for dessert—apple pie." He grinned for the first time since leaving Norwalk. "Two apple pies!"

The Galloways were suddenly aware of the rest of the hut's occupants, who had come in and were trying to make themselves look busy and uninterested while the father and sons talked things out. "And there's plenty for the rest of you, too."

Ezra broke into a big toothy grin and hopped up off his cot. "Bully!" he exclaimed as he made for the door. "I'll get the cook fire going."

The following day, Jack Galloway came and saw his sons march and drill with the rest of Company D. He stayed two more days—producing another picnic basket and paper bags full of socks and underwear for the boys. Unfortunately, no one imagined it would be so long before they were issued uniforms. And, while the socks and underwear were welcome, what they really needed was pants, shirts, and shoes.

So the next day, Daniel and Chris got a one day pass, and the three of them took a train into Cincinnati, where Jack bought them new clothes. The boys wandered about, craning their necks and gawking at the multi-story brick buildings and cobbled streets, the barge-clogged canal and bustling waterfront. At a general store, Daniel stocked up on ink and stationary, and Christopher bought a bag of hard candy. They stopped at a photography shop, where they had to wait an hour in a front room full of soldiers to have their image made on a tintype for Jack to take back to their mother.

Jack Galloway didn't buy them shoes. Before he left Norwalk, he'd made each of them a pair of brogans using the finest materials in his shop and cut to the shape and size of each boy's foot. Both Daniel and Christopher noticed he'd brought two pairs of shoes, and the topic of Christopher's three-year enlistment never came back up.

—m—

The days turned to weeks of almost constant drill. New recruits started coming in from the campaign to enlist three-year soldiers, swelling the ranks of the 8th. The increased size and influx of raw recruits put a particular burden on the regimental staff officers. The three-month men saw themselves as seasoned veterans compared to the newcomers, and were quick to help and correct with a sharp word and a shove on the field or a short lecture afterward.

Finally, as the Fourth of July approached, the three-month men were mustered out and the three-year men mustered in, and the 8th Ohio Volunteer Infantry was formed.

Then the uniforms, rifles, and other military supplies appeared. Companies B and D were assigned the right and left flank and designated skirmishers, so they were issued new Enfield rifles. The rest of the regiment received smooth bore muskets left over from an earlier war. Their uniforms were comprised of dark blue pants, waist-length jackets, and forage caps with small leather bills. They also got large leather belts with big brass buckles that bore the letters OVM (for Ohio Volunteer Militia), cartridge boxes with leather shoulder straps, haversacks to hold their rations and utensils, percussion cap pouches to hang on their belts, and knapsacks for their bedding and personal items.

Daniel was as excited as a kid at Christmas with everything but the knapsacks—too many memories of their painful punishment associated with that piece of equipment. The way Christopher bounced around as he went through his new equipment, Daniel could tell he felt the same way.

Their new equipment included brogans, but Daniel and Christopher preferred their father's shoes. They were much sturdier and more comfortable than the boxy, poorly made shoes the army issued.

The first morning the regiment marched onto the field in their new uniforms with real rifles tucked into the crook of their right shoulder, Daniel was almost overwhelmed at the pride that emanated off them—everyone's heads were high, chests out, and shoulders pulled back. There was a noticeable spring in their step despite the hampering of the prescribed twenty-eight-inch stride that kept them together. There was no grand review that morning—just a few regimental staff officers—but if Abraham Lincoln himself had been there watching, the boys could not have performed better.

Most of the three-month men did not re-enlist. So Daniel and Christopher had to say goodbye to many of the men they'd gotten to know during their time in the army—including the Fleharty brothers and Charlie Howe. Like the other boys who had stayed, Daniel took pride in being a "veteran" of the regiment and helped get the new men up to speed as fast as possible. When it came time to leave for the front on July eighth, Daniel was more than ready—and he was sure everyone else was as well.

CHAPTER NINE

TO WAR

Daniel looked up and down the company street. Despite the late hour, campfires burned everywhere. He knew everyone, like him, was too excited to think of sleeping. Tomorrow they would leave for the front. The trains that were to take them had shown up just a few minutes ago. Now, it all seemed so real. No longer was it a game of playing soldier on an empty field, marching back and forth and shooting at straw targets. After tonight, it would be the real thing with targets that shot back.

Daniel fretted about the fate of the company. Captain Sawyer was promoted to major and made executive officer of the regiment. Lieutenant Daggett was now Captain Daggett and in charge of Company D. Daniel had nothing against Daggett, he just worried about the sudden change on the eve of their departure.

He looked before him at their own campfire, its glow lighting the faces of his companions, then down at the cup in his hands, half full of lukewarm coffee laced with whisky. After only a couple sips, he felt lightheaded and melancholy. Not only would they be leaving this place, where they had done so much and met so many new people, they were also leaving their old lives. Once they'd seen the elephant, nothing would be the same.

Daniel looked back up at his drinking companions. There was Sergeant (formerly Corporal) John G. Reid. His promotion had, at first, created quite the conundrum for the men, as there already was a Sergeant John Reid (now First Sergeant since Hoyt had chosen not to re-enlist). Since the two shared not one but two names, they couldn't call him Sergeant Reid or Sergeant John, so everyone called him Sergeant G.

Then there was Ezra Rouse, who must have taken more than a splash in his cup because he was already loudly boasting of his exploits as the school bully back home. Looking over at Christopher, Daniel saw the topic was not going over well with at least one member of the audience. Next to Ezra sat twenty-year-old Alex Melville, whom most of the company called Ishmael despite his protests. The Jump brothers, Joe and Nate, Daniel knew from back home. They came from a poor family and had left home at an early age, living in boarding houses and working odd jobs to make a living. Their joining the army must have been a boon for the family—now that they didn't have to pay room and board, the lion's share of their thirteen dollars a month would go home, and the Jumps wouldn't have to worry where there next meal would come from. And last, Corporal Charlie Locker from Germany. A farm laborer, he lived with an American family and spoke English well. Which gave Daniel an idea.

"Hey, Charlie. I've got a question for you."

Ezra continued his story, but everyone else looked over at Daniel.

"Ya, shoot," Charlie replied.

"What's feestling mean?"

"What? Firstling?"

"No, feestling. This German called Chris and me that when we ruined his supper."

Charlie shook his head. "I do not know this word." Charlie frowned. "You say you ruined his supper?"

Daniel nodded.

Charlie broke into a large grin. "Ah, he probably called you a *fiesling.* If you ruined my supper, I would call you a *fiesling* too."

"But what does it mean?"

"Bastard."

"What?"

"Or slob. Either would be right."

Everyone broke into laughter. Ezra bellowed, "Danny, you old feestling, how you doing?"

"*Fiesling*," Charlie corrected. "There is no t."

Sergeant G grinned. "I'll add that to my list of names to call you sorry bunch of *fieslings* when you're malingering or blundering around the field."

Christopher moaned. "Ah, Danny, why did you have to bring that up. I'd hoped everyone would forget all about it."

The new men looked at Christopher, then Daniel. When neither said anything, Sergeant G laughed and told them the story of their fight with the German and their punishment. His audience didn't know how to respond. As former three-month men, the new men respected the Galloways. It was like hearing a story about how Moses was spanked as a little boy.

Daniel smiled and said, "I tell you, a bedroll and some extra rations and rounds seems pretty light now. Hey, Chris?"

Christopher smiled wanly and nodded.

"Anyway, all that's behind us," Daniel continued. "Soon we won't be fighting overgrown Dutchmen—no offense, Charlie—but actual secesh rebels. And it won't be fisticuffs and wrestling, but bullets and shot and shell."

"Think any of us will be killed, Sergeant G?" Nathan Jump asked.

Sergeant G nodded. "That's a possibility, Nate. But that's what we signed up for. To do what needs to be done, or die trying."

Ezra raised his cup. "Here's to doing what needs to be done, and not the other."

Everyone took a drink and sat in silence. The murmur of voices filled the air as all around them, similar conversations took place around similar campfires.

"Well, boys," Sergeant G said. "Tomorrow is a big day for us. Into the breach, as they say. I say we try to get some sleep."

"I don't know if I can," Nate Jump said.

"Don't worry, Nate," Joe Jump said. "After drinking that whiskey, you'll sleep like a baby."

"I don't think I wanna die," Nate whispered, looking into the fire.

Joe threw his arm around his younger brother. "Don't worry, bub, you have me to look out for you. Now come on."

Together, the Jumps headed back to their cabin. Melville stood up next.

"I guess I'll be retiring as well," he said, throwing the dregs of his cup into the fire.

"Get a good night's rest, Ishmael," Daniel said with a smile.

Melville shook his head. "Don't call me Ishmael." Everyone burst out laughing and, with a wave of his hand, he turned and left.

The rest of the group then stood as one—all except Charlie Locker. Daniel looked over at the German and saw he was fast asleep sitting up.

Daniel kicked his shoe and yelled, "Charlie, fall in! We're under attack."

Charlie fell back, spilling the remains of his drink in his lap. He sat up and shook his head. Looking around, he saw his companions laughing at him and mumbled, "*Fieslings*."

"Watch it, Charlie, we know what that means," Daniel replied.

"Ya, that is why I said it," Charlie grumbled.

—⧟—

Two days later, their train crossed the Ohio River into Virginia. Though that part of the state had voted to secede from the state instead of the Union, there was a large Confederate force in the area.

They were now in enemy territory.

The men celebrated by singing several ribald verses of "Dixie." At first, Daniel joined in the singing, but as the verses became increasingly vulgar, he felt embarrassed and eventually fell out. He noticed his brother continued singing with gusto to the last verse. Daniel looked at Christopher, laughing and singing about bedding a "Dixie lass," and assumed his brother had only a vague idea what he was singing about.

Once into Virginia, their progress slowed to a crawl as the train worked its way up steep inclines and around sharp curves carved out of the mountainous terrain. Most of the regiment consisted of men from northern Ohio, where the country was flat farm land. The hilly country surrounding Cincinnati had impressed them, but that paled in comparison to the mountains they now found themselves in. They passed through valleys already cast in dark shadows even though it was hours until sundown. On either side of the train, the woods were thick and the cliff walls steep. This almost claustrophobic environment added to a growing unease among the men as they contemplated what it meant to be in a state that had declared open rebellion to the United States.

Some men donned their trappings and, rifles in hand, moved to the sides of the cars. Those that could find a space along the wall stared out at the passing countryside. Those that couldn't stood ready to step up and take the place of their comrades if they should fall. Though their rifles weren't loaded, they all felt better having them ready—just in case.

Because of the single track, the train had to stop several times to let other trains pass. All the passing traffic seemed to have something to do with the US Army, and soon everyone realized being inside a state in active rebellion wasn't as exciting as it sounded. Except for a few cautious souls, everyone went back to playing cards or gathering in groups to gab about girls, horses, guns, and the war. Still, they kept their rifles and traps close by—just in case.

The train stopped in the middle of the night, and the troops disembarked and lined up for roll call.

"It seems we line up and take roll call before and after we do anything else," someone said.

"Hey, Captain, where we at?" someone else called out.

"Quiet in the ranks!" First Sergeant Reid yelled at the men. "If you need to know something, the army will tell you. Otherwise, keep your trap shut."

Daniel couldn't see much, but he could tell they were near a large encampment. Though it was late, scattered campfires lit the surrounding woods, and several pickets were posted around the track. "Gentlemen, I believe we have reached our destination," he said.

"Too bad, I could use another big meal and a few more huzzahs," someone replied.

"Well, now I guess we'll earn our nickel," another boasted.

After roll call, Captain Daggett stepped forward to address Company D. Other captains did the same for the rest of the companies up and down the line. "Gentlemen, we are now inside the state of Virginia, at a place called Fetterman, near Grafton. If you are not familiar with these place names, do not fear—you will be soon enough." The men gave him a good-natured laugh.

"From the continuous sounds coming from the boxcars and reports from the non-commissioned officers, it would appear none of you have slept much the last couple days. I appreciate your levity and applaud your bonhomie on your way to a theater of war. But, playtime is over. You are now in the thick of things, with enemy troops not far from here.

"You will have the rest of the night and morning to sleep and get yourself something to eat. Cook from whatever you have in your haversacks for now, and tomorrow we'll get the commissary set up. The executive officers will meet with General Hill to receive our orders. I urge you, get some rest—only the Good Lord above and the general staff know what we'll be facing tomorrow. Good night, gentlemen."

"Three by three for Captain Daggett!" someone called out. And the company responded.

"Hip-hip-HUZZAH!"

"Hip-hip-HUZZAH!"

"Hip-hip-HUZZAH!"

Followed by a tremendous roar. "And a tiger too!" Christopher yelled, waving his forage cap.

Captain Daggett smiled and waved as he walked away, but he gave First Sergeant Reid a pointed look.

"Quiet down, you lunkheads, people are trying to sleep," Sergeant Reid said. "Now, I suggest the rest of you do the same. Company! Dis—MISSED."

As the men dispersed and headed for the tree line, Christopher, Ezra, and Daniel looked for a good spot to build a fire for supper. Corporals Locker and Bonnett, whom Daniel had invited into their mess, joined them.

The five men headed into the trees and found a flat clearing where they could build a small fire and sleep. Corporal Bonnett dug a fire pit with his bayonet as Christopher and Ezra went in search of dry wood. Corporal Locker laid out a gum blanket, and he and Daniel spread out the contents of their haversacks. Soon they had a fire going with coffee boiling and salt pork frying and a small pot of odds and ends left over from the Zanesville feast. Christopher generated a chorus of huzzahs when he pulled out the pie he'd gotten in Zanesville and displayed it to the rest like a prized jewel.

After a satisfying meal, Ezra produced a flask with a small amount of whiskey still in it and passed it around. "Just a nip to help us sleep."

"I won't have any problems sleeping myself," Christopher said though a yawn. "I think I could sleep a week." The men dispersed, and soon the only sounds in the clearing were those of snoring.

—⚇—

The next day, reveille was not sounded until mid-morning. Daniel had grown so used to getting up before dawn, the bright sun shining through the canopy of leaves above their heads surprised him. He sat up and saw men moving through the trees. Then, the greater sounds of a large encampment—orders being shouted, horses neighing, wagons creaking, and the tramping of many feet at drill—caught his attention.

He looked at Christopher lying next to him and saw his brother was still trying to sleep. Daniel rose to his knees, grabbed the edge of Christopher's blanket, and gave it a sharp, hard tug. The blanket came up, and Christopher rolled over onto the remaining firewood.

Christopher sat up, sputtering and cursing.

"Up! It's time for roll call. And watch your mouth. Imagine if Ma could hear you," Daniel said.

"Yeah, well she ain't here, and roll call or not, that's no way to wake a body."

"It's the only way to waken you. I swear, you'd sleep through cannon fire."

The brothers continued their bickering as they straightened up their area and headed for the sound of men congregating. As they walked out of the trees, they stopped and stared at the sight before them. In the distance they saw a small mountain town. Between them and the town were hundreds of tents, lined up in neat rows.

There were cavalry and artillery units with makeshift stables full of horses. Wagons and cannons, along with their limber chests, were lined up in neat rows by the hundreds. There was the ubiquitous drill field. And soldiers were everywhere, some moving about on personal or official business, some grouped together around small campfires, idling the morning away.

While the encampment was much like Camp Dennison in size and scope, to Daniel there seemed to be something much more serious and official about this camp. These weren't a bunch of raw recruits learning how to march in a field, these were real soldiers going about the business of war.

The boys rushed over to where the company sergeants had positioned themselves to act as guides for the lines. With an efficiency born of repetition, the regiment lined up. Roll was called, and the men were assigned their duties for the day.

With few exceptions, the entire regiment went to work preparing their camp. They paced out an area for the company streets and erected officers' tents first, followed by the large tepee-shaped Sibley tents for the enlisted men. Each Sibley tent held up to twelve men, with a space in the middle for a stove that was left on the wagons. Instead, fire pits were dug on the company street for cooking.

Daniel and Christopher both had picket duty that night. So, after drill they were free the rest of the day. Daniel took advantage of his free time to write letters home to Susan and his parents. He also tried to get some sleep before he had to stand guard that night.

Christopher spent his free time exploring the camp with Ezra. After visiting almost every cavalry and artillery unit, petting the horses, admiring the field pieces, and chatting up anyone who would listen, the two returned to camp just in time for Christopher to grab his traps and rifle and head out to the picket line.

CHAPTER TEN
THE 8ᵀᴴ MOVES OUT

Despite his extra hours of sleep, the darkness and monotony of picket duty lulled Daniel into nodding off. His head was drooping and eyes closing when he heard the gunshot. It took a second for him to realize what it was, but when he did, it was like kerosene on an open flame. His breath caught in his chest, and every muscle in his body tensed. Somewhere on the line, a picket had encountered the enemy. This was the real thing.

All thoughts of sleep disappeared as Daniel retrieved a percussion cap and placed it on the nipple of his rifle.

The moon was barely a sliver in the sky, so it was too dark to see more than vague shapes. Daniel stared out into the field before him for any movement or shape that didn't look natural. He considered calling the corporal of the guard, Ebenezer Bunce, but at this point he had nothing to report and, if something were happening, they would come get him.

After what seemed hours, he heard movement to his left. Someone was coming down the picket line. Daniel turned that direction and waited until he could see the outline of a man walking toward his post.

"Halt! Who comes there?"

"Friend, Galloway. It's me, Bunce."

"Advance, friend, with the countersign."

"I told you it was me."

"Then give the countersign—Scrooge."

"Dammit, Galloway! You know I hate that name!"

Daniel laughed. "That couldn't be anyone but you, Ebenezer."

Corporal Bunce walked up to where Daniel could make out his features. "Monterey. Damn you," he grumbled.

Daniel smiled. "I guess you know the countersign."

"We got bigger things to worry about than countersigns. Your brother took a shot at something in the field. You seen anything?"

Daniel shook his head. Then it occurred to him Bunce might not have seen it in the dark, so he responded, "Nothing here. All quiet. Chris all right?"

"He's fine. Sutton's with him, trying to figure out what he saw. Chris said something in the field charged at him. He fired and took off like a scared rabbit. At least he had the presence of mind to call for the corporal of the guard. No one else has reported seeing anything. So it sounds like it may have been a false alarm."

The sound of the long roll blasted from the camp. If it was a false alarm, everyone was being woken up for nothing. He couldn't decide whether to hope it was nothing and Christopher was safe, in which case his brother would face the ridicule of the whole regiment, or to hope it was something so Christopher could be the hero of the hour.

He then heard someone else approaching from farther up the picket line. Both he and Corporal Bunce looked in that direction. Daniel brought his rifle up across his chest and called out, "HALT! Who comes there?"

"Friend."

Daniel recognized the voice of Lieutenant Sutton. "Advance, friend, with the countersign."

Lieutenant Sutton walked up and noticed Corporal Bunce. "This the last picket?" he asked.

"The countersign, sir," Daniel interrupted before Bunce responded.

The whole regiment knew one of Colonel DeVillier's favorite tricks back at Camp Dennison was to trick pickets into breaking protocol or surrendering their weapons, and then writing them up. Sutton took no offense at the interruption. "Monterey," he said.

"There's two more posts, sir," Bunce said.

"Good. Make your rounds. Tell everyone everything is all right. Galloway, the younger, took a pot shot at a cow is all."

"A cow? How the hell did he mistake a cow for an enemy soldier…sir?"

Sutton shrugged. "The night plays tricks on your eyes, I guess."

Sutton looked at Daniel and continued. "I heard the long roll. By now the whole regiment is awake. I need to get back and tell Colonel DePuy everything is all right. Your brother's in for a snootful of ribbing come tomorrow."

Daniel looked away and nodded. *Leave it to Christopher to get in trouble the first night. And somehow he'll drag me into it.*

—⁓—

The next morning, as Daniel stood in line, he heard the gossip. "False alarm.." "Some damned fool shot at a cow…" "Who was it?" "Did he hit the cow?" "We having beef for breakfast?" Then Daniel's stomach did a flip-flop at the word he'd been expecting. "Galloway…" "It was Galloway…" Soon, everyone around Daniel was looking at him. The icy cold in his innards grew until he thought he would puke icicles, but his cheeks were on fire.

Someone slapped him on the back. "The Galloway boys strike again."

It took all Daniel's willpower not to turn and strike the man who'd spoke. Daniel wouldn't suffer any direct consequences for Christopher's actions this time, but everything Christopher did reflected on him. They'd almost overcome their reputation as brawlers, now everyone would see them as trigger-happy.

Sergeant Rust was taking roll that morning. Apparently, the officers didn't appreciate their beauty rest being interrupted. Finally, he said, "Everyone is dismissed. Those of you coming off picket duty, as you fall out, unload and clean your rifles. Corporal of the Guard, make sure everyone's rifle is clean before they go back to bed. That's it. Company! Dis— MISSED."

Daniel turned to go to Christopher. As he did, the man who'd slapped him on the back and made the earlier comment came up and said, "You need to put your little brother on a leash, Galloway."

Daniel turned on the man and raised his fist to strike. Then Sergeant Rust appeared and placed a hand on his shoulder. "Walk with me, Galloway."

Daniel locked eyes with his tormentor and held them for a moment. Then he turned and fell in beside Sergeant Rust as he made his way through the men. As he did, Rust made sure everyone was doing something—either cleaning their rifle or preparing breakfast. He encouraged other corporals to help Bunce with the men coming off picket. On any other occasion, Daniel would have been soaking up everything Rust said and did, trying to learn how to be an effective leader, but that morning he was too preoccupied. His brother seemed to have disappeared.

"Don't be too hard on your brother, Daniel," Rust said. "What happened could have happened to any of us."

"Christopher shot at a cow. How do you mistake a cow for a Confederate?" Daniel said, repeating Bunce's reaction from last night.

Sergeant Rust shrugged. "It's our first time in the field as soldiers. We don't know what to expect or what it'll be like when we face the enemy. Did your brother err? Yes, he did. But he did so on the side of caution. When you're encamped in enemy territory, that is the right thing to do. Imagine if he had not fired, and it was a host of secesh creeping up on us. Your brother would now be dead or a prisoner, and we'd be routed. Then it wouldn't be just one soldier disgraced, it would be the whole regiment—at least what was left of it."

Daniel nodded. He appreciated the words, but this would still be something they would have to live with for a while.

"Clean your rifle, private." Sergeant Rust left Daniel to his last task as picket. Daniel reached into his cartridge box for his worm—the tool that screwed onto the end of the ramrod for extracting an unfired ball.

—⚬—

Breakfast was a quiet, uncomfortable affair. Christopher appeared shortly after the coffee came to a boil and sat down without a word.

"I wonder if we'll be doing drill today?" Ezra said.

"Probably," Bonnett replied. "We usually do."

"Company drill?"

"Of course."

"Regiment?"

"Maybe."

"Battalion?"

Bonnett spit tobacco juice into the fire. "What are you doing, Rouse, writing a book?"

"Maybe. What's wrong with that? Someday people will want to know what happened here."

"I doubt it," Bonnett said. "And if they did, they wouldn't be reading about it from the likes of you."

Ezra ignored the slight as they dug into breakfast. Afterward, he brought up the various methods of drill and, after that, the weather.

Daniel breathed a sigh of relief when the drumroll to line up interrupted their breakfast. "Thank God," he said. "If this had gone on any longer, Ezra would have described his morning constitutional."

They lined up and received their orders from Lieutenant Barnes.

"Boys, we are moving out. Gather your gear and report for duty in full kit. You will be issued three days' rations and forty cartridges. Make sure your canteens are full and that you have a full cap box. Company, dis— MISSED."

Daniel made a beeline for his Sibley, looking around for his brother as he moved through the camp. As he approached, he saw a lot of familiar faces, but no Christopher. Eyeing Ezra Rouse in the crowd, he called out, "Ezra, where's Christopher?"

Ezra turned and jutted his chin toward the tent they all shared.

As Daniel entered the tent, he saw Christopher on his knees buckling his knapsack.

"Big night," Daniel said, moving toward his area.

Christopher nodded but said nothing.

"I wish we could get some sleep before moving out."

Christopher nodded.

Daniel kneeled and rolled up his blanket. He'd been thinking what he'd say to Christopher when they met up, but now he was at a loss for words. As Daniel filled his knapsack with his personal items, Christopher stood, slipped on his knapsack, and fumbled with the clasps.

Daniel rose and moved across the tent, reaching to help. Christopher took a step back and shook his head. "I got this," he said.

Daniel let his arms drop and stood, feeling awkward. It was a strange, uncomfortable feeling. He wasn't used to being awkward and tongue-tied before his brother. "Anyone say anything to you this morning?"

Christopher shook his head. "They don't have to. I know what they're thinking."

"Who cares."

Christopher looked up at that, and Daniel's heart broke at the hurt look in his brother's eyes. "I do."

"You know what I'm thinking?" Daniel asked.

Christopher shook his head. "Don't tell me."

"I'm thinking what you did was brave and true to your regiment."

Christopher looked up again, this time the hurt was tempered with confusion. "Don't feed me a load of blarney, Danny. I know I did wrong."

"You made a mistake, Chris, but you did nothing wrong. Why, Sergeant Rust told me if you hadn't fired, and it was an enemy attack, we would probably all be dead or in chains by now."

Christopher shook his head. "Doesn't matter. The boys will hate me."

"A few might. But not me. And if anyone wants to push you around over it, they'll have to answer to me."

Christopher started to say something, but at that moment Ezra stuck his head in and said, "You better get out here, they're fixin' to call roll."

Daniel resumed packing as Christopher moved toward the door. Before exiting the tent, he stopped with his hand on the tent flap. Without looking back, he said, "Thanks, Danny." Then he was gone.

―⁂―

The 8th traveled by train to Oakland, Maryland, where they stayed long enough for the regiment to dismantle every fence within walking distance to the depot for firewood. While the quartermaster staff rounded up wagons and saw to the transfer of supplies from the train cars, the rest of the regiment ate a meal of hardtack, salt pork, and desiccated vegetables (called desecrated vegetables by the men because of how bad they looked and tasted).

Daniel noticed the wagons and realized they would be marching from that point on. He was starting to understand the importance of a soldier in the field to take food and sleep wherever and whenever he could get it. So, after he finished eating, he lay down in the grass and let the late-morning sun and the rhythmic chuffing of the locomotive lull him to sleep.

Later that afternoon, they started walking. All they knew was that they were heading for some place called Union Town, or West Union Town, or something like that, a two-days march away. Once they were on the road, Daniel realized they were walking toward the setting sun. That morning, as they rode the train, they'd been heading toward the rising sun.

Daniel spotted Sergeant Reid walking along beside the column, headed toward the rear of the company. "Hey, Sergeant Reid?" he called out. "Aren't we going back the way we came?"

"You know as much as I do, Galloway."

"But, why didn't we just take the train back?"

"You see any tracks around here?"

"But—"

Sergeant Reid held up a hand, palm out. "I haven't got time to chat now. All will be revealed in good time."

They continued to march the rest of the day, with only short breaks to catch their breath, but not time enough to take off their knapsacks. Soon, the pace was taking its toll on several of the men, and the column got longer and longer as men fell behind the main body.

"If we don't stop soon, it'll be midnight before some of these boys make it to camp," Corporal Bonnett said.

The rugged terrain made it worse. Sometimes they would struggle up a steep incline for what seemed like hours. Going uphill, Daniel's thighs would burn and his breath came in ragged gasps. Then, when he crested what he assumed was the top of the hill, he would discover, to his great disappointment, that it was just a temporary leveling of the ground before the road started uphill again. After several hours of this, he was sure they had spent twice as much time going uphill as down.

As the sun set, Daniel wasn't sure how much farther he could go. His legs were like lead, his arms were numb, and his rifle felt twice as heavy as when he started.

A fine dust covered his face and body, making it hard to breathe. The sweat that dripped off his brow created brown streaks on his forehead and cheeks. Even with the well-fitting shoes his father had given him, he had quarter-size blisters on both heels. This march might be worse than the disciplinary march with the knapsacks full of rocks he and Christopher had to endure—at least that had ended quickly compared to this endless torture.

With that thought, he looked back over his shoulder and tried to spot his brother. The regiment was spread out on the road for miles. Everywhere he looked men walked slumped over, slack-jawed and despondent, staring at the ground or the back of the man before them. The line went on until it wrapped around a bend and out of sight.

Then, like a call to glory, the bugle call for halt was sounded somewhere up ahead. Sergeants and lieutenants came trotting down the road calling out, "Keep moving! Keep moving! Guide on the man in front of you."

"Well, there's an end to this hell after all," Corporal Bonnett said.

"Yes," Daniel responded, "but when? Have you looked behind us?"

Bonnett looked over his shoulder and nodded. "It'll be all night before all those Sunday soldiers make it into camp."

Eventually, most of the regiment came together, and the men were dismissed. A few corporals were volunteered to go back and round up stragglers. Corporal Bonnett was one of them. As he set to leave, Daniel smiled and said, "I guess you'll earn your two extra dollars this month."

Bonnett frowned at him and said, "Next opening comes up, I'll put your name in the hat. It's not fair I have all the fun."

Daniel laughed as Bonnett walked away, but inside he felt a thrill. Corporal. That would be a feather in his cap for old Johnston to choke on.

CHAPTER ELEVEN
RED HOUSE

Christopher hadn't even had time to get any sleep after his disastrous night of picket duty before they moved out again. He'd tried to sleep on the train, but that's when the ribbing started.

He had made a bed of straw, using his haversack as a pillow, and was letting the rocking of the train car lull him to sleep when he heard the first "Mooooo…" It was just one person, and it was quiet, but once it started, others took up the call until there were several "moos" of different pitch and duration, followed by a raucous outburst of laughter.

Christopher remembered how his cheeks blazed, and his body tensed. His hands balled up into fists and his jaw clenched so tight his teeth hurt. He rolled over and threw his arm up over his head to block out the sound. He wanted to jump up and thrash the lot of them. But, he couldn't fight everyone. That was just the beginning. He would have to ride it out.

"Hey, Galloway," a voice called from somewhere in the crowd, "come over here by the door so you can keep an eye out for bovine attacks." Everyone laughed again.

Suddenly, Ezra shot bolt upright, as if shocked. "Who said that?"

The laughter stopped. No one said anything.

Christopher put a hand on Ezra's arm. "Forget it, Ezra. It doesn't matter."

"Like hell," Ezra replied, frowning at the surrounding men.

Christopher shook his head. "Let it go. Like the Good Book says, this too shall pass."

"I don't like it," Ezra said. "Wait'll it's their turn. They'll get theirs."

"I'm sure, but we can't take on the lot of them."

"We can try," Ezra mumbled. Then he burst out in a loud voice, "Just remember, ye shall reap what you sow!"

After that, no one had bothered him, and Christopher had drifted off in into a semi-sleep, just before they reached their destination.

Now, after hours of marching, Christopher's whole body hurt—his back was knotted, his thighs burned, and his feet shot sharp pains up his legs with every step. He'd been telling himself he couldn't take another step for about a half hour when the bugle call to halt sounded somewhere in the distance. He lifted his head and peered into the darkness, but the bugle call was far ahead, and he knew he had a ways to go before he could relax. He was somewhere near the back of the column, marching with strangers, and had no idea how far he'd have to walk to find Company D.

The only familiar face nearby was Ezra's. The steady, easy gait and relaxed manner in which Ezra marched didn't match the sloop-shouldered, slack-jawed, shuffle of the other stragglers. It occurred to Christopher that Ezra was not straggling because he had to.

Soon, he heard calls from up ahead.

"Company A to me!"

"Company B to me!"

When they heard Company D called, Christopher and Ezra picked up their pace and moved toward the sound of the voice. They came upon Corporal Bonnett, who was moving through the men, calling for Company D in a bored and frustrated tone.

"Here we are, Corporal," Christopher called out.

"Oh, thank the Lord, Galloway and Rouse are found. The company is whole once more," Bonnett sniped. "Fall in with me. Once we've rounded up the rest of you laggards, I'll take you in."

Corporal Bonnett rounded up over a dozen men from Company D and led them to where the company had made camp.

They found their mess site, with Daniel and Charlie Locker resting next to a fire and a pot of hot coffee. Christopher scrambled to get off his knapsack. Once free of the weight on his back, he thought he'd never experienced such blessed relief. His hands tingled as the blood rushed back into them, and it almost seemed he was floating. He fumbled through his haversack, looking for his cup, when the call to fall in filled the air.

"Damn it all to hell!" Christopher said, shocking himself with the sudden curse. He groaned, and his whole body seemed to sag. He was certain he couldn't get back up.

Then Lieutenant Sutton came and gave him hope. Companies A and D were just taking roll call; they would stay under Major Sawyer's command to guard the crossroad while the rest of the regiment marched ahead to their original destination.

"Thank you. Thank you, thank you, thank you," Christopher said to no one in particular. Then, self-conscious of his swearing, he said, "Thank you, Jesus," and followed it up with a silent *forgive me my sins* as he crossed himself.

Daniel helped him up, and Christopher was able to stand long enough to make it through roll call. Only two names from Company D went unanswered. Sergeant Reid informed Captain Daggett that those men were in Company Q—sick call.

As the sun set, a heavy mist rolled in. As Christopher ate his dinner, the mist turned to a light rain. Christopher saw one of the 8th's chaplains, Father Freeman—except he didn't like to be called Father—pass. Pastor Freeman led a group of sick men, some using their rifles as a crutch, others being assisted by their pards, and some being carried on stretchers. They appeared to be heading for a house, lit up bright and warm in the cold, dark night.

Ezra let out a loud fart. "I think I'm getting sick. I'd better head up there with them boys," he said.

Bonnett looked at him. "Stay where you're at, Rouse. You have picket duty coming up."

"What?" Ezra said, panicked. "When? How do you know? No one's passed down orders yet."

"I feel it in my bones."

"Ah, you're just makin' that up."

"We'll see."

—⁂—

The next morning, Companies D and A were back on the road before sunrise. It continued to rain off and on all morning as they marched through the mountainous countryside. Late in the morning, they reached West Union and joined up with rest of the regiment and the 16th OVI.

As the officers parleyed, the men mingled and shared what they knew. Christopher learned that a rebel force led by General Garnett was retreating and could pass by their location at any time. So everyone was trying to catch the secesh army before it got away.

It was afternoon and still raining off and on. The two regiments spread throughout the town, collapsing wherever they could find a spot. The men were worn out and depressed from the weather, the exertion, or both. They looked like a bunch of invalids, not an army ready for battle. That night, since they didn't have tents, they sought shelter on porches, under wagons, or anywhere they could to escape the seemingly unending rain.

The next morning they were again up and marching before sunrise. Christopher didn't know which was worse, the lack of breakfast due to their speedy departure—or Ezra's constant griping about the lack of breakfast.

After marching most of the morning, they arrived at a town called Red House. Ezra looked around, took a swig out of his canteen, and spit half of it back out. "I don't see any red houses."

"Maybe they were painted. I don't know if I'd want to live in a red house," Christopher replied.

"Oh, I don't know. It wouldn't be so bad—kinda spooky, maybe."

The soldiers wasted no time gathering up firewood from wherever they could find it before making campfires, boiling coffee, and frying salt pork.

The sun returned the following morning. By the time they had finished eating and were starting on their second cup of coffee, Christopher was nearly dry. Except for the fact that he stank, was covered in mud, his socks were stuck to his heals by dried blood and pus, and every muscle in his body ached, he felt almost restored.

Christopher finally got his socks off, washed them, and draped them over the bayonet of his rifle to dry. The rifles were stacked together in a tepee shape, interlocked at the bayonets to keep the breeches out of the dirt. Christopher inspected the blisters on his heels while Ezra picked lice out of the jacket draped across his lap. Each louse he found, he brought up close to his face for inspection, pinched it between his thumbnail and finger, and flicked the carcass into the fire.

Without looking up from his task, Ezra said, "You better hope you don't knock those rifles over getting your socks back on or there'll be hell to pay."

"Don't worry about it——"

"Damn it all to hell! Who's hanging their laundry on the rifle stacks?"

Christopher and Ezra both jumped as Sergeant Reid came storming up, pointing at Christopher's socks.

"Those are mine, Sergeant," Christopher said.

"Well, get 'em off there…And if you knock over the stack, you'll spend the afternoon running up and down the road here in full gear. Got that?"

"Yes, Sergeant," Christopher said, scrambling to his feet.

"Told ya," Ezra said as the sergeant walked away.

"Told ya," Christopher whined back at him.

—⚏—

Christopher had just finished tying his shoes when the bugle call for assembly sounded, followed by Sergeant Reid's voice. "Company D, fall in." As he limped over to his spot in the line, Christopher noticed Company A was also falling in, but no one else.

"Looks like we got the short straw again," Ezra said.

"Maybe Major Sawyer is bucking for a promotion," Chris replied.

After roll call, Major Sawyer addressed the two companies under his command.

"Gentlemen, we have received reports of Confederate troops in the area. If you didn't hear, there was a battle the other day at a place called Rich Mountain. That battle was an indubitable victory for the Federal

Army, and the enemy is on the run." That announcement got a rousing cheer from the men.

"What does 'indubabble' mean?" Ezra asked.

Christopher shrugged. "Big?"

"Undisputed, certain," someone said.

Christopher looked around to find the unknown scholar as Major Sawyer continued.

"What you probably haven't heard is that they are on the run right through this area. In fact, they were just here in this valley last night—passing through on their way south. They are right down that road." He pointed, and every man strained to look as if they would somehow see the rebel soldiers scurrying away. "It has been tasked to us to pursue them down said road, ascertain their strength and condition, and engage if conditions are favorable."

"Yep, he's a lawyer," Christopher mumbled.

After some private discussion amongst the officers and sergeants, Major Sawyer began issuing commands.

"Attention!"

Everyone came to attention, backs straight, heels together, toes pointed out forty-five degrees, eyes looking ahead just above the horizon, and rifles straight up and down at their side.

"Company!"

Christopher's muscles tensed in anticipation.

"Shoulder—ARMS!"

The soldiers raised their rifles together with a precision Christopher did not think possible two months ago.

"To the rear, open order!"

The sergeants at either end of the company in the rear rank stepped back four paces.

"MARCH!"

The rear rank stepped back until they were aligned with the sergeants.

"Inspection—ARMS!"

The soldiers pulled the ramrods out of their slots and dropped them down the barrel of their rifles. Then they unlatched their cartridge boxes.

Once the officers inspected each man to insure his rifle was in working order and he had plenty of cartridges and water, they closed ranks.

They loaded their rifles, attached their bayonets, and brought their rifles back to their right shoulders.

"Company! Left face! MARCH!"

"Guide on the first sergeant! Forward! MARCH!"

Everyone stepped out and followed Sergeant Reid out into the middle of the street and to the edge of town. Unlike the shuffling route step of the last several days, they marched with parade ground precision. Company D was in the lead, and Company A followed.

As they exited the town, Major Sawyer issued the command to shift into battle line. To the citizens of Red House, it must have looked like pandemonium, but every man knew what to do, and in a matter of seconds, each company went from four columns marching down the road to two lines, two men deep, spread out in battle formation—without slowing their forward pace.

Next, Major Sawyer had them break into platoons. The left half of each company stopped stepping forward but continued marching in place. The right half continued forward, with the sergeant guiding them to the left oblique until they were centered on the road. Once the first platoon was far enough ahead, the second platoon stepped out, moving to the right oblique until they were behind the first platoon.

Christopher, in Company D's second platoon, had to fight the urge to look behind him to see how close Company A's first platoon was the entire time he marched in place. But he knew he had to stay focused and trust the officers, or he would create the collision he feared.

The two companies had created four battle lines, each containing close to fifty men. In the lead, Company D's first platoon deployed as skirmishers. Christopher watched as the battle line in front of him spread out into a single line, each man approximately five paces from the man next to him. This maneuver didn't go as smoothly as the rest because the men had to contend with fences and the rocky, tree-covered landscape. They still performed the shift admirably, Christopher thought, and felt a burst of pride for his company.

The skirmishers moved across the open fields as best they could, their rifles held at the ready position. The following platoon leaders slowed their men to avoid getting too close.

Christopher saw Daniel on the skirmish line, leaning forward with his back hunched, his head swiveling left and right. He wondered what his brother was thinking, being out in front and knowing the enemy was somewhere ahead.

Christopher shifted his rifle and wiped his sweaty palms on the front of his jacket. It had gotten hot out, he noticed.

The skirmish line stopped, and they all kneeled down on one knee. The command to halt echoed across the battle lines. Everyone stopped and listened.

For a moment, it was quiet. Not even the sound of birds or insects broke the silence. Then the tree line fifty yards before the skirmish line erupted in a cloud of smoke. Christopher heard the thunder of rifle fire and another noise he couldn't quite place. It sounded like the buzzing of bees—but fast, the sound coming and going in an instant.

The skirmish line returned fire and began falling back. They worked in pairs. One man would fire, drop back ten paces, and reload; once his rifle was loaded, the second man would fire and run back ten paces behind his partner.

The unseen enemy, meanwhile, continued to fire. But, after the first volley, they shot individually, so the fire was sporadic and less unnerving. At the first volley, Christopher hunched over, and his head ducked down between his shoulders as low as possible, but he stayed in the line. He still thought he heard an occasional bee buzz past, but he was too focused on what was going on to give it much thought.

Christopher kept alternating his attention from the tree line to his brother and back. At one point, he thought he caught a glimpse of gray cloth in the trees behind the expanding cloud of smoke, but he couldn't be sure.

Once the skirmishers had moved back to the front of the second platoon, Major Sawyer ordered them to the rear. Then, nothing stood between Christopher and the enemy. Lieutenant Sutton, who commanded the second platoon, ordered them forward at the double quick.

For a second, Christopher wondered if he'd be able to move. His head said go, but nothing happened. His file partner gave him a shove from behind and he jogged forward, still hunched over.

"Second platoon—HALT! Dress your line!"

Christopher skidded to a halt and looked to his right toward Lieutenant Sutton. Everyone adjusted until their lines were straight, ignoring the fire still coming from the trees.

"Firing by rank! Front rank—READY!"

Christopher fumbled a percussion cap until he had it seated on the breech nipple and tucked the rifle butt into his shoulder.

"AIM!"

He raised the muzzle and pointed it in the general direction of the trees. Since he couldn't see through the smoke, there was nothing specific to aim at.

"FIRE!"

Christopher pulled the trigger. His rifle bucked into his shoulder, and the muzzle flipped up, but he regained control and brought it back down. He tried to peer through the smoke but could see no sign that the volley had any impact.

"Front rank—LOAD! Rear rank—READY!"

At that moment, the enemy fired another volley. *There are the bees again*, Christopher thought. He'd just figured out what the buzzing really was, when the left side of his head exploded with a sharp, tearing pain. He put his hand up over his ear, and blood gushed over his fingers.

Christopher's breath caught in his chest, and he looked around for reassurance. Ezra, in the rear rank behind him, put his hand on Christopher's shoulder and turned him around. Ezra's face was pale, almost white, and his bloodshot eyes were open wide and unblinking.

"Y-Y-Y-You've been shot!" As Ezra spoke, his voice rose in both pitch and volume, and the word "shot" came out as a loud squeak.

Christopher's knees threatened to buckle, and his vision blurred. As if from a distance, he heard the command "AIM," and was overcome with indignation that no one other than him and Ezra seemed concerned that he was shot and bleeding.

"FIRE!"

The rear rank erupted in a single explosion of noise, smoke, and fire—all except Ezra, who still stood ashen faced, staring at Christopher's ear. Christopher jumped at the noise and started to shake.

Then a firm hand grasped his upper arm. Christopher was once again pulled around until he found himself staring into Corporal Bill Gridley's eyes. The corporal tried to look both concerned and nonchalant at the same time. "How bad is it?"

Christopher shook his head, and blood speckled his shoulder. He winced at the sudden pain. Gridley pulled him back behind the line, retrieved a bandana from his haversack, and wiped the blood from Christopher's ear.

"Looks like it scraped the side of your head and took a little chunk off the top of your ear, but you should be okay. Probably want to wear your hair a little longer from here on out," he said with a smile.

He pressed the bandana against Christopher's head until it stung. "Here, hold that there until the bleeding stops."

"Thanks," Christopher mumbled.

The line was moving again—jogging forward at the double quick. Ezra tried to look over his shoulder as he jogged. His foot hit a rock, and he stumbled forward. Those around him jerked back, and the line crumbled.

"Close up that line! Where's my file closer?" Lieutenant Sutton looked around until he saw Corporal Gridley several yards behind the line with Christopher.

"Gridley! Get your sorry ass up here and help me corral these skittish colts!"

"Coming, Lieutenant!"

Turning to Christopher, he said, "Come on, you'll be all right. We have some secesh to catch."

They trotted forward, Christopher holding his rifle in one hand and the other pressed against the side of his head. He was dizzy and off balance and stumbled and swayed like a drunk hurrying for the outhouse.

They stopped once more and poured another volley into the tree line. Christopher's wound was still oozing, and his hands were sticky with blood. As he tried to load his rifle, the paper of the cartridge stuck to his shaking fingers and it came apart, spilling gunpowder over his fingers and hand. He retrieved another cartridge and managed to get most of the powder down the barrel. He had just finished ramming the minié ball home when he heard the command he dreaded the most: "Charge bayonets!"

They had discussed the concept of close combat at Camp Dennison, and he had performed bayonet drills until he could jab straw men in his sleep. But in all their drills, the straw men had never jabbed back.

Christopher had always avoided physical confrontation because of his small size. He had never been in a serious fight in his life, and he was still lightheaded and shaken from having been shot.

He wasn't ready for this.

Regardless, Christopher stepped back with his right foot, so his body was bladed forty-five degrees to the enemy, and raised his rifle until the bayonet was at eye level. He looked around for Ezra, and their eyes locked for a fleeting second. Were his own eyes as wide and wild looking as his pard's?

"Platoon. At the quick step. Forward—MARCH!"

They set off for the trees at a brisk jog. Christopher tried to keep an eye on the lieutenant and sergeant acting as guides at either end of the line to make sure he didn't get out ahead or drag behind. But, it proved much more difficult to do in actual combat than in drill. There were too many distractions—like men wanting to kill him.

When they reached the woods, they slowed down, but still managed a brisk pace as they wove their way through the trees and undergrowth. Christopher imagined a rebel soldier behind every tree he passed, waiting to step out and skewer him on his bayonet. Sweat dripped down from his hat band and into his eyes. His breathing was fast and shallow, and he couldn't see beyond a small tunnel of light directly in front of him.

Lieutenant Sutton called a halt, and the woods fell into complete silence. The enemy was gone. But, looking ahead, they saw discarded equipment scattered among the trees—haversacks, knapsacks, belts and cartridge boxes, hats and jackets, and even a few rifles.

"They're on the run, boys!" Lieutenant Sutton bellowed.

"HUZZAH!" the men cheered. Some took off their caps and waved them in the air. Christopher took off his cap and wiped his brow. He sucked in great gulps of clean-smelling air and leaned on his rifle.

The secesh couldn't be too far ahead, and Christopher was wondering if they would go after them when a runner came up and handed a piece of paper to Lieutenant Sutton.

After reading the message, he looked up and addressed the platoon. "Boys. You did a bang-up job today. The enemy is on the run, but Company A will take it from here.

"Platoon! Attention! About—face. Forward—MARCH!"

As the platoon exited the woods, Christopher saw that Company A had come up to the tree line and eagerly waited to take their place.

Ezra called out, "We got the secesh on the run, boys. But you can clean up the mess."

"Step aside, children. The men are here to take over," someone responded.

That led to a blast of good-natured boasts and insults from both companies as they passed one another.

Then they passed Company D's first platoon, who had re-assembled behind Company A after being pulled back. Christopher saw his brother in the line, face and cheeks blackened with powder, staring at him. Daniel's face was contorted in grief, and he looked as if he would keel over at any moment. Christopher wondered if he'd been shot too, when it occurred to him how he must look with the side of his head and hands covered in blood. He mouthed "I'm okay," as he walked past.

The second platoon fell in behind the first. Daniel twisted around and tried to get Christopher's attention until a sergeant barked at him to get his eyes front. There was a lot of excited chatter in the platoon, including Ezra poking Christopher in the back and talking about his "red badge of courage," until Lieutenant Sutton ordered them to be quiet.

That was all right with Christopher. He didn't feel like talking or celebrating. His ear hurt, he was dirty and sticky from all the blood, and he was so drained it was a wonder he was still standing. But mostly, he was in awe of what had just happened. He'd been shot at. Hell, he'd been shot. He'd have a notch in his ear from this day forward to remind him of the first time he'd experienced combat.

He'd seen the elephant.

CHAPTER TWELVE
CAMP PENDLETON TO HANGING ROCK

Daniel stood with a shovel in one hand and a tin cup of water in the other as he stared at the log walls being built around the newly christened Camp Pendleton, better known as Camp Maggoty Hollow. As he thought about the events of the last two weeks, he wondered how he had become so demoralized so fast.

The company had been in high spirits after that skirmish outside Red House. They had chased the enemy for two miles, capturing nine prisoners, several horses, and a variety of discarded equipment. They even captured a wagon full of rifles and pistols. Several members of Company A, who weren't issued the rifled Enfields, took advantage of the find to replace the old Austrian smoothbores they carried.

The prisoners said they were part of the rear guard and that the rebel army was long gone, so Major Sawyer turned the expedition around and headed back to Red House. From there, they took the main road eastward to hook up with General Hill's brigade and the rest of the 8th.

Daniel had gotten into the rhythm of the march and had resigned himself to a long, hard hike, when they met the brigade going the other way at the quick step. Daniel thought they had missed out on a major battle, but found out later that General Hill had turned and ran based on false rumors, never having seen the enemy.

They returned to Red House with the rest of the brigade. Everyone who had taken part in the skirmish at Red House knew that the enemy was on the run. Daniel didn't understand why General Hill had called a retreat—nor did any of his friends.

"He is a coward, plain and simple," Charlie Locker had said.

"There's a lot that goes on we don't know about," Parker Bonnett countered.

Daniel didn't want to admit it, but he agreed with Charlie. Based on the lack of conviction in Parker's voice, Daniel thought he did too.

They camped at Red House for a day and a half before setting out "in pursuit" of the rebel army. Daniel figured it had taken that long for Major Sawyer and the other officers to convince General Hill that the enemy was, in fact, retreating.

They marched until midnight and all the next day. By the second morning, Daniel and everyone he talked to was tired and disgusted with General Hill and the toadies with which he surrounded himself. Daniel believed the march was a waste of time, the enemy being long gone.

At assembly, General Hill gave a speech, hoping to lift the boys' spirits. Daniel heard nothing the general said, but he gathered from the cheers and hat waving at the front of the crowd that it was a rousing speech. The general was interrupted by a rider with an urgent message and stopped his speech to read the written note. He then stepped down from the box he was using as a stage and walked away without another word. Two hours later, the brigade was marching back to Red House.

The men marched in silence. No one tried to start up a marching song. Whenever someone tried to spark a conversation, all he got was a one-word response if he had stripes on his sleeves, or silence if he didn't.

From Red House, General Hill marched the brigade to Oakland—except the 8th, which he left to occupy the town. They spent five days in Red House digging trenches that were never occupied and sharpening logs for abatises that were never completed. The army paid for the property they took to build the defenses with government IOUs.

To make matters worse, while in Red House, the men stole pigs and chickens, raided gardens, and destroyed almost every fence in town for firewood. Red House was a pro-Union town, but by the time the 8th left, they had destroyed any goodwill the citizens had toward the army.

As they marched out of town, the hard stares they received from the citizens made Daniel ashamed. As he looked over at the small crowd, his eyes met those of a grizzled old farmer, who spit on the ground and turned away.

Now they were at Camp Maggoty Hollow with the 17th Indiana, the 4th Ohio, and an artillery battery. They were constructing a new fort to protect a major east-west thoroughfare and a bridge over the Potomac River.

As Daniel returned the tin cup, he looked at the blistered palms of his hands and wondered why he ever joined the army. It wasn't to dig ditches.

After dinner, Daniel sat by the fire, sipping coffee and picking at the blisters. "Wasn't this war supposed to be over by now?"

"Ya," Charlie agreed. "We should be home now, dazzling all the pretty women with our big brass buttons and tales of glory."

"Ha!" Daniel laughed. "My only war tales involve marching back and forth down the same road and digging ditches. That won't impress any pretty women.

"Or their fathers," he mumbled under his breath.

Parker took a draw on his pipe and said, "You should get shot like your brother. That seems to be what it takes to make you the belle of the ball."

Companies D and A enjoyed a fair amount of renown, having seen and fought the enemy. Christopher, with his notched ear and ragged scar along the side of his head, was enjoying his newfound popularity and spent less and less time with Daniel and their messmates.

"Where is the belle tonight?" Charlie asked.

"Notch," Daniel sneered. "Everyone's calling him 'Notch' now on account of the chunk outta his ear. I saw him and Ezra over by the artillery camp."

"Artillery." Parker spit a piece of tobacco into the fire. "There's the life. Ride a wagon into battle, yank a lanyard a couple times, then ride back to camp for a meal of fresh meat and vegetables and warm, soft bread."

"That is one thing about camp life," Daniel agreed. "We get vegetables and soft bread with our meals. I might starve on a long campaign with nothing but salt pork and hard crackers."

"I hate that salt pork," Charlie said. "I don't think there is enough water in the world to slake your thirst after a meal of that stuff."

"I thought you Germans liked preserved meat," Daniel said, knowing a dig at Charlie's heritage would get his hackles up.

"When done right," Charlie replied. "We grind it up with lots of seasoning." Then he grinned and winked. "That way, it tastes so good you're not too particular about what's in it."

Christopher and Ezra appeared long after the bugler sounded the evening tattoo. They entered the tent, giggling and stumbling. As they made their way across the tent, they stepped on more than one leg or hand.

Soon, everyone was awake.

After dodging a chorus of curses and flying shoes, Christopher lay down in his spot next to Daniel and let out a big sigh that ended in a stifled guffaw.

"You need to lay off the bark juice, Chris," Daniel said. "It will get you in trouble."

"Pshaw," Christopher replied. "I'm just taking the edge off is all."

"At your age, there is no edge to take off."

"How would you know, you ever been shot?"

"It was just a scratch. You didn't even spend any time in the hospital."

"That's beside the point. What's it to you, anyway?"

"I don't want you getting in trouble. What if you get caught out of the tent in the middle of the night?"

"What's the matter? Afraid I'll hurt your chances for some stripes?"

Daniel felt his cheeks redden and was thankful for the darkness. "The only one going to get hurt from your behavior is you."

"Yes…well…it's war. That's what happens."

"What kind of dumb thinking is that? You need to settle down before something happens and you end up in the guardhouse." Daniel paused. "I'm just trying to look out for you, Chris."

Daniel looked up at the smoke hole at the top of the tent. The camp was so far down in a ravine it seemed like the days were all dawn or dusk with little in-between. But when it wasn't cloudy and raining, they could look up at night and see the stars.

After a time, he continued, "Frankly, I don't like worrying about you all the time. We're soldiers. We both have a job to do. I should think of you as just another pard and messmate. But, I can't. You're my little brother, and that means something."

Daniel waited for his brother to respond. The only answer he got was the sound of snoring.

—⁂—

The next day, Daniel couldn't get out of bed. He woke to a pounding head, aching muscles, cold chills, and intense sweating. He had the disease of Camp Maggoty Hollow.

Since setting up camp in a ravine rarely graced by direct sunlight, an illness had swept over the men. The last Daniel heard, over two hundred were out sick. But more got sick every day, so the current number was probably much higher. Now, they would have to add Daniel's name to the list.

He looked over at Christopher who, despite the blast of a cannon, a bugle call, and the shouts of several sergeants, still slept. He reached over and shook his brother's shoulder. "Get up," he croaked.

Christopher snorted and shook off the hand. "No, Da. Let me sleep a little longer," he mumbled.

"I'm not Da, and you can't sleep a little longer," Daniel replied. "Sergeant Reid will poke his head in here any minute, and if you're not up, you'll be spending the day in the guard tent."

Christopher opened one eye and looked over at his brother. "You don't look so good."

"I don't feel so good. I think I need a transfer to Company Q."

Christopher sat up and grabbed his head. "Ow," he moaned. "I'm ready for Company Q too."

"Hangovers don't count. You'll be branded a beat and sent back. You wouldn't want to hurt your reputation as the hero of Red House, would you?"

Christopher struggled to his feet. "Anyone else called me the 'hero of Red House,' I'd almost take him serious, but when you say it, it sounds hateful."

He reached his hand down to Daniel. "Here, let me help you. We'll get you down to the surgeon so he can give you some quinine. You'll be up and about in no time."

Daniel didn't get better. Nor did he get worse. He lingered for days in the hospital tent somewhere between coherence and delirium. He lay and watched new men report sick every day. Fewer men left—some on their own, most on a stretcher, their dead faces covered by a blanket. Every day, as they removed the bodies, Daniel feared he would be next. *I wouldn't mind so much dying on a battlefield*, he told himself, *but to die of fever seems such a waste.*

Eventually, Daniel's fever broke, and he was able to sit up long enough to eat. Christopher tried to visit, but was not allowed in the tent for fear of contagion. Once he had the strength, they let Daniel leave the hospital for short walks with Christopher's help.

One evening, Christopher came to walk with Daniel and brought news.

"We're heading out tomorrow," he said. "I hear those who aren't too sick will come along in wagons. So, I guess you'll be with us. We'll be stopping in Grafton, and then on to Huttonville. I imagine we'll be back in the action soon."

Daniel frowned at the thought of Christopher marching off to battle without him.

"Major Sawyer is even sicker than you," Christopher continued. "He got to go home on leave though. I imagine while you're here languishing in a stinking hospital being waited on by orderlies who would rather be somewhere else, he's in his own bed under the tender care of his wife.

"Colonel DePuy's still out too." The regiment's commander had fallen off his horse and broke his arm. "Funny, I didn't see him in the hospital tent either. Must be rough being an officer."

Daniel smiled at his brother. "Why, Christopher, you've become a cynic. I knew they'd make a real soldier out of you."

Christopher let out a sigh. "I don't know. Maybe it's this camp. There's nothing to do but sit around and wait to get sick."

"And drill," Daniel added.

"And picket." Christopher laughed. "Everything but fight."

"Careful what you wish for," Daniel said, frowning. "After Bull Run, it looks like there will be plenty of fighting to go around."

"I told Da not to worry about the three-year term, we'd be home by Christmas."

Daniel squeezed his brother's shoulder. "I did too. We were just repeating what they told us."

Christopher shook his head. "Well, I got to get back. I got to pack both my kit and yours."

As Christopher turned to leave, Daniel grabbed his arm. "How are you doing, brother?" he asked. "How's the drinking?"

Christopher would not meet his gaze. He only shrugged and said, "Don't worry about me. I'm doing fine."

"And the drinking?"

"Under control."

Christopher walked away. A little too quick, Daniel thought.

—⚍—

On the march to Grafton, so many men fell out, including Daniel, that soon the wagons were overflowing. Many who made it all the way collapsed almost as soon as they were dismissed. The next day, they learned that the 25th would take their place, and the 8th would stay in Grafton. That was fine with Daniel. Though well enough to leave the hospital tent (where men continued to die daily) and handle light duty, he knew he wouldn't be able to keep up on a long march.

After a few days in Grafton, the regiment was broken up, and all the companies were assigned to different locations. Company D was moved to Oakland, Maryland on the Virginia border. With Colonel DePuy and much of the command staff out sick, the regiment's future seemed uncertain.

"I just know they're going to break us up," Charlie Locker said over evening coffee. "They can't have a regiment with no leadership."

"DePuy and Sawyer will be back, have no fear of that," Parker responded. "Once we're whole again, we'll tear 'em up…provided we get the chance."

"There's the rub," Daniel said. "We need a general that will fight."

The men all nodded. The Red House skirmish had gone so well, they were ready for more—maybe even a real battle.

After several weeks of drill and picket duty, they received orders to make ready to move out. As he lined up to receive his marching rations and ammunition, Daniel worried how far he'd make it. Could he keep up on an extended march? Even a trip to the commissary left him aching and worn out.

Fortunately, they departed by train and Daniel spent the day relaxing on a pile of hay, letting the rocking of the car sooth his aching body.

When they arrived at their destination, the men of Company D learned they were to be part of an expedition to take the town of Romney, Virginia. The total force was to include Companies B, D, G, and I of the 8th, led by Lieutenant Colonel Park, several companies from the 4th Ohio, a company of cavalry, and a single cannon and crew. Colonel Cantwell of the 4th was in command.

Once they were lined up awaiting inspection, Charlie leaned over and whispered to Daniel, "Keep an eye on that Cantwell, he may be our new commander."

Daniel shrugged. "As long as they keep Company D and the Norwalk boys together, I'm okay with whoever they put over us—as long as he'll fight."

Most of the expedition force spent the day trying to sleep. During that time, Daniel found out what he could about Romney. The town lay on the other side of the Potomac, reachable only by a single covered bridge. Its location—at a crossroads perfect for a supply line into the Shenandoah Valley—made it a desirable objective.

It was almost midnight when they set out on foot, heading east toward Romney. The first few miles weren't bad, but with each step, Daniel's back and legs ached a little more, and his breathing became a little more labored. By the time they made their first rest break, his clothes were soaked through with sweat, and his breathing was shallow and raspy. He half sat, half fell onto the ground where he stopped. After that, the rest of the march was a blur. At some point, someone took his rifle and pack, and he stumbled on unencumbered.

Shortly before dawn, they stopped at a fork in the road just outside Mechanicsburg, at the entrance to a gap in the high, steep ridge between them and Romney.

Colonel Cantwell sent the cavalry company ahead to scout the main road. Daniel appreciated the delay. Despite the noise and tension, he had no trouble taking a nap.

The cavalry had been out of sight for only a few minutes when the sound of gunfire woke Daniel. His rifle and pack lay on the ground next to him. Almost everyone else was standing and looking toward the pass.

Then, the cavalry came charging back up the road at a full gallop. Their captain reported to Colonel Cantwell while the troopers sat on their nervous horses and took guff from the surrounding infantrymen.

"Hey, trooper. Here's your mule!"

"The reverse charge! The cavalry's best maneuver."

"Any of you boys need your saddles washed? Two bits a saddle. You'll have to clean your own drawers though."

Angry shouts from company commanders cut the harassment short, followed by orders to fall in. After marching through Mechanicsburg, Companies D, G, and I of the 8th spread out on the left side of the road while the companies of the 4th spread out on the right. The 8th's Company B moved down the road, spread out in a skirmish line. The cavalry and cannon crew stayed back, watching the infantry companies maneuver from a safe distance.

Company B had gone down the road a hundred yards or so when pickets, hidden alongside the road, opened fire on them. The men took cover where they could and returned fire. After a few minutes, the shooting stopped. After a few more minutes, Company B started forward again. Soon, they were around the bend and out of sight.

As he knelt in the grass alongside the road, Daniel yawned and struggled with the urge to lie down and go to sleep. At the same time, he unconsciously bounced his knee up and down and twisted his hands on his rifle.

While they waited for Company B, a civilian approached Colonel Cantwell, and the two talked. The news quickly spread throughout the command that there was another way to Romney—a ford about ten miles north along a rugged mountain path. The colonel sent the civilian down the road to tell Company B to fall back. They would take the ford.

By the time Company B returned, the sun was high in the sky and no one had slept or eaten since the day before. After withdrawing a short distance from Mechanicsburg, the expedition fell out to fix something to eat and try to get some sleep. They would resume the march that night so they would reach the ford at first light.

Despite his nervousness, Daniel had no trouble sleeping. When he woke, he knew from the length of the shadows that it was late afternoon. After getting himself some coffee and hardtack, he realized he felt much better. His muscles still ached, especially his back and legs, but not as bad as the previous night. It would seem all he had needed was a good, long march.

—⁂—

They reached the ford at around four in the morning. It was dark, and a heavy mist covered the area. Daniel could barely make out the shoreline of the river. As the column came to a halt, he heard voices on the other side. Suddenly, the voices got loud and angry, followed by gunshots. Then, there were splashing sounds, and every man in the column raised his rifle, ready to shoot whoever came out of the ford.

But, it was a single man in blue who came out of the mist. Daniel recognized him as a member of Company B. He reported to Colonel Cantwell, who then ordered the column forward at the double quick. There were close to a thousand men in the colonel's command, and they hit the water running. As they slogged through the ford, they filled the mist-shrouded valley with splashing, shouting, and laughter.

Even at the ford, the river was deep and fast enough to make some of the shorter boys struggle. The current threatened to sweep them off their feet, but their taller comrades caught them and pulled them to shore.

Daniel realized much of the laughter was at these boys' expense. He looked over his shoulder and watched Christopher straining to stay upright as he reached the middle of the river. But the younger Galloway pulled through and made it to the other side without help.

They continued down the road at the double quick. It was apparent that Colonel Cantwell wanted to get to the town as quickly as possible, but if the distance was as far to Romney as it was from the Mechanicsburg, Daniel knew they would never make it all the way jogging.

Soon, they were out of the flat open area surrounding the ford and back into the woods. Colonel Cantwell ordered them to slow to a route step.

As the sun came up, it burned off the mist, and Daniel could see a tall ridge to the left, towering over the road. Colonel Cantwell did not deploy skirmishers, which surprised him. As they moved forward, the road got narrower, the ridgeline higher, and the trees thicker.

"If they're going to jump us before we get to Romney, this would be the place to do it," Daniel said. There were several nods and a chorus of nervous agreements in response.

Rounding a bend, the front of the column came to an abrupt halt, causing a ripple down the line. Daniel stepped out to the side so he could see ahead and knew right away they were in trouble. Across the road lay a downed tree. From its still green leaves, it was obvious the tree had only recently fallen—or been cut down. Just on the other side of the tree, a large flat rock covered the ridgeline that jutted out over the road. The ground below was covered with large boulders and thick underbrush.

A cold sweat broke out on Daniel's brow, and his feet felt like lead. The wide eyes and open mouths of the boys around him told him they shared his fear.

Colonel Cantwell sent squads out on either side of the road to look for a path around the tree for the cannon and cavalry. He ordered the rest of the column forward over the tree.

As the men before him climbed over the tree and continued down the road unmolested, Daniel relaxed. Maybe it would be all right.

The tree trunk was high enough that Daniel had to use his hands to climb over it. As he leaned his rifle against the trunk, the fear returned. Before pulling himself over, Daniel's eyes again swept the boulder-filled landscape on the other side.

As Daniel retrieved his rifle and turned to continue on, the world before him exploded. Daniel heard the buzz and ping of bullets flying past and ricocheting off rocks. All around him, men jerked and cried out, dropping their rifles and clutching at wounds.

Daniel found himself on his knees with his back pressed against the tree trunk. From the pain in his back, he realized he must have fallen into the tree, though he didn't remember doing so. He patted his chest and looked down, but saw no holes or blood.

The thought occurred to Daniel that he should do something, but he didn't know what. The whole column was in chaos—even the officers seemed at a loss for what to do. A few men returned fire, though there were no visible targets. Most though, ran back the way they'd came. Daniel capped his rifle, but he was on the wrong side of the road, and the steady stream of men running past blocked any potential targets.

After the initial volley, the hidden rebels continued shooting individually. Most of their shots were going over their heads, and Daniel realized the rebs were too high. They were on the flat overhanging rock at the top of the ridge, and the angle was too steep. Only the men by the fallen tree or farther down the path were in their line of fire. Those farther ahead were safe, but had the same problem in reverse—their shots hit the rock and ricocheted away.

Then the rebels along the ridgeline started throwing down large rocks onto the heads of the men below. At that, everyone gave up trying to return fire and joined the retreat.

Soon, everyone was over the tree and down the path. Daniel found himself alone, still on his knees, leaning against the trunk. With a pang of shame, he realized that since the first volley he'd done nothing more than cap his rifle. He'd not run, he'd not returned fire, he'd done nothing.

Then a bullet slapped the trunk to his left, showering him with bits of bark. That gave Daniel the motivation to scramble to his feet. He threw his rifle over the trunk and crawled over.

Once on the other side, he retrieved his rifle and steeled himself to run through the rebels' line of fire. He watched the last of his companions disappear around the bend. His eyes followed the road he would have to run down and stopped. About ten yards before him, a single Federal soldier lay in the middle of the road.

Daniel felt the weight of a hundred rifles pointed at him, but there was a fellow soldier lying out there in need of help. He looked over the trunk. The road was empty, but looking up he could see the tops of some heads and rifle barrels sticking out over the ridgeline.

His breathing was fast and shallow, and he started to get lightheaded. Sweat stung his eyes, and his palms were damp against the wood of his rifle. His muscles soaked up weakness like a rag soaked up water.

He thought of Susan and her father, of Christopher and his sisters, of his ma and da. He said a brief prayer. He was sure he would be shot as soon as he left the protection of the tree. He crossed himself, pushed himself up, and ran down the road to the fallen soldier.

Daniel felt his body expand as he ran until he was so large he couldn't be missed. But no one fired. With each step, Daniel's amazement at still being alive grew.

He reached the fallen soldier and dropped to his knees. He looked down at the man and recognized the vacant stare of death. The man's eyes were wide and unblinking, the mouth shaped in an O as if death caught him by surprise. His cheeks were flecked with blood, but his neck was soaked in it. Under all the blood was a gaping hole where his esophagus had been.

What energy Daniel had mustered to make it this far drained from his body. His hands shook as he realized he might still die here in this isolated path outside Romney, Virginia, and it would be for nothing. The man he came to save was already dead, the expedition in shambles.

Then he heard footsteps running toward him. His fear of death switched to that of capture, and he imagined spending the war in a Southern prisoner-of-war camp. He shifted his feet to rise when he realized the footsteps were coming from the wrong direction. Then, Christopher dropped to his knees on the other side of the dead man.

"What are you doing here?" Daniel screamed. He grabbed his brother by the collar and shook him. "God damn it! You want to get killed?"

Christopher knocked his hand away. "Quit your blasphemy. You want to die having just blasphemed the Lord's name? Besides, I'm not doing anything you're not doing." He looked down at the man they'd come to save and blanched. "Looks like we're too late."

A rock the size of a rounders ball hit the road beside them. "You Yanks get out of here now! You ain't wanted around here!"

They looked up and saw hundreds of dirty faces looking back at them from the ridgeline. They all had rifles raised but, thankfully, not pointed at them.

"Help me lift him up and let's do like the man said," Daniel grunted as he pulled on the dead soldier's arm.

Christopher took the other arm and together they lifted the dead man up and trotted down the road.

The same voice called out from behind them. "You boys are the only brave Yanks we've seen yet. Sorry about your pard."

He wasn't even their pard, Daniel thought. The dead man was with the 8th, but he was part of Company I, who had joined the regiment after they were already in Virginia. He didn't even know the man's name.

CHAPTER THIRTEEN
ROMNEY

When they got to the ford, Christopher and Daniel dropped the body and collapsed. Dirty and drenched in sweat, they lay on their backs, muscles quivering and breathing ragged. With shaking hands, both reached for their canteen at the same time.

Everyone else was already on the other side of the river. A cavalryman rode across and took the body back on his horse. The two brothers helped each other cross to the other side where they were surrounded by the smiling faces of men heaping them with praise. Except for Company B, who'd been receiving all the praise as the last ones back until Christopher and Daniel arrived. Captain Allen, of Company I, approached the boys and thanked them for bringing back his man.

Once they'd recovered, Christopher regaled anyone who would listen with the details of their retrieval of the body and the threats and grudging respect they'd gotten from the rebel soldier. But Daniel retreated into himself and wanted nothing to do with the small celebration. Only when Captain Daggett asked for a report did Daniel recount the events that transpired after everyone else turned and ran.

Daggett assured the brothers that Lieutenant Colonel Park was aware of their actions, and Colonel DePuy would get a full report as soon as he returned from sick leave.

—m—

Except for the cavalry and artillery piece, the expedition stayed on the bank of the Potomac. The cavalry and artillery returned to Mechanicsburg, the wounded riding double with the troopers or crowded together with the dead body on the cannon's ammunition limber. This gave the soldiers time to relax and eat and ruminate after what, for many, was their first experience in combat. The Galloway brothers ate with their messmates in silence.

Finally, Christopher asked the question on everyone's mind. "I wonder what they'll do next?" No one responded, so he continued. "I mean, we've tried both approaches to Romney and got pushed back both times. But the big bugs seem set on taking that town."

Daniel shook his head. "We tried both approaches, but how hard? First sound of gunfire, we skedaddled."

"The smart ones did," Christopher responded. "The dumb ones stayed behind picking up dead bodies on the way."

Daniel glowered at his brother and started to say something when Charlie interrupted. "I think we need more soldiers. The town is too heavily guarded."

Parker nodded. "Whatever we do, we need to do it soon. Eventually, the secesh will decide we're not serious and mount a counterattack to send us packin'."

Daniel turned his attention away from Christopher and said, "They send us the rest of the 4th and the 8th, we could take that town by sundown."

"And artillery," Charlie said. "You can't forget artillery, General Galloway." Charlie winked at Christopher.

"I don't think any artillery will get to Romney this way," Parker said. "We'll need to take that pass."

"How about they send the artillery and cavalry down the main road while we go in from this direction?" Ezra said.

"That's it!" Daniel exclaimed. "A two-pronged attack. The cavalry and artillery go down the main road and attack the enemy from the pass, while we cross the ford, carry that hanging rock, and flank the enemy from the north."

"Napoleon got nothing on you," Charlie said, smiling.

"Napoleon's too much of a mouthful," Parker said. "You prefer Nape or Leon?"

"I prefer Daniel," Daniel said.

"Too bad…Nape."

Ezra laughed. "Notch and Nape Galloway. Wait'll they get a load of that back in Norwalk."

Daniel threw down his tin cup and stood. "You can call me Nape all you want, but that doesn't mean I have to answer to it." He then turned and stormed off toward the tree line downstream.

"So long, Nape!" Ezra called, waving and laughing. The others chuckled.

Several hours later, a lone cavalry trooper arrived and reported to Colonel Cantwell. They broke camp within the hour. Colonel Cantwell and his staff took the 4th OVI companies back to Mechanicsburg, and Lieutenant Colonel Park led the 8th companies back across the river and down the path toward Romney.

As they marched, Parker fell in beside Daniel. "Danny, you won't believe this," he said, smiling. "Apparently, Colonel Cantwell heard of your two-pronged battle plan and intends to implement it."

Daniel looked confused. "What are you talking about? What battle plan?"

"Why yours, Nape!" Parker slapped Daniel on the arm. "Cantwell went back to Mechanicsburg to lead the cannon and cavalry down the pass while we go this way and take Romney from the north. Just like you said!"

"That's not exactly what I said," Daniel replied. "We don't have enough men. How are we going to get past that hanging rock?"

Parker shrugged. "How about by not running at the first sign of resistance?"

Daniel nodded his head toward Lieutenant Colonel Park at the head of the column. "I don't see that happening with Park leading us."

Bonnett laughed, but there was no joy in it. "You have a point there."

When they came to the fallen tree, Lieutenant Colonel Park had Company D form up behind the trunk and fire several volleys into the tree line on the other side. While they did that, Companies A and B went around the tree at either end. The rest of the command watched for rebels on top of the hanging rock.

There was no response. The rebels had already left. "This is it, boys!" Park raised his sword and cried. "Onward to Romney!"

—⁓—

After marching for a couple more hours, they found themselves in a line of hills just to the north of town. Park deployed his force in a battle line at the top of a hill. He then sent Companies D and B ahead as skirmishers. The men spread out and leap-frogged forward until they were within fifty yards of the enemy pickets. Once they were in range, the pickets started firing at them, and Christopher heard the buzz of a passing minié ball. Half the skirmishers returned fire. The other half waited for their partners to reload before firing. But, before they had the chance, the enemy pickets turned and ran back to town.

The skirmishers moved forward to the rebel picket line and dropped to a kneeling position. Christopher watched the retreating rebels and those manning the defensive line guarding the bridge on the road to Mechanic-sburg. It was his first good look at the enemy other than the few prisoners they'd taken at Red House. The first thing he noticed was how rag tag they looked. There was no military uniformity at all. Most of the men were in jackets of various shades of homespun butternut. Mixed in with them were militia and military school students in tight-fitting gray jackets with gold piping. They appeared to be well armed though. Besides their rifles, many of the men carried pistols and large knives in their belts. He hoped, what-ever happened, it didn't come to hand-to-hand combat.

From their vantage point, they sat and waited. Park brought the rest of the men forward to join the skirmishers. The colonel stared at the en-emy through a spyglass for several minutes. He then consulted with several company commanders. At one point, the conversation appeared to become heated. But nothing happened.

And they waited.

The rebels sent up skirmishers and cavalry to drive them off. Once the enemy was within range, Park had the men fire a volley by rank—rear rank first, front rank second. Several of the approaching Confederate soldiers stumbled, and one fell to the ground. The others stopped and returned fire. Christopher heard the bullets passing high above him. Instead of reloading for another volley, the Confederates turned and ran. Christopher and the rest of the men gave a rousing cheer, followed by a stream of insults toward the retreating men. Christopher wondered if the man who'd spoken to him and Daniel from the hanging rock was among the men they'd just shot at.

And they waited.

As the day passed with no activity, men became bored and wandered off, attracted by garden plots in the homes nearby and the call of fresh vegetables. At one point, an argument broke out over some cabbages taken from someone's garden.

Still, they waited.

Finally, Park gave the order to fall in. But instead of attacking, once they were lined up, he ordered the men to march back the way they'd come. The men broke out into a cacophony of questions and exclamations that the company commanders ignored. Instead, they left it to the sergeants to restore discipline.

Christopher looked over at his brother. Daniel was squeezing his rifle so tightly while staring at Lieutenant Colonel Park that his knuckles were white. He looked as if he wanted to skewer the officer with his bayonet. Christopher then looked at his file partner. Ezra just shrugged.

As they marched back to the ford, the officers and sergeants had trouble keeping the men quiet. Everyone wanted to know why they were retreating. Many of the comments were extremely insubordinate and insulting to Lieutenant Colonel Park, who marched ahead of the men and refused to look back.

"We had 'em," someone yelled.

"We coulda taken 'em," someone else cried.

"I don't know, there were a lot of them—and did you see the artillery battery?"

"We coulda taken it too!"

"Shut up, private," Sergeant Reid barked. "You ever seen what canister from a line of cannon does to a battle line up close?"

"But we coulda flanked 'em."

"I said shut up! One more peep out of you, you'll be wearing a barrel shirt all night."

Fatigue eventually did what the sergeants couldn't, and they marched the rest of the way to Mechanicsburg in silence.

When they arrived, it was well after midnight. At some point Cantwell and the cavalry had given up waiting on Park and bivouacked just outside of town. A full battery of artillery as well as hospital personnel had joined them, but no other reinforcements.

—ᴨ—

They were up the next day well before dawn. As Christopher rolled over to push himself up, his back spasmed. His thighs hurt so bad they throbbed, and his neck and shoulders ached even when still. He pushed up onto his hands and knees, wondering how he'd gotten so bad so fast.

"I feel like I've been run over by a locomotive," he said to Daniel, who also seemed to be in a lot of pain.

"Me too," Daniel replied. "I don't know why. I thought we were getting used to this camp life."

Christopher shook his head. They'd marched yesterday under light marching orders and, though they'd marched over twenty miles, they'd done worse. "Maybe it was carrying that dead body all that way," he speculated.

The call for assembly pierced through the growing sounds of men rising and going about their morning rituals. Christopher fell onto his back and threw his arm over his eyes. "I don't know if I can make it, brother. You must go on without me."

"You'll make it, and then some," Daniel replied. "I won't have anyone saying my brother is a deadbeat." Daniel smacked Christopher's legs with his forage cap. "UP!"

Christopher climbed to his feet, groaning all the time. "I ain't no beat," he said.

They dressed and headed toward the assembly area. Christopher mumbled to no one in particular, "I sure hope we have time to eat and pee—I have to do both."

"Just not at the same time, little brother," Daniel replied. "The Sanitation Commission frowns on that sort of thing."

As the men went about their routines, the rumor mill was working overtime. The most repeated rumor was that they had not attacked the day before because Lieutenant Colonel Park had refused despite the urging of his company commanders. Most of the men thought of Park as a Sunday soldier who didn't deserve the rank he held, so the rumor quickly took hold. Christopher figured they would never know the real reason for yesterday's aborted attack.

The second most repeated rumor of the morning—that they would attack Romney again—soon proved correct. Christopher had time to complete his morning constitution, then they lined up and marched down the pass toward Romney. Company D went ahead as skirmishers, and Company B acted as rear guard. In between were Companies G and I of the 8th Ohio, several companies from the 4th Ohio, a company of cavalry, and a full battery of six cannons.

They soon met the rebels' forward position. Several pickets stationed along the side of the road emptied their guns and ran. After a time, they met the same pickets, who repeated their shoot and run tactics.

Christopher saw a rebel pop up from behind cover before him and immediately fired his rifle at the man. Ezra fired as well.

"Damn it, you two! You want to die?" Corporal Gridley yelled. "Now you're both empty. What are you supposed to do if they counterattack?"

Christopher and Ezra exchanged guilty glances as they reloaded.

As the 8th came out onto the open land before the bridge and deployed into the battle line with the rest of the infantry, Christopher saw the same defensive position with its crude dirt parapets. This time from the front.

The infantry and cavalry halted as the battery lined up across the plain and engaged the enemy's artillery set up in the town cemetery on the other side of the bridge.

Christopher had seen plenty of cannon fire in training, but this was the first time he'd witnessed a full battery firing on an enemy position in earnest. Six cannons firing at once created an explosion that was ear splitting, and the flame and smoke that shot out the ends made Christopher think of hellfire and brimstone. They started out firing solid shot—the large iron balls that were the mainstay of artillery before the fuse lit case shot was created. The cannonballs sounded much like the buzz of a minié ball as they passed by, but deeper and angrier, almost as if they were ripping holes in the air as they passed. He shuddered at the thought of being on the receiving end of such a volley.

The battery exchanged fire with the enemy artillery for some time—both firing a mix of solid shot and exploding case shot. As Christopher watched, a cannonball hit the ground twenty yards before the Federal battery and bounced off the ground. It then shot forward, decapitating a gunner in its path. A shell exploded over a brace of horses, injuring several and disemboweling one with its shrapnel. The incoming fire caused Christopher to flinch, though it came nowhere near him.

After exchanging fire for almost an hour, the incoming artillery fire slackened, then ceased altogether. The enemy battery limbered up their cannon and retreated. The entire Federal force let out a deafening roar. Men waved their hats and rifles in the air and screamed their approval at the artillery battery—who responded by waving their own hats and cheering back. The battery captain stepped forward, swept his hat up in a wide arc over his head, brought it down to his waist, and bowed at the infantry and cavalry, who would now have to finish the job.

The cavalry moved forward at a trot, their lines as straight and uniform as any infantry's. Christopher wondered what it took to maintain that much control over a horse. He was just glad if the animal took him where he wanted to go.

The bugle command to charge pierced the air, and the cavalry took off at a gallop. As they increased speed, their lines wavered but held straight. Christopher craned his neck to see and muttered encouragement to them under his breath. It was like race day, only better.

As the cavalry raced across the field, a few of the troopers fired their carbines single handed, though their chances of hitting anything on the move were next to none. As they neared the bridge, the enemy line opened fire from behind their parapets. The volley seemed to have little effect other than to rattle a few troopers, causing them to swerve and break formation. They quickly recovered and straightened their lines.

When the cavalry reached the bridge, they slowed back down to a trot and, as Christopher and the rest of the infantry watched in admiration, maneuvered from battle line back into column and continued across without stopping. The command for the infantry to advance at the double quick was almost drowned out by another round of cheers.

Christopher's legs were still sore from the previous day's marching, so his thighs sent a painful wave of protest with each step. His cartridge box and haversack both bounced wildly, though he wore them high and tight. He remembered all the knives and pistols he'd seen the day before and wondered what being stabbed felt like. Did it hurt more than being shot?

When the infantry reached the bridge, they too had to slow to maneuver back into column. This gave Christopher a chance to look ahead, and he smiled at what he saw. The cavalry was already on the other side of the parapets, and the enemy was skedaddling back to town. *This is the way to do it*, he thought. *Let the artillery and cavalry do all the work, and we come in and clean up afterward.*

The companies of the 8th occupied the enemy defenses while the 4th and the cavalry continued into town. As soon as they were out of sight, dispersed among the buildings, a battle erupted within the town. Christopher listened with growing apprehension to the steady cacophony of gunfire of all kinds—rifle, pistol, and carbine.

The trench they occupied only came up to their knees, and the earthen parapets were worthless to them, as they faced the wrong way. Instead, they presented an obstacle that the men would have to climb over or go around if they had to make a hasty retreat.

Soon, the firing stopped, and all was quiet. They waited for word from the town, but none came. After an hour, most of the men relaxed. A few men produced cards and tobacco, and several wondered what was in the backyard gardens of some of the houses on the outskirts of town. After another hour, the cavalry came riding out of the town at a fast trot. They stopped at the parapets while their commander reported to Lieutenant Colonel Park. Christopher strained to listen to what the captain had to say.

"Compliments, Colonel," the cavalry officer said. "It would appear a large rebel force—possibly an entire division, has entered the town from the north."

Even from where he stood several feet away, Christopher could see the color drain from Park's face.

Moments later, Sergeant Reid came down the line. "Watch your fire, boys. Our boys will be coming back this way in a hurry, and we don't want to shoot any of them."

"I thought we had 'em whooped, Sergeant," Ezra said.

"They brought friends," Reid replied. "We'll be the rear guard covering the retreat. We hold here until everyone has passed. Then we will follow in a coordinated retreat to try to slow down the enemy as much as possible."

"How are we going to do that?" Ezra asked.

Reid spit tobacco juice on the ground and glared at Ezra. "I don't know, Rouse. Why don't you distract them with some card tricks."

Ezra turned bright red and put his cards away. Everyone in hearing distance laughed.

Reid started to say something else when someone yelled, "Here they come!"

The Federal troops who had entered the town in pursuit of fleeing rebels came spilling back out of the town, Colonel Cantwell, leading the way atop his horse. Christopher noted that, unlike the day before at the hanging rock, no one was panicking, but they were making a hasty retreat.

It took several minutes for the Federals to pass. When they reached the bridge, the discipline and control they exhibited earlier was gone. Instead, everyone tried to cross at once, and the officers had to yell and scream to regain control of the men.

The enemy forces streamed out of the town and formed into a battle line, whooping and cheering like the Federals had earlier.

"Fire by file!" someone yelled. Christopher assumed it was Captain Daggett, though he was too focused on the battle line in front of him to be sure.

"Company! Ready!"

Christopher brought his rifle up with the breech above the cap box on his belt and pulled the hammer back to half cock. He unfastened the flap over the cap box on his belt, reached in, retrieved a percussion cap, and placed it on the nipple of his rifle. Christopher inwardly sighed, somehow taking comfort from the actions drilled into him at Camp Dennison. Actions he thought trivial and unnecessary at the time.

He then brought the rifle to his shoulder, taking aim at the enemy, who still seemed impossibly small in his sights.

"Commence firing!"

The two men at the right end of the battle line fired, followed at once by the two to their left, and on down the line. It seemed forever for the sequence to reach Christopher, but he knew it could sneak up fast if you weren't prepared, so he watched the man on his right out of the corner of his eye, ignoring the danger in front of him for fear of messing up the command.

He saw Ezra's rifle barrel come alongside his head. Then, the man two files to his right fired, followed by the man to his immediate right. Christopher fired. And at the same time, the barrel beside his head belched smoke and flame.

Though his view was obstructed by smoke, he could still see the enemy advancing—now less than a hundred yards away.

The men on the far right of his own line had already reloaded and fired a second time. The sequence was once again almost upon him, so Christopher hurried to reload. He had just gotten the percussion cap on and brought the rifle to his shoulder when the man on his right fired. Christopher's second shot followed. Ezra fired a split second later.

"You slowing down back there, pard?" Christopher asked without taking his eyes off the advancing enemy.

"It's these damn cartridges," Ezra responded. "The paper keeps tearing too low."

Christopher got one more shot in during the fire-by-file sequence. As he was loading for a fourth shot, he heard the command to cease fire. He finished reloading and brought his rifle to shoulder arms.

He then noticed the sound of minié balls passing through the ranks. His breath caught and every muscle in his body screamed run, but he held. "*This is insane!*" The words looped through his brain as he strained to hold still.

"Company! Ready!"

Christopher took a half step back and brought his rifle down to the ready position.

"Aim!"

He raised the rifle to his shoulder and looked down the sights, picking out a man in the front rank before him.

"FIRE!"

Christopher pulled the trigger, and the man disappeared in an explosion of smoke and flame. He couldn't see if he'd hit him or not, and he didn't care. Just to be doing something was enough. He brought his rifle down and reloaded.

"Company! Reload and come to shoulder arms!"

This is ridiculous, Christopher thought. We need to be shooting. He looked around for an officer to voice his frustration, but all he saw was a corporal.

"Company! By files, right face! March!"

Everyone turned to their right into two columns.

"Guide on the colors. At the quick step. MARCH!"

The rebels cheered and started forward. As Christopher followed the man in front of him, he saw that Company B was already on the other side of the parapet and in line, aiming their rifles at the enemy. Company B fired by rank, and the rebel advance came to a halt. The rebels returned fire as Companies I and D passed through a gap in the parapet and onto the field before the bridge.

Almost home, Lord, Christopher prayed silently. *Please don't let me get hit in the back.*

The rest of the Federal force was now on the other side of the bridge and marching in columns of four toward the pass to Mechanicsburg. The three companies of the 8th were now alone to face an enemy force large enough to chase away over one thousand men. Despite the hundreds of men around him, Christopher felt alone and exposed. He realized he was hunched over like an old man, so he straightened up, only to hunch over again when the next bullet buzzed past his ear.

The three companies took turns covering each other as they leap-frogged up the road to the bridge. The Federal battery gave them covering fire with their own version of fire by file—each cannon firing individually starting on the right. They were firing case shot, but the fuses were long, so the ordinance was exploding behind the enemy. As the artillery adjusted their range, Company D fired a volley and followed Company B over the bridge. After their own volley fire, Company I was right behind them.

Once over the bridge, Christopher started to relax and his energy waned. As he started to wonder if he could keep the pace any longer, there came from behind him a screeching yell. Christopher looked over his shoulder and saw that the rebels were charging the bridge.

At that point, all order disappeared as each man took off running for the pass as fast as he could. Christopher saw the battery limber up and make its escape. Everyone left on the field was in full route, their lines breaking apart into a mob of running men. They ran all the way to the entrance to the pass, where the exhausted and out-of-breath soldiers slowed to a shuffle. Christopher looked back again and saw that the rebels had stopped pursuing them and had returned to their trenches.

In a slow dejected shuffle, they made their way back to camp. A few tried chattering about the battle they had just taken part in, but most were too tired and embarrassed at being routed two days in a row. By the time they got back to camp, they were all too exhausted to talk. After being dismissed, Christopher searched for the first comfortable plot of ground he could find and fell asleep while halfheartedly chewing on a hard cracker.

—⁂—

A month passed before they attempted another attack on Romney. This time, Christopher knew what to expect. The events from last time played over and over in his mind all the way to Mechanicsburg.

Up until the moment they reached Romney, everything happened almost like the last time. There was a brief artillery duel, followed by a charge of the bridge. Once the Federals reached the defensive works. they found them empty. They then marched into the town itself and were met by nothing but civilians. While the artillery was having its duel, the main Confederate force occupying the town had slipped away.

Romney was theirs.

CHAPTER FOURTEEN

CHRISTOPHER AND EZRA GET IN TROUBLE

Within two weeks of taking the town, almost every available room in Romney was occupied and the surrounding area covered with tents. The small town of four hundred and fifty was overwhelmed by a Federal force of over ten thousand men.

So, despite being stationed in Romney, Daniel and Christopher had never entered the town itself. Instead, they spent most of their time drilling or picketing the perimeter of the Federal encampment. It was a dangerous, stressful duty, as the surrounding woods and hills were full of Confederate guerrilla fighters. Pickets were shot at from the trees and ridgelines almost daily and several had been wounded though none had been killed. Yet.

On a cool November evening, Christopher and Ezra sat at a fire, passing a flask around with a group of artillerymen. Christopher was drinking again; when he wasn't on duty, there was little else to do except drink and play cards. It helped to ease his mind from the constant back and forth between fear and boredom. That's what he told himself, at least.

One of the artillerymen told them of a shack in the hills a couple miles south of town where you could find plenty of hooch and a faro game most nights. He was a short, stocky fellow named Jacob who talked with a lisp caused by a hair lip and several missing teeth. As he talked and drank, his lisp grew more pronounced.

"It's down the road a piesh, right before you get to the shushpension bridge. There's a path that goesh off into the woods," he slurred. "I been there a couple times when we got furlough."

"We ain't had no furlough yet," Ezra groused.

"Well, you boysh guard the camp. Shomebody has to keep all them bushwhackers at bay."

Jacob took a drink of the flask and passed it to the next man. For a minute his eyes got a glassy, faraway look to them. Then, he snapped out of it and said, "We wash looking for some fancy girls, but there weren't none. They had some fine bark juice though."

Ezra shook his head. "That's one thing this army don't have, is fancy girls. I hear them boys down by Washington City have more camp followers than they know what to do with. All we got is wives and old biddies."

When the flask reached him, Ezra managed to stop pouting long enough to take a drink.

"I'd know what to do with 'em," someone said, and everyone laughed.

Christopher yawned and looked around. He was getting bored and already had drank enough that the odds of making it back to their tent were getting slim.

Ezra slapped him on the arm.

"I think I know where these boys are talking about," Ezra said to Christopher. "You know that suspension bridge down the southern road about two miles? Company B's posted down there. I bet them boys know where that shack might be."

Christopher shrugged. "I'm not so sure. A couple miles down's no big deal. But then we'd have to walk back. Drunk. In the middle of the night. Sounds like a good way to get yourself killed."

"We'd need an overnight pass," Ezra mused. "So we wouldn't have to travel after dark. Maybe we could get ourselves attached to Company B somehow."

Christopher's eyes got wide, and he threw up his hands. "Attached to Company B! I'm not leaving the boys in D just to go get drunk and play faro."

Ezra shook his head. "No, no, no. Just temporary. Just to help out overnight or something."

Christopher frowned into the fire. It seemed like a lot of effort just to get drunk. But then what were the odds of them actually pulling it off?

"There's a lot of wagon traffic on that road," Jacob said. "Mebbe you could hitch a ride."

Ezra nodded enthusiastically. Christopher wondered how he could move his head like that without passing out.

"That's the ticket. What ya say, pard?"

Christopher continued looking into the fire for several seconds, then nodded. "If we can get a twenty-four-hour pass and hitch a ride both ways, I'm in."

Ezra laughed and slapped his knee. "Whoo-eee! We're gonna have a good time!"

Christopher looked toward their tent. It was a lot less than two miles, but tonight it seemed much farther. A trip to the nearest sinks might help. It would at least give him an idea of how far gone he was.

"I'm going to the sinks," he said, rising.

As he stood, the world spun, and he had to pause until it stopped before risking a step. He turned and walked in the direction he thought the sinks were in, taking slow, deliberate steps to avoid stumbling.

"They're over there," Jacob said, pointing to Christopher's left.

"Oh, yeah," he mumbled.

Christopher turned to his left and almost fell.

Ezra stood and stretched. "I think I'll join you. Then we can head back. It's getting late, and I have picket in the morning." He came up beside Christopher and took his arm. "Let's go, pard."

Ezra seemed much more stable, and Christopher appreciated the support. "Upward and onward," he said, trying to appear nonchalant.

"You boysh watch out for provosht guardsh. Ya hear?" Jacob called after them as they disappeared into the maze of tents and fire pits.

—⁂—

Almost a week later, Christopher had all but forgotten the conversation about the drinking establishment at the suspension bridge when Ezra came to him, excitedly waving two pieces of paper.

"Now we're in clover, pard."

Christopher took a sheet and saw it was a twenty-four-hour pass, signed by Lieutenant Colonel Park. His eyes widened as he looked up at Ezra. "How did you get this?"

"A fellow on their staff says Park and DePuy are on their way out and will sign pretty much anything—no questions asked. But, we gotta act now 'cause Sawyer's coming back, and he won't put up with no shenanigans."

Recalling his punishment detail for fighting back in Camp Dennison, Christopher nodded. "Don't I know it…"So, when do we go?"

"Two days' time," Ezra replied. "There's a wagon train leaving down the southern road, and we can hitch a ride to the bridge. Once we're there, we look up Company B and find out where the liquor shack is. Next day, we see who's heading this way and hitch another ride. If no one's coming back this way, we'll just walk. It's only a couple miles. We'll be back before they notice we're gone—and if they do, we got papers." Ezra waved the pass again.

Two days later, they were in the back of an empty wagon headed south. From the white, dusty crumbs that covered the bottom, it looked to have been hauling hardtack. They had agreed to act as extra security for the wagon train, so they had their rifles and full kits, including twenty rounds of ammunition.

The wagon train reached the bridge at the same time as the 14th Indiana, marching toward Romney from the other direction. There were close to a thousand men with their own supply wagons going one way, and about one hundred wagons going the other way. When both sides insisted on crossing the bridge first, a shouting match broke out, complete with shaking fists and threats of violence.

The sergeant of the guard detail from Company B sent a runner back to camp for the company commander and reinforcements.

Christopher and Ezra took advantage of the chaos to jump out of the wagon and head to Company B's camp. They entered the camp only to find almost everyone gone. The officers and first sergeant had taken a detail to the bridge. Those who remained behind looked at the newcomers with suspicion.

There was a large group clustered around a fire pit. As they approached the men, Ezra spoke first. "Hey ya, boys. How are things?"

One of the loungers gave a half smile and said, "Can't complain."

Ezra nodded. "Yeah, I tried that once. Got extra picket duty for a week." The men all chuckled.

"You boys loaded for bear. You expecting an attack?" One of the Company B men asked.

Christopher reached into his haversack. "We were guarding a line of wagons coming this way. Figured we'd drop off and have a snort of red-eye with our fellow members of the mighty 8th." With a nod of his head toward Ezra, he continued, "We're with Company D."

Christopher produced a flask and, uncorking it, took a long swig and passed it to one of the men sitting around the fire. "We've been scattered all over Northern Virginia so long, it's easy to forget we're still part of the same regiment."

The man who took the flask from Christopher took a swig, nodded, and said, "You are correct, sir. We've been down here by this accursed bridge since we took Romney. At least you fellows have a town to go to."

"You ain't missin' anything," Ezra responded. "Romney's a one-horse burg and off limits to us anyways."

"At least it would be nice to take a stroll down Main Street sometime and see a pretty girl," someone said wistfully.

"You boys have any fancy girls up there?" the first man asked.

Ezra and Christopher shook their heads. After that, the loungers seemed to lose interest in the two newcomers. The group continued to pass the flask around, but an awkward silence had descended upon the group.

Christopher decided it was time to get to the point. "Hear tell you boys have a reliable source for whiskey cheaper than what one can get at the sutler's—not to mention a possible game of chance."

The first drinker looked at Christopher askance. "Who you been talkin' to, son?"

Christopher smiled and jerked his thumb in Ezra's direction.

Ezra said, "Come on, now. All the traffic over this bridge, you don't suppose a little detail like that wouldn't slip out, now do you?"

"You boys got the spondulix for a little fun?"

"We got our pay, same as you, but there's nothing to spend it on. We just told you there's nothing in Romney. Provosts break up a good game before it gets going, and if you go to a sutler, he'll sell you a little bottle of tar juice for a month's pay that'll only get you a little swimmy-headed is all."

The first drinker stood up and sauntered to the edge of camp. He stood there for a few minutes, reviewing the activity at the bridge. The 14th had moved aside, half on one side of the bridge and half on the other, the wagons having somehow won the right of way.

After a couple rounds, Christopher's flask came back to him empty. He replaced the cork and put it back into his haversack.

The Company B man came back. "My name's Walt. Walter Griffis. There may be a little shack up in the hills that offers refreshments and gaming, if you're smart about it."

"We're the model of discretion."

Ezra nodded and pointed to Christopher. "What he said."

"Well then, come on, boys."

Griffis and his compatriots led Christopher and Ezra to the base of the hills and up a small path, no larger than a deer trail. They'd not gone far when they came upon a ramshackle building made of old planks covered in tar paper. The roof sagged in the middle, and the sides had a thick layer of moss about the bottom.

Christopher looked at Ezra. "This is what we came for?"

Ezra shrugged.

Griffis overheard and said, "It ain't much to look at, but they have good stump liquor."

"Well, let's get the ball started," Ezra said, clapping his hands and starting for the shack.

Christopher followed him inside. It was dark and cramped, most of the space taken up by a bar comprised of a plank laid over two barrels, and three card tables. Every surface in the room was coated with a thick layer of dirt and black stains. But what set Christopher back was the smell—a mix of sweat, stale liquor, old vomit, and earthy scents he couldn't name. Christopher thought he'd gotten used to bad smells, but nothing had prepared him for this. It was like something physical that filled the room. A barrier you had to push through to enter.

The boys of Company B followed them in and there was just enough room for the group to stand around the tables. Christopher felt as if he were suffocating, pressed between two Company B men and the bar. He cast a menacing frown at Ezra.

"Mabel, you got customers!" Griffis yelled.

A short, stout, gray-haired woman appeared from behind an old blanket hanging over a doorway Christopher hadn't noticed before. "I didn't expect to see any of you boys 'til tonight."

"Trouble at the bridge got the officers all tied up, and these boys came looking for a good time. Naturally, we told them about your place."

The old woman looked at Christopher and spit on the dirt floor. "Trust 'em?"

"They seem on the up and up. They're with the 8th."

"I don't know nothin' 'bout that, but you vouch for them, I guess they're all right." She looked around and spit again. "Virgil, my faro dealer, won't be here until nightfall. But, I'll get you some cards and some corn liquor. Make yourself at home." She smiled, revealing toothless gums, and disappeared behind the blanket.

Mable returned a few minutes later with a clay jug and three decks of cards. The boys all chipped in and paid for the jug, and Mable put a deck on each table. The boys started up a couple games of poker and passed the jug.

When the jug got to him, Christopher dug around in his haversack and pulled out his tin cup. He'd put it away wet, so stuck to the bottom was a mix of rice, coffee grounds, white dust from hardtack, and green flecks he assumed were flakes of desiccated vegetables. After wiping out the cup with a bandana, he filled it halfway with corn liquor.

Christopher passed the jug to Ezra, then took a drink from his cup. It was as if he'd put a burning lump of coal in his mouth. It took all his will-power to not spit it back out. Instead, he swallowed. The liquor burned his throat as it went down and continued to smolder in the pit of his stomach. His eyes watered up, and he coughed. The boys of Company B burst out laughing.

"Takes some getting used to, don't it?"

Christopher nodded. "It must. I'm no wallflower, but that has to be the most potent drink I think I've ever come across."

Everyone pulled out coins and paper money saved up from several months in the field. Christopher had bought more than his share of the watered-down whiskey the sutlers sold and freely admitted to a sweet tooth he tried to satisfy every chance he got, but he still had saved up fourteen dollars and two bits. Since they were starting out penny ante, he felt that was plenty. Ezra, though, only had about nine dollars.

Soon, more boys from Company B and even a few from the 14th Indiana, still stalled at the bridge, came up the trail. Apparently, Mabel's faro dealer was out drumming up business. All three tables filled up with drinkers and card players and, since the building wasn't large enough to hold them all, they spilled out onto the ground surrounding the shack.

As the boys got drunker, the penny antes went to nickel antes, and occasionally someone would bet big on a hand he thought was a sure thing. After an hour of drinking and gambling, Christopher was down to eight dollars and sure his luck was about to change.

He took in his surroundings and felt a swelling of joy and wonder. The sounds were louder, the colors brighter, and his emotions higher, but the dirt and the smell had almost disappeared.

After another hour, Christopher felt the call of nature. He dropped out of the game, pocketed his money, and headed outside. Christopher looked at Ezra and saw his friend had lost most of his money and was engrossed in trying to win some of it back. As he passed, Christopher placed a hand on Ezra's shoulder. What he meant as a friendly gesture became a stabilizer as he pushed off toward the door.

Christopher stepped outside and took in a deep breath of fresh air. He smiled. The mountain air was invigorating after the smells of the shack. He didn't know why, but the woods in Virginia smelled different from the woods in Ohio. It was November and the days still had some warmth. He was sure the cold wouldn't bother him tonight.

The world seemed so in balance. He hadn't won, but he still had over a half month's pay. He was sure he would turn that around. He imagined going back to Romney tomorrow with a wad of cash and a flask full of nokum stiff.

Once in the trees, the darkness surprised him. The sun had already dropped behind the mountain, and shadows seemed to engulf everything.

As he peed, Christopher closed his eyes and tried to estimate the time, but the world spun and he stumbled, spraying his feet as well as the bush he was aiming for. He opened his eyes and put a hand on the nearest tree while he finished his business.

Christopher buttoned his fly while he stumbled back to the shack, whistling a tuneless melody. As he stepped out of the trees, a fight broke out in front of the shack. Two men, both too drunk to be coherent, were yelling loudly at one another. Christopher didn't know what the argument was about, but it was loud, and promised to get violent as the men started shoving one another and waving their fists.

Others tried to calm the men down, but the two drunks didn't care who they shoved, and soon the intended peacekeepers joined the brawl. It didn't take long for the brawlers to go from waving their fists to striking one another. Then, Mabel stepped out the door with a musket, pointed it up to the sky, and pulled the trigger.

Everyone stopped as if they were playing a school yard game and someone had yelled freeze. All eyes turned to Mabel, who yelled, "I'll not have fighting in my establishment! You boys straighten up, or git!" She shook the musket at the fighters and went back inside.

Everyone backed up and looked around with downcast eyes. Most looked confused, as if they weren't sure why they had been fighting.

Several men spilled out the door, looking around to see where the rifle shot had come from. Christopher saw one of them was Ezra, who had scooped up their traps and rifles on the way out.

Christopher approached Ezra, smiling. "It's all right, pard. Just Mabel keepin' the peace."

Ezra extracted Christopher's belt, cartridge box, canteen, and haversack from the bundle in his arms. "I figured we might have to make a quick getaway. Didn't want to report for duty tomorrow having lost our gear."

Christopher took his traps and draped them over his shoulder. "I think the storm has passed. Let's get a drink and sit out here for a bit. We can try our hand at faro later."

Ezra nodded. "It was getting a might stuffy in there."

After filling their tin cups, Ezra and Christopher were looking around for a place to sit when someone ran into the yard.

"Provost! Provost guards on the trail headed this way!"

The shack and surrounding area broke into sudden pandemonium. Men scattered in all directions—except down the trail. Ezra and Christopher looked at each other, took a deep drink from their cups, threw the rest out, and ran around the corner of the shack and into the woods.

"Where to?" Ezra asked.

"I have no idea. Let's head up the ravine aways and hold up until the provosts leave."

The ground was steep and rocky, the trees thick, and the boys drunk. Christopher shifted direction to go around a tree, stumbled, and hit his shoulder on another tree—sending him spinning. He fell on an exposed root and felt the wind rush out of his lungs. He tried to gasp, his lips making puckering motions like a fish out of water, but nothing seemed to work.

Ezra's back disappeared behind a tree farther up the ravine, and Christopher was alone in the darkening woods. Then, in a painful rush, his lungs responded and filled with air. He gasped and cried out, his mouth in a rictus of shock and pain. Christopher squeezed his jacket over his chest and for a moment wondered if his heart was failing him.

He rolled onto his side and lay still for a moment as the pain subsided and his body relaxed. He heard the provost guards rounding up men around the cabin. Then, the crinkling of dead leaves nearby made his stomach lurch.

Christopher forced himself to rise and continue up the ravine. The pain had sobered him up somewhat, but not enough for his body to adjust to the exertion. Soon his thighs and lungs were burning from lack of oxygen, and he pressed the palm of his left hand against his ribcage, trying to suppress a sharp pain.

The ravine ended at the base of a vertical cliff at least twenty feet high.

Christopher stopped and looked around in panic. There was no sign of Ezra and nowhere to go.

Voices rose from below, and Christopher dropped to a crouch.

"Stop, stop, stop already…" someone said, out of breath.

"Ain't no drunkards going to make it this far up the hill, and if they did, to hell with them. They deserve to get away."

"If you say so, Sergeant," another voice responded. "But this ravine's gotta end sooner than later. If there's anyone up here, we have them boxed in."

"And so?"

"And so we round them up."

"That's a solid plan except for the part where we keep climbing up this damn ravine."

"It can't be far——"

"No! It's almost pitch black out here. Pretty soon we won't be able to see our hands in front of our faces. Back. Let's go."

Christopher listened to the footsteps recede until all was quiet. He looked around for Ezra, but the unseen sergeant was right. It was too dark. Ezra might have been only a few feet away, and Christopher wouldn't be able to see him.

He waited a few minutes to be sure that the pursuers were out of hearing range, then he called Ezra's name in a loud hiss. "Ezra! Ezra! Where are you, dammit?"

There was no response except the scurrying of small creatures in the surrounding underbrush.

As the transition to darkness ended, the sounds of crickets and other night creatures began. Christopher stood frozen in indecision. He had seen no way out of the ravine, but Ezra had disappeared somehow.

Maybe he should go down and take his lumps. If he didn't report for duty tomorrow, the punishment would be a lot worse. Public drunkenness was one thing, absent without leave was a whole other kettle of fish.

It occurred to him he might avoid both. The best thing to do was to find a place to bed down for the night and head back to the bridge in the morning.

As his eyes adjusted to the darkness, Christopher was able to see enough to move around if he took his time and was careful. It wouldn't do to go too far though; at least now he knew where he was and would be able to retrace his steps in the morning. If he stumbled around all night without being able to see, he would be lost for sure come morning.

He found a spot of ground covered with leaves under an oak tree. The leaves were thick and stiff, but offered good protection from the cold ground and the dew that would come as the temperature dropped. It could be worse, he thought. Back home there might be a blanket of snow on the ground.

Back home. He thought of his ma and da and all those he'd left behind.

Thinking of his family led to thinking about his brother, and he wondered how Daniel would react when he got back. He'd not told him when he left, knowing his brother would try to stop him. Instead, he and Ezra had only shown the passes to Captain Daggett and First Sergeant Howe (First Sergeant Reid having been promoted to lieutenant). They'd both assumed Sergeant Howe would tell everyone where they'd gone.

—◊◊—

Christopher got little sleep that night. As the evening progressed, the temperature plummeted, and soon he was shivering, his muscles constricted from the cold. He dug out a space in the leaves and piled them around him for insulation, but it didn't seem to make much difference. Sometime before sunrise, exhaustion overcame cold, and he slept fitfully for a few hours.

He was up with the sun, stamping around and trying to warm his aching, tired muscles. He would find Ezra, and the two of them could head back down the ravine. With luck, they would slip by Company B's pickets and be back in Romney by noon.

Christopher moved up and down the ravine, looking for hiding spots Ezra might have slipped into. As he did, he noticed a small path leading off to the right, up and out of the ravine. Maybe Ezra had found another way out and circled back to camp. He figured he would follow the path a ways and see.

The path was even steeper than the ravine, and soon, despite the morning chill, Christopher was sweating and gasping for breath. He was about to turn around and go back when the path ended at a road. The road was large enough for wagons, and there were rotten logs laid across it, telling Christopher that he'd found an old corduroy road, fallen into disrepair. It had to lead somewhere.

He was wrong. He followed the road first one way, then the other, but both directions ended in new growth forest. Once he was back to the trail head, Christopher looked around. A sense of despair, bordering on panic, clenched his chest and throat. Christopher had the sense he was somewhere in the hills about the main road leading to Romney, but there didn't seem to be a way back to the main road other than the way he'd come. Besides, he still needed to find Ezra.

He turned to follow the trail back down to the ravine when he heard a voice with a thick southern accent.

"Hold it right there, Yank."

Christopher stopped breathing. Every muscle froze. He knew he should run, but he couldn't move his feet.

"Drop the rifle, boy."

All around him, a band of armed rebels stepped out of the bushes. Christopher quickly dropped his rifle.

"The commotion coming up that deer trail, we figured it had to be a sick cow, or a blue belly," the man who'd spoke continued. "I guess it was the latter."

Two of the men stepped forward and grabbed Christopher, pulled him back until he was off balance, and threw him to the ground in the middle of the road. Another retrieved his rifle.

"Lookit here, Ira. A '53 Enfield."

The man giving orders, Ira, looked at the rifle and nodded. "Nice piece. What else you got, boy?"

Christopher raised his hands in front of him. From where he lay, all he could see was a bunch of muzzles pointed at him. The men themselves seemed to fade into a gray background. "N-N-N-Nothing."

"N-N-Nothing, my ass." Someone kicked him in the side, and Christopher doubled up in pain. Hands were grabbing him, pulling off his belt,

cartridge box, haversack, and canteen. As they relieved him of his posses-
sions, they slapped and hit him, though he offered no resistance.

Soon, they stopped and stepped back to review their take. Christopher
lay on the rotten logs of the old corduroy road in a fetal position, whimper-
ing. "This can't be real, this can't be happening," he repeated in a chant-
like whisper.

"I got twenty rounds for the rifle," someone said.

"Look at all this food," someone else said. "No wonder them Yanks are
so fat."

The man pulled out a huge knife—it had to be at least a foot long—and
Christopher scurried away from him.

The man laughed and struck a piece of hardtack he held in his other hand with the hilt, breaking it into pieces. He distributed the hardtack
among his comrades and kicked Christopher in the side of the leg. "You're
a skittish little brat, ain't you?"

"We ain't got time for this," Ira said. "Where there's one of these devils,
there's a hundred."

"You want me to stick him?" the man with the knife asked.

"Not unless he tries something. Up, Yank. We gotta move."

Christopher looked at him as if he didn't understand.

Ira kicked him again. "I said up."

Christopher responded by flinching, but did not try to stand, still staring
at the man. Someone grabbed him by the hair and pulled him to his feet.

Christopher cried out. Ira stepped up to him and grabbed his jaw, his
fingers and thumb digging into his cheeks. He pulled Christopher's face up
to his.

"You're comin' with us. Understand?"

Christopher tried to nod, but the hand grasping his face held him im-
mobile.

"And if you try to get away, ol' Johnnie here will bury that pig sticker in
your ribs. Got it?"

Ira shoved Christopher back and turned to go. The others formed a
cadre around him, and the group moved out, following Ira down the road.
Away from the Union encampment.

CHAPTER FIFTEEN
THE SEARCH FOR CHRISTOPHER

Daniel was used to not seeing Christopher for long stretches of time. Sometimes their schedules were such that they didn't see each other all day. So, it wasn't until evening roll call, when neither Christopher nor Ezra showed and Sergeant Howe didn't call their names, that Daniel got curious. No one had picket duty for that long—even as punishment. Maybe they were in another part of camp on a special work detail.

After the company was dismissed, Daniel approached Sergeant Howe. "Sergeant, have you seen my brother?"

Howe looked at him curiously. "Didn't he tell you?"

"Tell me what?" Daniel felt nauseous. He knew this would be bad.

"He and Rouse got two-day passes signed by Colonel Park. They left camp this morning."

Daniel's head exploded in a thousand different directions. Left camp? With Ezra? Anything those two were up to couldn't be good.

"Where did they go?"

Howe frowned at Daniel. "How the hell should I know? They're not my problem until tomorrow evening."

"But, what's around here to go to? There're just small towns and farmsteads. Nothing to attract the likes of those two."

"You mean whorehouses and saloons?" Howe smirked.

Daniel blanched. Then blushed bright red. Drinking was one thing—

but he couldn't imagine his little brother in a brothel.

Seeing Daniel's discomfort, Howe softened his tone. "I'm sure they'll be all right. They know to stay on the main road and populated areas. And there aren't any houses of ill repute around here that I'm aware of. They probably just took up with a couple boys from another regiment and they're off visiting. That's all."

Daniel sighed. "They're gone overnight?"

"I'd imagine. They don't have to report in until tomorrow evening at sundown."

Daniel left the sergeant and headed back to the Sibley tent he shared with his messmates and several other members of Company D. As he moved through camp, he barely saw anything around him. He couldn't stop thinking and worrying about what Christopher may have gotten himself into this time. Whatever it was, Daniel was sure it involved alcohol.

When he arrived at the tent, Parker and Charlie were already at work, dividing up the rations and heating two pots of water—one for coffee and the other for rice.

"You don't need that much food," Daniel said. "It'll just be the three of us for dinner."

Parker and Charlie exchanged a glance, then looked at Daniel.

"Where are the troublemakers?" Parker asked.

"Somewhere making trouble, most likely," Daniel said, spitting out each word as if it left a bad taste in his mouth.

"Did they say anything to either of you about leaving camp?" he asked. Both shook their heads.

"Don't worry, Dan," Charlie said. "They'll be all right."

Daniel nodded. But he didn't believe a word of it. Wherever they were, he was sure they were getting into trouble.

That night and the next day, time seemed to stand still. Each minute slowly crept by, reluctantly passing on to the next. Picket duty, where Daniel had little to do to occupy his mind, was the worst. He had been assigned an area near the Mechanicsburg Gap. Most days he would have been nervous and hyper-alert so far from camp. But that day, all he could think of was Christopher and where he might be.

His inattentiveness almost got him in trouble. When the captain of the guards approached his area, Daniel didn't hear his footsteps until the officer was almost upon him and didn't sound the challenge until the last second. The officer, a stranger from another company, frowned at the late response but let him off with an admonishment to "be vigilant."

When Daniel got back to their tent, he saw Ezra standing by the fire pit, facing Parker and Charlie. Ezra appeared cowed and submissive, Parker and Charlie coiled as if ready to strike. Daniel rushed up to the three and his head swiveled around, taking in his surroundings. He was blatantly aware of his brother's absence but didn't want to accept it.

"Where's Christopher?"

"I thought he'd be here," Ezra responded, eyes downcast.

Daniel gulped. He tried to fill his lungs but couldn't draw a deep breath. His perception dwindled until the camp disappeared and all that remained was Ezra's face. He whispered, "What do you mean by that?"

"Just that," Ezra said, standing up a little straighter and raising his chin. "We got separated last night, and he knew we had to be back today by sundown, so I assumed he would have made it back to camp, same as me."

Without thinking, Daniel was across the fire and had his hands around Ezra's throat. When he spoke, his voice was loud and high pitched. "You got separated? Where? Did you even look for him, you lazy, no good Dutchman?" He squeezed Ezra's neck and shook.

Ezra raised his hands and tried to push Daniel away, but the older boy's feet were firmly planted, his muscles rigid with anger, fear, and frustration. Ezra fell back, and Daniel landed on top of him, never taking his hands from his neck. Ezra's eyes and tongue stuck out, and he flailed at Daniel's head and face. Then, Daniel released Ezra's neck and began punching, his arms moving like pistons as all the strain and anxiety of the last twenty-four hours flowed out of him with each strike.

Parker and Charlie moved in and separated the two. Parker grabbed Daniel, and Daniel responded by taking a swing at him. Daniel kicked and thrashed about, swinging at Ezra as Parker got his arms around his waist and pulled him back. Suddenly, Daniel stopped.

Daniel stood, body limp, but hands curled into fists and eyes blazing.

Parker stepped back, hands raised in front of him. "You will tell me everything," Daniel said to Ezra. "You're going to leave nothing out. And, if anything's happened to Christopher, I will kill you."

Everyone froze in stunned silence. None doubted Daniel meant what he'd just said.

Parker stepped forward and took Ezra's arm in a firm grip. "Don't worry, Danny. We'll get your brother back."

He nodded his head toward the captain's tent at the end of the company street. "Come on, let's go see the captain.

All four messmates walked down to the end of the street. When they got to the captain's tent, Parker called out, "Captain Daggett, sir? Can we have a moment?"

"Enter."

The four exchanged glances. The voice that answered was not Captain Daggett's.

When they stepped inside the tent, even Daniel felt a moment of relief and excitement. Sitting at the desk going over reports with Captain Daggett was Major Sawyer, returned from three month's sick leave.

Major Sawyer still looked pale and drawn, and he had lost considerable weight from his bout with typhus, but he looked at them with the same intense stare they had all come to fear and respect.

"Major Sawyer, sir! It's good to see you," Parker said.

"Thank you, Corporal Bonnett. It's good to be back." Major Sawyer surveyed the four soldiers before him and frowned. "What's this about?"

Daniel opened his mouth to speak, but Parker beat him to it. Daniel frowned at Parker, who responded with a slight shake of his head as he laid out the entire scenario to the captain and major.

When Parker got to the part where Ezra came back alone, Sawyer looked over at the sheepish young man and said, "What do you have to say for yourself, soldier?"

Ezra bowed his head. "We was just having a little fun, sir. We heared of this drinking establishment down by the suspension bridge and thought it would be fun to go see for ourselves."

Ezra relayed the events leading up to that moment. After they became separated, he had spent the night hidden in a rocky outcropping. That morning, when he could not find Christopher, he returned to camp, expecting to find him there.

By the time he finished, the major's pale face had become bright red. He held out his hand. "Let me see that pass."

Ezra handed it over, and Sawyer looked at it for what seemed to be several minutes, but was probably just seconds.

Without looking up, he said to Captain Daggett, "Dan, would you have Sergeant Re—I mean Howe—assemble the men?"

Sawyer looked up at the four men before him, his eyes boring into Ezra. "You four, go line up."

As they turned to go, Sawyer said, "Galloway."

Daniel turned and met the captain's stare.

"I'm sorry, son. We'll do everything we can to get your brother back."

Daniel nodded and ducked under the tent flap into the cool but sunny November air.

Once the company was assembled, Major Sawyer strode out of the tent and stepped before them. As soon as they saw him, the men cheered.

"QUIET!" Lieutenant Reid yelled, forgetting for the moment he was no longer first sergeant. The cheering stopped and everyone exchanged worried glances.

"Company—attention! Eyes—front!"

When the men were at attention and staring straight ahead, Major Sawyer addressed them.

"It's good to be back with my beloved 8th—and Company D in particular. I had hoped our reunion would be a happy one." Sawyer put his hands behind his back and paced in front of the company.

"But that was not to be. It would appear that, in my absence, things have fallen into a shambles." He stopped and looked over at Captain Daggett, lined up on the right of the company, looking red-faced and angry.

In a more conversational tone, Sawyer continued. "This has nothing to do with Captain Daggett, who has led his men admirably during my long illness and recovery. There are issues at play that are beyond his control and level of responsibility." Daggett blew out the breath he'd been holding and let his shoulders slump just a little.

"But," Sawyer continued, his voice rising to address the ranks, "discipline has faltered. There has been too much drinking and gambling, and Lord knows what other vices going on.

He stopped and turned toward the men. "From this point on, and for the foreseeable future, unless your duties require otherwise, Company D is confined to the company street. Sutler's Row is off limits." A palatable tension rose among the ranks as the men took in this news.

"This wanton behavior has led to trouble for the company," Sawyer continued. "We have a man missing."

At that, discipline cracked, and men looked around and began talking among themselves. "Who?" someone blurted out.

"QUIET! You sorry bastards are at attention. Get your shoulders back and your eyes front. The major wants you to know something, he'll tell you." Howe glared at the men until everyone was back at attention.

Sawyer sighed. "Private Christopher Galloway disappeared last night at a drinking establishment down by the suspension bridge. Sergeant Reid will take a squad down that way and investigate," he said, referring to Sergeant John G. "Hopefully, he'll come back with our wayward son."

As the company was dismissed, Daniel made a beeline for Sergeant G, but Major Sawyer beat him there.

"John," Major Sawyer said.

"Yes, sir?"

"Make sure Dan Galloway is in your squad." His eyes flitted to Daniel's. "But keep him under control."

—⚉—

Along with Daniel, Reid took Parker Bonnett, Charlie Locker, David Ward, Joseph Taylor, and Ezra Rouse. The grabbed their rifles and traps, made sure they had ammunition and provisions for a couple days, and were on the road south within a half hour. Reid let Daniel set the pace so they were all a little winded when they arrived.

With Daniel shadowing him, Reid spoke with Captain Kenney of

Company B. Captain Kenney directed them to Sergeant Thomas Galwey, the provost sergeant the night before. Reid ordered Daniel to stay with the other men and set out in search of Sergeant Galway.

While he was gone, the men stacked their rifles and everyone but Daniel removed their traps and sat, trying to relax and catch their breath. Daniel remained in full gear, pacing back and forth.

"Danny, you will not be much help in the search if you wear yourself out before we even get started," Parker said.

Daniel took off his hat and wiped his brow with his sleeve. Despite the cool November air, he was sweating profusely. "I don't think I'll be able to rest until we find Chris," he said. "What'll I say to Ma and Da?"

Daniel looked at the tree line, staring intently as if expecting Christopher to appear any minute. "I told them I'd look after him," he whispered.

David Ward, not much older than Christopher, chewed on the edge of a hardtack cracker and complained. "It's getting late and it don't appear likely we'll be getting any supper at this rate."

"Quiet, Davey," Charlie chided. "We're trying to find Nape's brother."

David looked hurt. "I know that. Hell, I want to find him too. But a man's gotta eat."

Sergeant G returned. "I spoke with the sergeant of arms from last night. He wasn't even aware there were Company D men in the area. He rounded up some of his boys and a few from an Indiana regiment who were drinking in a shack up a ravine south of the river. Apparently, things got out of hand and someone got killed—bayonet through the throat."

Daniel felt the blood rush from his face.

"He was a Company B man. They have a man in custody they suspect of doing the deed—another Company B man. The two were drinking and playing cards, and the dead man was winning."

"I don't know nothing about no murder," Ezra said. "Like I said, Chris and me skedaddled at the first sign of provosts. Everybody looked all right to me."

"Well, that doesn't matter," Sergeant G continued. "Sergeant Galwey will take a detail and scout the immediate vicinity. He's not too happy about it—doesn't think our Galloway is anywhere around here that they wouldn't know, unless…" He broke off and looked away.

He made a point not to look at Daniel as he continued. "We're going back to the shack and up the ravine to look for him there. Daylight's burning, and we don't want to be outside the pickets after dark. There's too much rebel activity. We might be beset by bushwhackers or shot by a trigger-happy picket coming back. So, grab your gear and let's go."

As they rose and put on their traps, David Ward said under his breath, "I told you we weren't getting no supper."

They made their way to the cabin—trotting most of the way. The provost guard had not been gentle with the men they'd taken into custody and didn't mind dragging them through the underbrush, so the trail was wider and easier to navigate.

As they entered the clearing, they saw the cabin door hanging half on its frame and the chairs and tables strewn about the yard. Around back, they found a pile of broken glass and the strong odor of spilt whiskey.

"Damn waste, you ask me," Ezra mumbled.

"No one did, Rouse. So shut it," Sergeant G responded.

Inside was more broken bottles, boxes, and furniture. There was no sign of Mabel, the proprietress.

Back outside, they broke up into three groups and started up the ravine. Locker and Taylor took the left side, Daniel and Ward took the right, and Reid and Ezra went up the middle.

The ravine was only fifty yards wide at its widest, and narrowed as they climbed, but the trees and undergrowth were so thick the three groups couldn't see one another. Daniel called Christopher's name every few minutes. The others took up the cry as well until calls of Christopher, Galloway, and Notch filled the air. Finally, Sergeant G called out in exasperation, "Quiet! Me and Dan will do the calling. The rest of you, just keep your eyes peeled."

It was already getting dark in the ravine. Daniel was starting to worry that Sergeant G would call off the search, when Locker called out from the other side of the ravine.

"There's a trail over here."

Everyone converged on his location. Daniel furiously thrust himself through the underbrush, breaking branches and scattering leaves.

"Good Lord, Nape, you make more noise than a herd of buffalo," Ward said.

"You ever heard a herd of buffalo, Ward?" Sergeant G asked.

"Well…no. But if I did, I imagine it would sound a lot like Nape here."

What Locker found appeared to be a deer trail. They followed single file, the branches on either side tugging at their rifles and traps. The trail rose steeply out of the ravine, and they found themselves on an old corduroy road.

"I wonder where this goes," Locker mused.

Sergeant G shrugged. "Probably an old logging road."

Daniel rushed up the road one way and then the other. He stopped and looked at Sergeant G. "We have to split up—look both ways."

Sergeant G looked up at the patch of sky visible through the trees. There was still some blue, but not for long. He shook his head. "We need to get back to camp. It's almost dark."

Daniel's eyes got big, and he gripped his rifle so hard his knuckles turned white. "We can't stop now. We're on to something here. He might be somewhere on this road, lost or hurt."

"If we stay any longer, we'll be in the same boat, and that won't help your brother none," Sergeant G shot back.

Daniel spun around, took several steps, and stopped. His whole body tensed and then relaxed as the truth of what Reid said shot home. His brother was out there somewhere, and there wasn't a damn thing he could do about it.

They all heard footsteps running down the road and spun around, bringing their rifles up to the ready position. Not that it would do any good, Daniel thought. None of them were loaded.

Ezra ran up to the group, and Sergeant G cussed him out.

"Dammit, Rouse. Where did you get to? I didn't give you permission to leave the group."

Ezra held up a belt, an empty cartridge box, and a blue forage cap with a brass 8 on the flat top. "I found these up the road a piece."

Daniel looked at the hat. The leather brim of each forage cap had a unique curl to it. Some men wet the leather and curled it for a more jaunty appearance, others worked diligently to keep the brim as straight as possible. Most just let the sun and rain have its way with the leather until it took on its natural shape. Daniel would recognize that hat anywhere.

"It's Chris's."

"You sure?" Sergeant G asked.

Daniel nodded.

"That does it. We need to get back to Company B's camp now. We'll figure out where this road comes out and send a larger search party in the morning."

Sergeant G looked at Daniel. "You know what this means, don't you?"

Daniel looked into the sergeant's eyes. He didn't want to know. Didn't want to be thinking what he was thinking. He shook his head, almost imperceptibly.

Reid's voice softened. "Your brother is probably a prisoner of the enemy, Danny. The secesh have him."

Tears came unbidden to Daniel's eyes. The lump in his throat made him gasp. He spun around and took two steps away from the group.

"Come on, let's go."

A gentle hand grasped Daniel's arm and pulled him along.

—⚏—

Daniel thought it was the longest night of his life. Worse than the time Christopher had gotten lost in the woods. Then he'd been a child, and his father had been there to shoulder the burden. He knew with his da there it would be all right. And it was. This time though, Christopher would not come wandering out of the woods in the morning. Daniel might not see him again until the war was over—if ever.

Daniel wondered how they were treating his brother. Were they feeding him and giving him shelter? Or were they beating and humiliating him? Daniel sought solace in the fact that the enemy weren't savages—they were Americans. Or were until recently. They had the same values he did, and his government didn't mistreat prisoners.

In the morning, Sergeant G sent David Ward and Joseph Taylor back to report to Major Sawyer, and to see if any locals were aware of an abandoned road in the vicinity. Captain Kenney sent his first lieutenant, William Delaney, with a platoon to accompany Sergeant G's squad in their search of the corduroy road.

It was slow going getting fifty men up the ravine and the deer trail to the road, so it was late morning by the time they were ready to begin the search. But it ended almost as soon as it had begun. The road dwindled to nothing in less than a mile both directions—reclaimed by the forest—and revealed no further clues as to Christopher Galloway's fate.

It was an exhausted and depressed Daniel who walked the road back to Romney that evening. He'd not slept the last two nights and was coming to terms with the fact that they were not going to find Christopher. He was thankful for the effort that Captain Kenney and Major Sawyer had made to find his brother. Usually, when a soldier went missing, they assumed he'd deserted and listed the man as Absent Without Leave.

That night, he tried to write a letter to his parents. But he couldn't get past the opening paragraph. How was he going to tell his parents their youngest son was missing, most likely a prisoner of war? How could he convey any sense of hope or indomitability when he had none? He knew he had to do it. He had to be the one to write them and tell them what had happened to Christopher before his name appeared on a list in the post office or the next *Harpers Weekly*.

But he couldn't. Not now. Maybe tomorrow.

He gave up, blew out the candle, and left the paper, blank except for the salutation and opening paragraph, for tomorrow. He lay in his bed with questions and self-incriminations flitting through his thoughts in a circular pattern with no end. Then, the tears came, and he cried as quietly as possible so his tent mates wouldn't hear.

Sometime in the middle of the night, he drifted off. For the first time since he'd discovered Christopher and Ezra had left the camp, he slept a deep, sound sleep until reveille.

CHAPTER SIXTEEN
PRISONER OF WAR

Christopher's capturers walked all day and into the night, with only one stop to build a small fire and eat all Christopher's rations. After walking only a short way, the road disappeared—the land reclaimed by the forest—and they spent most of the day following what once might have been deer trails, but now were used more by bushwhackers than wildlife.

The way was hard and the pace brisk. Christopher's head pounded like a hammer on an anvil with each step. After the first mile, he gagged and threw up the little bile in his stomach. He'd slept only an hour or two the night before. His eyes burned and he couldn't concentrate. His feet scraped the dirt with each step and his head hung low, his vision fixed on the ground before him.

He tripped over roots and rocks often. When he did, someone would grab him by the collar, pull him to his feet, and give him a hard shove forward. If his pace lagged, someone would push him again and tell him to keep moving. All the pushing resulted in more falling, followed by more pulling, resulting in more falling. Soon the palms of his hands were raw and swollen, crisscrossed with red scrapes. Rivulets of blood coursed down his shins from open cuts on his knees.

After one painful fall where Christopher's knee landed on a small, sharp rock sticking up in the trail, the leader, Ira, lost his patience. "Iffen you keep pushin' him, he's gonna keep fallin' and we ain't never gonna get back to camp."

At that, the one called Johnnie looped a rope around his neck, tied it in a slip-knot, and pulled Christopher along. This not only resulted in just as many falls, but also caused the loop to tighten around Christopher's neck every time. After falling, instead of trying to rise, Christopher would claw at the rope until Johnnie loosened the loop.

After several stops to save Christopher from choking to death, Johnnie gave up and removed the rope. He shoved Christopher forward and grumbled, "I shoulda just stuck ya back there on the old road."

Ira called a halt, and Christopher collapsed in a heap by the trail. "Robbie," he said to a young boy no older than Christopher, "get a fire going. I've a hankerin' for some sow belly and grits. Oh, and give the Yank a cracker." He chuckled to himself and sat, admiring Christopher's rifle.

"The boys down south got rifles like this. But we gotta make do with the squirrel guns and shotguns on hand when you yankee mudsills invaded." He spit on a spot of rust on the barrel and scrubbed it with a bandana.

The one called Robbie brought Christopher a piece of hardtack and a canteen. Christopher lay on the ground, his cheek in the dirt and his eyes closed, but he smelled Robbie's approach. He opened his eyes.

The young bushwhacker was tall and rail thin, and his clothes were filthy and threadbare. He had an old fashioned leather possibles bag draped over one shoulder, and he carried a double barrel shotgun. Nothing about him said soldier. Not in any sense Christopher had learned at Camp Dennison.

After giving Christopher his supper, Robbie moved back several paces and sat on the ground facing him, his shotgun draped across his lap. He never took his eyes off his prisoner.

Christopher tried to ignore the young man, instead concentrating on attacking the hard cracker that was all he would get to eat that night. He had no way to soften it, and he knew from experience that trying to bite off a piece would get him nowhere. Instead, he nibbled on the end with his front teeth, like a rabbit or squirrel. When he had eaten enough to expose the porous inside of the cracker, he tried to pour a little water from the canteen into it. He thought some water may have gotten down into the cracker, but most of it ended up on his hand and in his lap.

After a while, Robbie's constant staring bothered Christopher enough for him to say something. He looked at the boy and asked, "What are you looking at?"

"A shit-heel."

Christopher blinked.

"Why?"

"Why are you a shit-heel?" Robbie shrugged.

"No. Why are you staring at me?"

"I'm guardin' you. Makin' sure you don't 'scape."

"So, you think if you take your eyes off me for a second I'll disappear?"

Robbie frowned. "Shut up."

Christopher returned to nibbling on his hardtack. He grew frustrated at his lack of success breaking the hard lump of dough and set the cracker in his lap.

He looked at his capturers, all dressed and armed like Robbie, and a question entered his head.

"Why are you doing this?" he asked Robbie.

"What, taking you prisoner? Got me. We should a stuck ya and left ya back on that road."

"No. Why are you fighting? I bet none of you have slaves."

"Slaves! She-it, I don't know nothin' 'bout no slaves. Ain't got nothin' to do with slaves. We're fightin' cause you invaded us."

"We didn't invade—you seceded."

"So, what's that to you?"

"Nothing. Far as I'm concerned, you can take your bumpy old state and keep it. After this, I hope I never see another mountain. But your state seceded because Lincoln is an abolitionist."

"Abo-what?"

"Abolitionist. Someone opposed to slavery."

"Hell, then I'm an abo-lishon-ist too. All I know about slavery is it makes it damn near impossible for an honest white man to make a living."

"Then why are you fighting?"

"Cause we had to, dammit! Ain't no gubment back in Washington City gonna tell us how to live our lives."

Johnnie walked up, interrupting the conversion. Which was fine with Christopher. He didn't know how to respond to Robbie's statement.

This was crazy. Did anyone even know what they were fighting for? Christopher thought he did, but now he wasn't so sure.

"Git yur-sef sumpin' to eat, Robbie, I'll watch the p'isner," Johnnie said as he squatted.

Christopher saw Johnnie had a hunk of fresh-cooked sow belly stuck on the end of his knife, and his mouth watered. The hunger gnawed at his gut, but he couldn't stop thinking of the conversation he'd had with Robbie. That had probably been the deepest conversation he'd ever had about the reasons behind the war.

Johnnie gave Christopher a big, wicked-looking grin. Half his teeth were missing, and those that remained were gray and crooked. Christopher could smell his breath from where he sat. He thought with some satisfaction that Johnnie wouldn't have any better luck trying to eat that sow belly than he was having with his hardtack. He turned his back on the rebel band and went back to nibbling.

They reached the rebel encampment late the next day. Again, the lack of uniformity and military discipline surprised Christopher. Most of the men lived in small log shelters, but unlike the uniform rows and streets in a Federal camp, they seemed to have been built wherever was most convenient. The only uniforms in sight belonged to officers who, while treated with respect, were not saluted.

His appearance seemed to create a small commotion among the officers. After much yelling and barking of orders, he was strapped to the back of a horse and led south with a small troop of cavalry.

They arrived in Winchester after dusk. The sergeant of the cavalry troop turned Christopher over to the local provost guard, who took him to the courthouse, gave him a threadbare blanket that reeked of sweat and vomit, and locked him in the basement. Except for a couple small candle flames, the basement was pitch black.

As they closed the door on him, Christopher pushed back in desperation. "Wait! I haven't eaten anything all day."

The guard conveyed how little he cared with a single look. "Prisoners already ate. Next meal's in the mornin'."

"But, I'm starving…"

"Not my problem. You shoulda thought of that before you invaded our state."

He closed and latched the door with a loud bang and rattle that unnerved Christopher as much as anything that had happened to him in the last two days.

Christopher could tell by the sounds of rustling straw that the room was already occupied.

A voice came out of the darkness. "Try and get some sleep. There'll be food in the morning."

Though he couldn't see anything, Christopher eagerly looked around. "You have something a body could nibble on 'til then?" he asked.

His question was answered by a chorus of bitter laughter. Disappointed, Christopher felt his way along the wall and sank to the floor to await the dawn.

—⁂—

At breakfast the next morning, Christopher met the first of his fellow prisoners. A large man wearing a tattered artillery jacket with red sergeant stripes approached him as he was finishing his meal.

"I'm Spaulding," he said. "You just arrived, so I'm going to give you some leeway your first morning, but I am the ranking man here, the rest of you being lowly privates and webfeet to boot. In case you hadn't noticed, I'm larger than the rest of you. So, I need more nourishment. You understand?"

Christopher shrugged.

"You give me a quarter of your bread and some of your stew."

Christopher stared at the man, his last bite of stew-sopped bread forgotten in his hand. "I don't understand. There's hardly enough food here to survive as is."

"Exactly," said the big man. "And you're a little runt. Imagine how

I feel?"

"But, I'm sure they take that into account," Christopher reasoned.

"HA! You think so, do you? The dirty secesh, they give us the least they can get away with. It doesn't matter to them if we starve down here or not."

Christopher looked at the last piece of bread in his hand. Overwhelming hunger pains wracked his belly. Now this big ape wanted some of his food? He looked up at the man and shook his head.

"I don't think——"

Christopher saw the big fist coming in plenty of time to duck, but sat frozen by disbelief. Just before the strike landed, he reacted, trying to move his head out of the way, but it was too late. Spaulding's fist glanced off his cheek, violently twisting his head and knocking him over.

The piece of bread he'd been holding flew out of his hand and rolled across the floor, stopping at the feet of another prisoner. The man fervently reached down, grabbed the piece of bread, and popped it into his mouth.

Gone was any pretense of civility from the big man. Spaulding glared and jabbed his finger at Christopher with each word. "Now it's out there plain and simple! You will give me a part of everything they give you. What's yours is yours only because I say it is. Do you understand?"

Christopher didn't move. Didn't respond. After a few seconds, he sat up, rubbing his cheek. He looked around the room at the other four men. All of them avoided eye contact.

Spaulding slapped him across the top of the head. "I asked you a question! Do you understand?"

Christopher looked into the eyes of his tormentor. He nodded once. Not because he agreed to anything, but to make the big man go away.

"Good." Spaulding smiled. "See you at dinner."

He turned and went back to his seat at the other end of the room.

Christopher brushed his hair back and glared around the room. It was just like his childhood, with Ezra smacking him around and taking whatever he wanted. But back then, he could retreat to the safety of his home.

Now there was nowhere to retreat. As bad as Ezra seemed to his childhood self, there had been limits. He didn't think the same was true for Spaulding.

Dinner came that evening—a watery rice gruel with little flavor.

Christopher watched the others pour a little of their gruel into Spaulding's bowl. The big man was looking at him. Christopher thought about refusing. He imagined himself staring down the bully and not giving in.

Then, he took in the size and strength of the man, and the complacency of the other prisoners, and he knew he couldn't stand against the man alone. He walked across the room, each step a blow to his pride. He poured some of his gruel into Spaulding's bowl, which was already almost overflowing.

Spaulding nodded and gave him a smug smile. As he returned to his seat, Christopher's face burned with shame. That smile hurt worse than the blow he'd received that morning.

—⁓—

As the days progressed, Christopher thought about how he could get the others to stand up to Spaulding, but they were all locked up in one big room—there was nowhere he could go to be alone with any of the other prisoners. He thought about who would be the best candidates for an alliance—there was Isaac and Frederick Mann from Indiana, Jacob Spindleman from Ohio, and Stephen Cole from West Virginia. The Mann brothers were in their twenties, strong farm hands, but docile. Spindleman was in his thirties and a clerk from Cincinnati; to him, violence and graft was something the police handled. Cole was a miner, by far the strongest of the bunch, but Christopher learned from Isaac that Spaulding had given Cole so severe a beating that the man could hardly move for a week.

As December approached, it got much colder. The guards put the prisoners to work bringing in coal and firewood to heat the courthouse. One day, Christopher was out with Cole, collecting firewood, when he decided it was time to broach the subject of Spaulding.

"Stephen, we need to do something about Spaulding. We're starving."

Cole shook his head. "I tried that. He almost killed me. Probably would have if the Mann brothers hadn't talked him out of it."

"He's big, but there's only one of him. The five of us together are stronger."

Cole looked Christopher in the eye. "And do what, Galloway? We gonna kill him? That's the only way to stop him."

Christopher didn't respond right away. He'd not thought of anything so extreme. In fact, he realized he'd not thought through what they would do to get Spaulding to stop.

"Surely, a good thrashing will make him see the error of his ways."

Cole snorted. "You think so? You ever dealt with a man like that?"

Christopher thought of Ezra and shook his head.

"I tell you, he won't stop. He'll just go off, lick his wounds, and wait for the time he can get his revenge. He'll probably kill one of us to show he means business. Most likely you or Spindleman cause you're the smallest. Maybe me, cause I'm the biggest. It'll be like sharing a room with a tiger."

—⁂—

One day, some ladies from the local auxiliary came with extra blankets and some pies for the prisoners. The prisoners erupted in a chorus of God-bless-yous and thank-yous and rushed the women. The well-meaning ladies, all smiles and assurances as they entered the room, shrank back in fear as the filthy skeletons (except Spaulding) came at them. One woman gagged, put a handkerchief over her nose, and rushed out of the room.

The guards stepped forward, pointing their bayonet-mounted rifles at the overenthusiastic prisoners. That stopped their approach, but didn't dampen their thanks. Christopher dropped to his knees and crossed himself. Spindleman wept. Spaulding stayed back, watching the activity with his arms crossed and a smile on his face.

Each man got a new blanket and half a pie. After the ladies and guards left, Spaulding reminded them of their tithing requirements. Christopher sighed and silently cursed his cowardice as he broke off a piece of pie and brought it over to the big man. Everyone else followed suit.

Christopher ate the rest of his pie as fast as he could. Afterward his stomach cramped—a sharp pain that doubled him over. For a moment, he was so overcome with nausea he feared he would throw up his pie. But he held it down. He lay on the pile of straw that was his "bed" and relished the full feeling in his stomach, despite the pain.

The only one who did not keep his pie down was Isaac Mann. He just made it to the slop bucket when his pie came back up in a rush, splashing vomit and urine all over his feet and the floor. The smell wafted through the air, causing Christopher's stomach to roil. He pressed his new blanket over his nose and mouth until the urge to vomit passed. "Lord, Isaac, did you have to do that?"

Isaac, hunched over the slop bucket with his hands on his knees, responded with a slight nod. When it was clear he would not throw up any more, his brother helped him back to his spot to lie down and covered him with his blanket.

Frederick placed his hand on his brother's forehead and said, "You don't look too good, brother."

"I don't feel too good," Isaac responded.

"Must have been too much rich pie," Frederick said. Isaac nodded.

"Get some sleep, you'll feel better in the morning."

But Isaac didn't feel better in the morning. Instead, he got worse. He tried to eat, but only managed to get down a few bites. Spaulding took the rest.

As the day progressed, Isaac got so weak he couldn't stand. His diarrhea was so bad, he had to leave his pants off. His brother had to scoop up the soiled straw and take it over to the slop bucket.

The smell was so overpowering that everyone tried breathing only through their mouths. Christopher made frequent trips to the door to suck fresh air in through the doorjamb.

That afternoon, Spaulding stood up and glared at Frederick. "Dammit, Mann, do something about your brother or I will."

"He can't help it, Spaulding. He'll be better tomorrow."

Spaulding pointed his finger at Frederick. "He'd better be, or there'll be hell to pay."

That night, Christopher dreamt of chopping wood outside Norwalk. He'd been chopping for hours but couldn't stop. The air was unseasonably cold and the sound of the ax striking the log echoed through the trees. As he continued to chop, it got darker, and a deep chill penetrated his back. The cold Ohio air, the woodlot, and the ax all faded away to the underground darkness, cold floor, and stink of his prison cell. But the striking sound continued.

Christopher sat up and looked around. In the darkness he could make out a large shape leaning over Isaac Mann, whose flailing legs hitting the wall and floor were making the striking noise. He lit a candle in time to see Frederick Mann jump onto Spaulding's back. Frederick struck the larger man twice on the back and grabbed his hair trying to pull him off his brother. Spaulding roared and spun around, striking Frederick in the ribs with his elbow as he turned.

The smaller man doubled over and stumbled back, giving Spaulding room to follow up with a haymaker that dropped Frederick senseless.

Spaulding looked over at Cole and Christopher. "I'm sick of smelling his shit," he said, pointing at Isaac. "The man's dying anyway, I'm just helping him along."

Christopher looked over Spaulding's shoulder and saw Isaac's blanket bunched up at his chest, where he'd pushed it down as he gasped for air. He looked over at Cole, who had lit his own candle. Their eyes met, and they stared at each other, probing. Spaulding turned back to the sick man, and they both nodded and stood.

"No," Cole said.

Spaulding looked over his shoulder. "You say something, cracker?"

"I said no."

"No what?" Spaulding stood and faced them. "No, please don't hurt me, Mr. Spaulding? Is that what you're saying?"

Cole moved to the middle of the room. "No, I won't let you kill that man."

Without another word, Spaulding rushed Cole, who responded by crouching down and diving for the other man's legs. He got his arms around Spaulding's legs and drove his shoulder into the big man's crotch. But Spaulding didn't move until Christopher leapt over Cole and wrapped his arms around the big man's neck.

The weight of both men pushed Spaulding over. He fell straight back, striking the back of his head on the floor as he hit. Christopher was up at once, straddling Spaulding's chest and striking him in the face with both hands. Cole stood up and drove his heal into the big man's crotch. Spaulding's whole body spasmed in response to the blow to his genitals, almost throwing Christopher off.

Christopher held on by squeezing his knees around Spaulding's chest. He continued to hit his tormentor in the face, driven by fear and frustration until his arms tired and his blows weakened. By then, Spaulding's face was bloody and showing the first signs of swelling.

Frederick recovered and joined Cole in kicking Spaulding's legs and midsection. Once the fear and adrenaline passed, the three men stopped, their muscles quivering as they collapsed to the floor.

The basement was quiet except for the sound of their ragged breathing. Once they'd all recovered enough, they stood and looked down at Spaulding, who wasn't moving. His swollen, blood-covered face was almost unrecognizable. His nose had been smashed to the side, and there was a small puddle of blood under his head from where he'd hit the floor.

"Is he dead?" Christopher asked.

Cole knelt down and placed a hand on Spaulding's chest. After a few minutes, he shook his head.

"What do we do now?" Cole asked. Christopher would not meet his gaze.

"What do you mean?" Frederick asked.

"With him," Cole responded, pointing at Spaulding. "He won't let this stand. He'll come back at us as soon as he's able. And he won't stop with just a beating."

"You're talking cold-blooded murder," Christopher said.

"I'm talking preservation."

Christopher paced the room, shaking his head. "I don't know," he said over and over.

Frederick was quiet for a moment, then said, "The son of a bitch tried to kill my brother."

Christopher stopped and looked at the Indiana farm boy. He knew what they said was true. Given the chance, Spaulding would kill one or all of them. But, he couldn't bring himself to accept committing murder.

"I just don't know."

"Damn it, Galloway!" Cole exploded. "What don't you know? It's him or us? Who's it going to be?"

"Kill him," came from across the room. Christopher looked in surprise at Jacob Spindleman, who sat on his bedding with his legs pulled up to his chest, arms around his shins. He looked to Christopher like a small child, afraid of the monsters under his bed.

After another moment, Christopher reached a state of acceptance, if not agreement, much like that first day when he'd given Spaulding part of his meal. He gave in to the inevitable and nodded.

"How are we going to do it?"

"Beat him to death," Frederick spat.

Cole shook his head. "It'll take all night to kill the big ox that way. And even then it may not be a sure thing."

"Strangle him," Christopher said.

Cole and Frederick nodded and looked around for something they could use to strangle Spaulding.

"His suspenders," Christopher said, pointing.

Cole dropped next to Spaulding and unbuttoned his suspenders. They rolled him half over and unbuttoned the back. Cole stood up and held the suspenders out before him.

"All of us together," he said.

Christopher and Frederick nodded.

Cole wrapped the suspenders around Spaulding's neck and took one end. Christopher and Frederick took the other end, and all three pulled.

Spaulding twitched, then convulsed. They pulled harder. Spaulding's eyes shot open, and he thrashed about, his fingers trying to grip the suspender material that was now deeply embedded in his neck. His thrashing slowed and his eyes started to flutter, but then the suspenders broke and the three would-be killers flew back.

Spaulding sat up and removed the broken suspenders from around his neck. "I'll kill you all," he croaked, trying to rise.

The three jumped up and were on Spaulding before he could get up, pounding him with their fists. Spaulding roared, and Christopher thought for sure the guards would come in any minute. But the four continued to thrash about on the floor for several minutes more before Spaulding got his hands and knees under him. He mustered everything he had and pushed up with another roar, sending his attackers sprawling in all directions.

Spaulding leered through the blood and the swelling and leaned forward to push himself up the rest of the way. Christopher was the first up and blindly kicked at the man, catching him just below the chin.

Something gave in Spaulding's throat, and his face went from triumph to pain and fear. His fingers fluttered over his broken esophagus, and his mouth opened and closed like a fish out of water.

The three smaller men scrambled back and watched as their tormentor toppled over. They watched him struggle by the weak candlelight for several minutes. His face turned a dark blue beneath the blood and swelled out even more. His tongue too, swelled until it was sticking out of his mouth like a hunk of meat. They watched in horror as his eyes seemed to protrude out of his head.

Spaulding reached toward Christopher. Their eyes locked—the big man's full of both pleading and accusation.

A sob broke forth and caught in Christopher's throat.

Then, the hand dropped. Spaulding seemed to deflate before them. His eyes were empty.

The silence was overwhelming. None of the men in the room could look away from the horror before them. Christopher's stomach heaved, and he tasted bile in the back of his throat.

A low moan shattered their paralysis and made all three jump. But it was Isaac.

Frederick went to his brother and straightened his blanket.

Cole and Christopher got their candles and went to Spaulding's spot on the floor. They found a stash of bread equivalent to three days' rations for the four of them. It appeared Spaulding was eating even better than they thought. They took the bread and divided it evenly. Cole gave Frederick both his and Isaac's share.

They all returned to their spots and ate the bread in silence, unable to take their eyes off the dead man in the middle of the floor. Cole got up and approached the body. "Come on, Galloway, give me a hand."

"What? What are you going to do?"

"We can't just leave him here in the middle of the floor. Give me a hand and let's drag him back to his bed."

They dragged Spaulding's body to his spot and covered it with his blanket. Afterward, each man returned to his own spot and waited sleeplessly for morning.

—⁂—

When the guards came in the next morning with breakfast, Frederick, Cole, Spindleman, and Christopher met them at the door. As they were distributing the food, one of the guards called to Spaulding. "Come on, Spaulding, come get it or go without."

"He won't go without. He'll just beat it out of one of these others," the other guard said.

The first guard shook his head. "Not today. I'm sick of this shit. And you boys should be too," he said, pointing to the four prisoners standing before him.

The first guard looked at Spaulding and noticed his blanket was pulled up over his face. He looked at the four before him, an unspoken question in his eyes.

"Just what's wrong with Spaulding this morning?" he asked.

All four shrugged.

"I think he's under the weather," Cole said.

The guard approached Spaulding, reached down, and pulled the blanket back. Spaulding's whole head had swollen in the night until it looked like a large purple ball with a tongue and two eyeballs sticking out. The guard dropped the blanket and jumped back.

"Good Lord, boys. What have you done?"

"He was trying to kill Isaac," Christopher whispered.

The guard looked at Isaac, shivering and sweating on what remained of his straw. He looked back at the corpse. "About time," he said under his breath.

151

He walked back to the door and said to the other guard, "Give them Spaulding's share." Then he looked at the four prisoners. Jerking his thumb at Spaulding's body, he said, "That's why we'll win. You Yanks are savages."

—⚍—

Two days later, Isaac died.

Christopher spent his days thinking about how Spaulding's neck crumpled under his foot. When he closed his eyes, he saw the dark blue swollen face with its swollen tongue and protruding eyes. At night, he listened to Frederick cry himself to sleep and thought of Daniel.

One day, the guard mentioned that they might be paroled through the prisoner exchange program. Another day they were to be transferred south to Richmond. Their rations continued to be just enough to keep them alive, and the Ladies Auxiliary did not return. Christopher's emotions went up or down depending on the rumor of the day until constant hunger and disappointment became so commonplace that he stopped caring.

Then, just before Christmas, the four prisoners were marched to the depot, put on a train, and shipped south to Richmond.

CHAPTER SEVENTEEN
WINTER CAMP

The army listed Christopher as missing, assumed captured by the enemy. Daniel pleaded with Major Sawyer to continue the search, but he refused, saying Christopher was most likely captured or dead. Everyone told Daniel he should be thankful Christopher hadn't been branded a deserter, but he saw little to be thankful for.

He tried to see Colonel DePuy, to ask him to intervene, but his adjutant said he wasn't "accepting appointments" at this time. Major Sawyer announced a few days later that Colonel DePuy and Lieutenant Colonel Park had both resigned and that he would assume temporary command of the 8th. The news came as a surprise to no one, and a relief to most. The men of Company D were particularly proud of the rise of their former captain.

Many of the enlisted men had a minor celebration to mark the occasion. There was drinking—despite Major Sawyer's injunction against alcohol—and plenty of boasting about how everyone would now see what the 8th could do.

The officers abstained and offered no comment on the matter, but they didn't interfere with the reverie and the sniping about Sunday soldiers and worthless big bugs as long as it wasn't too vulgar or disrespectful to the army leadership—past and present.

Major Sawyer received a promotion to lieutenant colonel and Captain Winslow of Company A was promoted to major. Daniel had a moment of hope that their promotions might result in some vacancies in the ranks. But, there were no promotions in Company D. He resigned himself to being a private for a while longer.

Despite being part of the ninety-day regiment, Daniel had been passed over for promotion when the three-year regiment was mustered in. Others who had joined up after him came in as sergeants and corporals. He'd blamed Christopher and the fight with the German at the time, and had seethed for days with frustration and envy. Then, Captain Sawyer was promoted to major, resulting in a chain reaction of promotions through Company D. Again, Daniel was passed over.

Daniel started to think that maybe it wasn't Christopher and his antics that were the problem, but that there was something wrong with him.

Maybe he should be content with just being a private. His drive to rise in the ranks had been motivated by a vague promise from Susan's father. Not even a promise—more an implication. He had to be honest with himself, victories and promotions would not win Susan's hand. Either she loved him for who he was, or she didn't. And it seemed more and more likely that she didn't.

Her letters had become bland and matter-of-fact. She spoke of local events, reactions to the war, who was dating whom…But she had stopped expressing her feelings. She never talked of the dreams they had shared, never told Daniel how she felt about him. The closest she came to expressing a feeling was to sign the letter, "Most Affectionately Yours…"

Daniel thought of the emotion and effort he'd put into their relationship. But he had been gone less than a year, and she had already lost interest.

He wished Christopher were there to talk to. He dared not try to discuss what he was going through with anyone else.

Strangely, if not for Christopher's disappearance, he would probably be more upset about his waning relationship with Susan. Daniel didn't have the energy to worry about someone who clearly didn't care for him the way he did for her when so much of his emotional energy was focused on worrying about his brother. He would trade a chance for a generalship to get Christopher back.

But, Christopher was gone, and Daniel had nothing to trade that would change that. He'd failed at his most important duty—keeping his little brother safe. The rest seemed trivial.

November turned into December and care packages from home arrived more often as the holidays approached. Mail call, always a welcome diversion, became a major event.

But not for Daniel.

Before, he had always been one of the first to arrive, watching as the quartermaster sergeant sorted the envelopes. But now, instead of rushing to mail, he ambled along, not caring if he got there in time—or at all.

As he stood staring at the back of a man in front of him, Daniel was drawn out of his lethargy by the calling of Christopher's name. The crowd became quiet, and Daniel looked up at Quartermaster Sergeant McConnell, who looked back at Daniel, abashed. McConnell held the package out to Daniel.

"Here, son, you had better take this," he said, trying to hide his embarrassment.

After handing Daniel the package, McConnell looked down and saw another package with Daniel's name on it. He picked it up and held it out before Daniel could retreat into the crowd.

Daniel stepped back, eyeing the packages. They were both from their parents, probably full of the usual assortment of socks, undergarments, and assorted treats. Daniel thought of the letter he'd finally written and mailed to his parents informing them of Christopher's disappearance. It had clearly not gotten to them before they mailed these packages.

Daniel stood staring at the parcels, wondering what to do with Christopher's as McConnell completed mail call. He looked up and watched the quartermaster sergeant as he packed up to leave. There had been no letter from Susan.

Daniel returned to his tent, sat down by the cook fire, and opened his package. As he surmised, it contained two pairs of socks, undergarments, a package of jerked beef, some dried fruit, a package of cookies (all broken), a small apple pie, and several back copies of the *Norwalk Reflector*.

A letter sat on top of everything. Daniel read the letter, recognizing his mothers handwriting. It contained the usual news about the weather (cold), his father's health (he was slowing down, but too stubborn to accept he was now approaching fifty), the health of the rest of the family (little Rachel had a bad cough and they were all praying it didn't worsen), and the business (Jack Galloway was in negotiations with the War Department to supply the army with shoes).

Despite himself, Daniel smiled at that. Surely they would be better shoes than the ones now being issued.

There were also proclamations of eternal love and affection, and how much he was missed. The last thing his mother wrote was, "Please be careful and look after your brother."

Daniel crumpled up the piece of paper and threw it in the fire.

Christopher's package was the same, except without the newspapers, and the letter did not ask him to look after his brother.

Daniel shared his largess with his messmates, including Ezra. Though still angry with the younger man he partly blamed for his brother's disappearance, he had to accept that Christopher was his own man and hadn't been forced into going down to the suspension bridge looking for alcohol and trouble. Besides, Ezra was still a messmate and just as entitled to a share as anybody. Daniel either shared with Ezra, or convinced Parker and Charlie to join him in kicking Ezra out of their mess.

—⁂—

On the sixteenth of December, a new commander for the 8th arrived in camp. Colonel S.S. Carroll was a West Point man and a regular army officer before the war.

"Now you'll see some spit and polish, for sure," Charlie Locker said in his rich German accent.

"If by 'spit and polish', you mean drill and more drill," Parker Bonnett said with a wink.

"Arrgh!" Ezra, sitting by the fire, groaned. "Not more drill. Please."

"It'll go with your newfound sobriety," Parker said.

"That sobriety will go out the window just as soon as he finds a new source," Daniel said.

The next day Daniel went to mail call. Again no letter from Susan.

He'd received one letter from her since Christopher's capture. In it, she offered her condolences regarding Christopher's fate and said she was praying for his safe return. She'd also made all the usual small talk one would find in a letter from a friend or acquaintance.

In that letter, she wrote that she had to be careful, that sometimes her father read her letters before being mailed. But that hadn't seemed to be much of a concern last summer.

He looked up and saw Sergeant Elijah Rust staring at a tintype. From the oversized envelope he held in his other hand, Daniel surmised he'd just received the photograph. The man looked ecstatic. *At least someone has something to be happy about,* Daniel thought.

Daniel approached Rust and looked over his shoulder. The picture was of a pretty young woman seated with a boy of about three or four standing next to her, and a girl of about one or two sitting in her lap. Daniel assumed they were Rust's family. He smiled and put his hand on Rust's shoulder.

"That's a fine-looking family you have, Sergeant," he said.

Rust looked up with a start. "Why, thank you, Daniel. They mean everything to me."

"It must have been hard to leave them, with the little ones so young."

Rust nodded. "Especially little Julia, she had just turned one when I left," he said. He looked away, his voice dropping to a whisper. "I miss them terribly, though. I didn't think it would be so hard being away from them. Or I'd be gone so long."

Daniel nodded. "I know the feeling. Chris and I felt sure the war would be over by now."

"I pray your brother makes it back all right. Hopefully, he'll get lucky and be paroled."

The two talked for a time, sharing their concerns about the progress of the war and their families' well-being before parting ways and going back to their respective messes. For a few moments, Daniel had put Susan and Christopher in the back of his mind and relaxed.

—⁓—

As predicted, Colonel Carroll proved to be a strict disciplinarian. He extended the prohibition on alcohol to the whole regiment and made sure it was strictly enforced. Surprise inspections of the pickets became common, drill was once again part of their daily routine, and the regiment held a dress parade and inspection every Sunday morning.

Daniel received confirmation of Christopher's fate by letter. He'd returned from mail call with the customary letter from his parents, but as he started to read he abruptly stood and turned his back on the fire. He feared losing control in front of his messmates, but the flood of mixed emotions that came over him made it nearly impossible. He clenched his teeth to suppress a moan and squeezed the tears out of his eyes. Christopher was alive.

The Galloways had gotten a letter from Christopher letting them know he was alive and safe. He had been in Winchester, Virginia for a time, but was now in Richmond, being held in an old tobacco warehouse. He said conditions were miserable and getting worse as the prison population grew. After every battle or skirmish, more prisoners would arrive. Most of the prisoners he was currently housed with had been captured at the battle of Bull Run, outside Manassas, Virginia.

Daniel took a deep breath and turned around. Everyone was making a little too much effort to ignore him. "Christopher's alive," he said.

"Bully!" Ezra exclaimed and jumped to his feet. Everyone expressed their relief as Daniel told them where his brother was being held.

"Do you think they're feeding him well?" Charlie wondered.

Daniel shrugged. Christopher had described the conditions as miserable to his parents. After spending a few months campaigning both he and Christopher were more than familiar with miserable conditions, but they'd never tell their parents that. Conditions must be ungodly for Christopher to admit that much.

"It'll be Christmas soon," Parker said. "Maybe the ladies back home will send the prisoners some care packages. I've not seen any, but I hear that they do that sort of thing."

Daniel nodded, mumbled some excuses, and walked away. He didn't want to be around anyone. After the initial jolt of relief, the fear that

Christopher may be dead had been replaced by the fear he was locked up in a cold, dank warehouse, starving and freezing.

Christmas was a melancholy affair. It was the first time most of the soldiers had been away from home for any length of time. The holiday most were used to sharing with family and friends seemed the hardest on everyone.

Daniel thought of his family—decorating the house, buying or making presents, wrapping them, and then unwrapping them Christmas morning. Then he thought of Christopher, locked up in a cold, crowded warehouse without proper heat or food, and the happy images disappeared.

It was not a bad camp. They had warm tents, plenty of firewood, and a varied diet of fresh meat, vegetables, and soft bread all washed down with plenty of fresh-ground coffee. But the cold, snowy weather prevented campaigning, and complaints about the lack of progress toward ending the war were common whenever soldiers got together.

Christmas morning, the commissary baked hundreds of pies for the men. Most of them were burnt around the edges and doughy in the middle, but no one cared. They were something sweet and different from their normal diet. Jonathon, the wagon master for the 8th, worked hard to see as much mail delivered by Christmas as possible so the boys would get their packages from home.

Daniel had just finished a piece of cold apple pie and was washing it down with lukewarm coffee when a group of soldiers came by with a flyer for a jamboree that night. The sing-along would be held on the parade ground at dusk, and anyone not on duty at the time was encouraged to attend.

As the sun set, Daniel, along with Elijah Rust and his messmates (except for Ezra, who had picket duty), wandered over to the parade ground. Thousands of men already crowded the grounds. Someone attempted to distribute lyric sheets, but they quickly ran out. Daniel and his companions would have to sing from memory.

They started with patriotic and marching songs almost everyone knew well. Except for a new song, sung to the tune of "John Brown's Body," called "The Battle Hymn of the Republic." It was so new, no one knew the words from memory. But those with lyric sheets carried the verses, and everyone knew the chorus (which hadn't changed). After hearing the first verse, Daniel thought "Mine eyes have seen the glory of the coming of the Lord" much more appropriate for the occasion than "John Brown's body lies a moldering in the grave".

Then they moved on to carols. "Angels from the Realm of Glory," "The First Noel," "Good King Wenceslas," "God Rest Ye Merry Gentlemen," "Hark! The Herald Angle Sing"… Just about everyone knew them, and they were sung with gusto. But, they also reminded everyone of what they were missing. Daniel had to stop singing several times as the words caught in his throat. He looked around, and it seemed his companions' eyes all looked unusually bright in the light of the bonfires and torches.

Next they sang "Auld Lang Syne." Daniel remembered how his father would sing it, exaggerating the original Scottish pronunciations and swaying back and forth, his hands out in front of him has he pretended to hold the hem of a kilt. Daniel and Christopher used to laugh at his caricature until tears streamed down their cheeks.

Then, they sang "Home Sweet Home," and everything fell apart. They made it through the first verse, but the chorus fell to a whisper, then silence, punctuated by hundreds of throats being cleared. After that, the jamboree broke up, and everyone wandered back to their tents to spend the time with friends or alone with their thoughts.

—⁓—

The melancholy mood that settled over the camp didn't end until the first week in January, 1862, when they finally got the chance to do something about the bushwhackers still roaming the woods, taking potshots at pickets and supply wagons en route to and from Romney.

An expedition was mounted to attack the bushwhackers in their camp. It was a clear, bitter-cold night, and Daniel, along with the rest of the 8th (minus Company B, still stationed at the suspension bridge), had been ready to march since before noon.

As they waited, Daniel stamped his feet and watched his breath form misty clouds before his face. "A fire would be nice about now," he said. "My feet are numb."

"You know as soon as you got that fire lit, we'll get the command to move out," Sergeant Rust replied. "Hell, we've been waiting since this morning; the order has to come any time now."

Daniel barked a short, humorless laugh. "You been in the same army as me the last nine months?" he asked.

Rust nodded. "Yep. And I've done my share of waiting too. But this is ridiculous. We can't stand here all night."

At that, bugle calls to assemble blared throughout the camp.

"From your mouth, to General Kelley's ear, eh Elijah?" Daniel said with a smile.

"Exactly as we discussed over tea this morning," Rust grinned back.

Daniel looked over at the parade ground and saw Captain Daggett standing next to Lieutenant Lewis of Company C. Sergeants and officers of all the companies had already formed the framework to guide the enlisted men as they lined up in a brigade-size formation.

"I'd better get to my post," Rust said as he started off at a trot toward the assembly area. Without looking back he called out to Daniel, "See you in Blues Gap! We'll make the bastards pay for your brother!"

"The *fieslings*," Daniel shouted back.

Daniel lined up in his usual spot next to Parker. The two men stood in casual, bored stances, watching the regiment form into a battle line around them. Daniel continued to stamp his feet to get blood flowing to them.

Parker looked at the ground where he'd been stamping and said, "One good thing about marching at night—at least the mud will be hard."

Daniel looked at the snow piled up around the edge of camp and nodded. "And thank the Lord Almighty it's not snowing."

Ringgold's Cavalry, under Captain Keys, moved out first. Most of the boys of Company D knew them from around camp and their participation in both Romney campaigns and gave them a cheer as they rode by. The infantry loved to give the cavalry a hard time, but they appreciated the extended "eyes and ears" they provided the slow-moving columns.

An hour later the 8th moved out. They were the last regiment in line—

preceded by the 4th, 5th. and 7th Ohio. Behind them was an artillery battery and the unlucky company from the 7th acting as rear guard.

They reached Blue's Gap at dawn, tired but not as cold as when they started. Colonel Dunning, leader of the expedition, deployed the 4th and 5th in battle lines on either side of the road. Colonel Carroll asked for, and was granted, the opportunity to lead the 8th in the initial assault into the narrow canyon. The 7th remained with the artillery in reserve.

Hidden skirmishers shot at the 4th and 5th as they deployed into line. Daniel, along with almost everyone else, unconsciously hunched over and ducked his head down but, to his surprise and relief, he never heard the angry buzz of a passing minié ball.

Parker nudged Daniel and jutted his chin toward the front of the regiment. "Look there, that's a first for the 8th."

Daniel looked to the head of the column and saw Colonel Carroll take position at the front of his regiment. Daniel nodded in appreciation. "He's no DePuy, that's for sure."

Parker nodded. "I can finally write home with some pride in our commander."

Colonel Carroll gave the order to load and fix bayonets. It was echoed down the line by company commanders. Then, he unsheathed his sword and held it straight over his head.

"REGIMENT! At the double-quick—MARCH!"

Carroll brought his sword down, pointing it up the canyon, at the same time taking off at a run. His men gave a loud "HUZZAH!" and followed him into the enemy lair.

As they ran through the canyon, Daniel felt a charge of excitement. The way was uphill, but still his breathing came harder than the exertion warranted, and despite the cold, he was soon dripping with sweat.

Time slowed down, and Daniel watched the rocks and trees—possible hiding places—slowly pass by. Everything seemed in sharp contrast—even the trees in the distance were as clear as if they were right next to him.

Soon the canyon widened back out, and Daniel saw the flotsam of a retreating army scattered by the roadside—rifles, packs, articles of clothing, even two artillery pieces and some beef on the hoof—but no rebel soldiers.

Colonel Carroll called a halt, and the men stopped. Daniel leaned on his rifle, breathing hard. Then he remembered the weapon was loaded and quickly straightened.

Carroll deployed Company D in a skirmish line to search the immediate area and sent a runner back to report to Colonel Dunning.

Daniel crept through the area with Alex Melville (Ishmael) as his skirmish partner. Someone had been camping there for some time, but they had made their escape long before the Federals arrived.

Colonel Dunning and his staff arrived with the cavalry. Carroll brought Company D back, and the cavalry rode ahead to try to catch the rebel rear guard. For the first time, Daniel noticed several men in civilian clothing accompanied Colonel Dunning. As the officers milled about, these men dismounted and began writing in notebooks and drawing on sketch pads.

"Reporters," Ishmael said.

Daniel looked around at the empty camp and scattered debris. What could they be writing about? Nothing happened.

Parker spit on the ground. "That means within a week we'll find we've just experienced a glorious victory…or a devastating defeat."

The enemy camp was too small for the entire force, so the other regiments and the artillery battery remained at the mouth of the gap and the 8th broke ranks. Heavy pickets were posted around the perimeter while the bulk of the men settled down to cook breakfast and take a nap.

Midday, the cavalry troops returned reporting they could not overtake the enemy. The entire force formed up at the mouth of Blue's Gap and marched back to Romney—this time with the 8th in the lead.

Most of the men were in high spirits at the resounding and bloodless victory, but Daniel saw it all as a big waste of time. They'd spiked the cannon and burned everything else; the cavalry volunteered to drive the beef back to Romney for the commissary department to slaughter, and they'd found one dead rebel soldier. It didn't seem like much of a victory to Daniel.

Two days later, a General Lander arrived to replace General Kelley. Daniel, Parker, Charlie, and Ezra watched the new general ride into camp, followed by his staff. The man was tall, lean, and sported a perpetual scowl, as if the entire world existed just to irritate him.

"New bug, same shit," Parker said.

General Lander had only been in camp for a day when they found out he had brought with him orders to abandon Romney. Daniel remembered what Parker had said the day before and muttered under his breath, "Sounds like a whole new pile to me."

CHAPTER EIGHTEEN

THE CAPTURE
OF WINCHESTER

A s January inched toward February, Daniel's misery and disenchant-
ment increased. They had spent the last month going from cold wet
camp to cold wet camp, sometimes well ahead of their supply wagons, forc-
ing them to sleep on the semi-frozen ground with nothing but wool and
rubber-coated gum blankets for shelter.

To make matters worse, it had rained or snowed almost the whole time.

With the constant exposure, nothing had time to dry. Everything Daniel wore was soaked.

The snow soaked through his shoes, keeping his socks wet and cold
until his feet felt like stumps. He wore an overcoat and had made a cape
out of a gum blanket, but between sleeping on the ground and long sweaty
marches, his clothes stayed wet, clinging to his body in an icy caress.

And mud covered everything. Daniel's pant legs were stiff with the glue-
like sludge. As he marched, mud accumulated on his shoes until they felt
like lead weights, making each step an agonizing effort that left his legs
quaking with exhaustion by the time they stopped. He had a sheath for his
rifle, covered with the same rubbery coating as his gum blanket, but it still
took constant care to make sure his rifle remained clean and dry.

Even the food and coffee, besides being lukewarm, tasted gritty.

Other than being cold and gritty, the food was the only positive thing
about the current campaign. Thanks to the new general's foraging policy,

they kept the commissary well stocked with fresh chicken and pork, canned vegetables, even sometimes milk and sugar.

But the full meals did nothing to relieve the muscle cramps from constant shivering. Or the numbness, accented by sharp painful pin-pricks, that afflicted Daniel's toes and fingers—especially when he first rose in the morning or after a couple hours on picket duty. Or the misery when he warmed his hands and feet by the fire and the feeling came rushing back in flaming agony.

Many of the men had lost fingers or toes, or even parts of their noses or ears, to frostbite. Daniel became afraid to take off his shoes—fearful of what he would find.

On January fifteenth, the 8th joined the Second Brigade, along with the 4th and 5th Ohio and the 39th Illinois. Afterward, the brigade held a regulation review for the new commander, Colonel Dunning from the 5th.

The officers wore their dress jackets and coats, complete with gold braid and epaulets, but with the same muddy wet boots and pants. The men attempted to brush off the mud and shine their brass, but it did little to hide their miserable conditions. Constant coughing and sneezing filled the air throughout the review. Some men were so sick, they couldn't stand up straight without leaning on their rifles.

Despite their best efforts, mud still clung to everything. If you looked close enough, it was visible on every jacket, hat, and pair of pants in the entire brigade. Clean shoes were a lost cause, lasting no more than a couple steps outside the tent.

The officers praised the men with the cleanest uniforms as shining examples of soldierly discipline. The men thought no one pulling his weight could stay so clean and pegged those shining examples as shirkers.

And still more regiments kept arriving from all over the northern United States. The size of the army in West Virginia now surpassed any assembly Daniel had seen so far in Romney, Grafton, or even Camp Dennison. Three weeks after becoming part of the Second Brigade, the 8th and 4th were moved to an artillery brigade. Daniel didn't care what brigade they were in as long as they had the chance to fight.

But, their foe was always one step ahead of them. They continued to pursue the rebel forces, who continued to harass the pickets and supply wagons. But, the enemy always knew when they were coming and remained just out of reach.

The latest campaign was stalled on the bank of the Little Cacapon River, swollen and fast moving from all the rain and snow. They had come to this spot hoping to cross, but the bridge had been burned. General Lander sent scouts up and down river to find a ford, but they had returned hours later without success. Eight infantry regiments, along with a complement of cavalry and artillery and their accompanying supply wagons, were at a standstill for want of a bridge or passable ford.

Daniel could see the big bugs up ahead, gathered on the bank with orderlies holding their horses. General Lander appeared to be in a rage, pacing back and forth and waving his arms.

"That new general's an excitable cuss," Parker said.

Daniel nodded. "I can't say I blame him. Everywhere we've been, the rebels were just there. Now it looks like we aren't going anywhere anytime soon."

Both men knew if they didn't get across that river, General Lander would be in a rage for days. And a general's rage always found its way down to the private soldier.

Then, the wagon master, Jonathon, came striding up to the officers, hat in hand, with a confident yet respectful bearing. He spoke to General Lander for a few minutes. The officers huddled together and conferred. They talked with the wagon master. They conferred some more. Eventually, they reached a decision. General Lander nodded and shook Jonathon's hand.

Jonathon turned and walked back to his wagons. Given the length of the column on the road, Jonathon had to walk over a mile to get to his wagons, and nothing more happened for almost an hour. Then, the order to move to the side of the road rippled up the column.

Daniel stepped off the road into the snow and mud and watched the wagons rolling up to the river bank.

A rumble of animated conversation followed the wagons up the trail. As they passed, the column closed up behind them. Once at the riverbank, conversation came to an abrupt halt as the men watched Jonathon work.

The men at the head of the column unloaded the first wagon. While they did that, the wagoners behind Jonathon's wagon unhitched their mules and brought them forward to the lead wagon. Once Jonathan's wagon was empty, he had the men replace the supplies with rocks for ballast. He then took two long ropes and tied one end to his wagon and the other to the next wagon in line. They hitched as many mules as they could to the lead wagon, and Jonathon climbed up into the driver's seat.

Daniel and Parker looked at each other, mouths agape.

"Is he going to do what I think he's going to do?"

"I believe so."

Calls for bets rang out. It was even money on whether Jonathon made it to the other side. One man suggested a side bet on if he drowned, but angry threats from many in Company D shut him down.

Daniel could hear Jonathon's whip and his call to "git-up" all the way back at his spot in line. He held his breath as the mules stepped into the raging river, their heads bucking up and down, fighting the reins.

The first pair of mules stepped out into water too deep to stand, and then the river had them. The mules' heads jerked back and their eyes got so wide Daniel could see their whites from where he was standing. They swam with all their might as the river swept them downstream and out into the middle—pulling the other mules and wagon with them.

Once in the river, the mules swam toward the only safety they could see—the opposite bank. The wagon sped up as it rolled into the river, the front end diving until it appeared the wagon would be swamped before bobbing back up.

As soon as the rear wheels lost contact with the bank, the current turned the wagon to a forty-five degree angle and swept it into the middle of the river.

At the front, the mules continued to swim for their lives. On the near bank, two lines of men pulled with everything they had on the rope attached to the back of the wagon. The mules didn't seem to be making any headway, and the men pulling were being drug toward the river's edge. For a few minutes it appeared the whole she-bang—mules, wagon, and Jonathon, would be swept downstream.

The betting rose to a fever pitch. Never taking his eyes off the wagon, Daniel yelled for the surrounding men to shut up.

Then, the first pair of mules got a foothold on the opposite bank pulling themselves up and the rest followed. The whole column of men, winners and losers both, broke out cheering. The first pair of mules pulled the next pair up onto the bank, and so on until the wagon wheels hit ground. It wasn't until the wagon was on the other bank, water pouring out between the planks, that Daniel relaxed.

Jonathon stood up in the wagon, turned to the men on the other side of the river, removed his hat, and bowed. The men went wild. Daniel watched as General Lander slapped some unknown colonel on the back and waved his hat back at Jonathon.

Jonathon moved the wagon until it was well away from the water. He tied it to a tree and then unhitched the mules. Then he untied the two ropes hanging out the back of the wagon and across the river and tied them to the brace of mules. He then drove the mules up the road until they pulled the next wagon in line across.

When that wagon was behind the first wagon, its wagoner tied the two together. They repeated that process until there was a line of wagons tied together, spanning the width of the river. Engineers placed planks over the wagons, and they had a pontoon bridge.

The infantry marched across the river, their feet never touching the water. As each row of men passed Jonathon, they tipped their hats to the man and nodded.

The officers had their orderlies swim their horses across the river, and the cavalry followed suit. After a quick reconnaissance by the cavalry, they learned that the road soon dwindled down to a mountain path, so they had to leave the wagons and artillery behind as the column set out once more in search of the enemy.

They marched through the night up the mountain path, the column spread out for miles. General Lander rode on ahead with his staff, the cavalry, and Jonathon and several wagoners riding mules. The infantry was left behind to make their own time.

Sometime late in the morning, they reached the entrance to Bloomery

Gap—where they hoped this time to catch the enemy unaware. When Daniel trudged out of the trees, he could see something had already happened. Had they caught them this time?

Looking across the valley that led to the gap, Daniel saw several men being guarded by cavalry troopers—some in night clothes and some in Confederate uniforms. Next to them was a small pile of equipment. Farther up toward the gap was a small farmhouse, surrounded by several wagons, horses, and cattle.

Once again, General Lander was in a fury. This time the object of his wrath appeared to be Colonel Anisansel, the cavalry commander. Daniel watched the general yelling at the hapless colonel and gave thanks he didn't report directly to the temperamental commander.

That was the end of the 8th's involvement in the Bloomery Gap campaign. After a short nap and a quick meal of fried salt pork, hardtack, and coffee, they turned around and marched down the mountain path, across the Little Cacapon river, and back to camp.

Daniel found out later that General Lander himself had led the cavalry charge that captured the sleeping officers, and Jonathon and his wagoners had pilfered the enemy supply wagons until driven back by gunfire from the rear guard of the main rebel force.

While Daniel and the other infantrymen were slogging up the mountain path, the Confederates were escaping, and Colonel Anisansel had refused to pursue them without infantry support. That explained the general's wrath that morning. He'd had to stand by in frustration most of the morning, waiting for his infantry. By the time there was enough men in the valley to satisfy Colonel Anisansel, it was too late.

Just as well, Daniel thought. *Everyone was too exhausted to make it much farther anyway.*

—⁂—

General Jackson's headquarters were in Winchester. Jackson's fast-moving troops were the terror of the Shenandoah, and Lander's division received orders to take the town and deprive him of a base of operations.

On March first, the 8th took up position at the top of a ridge overlooking the road to Winchester in support of their brigade artillery. The ridge offered no protection from the wind, and they had come up with nothing but what they could carry on their backs. Daniel had his wool and gum blankets, and his great coat, but they offered little protection from the cold wind that never stopped.

The second morning on the ridge, it began to snow. It snowed all day. By dusk there was a white blanket, several inches thick, across the landscape.

As Daniel returned from picket duty, he saw that Ezra had somehow gotten a fire going and had a pot of coffee sitting on the coals. Daniel kicked most of the snow away from a spot by the fire and sat down on the frozen ground. "Damn the army, damn General Lander, damn this ridge, and damn you too, Ezra Rouse."

Ezra's eyebrows shot up. "Damn me! Why?"

"For good measure," Daniel shot back. "I'm so sick of this. I don't remember when I was warm last. I've been in the army a year and all I've done is freeze and march, march and freeze."

Ezra grinned. "You're forgetting last summer when we sweltered."

"Swelter, freeze—makes no difference. Misery is misery. And I'm sick of it!"

Ezra pointed to the coffee pot. "Have some slightly warm coffee and you'll feel better."

"We haven't even had a real battle yet," Daniel grumbled.

"How about the Battle of Blue's Gap?" Ezra responded, sneering the way they all did when mentioning that trumped-up nothing of a skirmish.

"I said a real battle. Not the shite the newspapers make up. Maybe if we can get a few real stand-up battles going, we can decide this thing once and for all."

"I'm not looking forward to no battles," Ezra said. "But just about anything would be better than this."

Daniel got out his tin cup and poured a cup of coffee. He brought the steaming, brown liquid to his lips and took a sip. It was lukewarm, but even so, it burned like fire on his frozen lips. That set off another stream of cussing.

As Daniel was cussing, Sergeant Rust walked up. He ignored Daniel's rant and poured himself a cup of coffee. He took a few sips, scrunched up his face, and poured the rest out. "Pack up, boys. We're heading back."

"What! We just got here!" Daniel shouted, forgetting for a moment how much he hated where "here" was. "What is it this time? Lander's boots not polished to his liking?"

"General Lander is dead," Rust replied and turned to go.

"Well, hold up just a minute," Daniel said, scrambling to his feet. "You can't just drop something like that on us and walk away. What happened? What about Winchester?"

Rust stopped, turned partway back to Ezra and Daniel. "What I heard, the fever got him. As to the Winchester campaign, no one knows. I guess we'll find out when we get back. Now, I gotta go."

Two days later, they had a ceremony giving Lander's remains a formal send-off before being shipped back to Washington City.

Then a new general named Kimball arrived and took temporary command of the division.

—ɯ—

A week passed, and spring was in full bloom when the 8th, along with the rest of the division, boarded trains south. The train ride took two days, as they had to stop and repair tracks every few miles. Then, at the end of the second day, a destroyed bridge at Battle Creek stopped the train for good. They spent the night next to the creek and set out on foot the next morning for Martinsburg.

When they reached the staging area for the assault on Winchester, the horses and baggage had already arrived. The men erected tents and settled down for a few days rest while they waited for the rest of the attacking force to join them. On March eleventh, a division led by General Banks arrived, and they headed out for Winchester.

They marched well into the night, then stopped and formed battle lines in the dark. Captain Daggett worked his way through the company, whispering for the men to keep quiet and rest on arms until dawn. Daniel couldn't see very far in the dark and had no idea where he was. He assumed the officers knew what they were doing, and the enemy was somewhere nearby.

The sight that Daniel awoke to the next morning left him speechless. They were in a valley, covered with thousands of men, lined up by regiment in battle lines. It was as if it had rained men in blue uniforms overnight. Daniel figured there had to be over ten thousand men. The sight of the battle lines reaching from one end of the valley to the other was impressive. *How could the rebels hope to win against all this?*

As the men rose, the officers and sergeants went to work straightening the lines. Daniel could see a defensive line of earthen breastworks with a wooden abatis erected in front. That, he was sure, was where they would attack.

Sergeant Rust was out front working with sergeants from other companies to make sure the 8th's line was straight.

"Hey, Sergeant Rust!" Daniel cried out. "I got to visit the sinks."

Rust looked at him. "There are no sinks, Galloway, and we're under orders to stay put. You'll just have to go where you are."

Daniel looked around. Several faces in the line looked back. "I don't think the boys behind me will appreciate walking through what I'll be leaving on the field."

"Well, Dan, unless you're going to shit out the River Nile, I'm sure they'll get over it."

Daniel settled on emptying his bladder. There was no way he was going to squat out here surrounded by all these people. Though, looking around, he could see others were doing just that.

Then, bugles blared, and the sound of thousands of men coming to attention was like rolling thunder. The first battle line stepped out onto the field and began their advance toward the defensive works.

Daniel saw a line of officers on horseback, watching the advance from a hill nearby. He was sure he saw Colonels Sawyer and Carroll among them.

The line advanced, and as it approached the enemy position, Daniel felt his stomach grow tighter and tighter. Any minute, he expected the earthworks to explode in fire and gun smoke.

The line reached the earthworks.

Then they passed the earthworks and kept marching. Daniel thought he heard a few solitary gunshots, but where were the volleys?

Men started talking, and Daniel realized how quiet it had gotten. It was as if the whole force were holding their breath.

But now they were confused. Where was the enemy? Where'd they go? Men speculated among themselves or called out questions to their officers. The morning sun inched along overhead, and the advancing battle line still did not return. Daniel looked up at the big bugs on the hill. They were leaning forward in their saddles, telescopes and binoculars to their eyes. They seemed as perplexed as the rest of them.

Then, the battle line reappeared from behind the earthworks, no longer as straight and disciplined as they were marching out.

Daniel shook his head. "They did it again."

The enemy was gone.

—⁂—

They marched into Winchester like a conquering army invading a foreign capital. Generals Banks and Kimball rode out front, with their staffs and color guard, followed by the cavalry, then each regiment, preceded by its own command staff and color guard, and last, the artillery and supply wagons. Daniel didn't feel much like a conqueror though. Just like at Romney, the rebels had retreated and left them to take the town without a fight.

As they marched past the courthouse, Daniel craned his neck to get a better view. He knew from the letter Christopher had written their parents that he had been held there for a spell. It just looked like a typical courthouse with big, white pillars in front. To Daniel, the townsfolk seemed curious, but not hostile to the new army taking over their town. He hoped that they had been kind to his brother.

As usual, the big bugs and their staffs occupied private homes, while the soldiers camped in the fields outside town. For the next two weeks, the 8th spent their time between picket duty and chasing Ashby's Cavalry. Ashby's constant harassment and ability to disappear made him almost as feared and hated as Jackson.

While in Winchester, a permanent replacement for General Lander named Shields arrived, and Kimball was given command of a new brigade that included the 8th Ohio.

CHAPTER NINETEEN
BATTLE OF KERNSTOWN

Daniel and his messmates had just finished their midday meal and were drinking coffee and smoking cigars when the sound of a massive artillery barrage thundered through the camp. Daniel jumped to his feet and looked south toward the sound.

"Sounds like the southern picket line is under attack," Sergeant Rust said.

"You mean the rebels have finally stopped running?" Daniel sneered. "That'll be a first."

Rust started to reply, but was interrupted by the long roll—the call to fall in under arms. The men dropped their cups, extinguished their cigars, and grabbed their traps.

Daniel was balancing his rifle in the crook of his left arm and finishing the last button on his jacket when Colonel Carroll rode up. He stood up in his stirrups and raised his voice to address the whole regiment. But, the companies on the end, which included Company D on the left flank, only heard fragments of his speech.

"Men! We are under attack! We will march out to the sound of the guns, relieve our comrades, and show the secesh what Ohio men can do!" He raised his sword over his head, and the men dutifully cheered.

They marched through Winchester along with the 67th Ohio, a battery, and General Shields himself accompanied by his staff and the 1st West Virginia Cavalry.

General Shields joined the battery as they moved into position to take on a Confederate battery firing from a distant hill. The 67th and the 8th deployed on either side of the pike leading out of Winchester and advanced toward Kernstown. Though the pike was macadamized and relatively dry, the fields on either side were covered with mud from a mix of spring rains and melting snow.

Daniel heard a shell burst, followed by a large explosion behind them. Then came one of the most horrific screams he'd ever heard. He looked over his shoulder, stumbled, and quickly looked away. Among the wreckage of a cannon, blood and guts and dismembered pieces of horse lay scattered around the hilltop where their battery had deployed.

The screaming continued and Daniel looked back again. General Shields's riderless horse pranced around, kicking its feet and bucking its head, blood spattered on its haunch. Near the horse lay the general's body, surrounded by his staff.

"Good Lord. They got the general," he said.

Parker's head whipped around to where Daniel was looking. "I wonder who'll take over?"

Daniel looked back and shrugged. "My money's on Kimball.

Parker nodded. "Good solid Indiana man. We'd be in good hands."

Carroll deployed Companies B, C, and D as skirmishers. As Daniel moved out ahead of the rest of the regiment, he and his partner, Ishmael, came under fire from rebel skirmishers protecting the Confederate battery.

The buzz of passing minié balls no longer bothered Daniel. He knew they were deadly—he'd seen firsthand their handiwork many times. But, being shot at had become a regular occurrence, and so far no one in Company D had been killed in battle.

Many had died of illness though. A fever or a bout of diarrhea scared Daniel more than bullets and artillery shells. This was, to him, just another day, another skirmish that would soon end in a quick retreat by the enemy.

As if to prove Daniel's assumption, the enemy battery limbered up their cannons and headed south. The cavalry and infantry supporting them soon followed.

"There they go again," Daniel said. "They saw the 8th approaching and skedaddled."

Ishmael chuckled. "Don't let it go to your head. They'll be back."

As they watched the enemy disappear down the road, a cavalry company rode past on the pike at full gallop, intent on catching the retreating rebels. Daniel watched as the passing horses splattered muddy water from puddles on several men by the side of the road. He let out a short laugh as the mud-spattered infantrymen cursed the cavalry and their "damn mules."

After returning to where the army had amassed south of Winchester, they learned General Shields was still alive, but badly injured. General Kimball had taken over command of the division.

That night, everyone slept under arms on what had been the picket line. Daniel spent most of the night staring at the sky, reliving the afternoon's events. Several men had been wounded but, again, no one had been killed in the skirmish. He wondered how long their luck would hold out.

The next morning, the Quartermaster Corps brought their tents from the camp north of town. They formed a new camp on the former picket line south of Winchester.

It was a clear, quiet morning, and cavalry scouts reported no signs of the enemy in the immediate vicinity. Colonel Carroll left to retrieve his family and bring them to Winchester, leaving Colonel Sawyer in command. The men kept busy laying out company streets, erecting tents, and digging trenches for defense and sinks for waste. To Daniel, Winchester was proving to be just another Romney. Somewhere for them to encamp for several months, drill, and hold dress parades.

Then, on the second day in their new camp, the enemy returned.

Daniel had just finished breakfast and was starting his second cup of coffee when the sound of incoming shells shattered the morning's peaceful quiet. Explosions sent shrapnel flying through the camp—tents were shredded, men ran in all directions, and horses neighed in fright. He sighed, threw out his coffee, and stood. This time, he didn't wait for the long roll to don his traps.

He was buttoning his jacket when Colonel Sawyer rode up, leading Companies B, E, and H. He had Captain Daggett gather his men and fall in.

As they marched out, they picked up Company C returning from picket. As Company C fell in behind D, Daniel heard two men talking about how they had seen rebel cavalry on the outskirts of Kernstown. Daniel wondered how since the picket line was nowhere near Kernstown, but he didn't bother to ask.

Instead, as Lieutenant Reid trotted down the edge of the column, Daniel called out to him, "Lieutenant, sir, where's the rest of the 8th?"

Reid raised his right hand and fluttered it toward the east. "Colonel Carroll has them over there somewhere."

"Carroll's back?"

Reid paused. "It seems General Kimball didn't agree with the consensus that the enemy was done with us. He called *Colonel* Carroll back yesterday, and he arrived first thing this morning."

Daniel noticed the emphasis Reid placed on the word "colonel." He quietly cursed himself for being too familiar with an officer. In his defense though, he'd known Reid longer as an enlisted man.

They marched once more down the pike toward Kernstown. They had not gone far when they spotted the enemy occupying a hill on the right that would be a perfect location for artillery. Colonel Sawyer shifted his troops into battle line across the field to the west of the pike, and they advanced at the double quick, bayonets fixed and at the ready. They shouted out huzzahs as a more civilized response to the rebel yell that had become so popular with the enemy.

Daniel used the excitement and fear of the charge to release all the frustration and rage that had been building inside him for the last several months. He ignored the mud as it splashed up into his face, the rocks and ruts that threatened to trip him. He ignored the minié balls that flew by so close he felt the breeze of their passing. His huzzahs turned to an angry roar.

The enemy did not try to hold the hill. They were too few. The the small battalion comprised of five companies of the 8th Ohio outnumbered them five to one. They fired a couple volleys and made a hasty retreat toward Kernstown.

At the crest of the hill, the 8th stopped, and the men began cheering and slapping each other on the back until the officers yelled for quiet.

"Save it, boys," Sawyer said. "You haven't done anything yet."

The men answered him with another cheer.

The height they found themselves on had a commanding view of the whole area, and even the least attentive private recognized its importance if the enemy should come this way. Soon, Sawyer's battalion was joined by several companies from the 5th and 66th Ohio and Daum's artillery. Daum spread his cannon across the hilltop, and the infantry occupied the slopes below. Then, General Kimball came up and established his command center on the hill behind Daum's batteries.

Daniel thought at first this would be another inconclusive skirmish. But, it was turning into a full-blown battle. An endless line of soldiers came down the pike. A steady stream of runners flowed to and from Kimball's command post. The roar of rifle and cannon fire came unceasing from the area around Kernstown east of the pike.

Colonel Carroll and the other 8th Ohio companies were over there somewhere. He wondered how they were faring.

From the top of Pritchard's Hill, Daniel saw the pike stretching out south with open fields of new spring grass spread out on either side. On the eastern side of the pike, battle lines of blue were forming across the valley for hundreds of yards.

It appeared Kimball was bringing up as much of Shields's division as possible. It was a temporary command for Kimball, and he was probably being cautious.

But, Daniel thought, this may be it. A chance to do something meaningful and lasting toward ending the war. Not another minor skirmish or frustrating pursuit of any enemy that always seemed to be just out of reach. This might turn into an honest-to-God, knockdown, drag-out fight—two armies facing each other on the field in open battle, and may the best army win.

Colonel Sawyer deployed Company D as skirmishers on the west side of the pike. He sent Company B to the east to join Colonel Carroll. The rest of his command spread out on the field west of the pike and started toward Kernstown.

Already uncomfortable with the small size of their force, Daniel watched the departure of Company B and muttered, "Why don't they tie one hand behind our backs while they're at it."

But a company from the 13th Indiana, returning from the picket line, fell in with them as a replacement for Company B, and Daniel's attitude was somewhat mollified. As Sawyer's battalion moved across the field, a rebel battery lobbed shells at them. The incoming fire flew over their heads and exploded behind them, sometimes peppering their backs with clods of dirt, but doing no damage.

Once they reached the outskirts of Kernstown, they were no longer in the battery's field of fire, and it found more promising targets. All around them, it became deathly quiet. The Confederate batteries to the east continued their duel with the Federal batteries behind them, and rifle fire would flare up here and there, but in Kernstown itself, there was nothing. No enemy soldiers, no civilians, not even a stray dog. The buildings were all closed up tight and shutters drawn.

They slowly made their way through town. Out front on the skirmish line with the rest of his company, Daniel's heart was pounding in his chest, and sweat ran down his forehead into his eyes.

As they passed each building, he expected to come face to face with an enemy battery or line of infantrymen ready to fire. What a way to die, he thought. One minute you're walking along and the next, you're gone. Just like that.

After what seemed like hours, they reached the other end of town and stopped on the front lawn of a church. From there, they had a view of the pike continuing south and the surrounding countryside. An occasional boom from the southeast told them there was a battery set up somewhere ahead. But, other than that, all was quiet.

The quiet of their immediate surroundings coupled with the increasing sounds of battle unfolding behind them made Daniel uncomfortable. They were too far forward and exposed. He hoped Sawyer knew what he was doing.

A partial Federal battery of two cannon rode up the pike and unlimbered across the road. Two companies from the 5th Ohio came up to support the artillery, and Daniel relaxed. Until Colonel Sawyer ordered them forward again.

Sawyer had his entire battalion deploy as skirmishers and head down the pike. The Confederate battery they'd heard firing from the southeast redirected its fire, and soon shells began exploding all around them.

The Federal battery fired back in response.

The enemy battery moved closer to the pike. They aimed their cannons and resumed their fire on the advancing skirmish line. There was no more than a company of infantry supporting them, so Daniel thought if they got close enough, they could take the cannon.

The Federal battery had to shift its fire, and soon shells were flying over the skirmishers from both directions. Colonel Sawyer called a halt. He turned his men around and returned them to the battery, where he deployed them on either side of the pike.

By now the sun had passed its zenith, and Daniel's stomach was rumbling. He knew Sergeant Howe would give him hell if he set down his rifle, so he balanced it in the crook of his arm while he rooted through his haversack.

"Rebs coming down the road," someone said.

Daniel looked up, expecting to see a few companies of Ashby's raiders. Instead, advancing down the pike was a sea of gray uniforms, spilling out on either side of the pike in lines that seemed to cover the earth. The many battle flags and other banners flying overhead said this was much more than just a few companies—or even a few regiments.

It was Stonewall Jackson's entire division.

A jolt of panic crawled down Daniel's spine, and thoughts of eating disappeared. The battery broke off its duel, limbered up, and rode north as fast as they could, their support infantry running behind. Sawyer had the battalion form up on the pike, and they headed up the road in a four-man column at the double quick.

There was no thought of deploying skirmishers or worrying what was behind the buildings they passed. Nothing they might face ahead could match what was behind them.

They left Kernstown to the rebels and returned to the hill with the federal command center. Prichard's hill, Daniel heard someone call it. There they were allowed to fall out and rest on the north side of the hill behind Daum's battery.

Soon, the volume of fire from Daum's cannon grew to a steady roar as the artillerymen ran to reload as fast as possible. From their spot on the north side of the hill, the men of the 8th couldn't see anything, but given the increased agitation of the artillerymen and the officers around Kimball's command, Daniel knew something was wrong.

Then, several artillerymen abandoned their guns and ran. The look in their eyes as they passed Daniel made him want to join them.

Daum strode through his battery, saber drawn, screaming threats that were swallowed up by the roar of his cannon. The remaining artillerymen worked their guns like madmen. No longer bothering to aim or check elevation, barely bothering to swab out the barrels between shots, they went through the motions of loading and firing like men who knew their actions would decide their fate.

The infantry command waiting behind the hill grew as a hodgepodge of companies from various regiments joined them. The company from the 13th had left to rejoin their regiment, but the men from the 8th lined up with the new companies, and together they marched to the top of Pritchard's Hill.

The quiet valley from that morning was now filled with men in gray. Several battle lines stretched out from one end of the valley to the other. It made Daniel think of the Federal force that had come together to take Winchester. He remembered how they filled the valley that day and he'd thought, *How could the rebels hope to win against all this?*

This was how.

Daniel wanted to run, to crawl behind the cannon limbers and hide, to freeze and not move until the danger passed. Instead, he marched down the southern slope and joined the battle line with everyone else.

The line before them was twice as long, and backed by several more lines behind it. Over the blast of cannon and the shrieking of flying shells, Daniel heard the rebel yell—a high-pitched wail from thousands of voices that wordlessly screamed, *We're coming to get you.*

Others were joining the line to the east of the pike, and shells shrieked overhead without pause, but was it enough? Daniel's hands were shaking, and his lips trembled. Was this what he wanted? What he'd been asking for the last year?

Bodies in gray lay scattered across the field. Those still upright marched on, undeterred.

As Daniel watched, the artillerymen lowered their guns and loaded with canister. He thought of the hundreds of lead pellets those guns were about to discharge and almost allowed himself a glimmer of hope. As the front lines of the advancing army entered canister range, Daum's guns fired. Huge sections of the advancing line disappeared as thousands of lead balls tore men to shreds.

The advancing line closed ranks and continued. Their bravery scared Daniel more than their numbers.

Since they were now in canister range, they were also in rifle range. The Federal infantry line fired a volley that almost matched the cannon with its roar.

Gun smoke swirled around Daniel, burning his nose and throat with its acrid stench and bathing the approaching enemy in an ethereal haze.

Then, the enemy got so close, Daniel could see the mix of fear and determination in their eyes. Some stood upright, shoulders back, heads high, their faces full of righteous indignation. Others scrunched over, heads down and shoulders rounded, their faces crumpled in anguish. But none faltered. Suddenly, they were more than just a line of infantry; they were individuals with homes and families, hopes and dreams, risking it all to take this hill.

But, after several more rounds of canister and rifle volleys, it became too much for even the most determined. The Confederate lines fell apart as each man reached his breaking point and stopped. They didn't all run at once. Many just stood there as if trying to make up their minds. Then, Daniel watched as fear won out over determination, and they turned and ran.

As the enemy retreated, Daniel stared out onto the field. Nothing in all the skirmishes he'd been a part of over the last year had prepared him for what lay before him.

Some bodies lay contorted in shapes he wouldn't have thought possible, frozen in a spasm of agony. Others, though still recognizable as human, had been torn apart, missing limbs or heads, or ripped into pieces. The worst were the victims of canister, reduced to red smears on a ground covered with unidentifiable pieces of flesh. Most though, just seemed to be sleeping.

But, what bothered Daniel more than that horror was the wounded. Hundreds of men lay writhing and screaming, some calling out for mothers, spouses, or children. Left by their comrades, surrounded by their enemy—consigned to a long, painful ordeal with little hope for relief.

Daniel looked around, but no one seemed to care. The artillerymen were lobbing shells at the retreating rebels. The men on the line went about reloading or drinking from their canteens, grim and silent, or jabbering in a fast, unintelligible voice that their comrades ignored. But none seemed to give the men on the field a second glance.

Daniel caught Parker's eye and nodded his head toward the field. Parker shrugged and spit gunpowder off his lips.

"Battalion! Attention!" Sawyer's voice cut through the continuing sounds of battle.

Daniel's eyes swept the field one last time as he straightened and brought his heels together. He said a silent prayer for the men he'd been trying to kill just moments before.

They returned to the area behind the hill, and for the next two hours, the companies of the 8th and several companies of the 67th Ohio took turns standing guard over the battery and Kimball's command station while the others fell out and tried to rest.

Daniel spent that time wondering why he had ever joined the army. There was no glory or honor in war. What beauty there was—in the colorful banners, the gleaming steel, and the precision of hundreds of marching men—masked the horror and destruction wrought by those men and that steel.

He didn't feel like eating, but breakfast seemed so long ago, and there didn't appear to be any letting up of the battle, still raging to the east on the other side of the pike. Daniel pulled out a piece of hardtack and chewed without enthusiasm. His canteen was almost empty, and he figured the hard, dry bread would just make him thirsty, but it was all he had.

Daniel turned his body to the west, away from the fighting, and noticed a ridgeline to the right that seemed to dominate Pritchard's Hill. It appeared empty, but if occupied by the enemy, it would take away the advantage of high ground they now enjoyed. Why no one had thought to send anyone up there seemed unfathomable to him, but he shrugged and assumed the big bugs knew what they were doing.

He no sooner finished that thought than the ridgeline exploded in flame and smoke, followed by a shower of artillery shells and solid shot on Prichard's Hill and the men behind it. Shrapnel ripped through the air. Cannonballs skipped off the ground, leaving deep ruts and missing men by inches. Everyone threw themselves on their bellies and tried to make themselves as flat as possible. And prayed.

"Where's that coming from?" Sergeant Rust cried.

Daniel looked back up and saw gray smoke wafting across the ridge. As the wind blew the smoke away, he glimpsed cannons before another volley covered the ridge top with smoke again. Pointing, he said, "From up there."

"Well, why didn't that dang fool Kimball take that ridge when he had the chance?" Rust asked.

"I guess someone will have to take it now," Daniel replied.

Daniel buried his face in the spring grass and watched the muddy earth beneath him quake at each hit from a cannonball. Clods of dirt peppered his back as shells exploded around him. Then First Sergeant Howe called out, "UP! UP! Line up!" Sergeants from the other companies joined in the call.

A jagged chunk of iron buried itself in the earth by Daniel's head.

He looked up at Howe and shook his head. "Are you crazy?"

Howe kicked him in the leg. "The sooner you get your sorry ass up, the sooner we'll get out of here."

At that, Daniel scrambled to his feet and ran to where Sawyer's battalion was assembling.

As Daniel took his place in line, Parker caught his eye and gave him a knowing look. "We're going up the ridge, I just know it."

Daniel looked up and saw that a large force of Confederate infantry had joined the batteries. As he watched, more infantry appeared, and he felt the blood drain from his face. "Lord, I hope not."

Instead, they marched to a battery set up northwest of Pritchard's Hill and at the base of the ridge now occupied by the enemy.

Relief washed over Daniel when he realized they would not be attacking up the hill. Muscles he didn't realize were clenched relaxed. Then guilt, like a punch to the gut, hit him. Someone would have to take that ridge.

Several cannons on Pritchard's Hill, along with the battery Sawyer's men guarded, returned fire on the Confederate cannon on the ridge. But the elevation was too high, and most of the return fire plowed into the ground yards before the enemy position.

Daniel watched the enemy amassing behind a stone wall that bisected the top of the ridge. He thought again of the field full of dead and dying before Pritchard's Hill and said a prayer for whoever would have to march into that.

Speculation over who would assault the hill grew. Someone suggested taking up a pool and placing bets, but they didn't have time.

On the other side of the rock wall the enemy was amassing behind was a wood lot. As Daniel and the others watched, several short ragged lines of men in blue, accompanied by the stars and stripes, walked out of the trees and straightened their line before the wall. A massive volley of rifle fire shattered their ranks, but more Federal soldiers appeared behind them.

"Who is it? Who is it?" everyone was crying out. "Can someone see the regimental colors?"

As a gust of wind cleared the smoke, they saw the regimental flags.

"It's the 7th!"

"Them's the boys we replaced at this here battery."

"Not just them. It's Tyler's whole division!"

Daniel crossed himself.

"God bless and keep those boys," Rust whispered.

For an hour, they watched Tyler's division slug it out with the Confederates behind the wall, with the 7th Ohio and the 7th Indiana in the front taking the brunt of the punishment. Men continued to drop. Even from the base of the hill, Daniel could see the bodies piling up. Several times the flags dropped, only to come back up again. Daniel's eyes filled with tears, and he repeated a prayer over and over for the dead and dying on both sides—but mostly for their side.

The rebel battery that had been firing on Pritchard's Hill turned to face the attack. Just as they'd done to the rebels earlier, canister shot obliterated dozens of Federal soldiers with each volley. More Confederate infantry arrived and re-enforced the rebel line. Tyler's men had to break soon.

It was near dusk when Sawyer ordered the men to load and fix bayonets. Everyone exchanged glances. They knew what was coming.

They were only four companies, and undersized companies at that. With the casualties they'd already taken that day and so many sick, they didn't even make two hundred men. But it didn't matter. For an hour they had stood by and watched their brothers on the hill being killed and mangled and did nothing. Now was their chance. They would no longer have to stand by while others died.

Daniel gasped as fear and anger engulfed him. His limbs got weak and his stomach jumbled in knots. He tried to draw air into lungs that would not cooperate. His breathing was fast and shallow. His head swam and his fingers shook as he loaded his rifle. Unable to concentrate, he went through the motions by rote, relying on his training to carry him through.

As they stepped out, the men cheered. They cheered for Colonel Sawyer, who walked before them. They cheered for the sovereign state of Ohio. They cheered for the boys dying on the ridge. They cheered to drive away the fear that threatened to consume them.

Daniel stumbled on the uneven ground, his vision a pinprick before him. He blinked and shook his head. Was he going blind?

A cannonball shrieked over their heads and plowed into a cannon behind them. Injured men and horses screamed in fear and agony. Daniel felt warm liquid run down his leg. He looked down to see if he'd been hit. To his shame, he saw that it wasn't blood that ran down his leg. He looked around to see if anyone had noticed he'd peed himself like a little schoolboy and stumbled again, almost falling forward. The man behind him grabbed his belt and pulled him back.

As the 8th advanced across the open field, they began to take cannon and rifle fire from the ridge. But the 8th was in a swale, and the shots flew overhead to explode behind them.

As they watched the shells sail over their heads, the men cheered again. As they neared the crest they shifted into quick step, and the cheering turned into an angry roar.

Just before they reached the top, they entered a dense woodlot. Daniel thought they would still be safe from the artillery fire until they came out the other side. But the exploding shells and passing balls shattered trees and sent down large splinters and branches onto the men's heads. Men cried out in surprise and pain, cursing the falling debris. One man was knocked out cold when a large limb hit him square on top of his head.

They exited the other side of the woods on top of the ridge and came to a rail fence. Sawyer ordered a halt, but Company C, on the left flank, went around the fence and continued on.

Daniel stared at the advancing company in confusion. He'd clearly heard Sawyer order a halt, but Company C continued on another two hundred yards and stopped on a raised knoll, halfway between Sawyer's battalion and the enemy. From there they opened fire.

Daniel looked over at Colonel Sawyer and saw the frustration on his face. Not only was the errant company endangering themselves, they were blocking the line of fire for the rest of them. The rest of the battalion took advantage of the respite to knock down the rail fence. They were ready to join their brothers on the knoll.

There were no more than fifty men in Company C. In a matter of minutes, a dozen had fallen. Then, a skirmish line appeared on their left and tried to flank them. If they stayed any longer, they would be wiped out.

"Come back, dammit, come back," someone yelled.

Company C did. Those who could turned and ran back to the rail fence and fell in behind the rest of the battalion, shaken and out of breath.

Now they could fire on the enemy. The 8th had come up at a right angle to the rebel line engaged with Tyler's division. If they could get past the battery and battle line they now faced, they would enfilade that line and give Tyler's men a fighting chance.

The two facing battle lines fired at each other as fast as they could reload. Men dropped at a fearful rate. Others staggered and clutched wounds as blood seeped between their fingers. Instead of the passing buzz of an occasional minié ball, a constant hum filled the air.

But the men before them were falling just as fast. As Daniel loaded and fired, the fear left him. He stopped worrying about the dead and dying. All he thought about was living—and winning. They were just numbers now: *two hundred of us, two hundred of them, whoever is still standing at the end wins.* Daniel was determined to still be standing.

Colonel Sawyer screamed, "Company D! Refuse the line!" Company D was on the left flank. Daniel looked to his left and saw the skirmishers who had tried flanking Company C were now flanking the entire battalion.

There was no time for proper commands, everyone knew what they needed to do. First Sergeant Howe screamed, "Guides! POST!" Sergeant Rust, on the far left end of the line, raised his rifle so all could see. "MARCH!" Rust walked backward, and the men next to him followed. On the other end of the company line, Sergeant Howe held his place and pivoted to the left. The men in between stepped back at different lengths of stride depending on where they were in the line, so the whole company rotated like a closing door, changing their facing to meet the new threat.

As they moved, the whole company was looking at Rust for guidance. Daniel was only a couple positions down the line, and he saw Rust's eyes, staring toward the other end, wide and glassy. Then Rust's chest blossomed in a fountain of blood just below the base of his throat. He staggered but managed two more steps before falling.

The line buckled as shock overwhelmed training. Men stumbled or sped up, and the line bowed and waved. Daniel's knees shook, and inside he cried out in anguish, but he kept going.

"Hold the line! Hold!" Captain Daggett and the two lieutenants were walking behind their men, sabers drawn and arms spread wide, trying to keep the line straight.

Sergeant Howe screamed, "Guide! I need a guide on that end!"

Parker left his position and moved to the end of the line, taking Rust's place and raising his rifle for all to see. Daniel's eyes were at first on Parker, but then they drifted to where Rust had fallen. He wanted to go to his friend, but the company had reached its new position just as the enemy skirmishers broke into a charge. Daniel took a half step back and raised his bayonet to meet the onslaught.

A few men got a shot off before the enemy fell upon them. At such close range, no one missed. Daniel fired point-blank into the face of a rebel soldier. The man fell behind a cloud of gun smoke, and Daniel was reaching for another cartridge when another rebel soldier appeared out of the cloud before him.

The man was holding his rifle by the barrel, swinging it like a club. Daniel brought his own rifle up to block the blow. Their rifles met with the crack of wood, and the shock numbed his hands. Their rifles still crossed, Daniel tried to push the man back, but he deflected the shove and drove his shoulder into Daniel's chest. He fell on his back, and the air rushed out of his lungs. Then the rebel fell on top of him.

All around Daniel, feet were shuffling back and forth like a macabre dance. Someone screamed, and blood spattered his face.

The rebel soldier hit Daniel several times with his fist, then took his rifle and tried to push it down onto his throat. Daniel was able at the last second to get a hand up between the rifle and his neck, and they stayed like that, as if frozen, the rebel pushing down and Daniel pushing up, until a swinging rifle butt caved in the rebel's skull.

Daniel pushed the twitching and moaning man off him and struggled to his feet, gasping for air. All around him was a picture out of Dante's *Inferno*. Men were shooting, stabbing, and clubbing each other in a frenzied orgy of violence. The smell of blood and gunpowder mixed with the smell of shit and burnt wool and flesh. For a second, he thought of running. Then he thought of Sergeant Rust, and all the men from Company C, and the 7th Ohio, and the rest of Tyler's division, and all those who would never see a sunrise. And he thought of those still alive around him, depending on him.

He reloaded his rifle, shot a rebel soldier from so close the man's blouse caught fire, turned the rifle over, and began swinging.

Company C came up to support Company D, and the enemy fell back, but not far. Everyone returned to shooting, now only a few yards from one another. Daniel felt his jacket tear more than once from a passing minié ball. A bullet struck his cartridge box and spun him around. He reached into the now bent and torn box and pulled out his last round.

The 8th faced a larger force on two sides. They had fought them off hand to hand, and now their ammunition was gone.

It was time to surrender, run, or die.

Daniel considered another option—charge. Take the bayonet to them. Show them Ohioans don't give up.

Then, a line of blue-clad soldiers came out of the woods on their left and fired a volley into the rebel skirmishers. Those still standing turned and ran. The newcomers followed them all the way to the rock wall. As the enemy before them fled, Daniel looked up and saw the regimental flag of the 67th Ohio pass them by. The 8th remained on the edge of the woods with no one to fight and no ammunition left to fight with.

Daniel stood shaking, his knees wobbling and tears streaming down his cheeks as the adrenaline coursing through his body suddenly had no outlet. His fists clenched around his fractured rifle. He thought of howling, of rending his clothes and screaming for revenge. Then he thought of Rust.

Daniel stumbled to the area where he thought the sergeant had fallen. There were dead and wounded all around him. The wounded men clutched at his pant legs as he passed, begging for help, but he ignored them. He was only thinking of one body; nothing else mattered.

Daniel realized that his friend had not died right away. Rust's jacket was torn open, the buttons scattered around him. In his bloody hands he held a tintype of his family—the one he'd shown Daniel at mail call that day before Christmas.

Daniel dropped to his knees and wept over the body of his friend, Elijah Rust, as the sun set on the battle of Kernstown.

CHAPTER TWENTY
CHRISTOPHER RETURNS

Christopher lay on the bundle of straw he called a bed, covered with a threadbare, hole-filled blanket, and felt the fever-induced shakes rack his body. He took a deep breath and tried to will his muscles to relax. For a few seconds, it seemed as though it might work, then his muscles seized up and the shakes started again. At least it was morning; that meant there would soon be a little warm April sun coming through the few windows set high up in the walls. Maybe if it warmed, he could get some rest.

He couldn't remember the last time he'd slept through the night. The winter nights in the drafty warehouse were so bone-chillingly cold, even the slop buckets would freeze. Christopher considered it a miracle he'd made it through the winter without getting sick. Then, two weeks ago, he'd woken from a nap with a sore throat and a cough that worsened throughout the day until he almost couldn't swallow.

When he'd first arrived in Richmond, the population of Libby Prison was small, thanks to an aggressive prisoner exchange policy enacted by two governments ill-equipped to handle the number of prisoners that grew with each battle or skirmish. Now, several hundred men were housed in an old warehouse on the docks of the James River, living off a watery gruel of rice and meat (or so they said—Christopher had never actually found a piece of meat in any of his meals) and a little soft bread.

Though the rations were meager, as Christopher's illness worsened, even that was hard to get down. His ragged clothing hung loose and billowed around him when he walked. Beneath them, his ribs and hip bones protruded. He'd always been on the small side—short and rail thin, but now he was sure he weighed well below a hundred pounds. Even his shoes were loose.

As Christopher tried to will himself to stop shaking, Cole arrived with their day's rations. Stephen Cole had been with him since Winchester and now took care of him while he was sick. Though he was from West Virginia, Christopher considered him as good a pard as anyone in the 8th—with the possible exception of his brother.

Cole looked around first to make sure no one was lingering too close, then set the bowls down and helped Christopher sit up. He picked up a bowl and tried to spoon some gruel into Christopher's mouth. Christopher shook his head. "You eat first," he croaked.

"I'll get mine, don't you worry," Cole responded. "But, first, I want to get some of this in you while it's still at least a little warm. Trust me. It'll make you better."

Christopher lifted a hand a few inches and fluttered it in dismissal, but he took the gruel without further argument. He managed to eat all the gruel, but not the bread. Afterward, he decided Cole was right. He felt better.

As Cole ate, he filled Christopher in on the latest rumors. "The guard said they are working on another exchange. Maybe we'll get out of here."

His eyes closed, Christopher responded, "I've heard that before. Somehow we keep getting overlooked—like the homely lass at the ball." He managed a small smile. When was the last time he'd laughed?

"Well, this homely lass is gearing up for a jig any day now," Cole responded.

"What's this about a homely lass?" A third voice broke in. "I hope you handsome young fellows are treating her right."

The two looked up as Major John Smith approached. Major Smith was a former pastor, the chaplain for a Pennsylvania regiment, and preferred to go by his civilian title.

"Father Smith," Christopher said, trying for another smile.

Pastor Smith kneeled down next to Christopher and put his hand on his forehead. "How many times do I have to tell you, Christopher. I'm not Catholic, so I'm not a Father. In fact, I have a wife and two darling daughters waiting for me back home. So, Pastor Smith will do."

"I still say we should be calling you Major Smith and saluting," Cole said.

Smith shook his head. "None of that here. Here we're all the same—prisoners in a war that grows more horrible with each passing day."

Cole leaned forward expectantly. Even Christopher sat up a little straighter at the hint of war news.

Smith frowned. "There was a battle down in Tennessee. Someplace called Pittsburg Landing. It lasted two days and they're reporting as many as ten thousand killed or wounded on our side and just as many on the other."

The boys didn't respond for a moment. They both looked at the older man with mouths agape. Christopher forgot for a moment about his pain as he tried to come to terms with those numbers. "My God," he whispered. "That's twenty regiments between the two—gone just like that."

Smith hung his head and shook it slowly—somehow expressing both anger and sorrow at the same time.

First looking over his shoulder, the pastor whispered, "Slavery is an abomination, and this war is our punishment."

The boys nodded.

"If I get my hands on a *Harper's Weekly*, I'll share it with you—that is, if you're still here." His voice took a more cheerful tone.

Cole scrambled up onto his knees. "Have you heard something? Are we going home?"

Smith smiled and nodded. "That you are. I've got official word you're both to be exchanged next week. They keep taking prisoners, and the Confederate government cannot afford to feed them all. So, they hope to clear out this facility and make room for the next big battle. I'm sure McClellan has something up his sleeve."

"That's right," Christopher said. "You can count on Little Mac."

"Anyway, brace yourselves, boys. They'll be coming to fetch you next Monday. So, be ready to go."

"I'll check my social calendar and make sure there are no conflicts," Christopher said.

Smith laughed. "I'm glad to see you still have your humor, Christopher. Here." Once again, Smith looked around before reaching into an inside pocket on his jacket and pulling out a small, shriveled-up lemon. He retrieved a small pen knife from another pocket and cut off the end.

"Here, Christopher. I want you to suck on this. It'll help make you better."

Christopher looked at the lemon and his mouth watered, but he shook his head. "Let Cole have some first."

Cole shook his head while never taking his eyes off the lemon. "No. You need it, Chris. I want to see you're still alive come Monday."

Smith squeezed Christopher's shoulder and handed the lemon to Cole. "Here, Stephen. Take a couple sips and make sure your pard drinks the rest." He smiled at the two. "You're good boys."

Both young men hung their heads. An image of Spaulding's dead, swollen face filled Christopher's thoughts.

"No, we're not, Fath—Pastor. But thank you for thinking of us anyway," Christopher said.

After squeezing a couple drops of lemon juice into his mouth, Cole held the lemon to Christopher's lips and squeezed. "Where do you get this stuff, Pastor Smith?" he asked.

Smith smiled and shook his head. "I can't reveal my sources." He put a hand on Christopher's forehead and brushed the greasy, matted hair out of his eyes. Pastor Smith lowered his head and prayed, "Lord, I ask that you keep these young men safe from harm. Keep them alive and well in these horrid conditions until they are free once more, Lord. And please bring this accursed war to a righteous conclusion, ending slavery and reuniting this country. In Jesus's name we pray. Amen."

"Amen," the boys echoed.

Smith put a hand on Cole's shoulder and gave it a squeeze as he rose to his feet. Then, his hand dug into Cole's shoulder as he started to sway.

Cole took Smith's arm and helped steady the older man. "Are you all right, Pastor?" he asked.

Smith nodded. "Stood up too fast. It's nothing. Thank you for your concern. Now, I have other patients to see. You boys be careful and look out for one another. I'll stop by again tomorrow."

"Thank you, Pastor Smith," they responded in unison.

Cole watched the back of the pastor as he made his way through the crowd, offering blessings and encouragement. "That man is a godsend."

Christopher nodded. He sucked on the lemon, ignoring the tingling in his jaw from the bitterness and thinking of its health benefits.

The list of those prisoners scheduled for exchange was posted later that day. As Pastor Smith had said, both Christopher and Cole's names were on it.

After laughing with joy and hugging Christopher, Cole looked closer at the list and frowned. "That's odd…"

"What?" Christopher asked. "Are there conditions?"

Cole shook his head. "No, nothing like that. It's just… just that, the list is almost all officers. There's only a few enlisted, and they're sergeants. We're the only privates on the list."

"Could be because I'm sick, and since you're my pard, you get to come with me," Christopher said.

"Maybe," Cole responded. "But, I've never known our jailers to be too concerned with our welfare. To them our deaths would mean fewer Federal soldiers they have to face on the field."

"Well, I don't care how or why," Christopher said. "I just know we're going home—or at least back to our regiments."

Cole nodded. "Hallelujah."

—⁂—

It was Monday. Christopher knew that because the guards had gotten Cole and him that morning and had them march out of the warehouse and line up behind the officers waiting on the dock. In the water sat a transport ship building up steam. Christopher assumed that would take them to a Union ship somewhere equally loaded with Confederate prisoners.

Christopher walked on his own most of the way, with only a little help crossing the gangplank onto the ship. He found a place on the deck and half sat, half collapsed there. The entire time he had a big grin on his face. He didn't think he could stop smiling even if he tried.

Pastor Smith had been there to see them off with a prayer for safe travel. He gave a letter for his family to another officer to pass along and wished every person who passed Godspeed and best wishes. When Christopher and Cole passed him, they stopped to thank him for his generosity and caring.

"Pastor, your congregation must be proud to have such a fine man guiding them," Cole said. "If I'm ever up in Philadelphia, I'll be sure and look up your church and tell them all what you did here. There's many a man here alive thanks to you, Chris included."

Christopher nodded, but he could not find the words to express how he felt. No one outside his family had ever treated him with the kindness and compassion this man, a stranger, had shown. He pumped Smith's hand and nodded as tears filled his eyes.

Smith brought him into a hug and said a quiet prayer. He stepped back and said, "You get on that boat and go. And tell your brother God loves him, and that I will be praying for your safety in the days ahead until this war is over and you can both go home."

Christopher nodded and moved on, his head high despite the pain that coursed down his back. This simple act was well beyond anything he'd been able to do for the last two weeks.

Once the line of prisoners being released had passed, the sergeant of the guard walked up and stood beside Pastor Smith.

"Smith, you're a fool. You know that?" he said.

Smith raised an eyebrow and looked at the guard askance. "Why, whatever do you mean, Sergeant Conner?"

"I know what you did, so don't play coy with me. I don't know how you did it, but you traded your spot for those two pups. That's you should be leaving today."

Smith shook his head. "I'm needed here. Besides, you know as well as I, if that Galloway boy hadn't gotten out of here, he'd have been dead before the month was out."

"Maybe so," Conner replied. "But it's your own hide I'm thinking of now. It's not right, a man of the cloth living in this pigsty."

"The founders of the church, and Christ himself, endured worse. I'll be fine."

Conner reached into his haversack and pulled out a loaf of bread. "Here, you need to put some meat on your bones."

Smith took the bread. It was soft and yielding in his grasp, still warm from the oven. When the smell reached his nose, his eyes watered and his mouth salivated. "Thank you, Sergeant Conner. I'll be sure and include you in my prayers."

"Don't worry about me, Pastor. Just pray for another exchange soon."

Smith put the loaf of bread in the inside pocket of his jacket. He marveled that there was room. His jacket—no, all his clothes—hung on him like those on a scarecrow that had lost its stuffing. *There's many still here that need this worse than I*, he thought. He looked at his skeletal hand as he pocketed the bread. *Maybe just one little piece.*

Smith nodded to Sergeant Conner and retreated into the dark warehouse that smelled of unwashed bodies and human waste—of death and pain. He stopped at the door, overcome by a coughing fit that bent him over. The coughs seemed to be coming from deep within his chest now. When it passed, he stood and continued on his way, the loaf of bread warming his side.

—⁂—

A month later, Christopher stepped off another transport ship in Bell Plains, Virginia, where he caught a ride with a supply wagon to the town of Falmouth, Virginia. This is where they told him he could find the 8th Ohio. If they were in this part of the state, the boys had made progress while he was gone.

In the last month, he'd seen the massive batteries protecting Washington City and army camps spread out to the horizon and beyond. He'd seen great generals riding through those camps accompanied by their staffs—including McClellan himself. Looking at the large groups riding by on their sleek and shiny horses, he thought you could make a whole company just out of a couple generals' staffs. By contrast, the southern army was stretched thin, a hodgepodge of uniforms and equipment. And desperate. They couldn't even feed their prisoners enough.

While in the hospital in Alexandria, Christopher had put on weight, though he still had a long way to go before he would be back to the size he was when he was captured. His cheeks were still hollow, and his bones still stuck out like a walking cadaver.

Christopher looked down at his new uniform. He liked the old one better—particularly the waist-length jacket, with its row of brass buttons and snug fit. To Christopher's eyes, it looked more soldierly.

He had to admit though, the shapeless new sack coat with no waist and only four buttons would be easier to get into during the long roll, and it was more comfortable. Unlike the old dark blue pants though, the new sky-blue showed every speck of mud and dirt and would look terrible during a grand review—no matter how much you brushed them.

What he missed the most was his father's shoes. The new brogans he wore had already started to fray at the seams, and he felt every pebble he stepped on through the thin, poorly cured soles. Worse though was the fit—there wasn't even a right or left shoe, just two square toed monstrosities that made his pinkie toes hurt. His next letter home, he would have to ask Da to send him another pair.

He thought of the correspondence he'd received from home and from Daniel while he was recovering in the hospital. The hospital had been like a prison of another kind—a converted hotel with a half dozen men per room. The fancy wallpaper and ornate woodwork didn't make up for the stench, poor food, and constant moans and cries that made sleep almost impossible. Bed-ridden most of his time there, the letters from family were his only escape.

His father's letters were just as he expected they would be—cold and perfunctory. There was the business—he'd gotten a contract with the government and was expanding. (That, his father explained, was why he could not come down to Washington City to see him in the hospital.) There were also admonishments to write his mother and sisters as well as the usual entreaties to "be strong," to "be brave," to "make the family proud." Christopher wondered if he knew of the events surrounding his capture. He hoped not.

His mother's letters were heart-wrenching. She wrote of her joy and relief on hearing of Christopher's release. But, she also worried that now he would be back in the fighting. She admitted the shocking casualty numbers from Shiloh had her on edge, and she wondered if he wouldn't have been better off staying a prisoner of war. (He could never tell her how bad it had been.)

She wrote about his little sisters—how they were doing in school, their health, and how they missed him and Daniel. Sometimes she would include a little drawing or short note from each of them. His favorite was the drawing Rebecca made of him decked out in a uniform that looked like something from the War of 1812.

Sometimes, his mother's writing became shaky and difficult to read; or a smudged word would show where her tears had dripped onto the page. He choked on his guilt when he thought of what his joining the army was doing to her. But, she had her duty, and he had his.

Most confusing were the letters from his brother. Daniel's letters were short and terse. Even his father seemed long-winded next to Daniel. In his letters he mentioned how they'd captured Winchester (without a shot); a battle outside Kernstown, south of Winchester; and almost daily skirmishes with Jackson's army as they chased him up and down the Shenandoah Valley. He wrote how they were now part of a brigade under General Kimball, a division under General Shields, and a corps under General Banks. He wrote of equipment, logistics, and diet. But he never wrote how he was doing or mentioned the events around Christopher's capture. Christopher wondered if Daniel was mad at him for staining his and Company D's reputation.

He would find out soon enough.

Christopher jumped from the wagon, thanked the wagoner, and looked around for the army headquarters. Like the camps outside Washington, this one was huge, and the task of trying to find the 8th among so many regiments seemed daunting. He wasn't even sure they had arrived yet. He might be looking for a regiment that wasn't even here.

A passing sergeant directed him to a large house just outside town. The building was three stories high, with a wraparound porch and multiple chimneys for heating its many rooms. A large lawn encircled the building, occupied by a couple dozen horses.

After climbing the steps and crossing the porch under the watchful eye of two pickets, Christopher opened the front door and stepped into the foyer. To his right was a drawing room, filled with several desks occupied by young but earnest- and officious-looking officers. Christopher assumed that the big bugs were probably upstairs or back in the dining area.

He entered the drawing room and approached the nearest desk. He came to attention before the lieutenant sitting there, his eyes looking out the window onto a fenced-in pasture where several thousand soldiers stood at attention, lined up by regiment and awaiting orders.

The lieutenant finally looked up from his paperwork. "Yes, private. What is it?"

Christopher looked down at the young man. The officer had thick, wavy blond hair and was trying to grow a mustache and goatee like McClellan's, but the sparse growth was more pathetic than dashing.

"Pardon me, sir. I've just arrived from Washington City and I'm looking for the 8th Ohio Volunteers."

"And what is your business with the 8th, private?"

"That's my regiment, lieutenant, sir. I was a prisoner of war, recently exchanged, and spent the last month in a hospital. I'm looking to get back with my people."

The young lieutenant looked across the room and yelled, "I say, Chapman! Do you know where they put the 8th OVI?"

"Never heard of them," Chapman replied. "What division are they with?"

The young lieutenant looked to Christopher, who had to think for a minute to recall what Daniel had written. Both young officers frowned at the young private and glanced at the piles of paperwork before them when Christopher blurted out, "Shields's division…sir."

"You mean General Shields's division, don't you, private?" the young officer responded, arching an eyebrow.

Christopher nodded. "Yes, sir. Sorry, sir. No disrespect intended."

The other officer, Chapman, smiled. "You're in luck. They just arrived." He picked up a piece of paper, scanned it, stood, and pointed out the window. "In fact, that's General Kimball's brigade out there. You're in time to help set up camp."

Christopher's eyes widened as he looked back out at the soldiers on the field. Officers were addressing the different blocks of men. One of them was the 8th.

Christopher saluted and profusely thanked the staff officers who had helped him. He ran out of the house and across the lawn toward the neighboring field, disturbing several horses as he passed.

After running a short way, his legs ached, and he developed a stitch in his side. Giving in to his weakened condition, Christopher slowed to a brisk walk.

Questions flooded his mind. Had they replaced him in the mess? How much trouble had Ezra gotten into after their escapade at the drinking shack? Would Daniel be glad to see him?

When Christopher reached the camp, several regiments were setting up their camps at once. Men were everywhere, going back and forth, marking their regiment's area and pacing out rows for tents. Several men were dismantling the fence and carrying away boards for firewood.

"8th Ohio!" Christopher called. "Anyone with the 8th Ohio."

Several men he passed shook their heads and kept walking. Eventually, someone stopped and pointed to the south end of the field. "They're down there. Just past the 7th Virginia."

As Christopher walked across the field, the closer he got to the 8th's campsite, the slower he moved. He recognized the signs—it was like walking into battle. He was afraid. How would he be greeted? Would he be dubbed a Jonah and shunned?

As he drew closer, he recognized a few familiar faces. No one from his company yet, but he knew he was getting close. He looked up and saw a regimental flag flying with old glory. That was something new.

He was spotted first.

From out of the crowd, Nathan Jump stepped forward. "Well, lookie here. It's young Master Galloway, returned from perdition."

"Nate," Christopher said, deadpan. "How are you?"

"Well, thanks. Three squares a day—most days. And these springtime strolls through the countryside are good for the constitution." Nathan laughed, patting his flat belly.

"You look like you're in need of a good square meal or six yourself."

Christopher nodded and broke eye contact. "Yes. They don't feed you too well in a Confederate prison." He gave Nathan a wink and continued. "My advice. Don't try it. The food, scenery, and company all leave a lot to be desired."

Nathan frowned and got a faraway look in his eyes. "Beats dead or mangled, I suppose."

Christopher didn't respond. "You seen my brother?"

Nathan half turned and pointed back the way he'd come. "Company D's setting up over there. He's around someplace."

Christopher thanked him and continued on. The closer he got, the more faces he recognized. There was Nathan's brother Joe, Will Parker, Lucius Hoyt, and Jim Fox. As he walked, he nodded or called out to those he knew. He was greeted with surprised hellos, followed by smiles and well wishes.

There was Alex Melville: "Howdy, Ishmael!"

Ishmael looked up with a frown which quickly turned to a grin as he recognized Christopher. "Notch, you old dog. Good to see you back." As Christopher moved on, he heard from behind, "And DON'T call me Ishmael!" Christopher smiled at the running joke.

All these familiar faces made Christopher even more self-conscious of his appearance. Where his uniform was new and clean, theirs were all threadbare and filthy. Several men wore the new uniforms like Christopher, but many still wore the original dark blue uniform, now so torn and ragged that the term uniform didn't seem to apply.

Christopher's skin was pale and sickly looking compared to the nut brown complexions of those around him. Everyone was thin, but they didn't have sunken, almost skeletal features like Christopher. Instead, they were lean and wiry, with a strength and quickness to their motions that made Christopher self-conscious in his weakened condition. These men had been forged and hardened by their experiences over the last six months. He was just worn down.

He saw Daniel, breaking down a length of fence rail into firewood with a hatchet. Next to him was Parker, digging a fire pit with his bayonet. As Christopher approached, Ezra and Charlie walked up carrying more fencing.

Parker saw him first. Their eyes met, then he said something that Christopher couldn't hear. Daniel's head shot up like he'd taken an uppercut to the chin. He saw Christopher and froze.

Christopher walked up and stopped. Daniel stood frozen in place, and the other three watched the two brothers, waiting to take their cue. It was like one of those Brady images—soldiers in the field, preparing supper.

Christopher looked Daniel in the eyes, but his brother was giving nothing away. There was a look of cold detachment in Daniel's eyes that Christopher had seen in many others—but never his brother.

"Well," Christopher said. "Aren't you going to welcome me back?"

Daniel coughed—a short explosive bark that caught in his throat.

"The prodigal son returns," Parker mumbled.

Daniel dropped the hatchet and the piece of wood he still held in his hands and stepped forward. "Chrissy…"

He rushed forward and put his arms around his little brother. Ezra cheered. Charlie and Parker smiled, and their shoulders relaxed.

Keeping one arm around Christopher, Daniel turned and pulled him toward the group. "Come on, little brother, you're just in time to help us with supper."

Christopher smiled. "I'm glad to see you didn't replace me in the mess," he said.

Everyone froze again. Christopher looked from face to face. "Did you?"

Daniel shook his head. "Not replaced. But, Sergeant Rust joined us for awhile."

Christopher looked around. "Where's he at? They make him an officer?"

"He was killed at Kernstown," Parker said.

Christopher stopped and looked at his brother. Daniel refused to make eye contact.

"Anyone else?"

"Ebenezer Bunce," Parker replied.

Christopher's eyebrows shot up. "Scrooge? Dead?"

Charlie shook his head. "Not right away. They amputated an arm— then the fever took him."

"Damn. The fever took a lot of men in the Confederate prisons."

"I bet it did, bub," Ezra said, dropping the wood he was carrying and stepping forward with an outstretched hand. "I looked for you, pard. Honest I did."

Christopher shook Ezra's hand and nodded. "I'm sure you did, Ezra."

Daniel stepped up to the fire pit. He stooped down to make a little tee-pee with the kindling he'd created. With his back to everyone but Parker, he said, "And when he didn't find you, he came back to camp like nothing had happened."

"I thought he'd have come back!" Ezra shouted.

Charlie stepped forward. "Gentlemen, what's done is done. I'm sure Ezra did his best. They're friends, for Christ's sake."

Ezra nodded. "That's true, Charlie. Me and Chris are pards. I wouldn't have left him to the secesh if I'd known."

Christopher nodded. "Charlie's right. It's done and I'm back now. And we're moving south, boys. Next time I go to Richmond, it'll be with a rifle in my hands. And we'll hang ol' Jeff Davis from the nearest sour apple tree!"

"Huzzah!" Everyone nodded and cheered.

Ezra slapped Christopher on the back. "We're on our way."

A week later, Kimball's brigade was ordered back north. Banks had been driven out of the Shenandoah Valley by Jackson.

CHAPTER TWENTY-ONE
PENINSULA CAMPAIGN

The transport ship moved lazily down the Potomac, the clanking of the steam engines offset by the rhythmic splash of its paddle wheel and the steady beat of waves against the bow. Daniel stood at the rail, watching as they passed Mount Vernon, the home of George Washington, the hero of the Revolution and the nation's first president. What would old George have to say if he were alive today to witness this struggle to hold on to everything he'd fought so hard to build? *How will we face those old heroes in the hereafter and explain what we've done to their legacy?*

Daniel didn't take his eyes off the stately old home, fallen into disrepair, as Christopher came to stand beside him.

"He was a slaveholder, you know. Probably would have sided with the secessionists," Christopher said.

Daniel shook his head. "I don't think so. I think he knew slavery was wrong."

"You can't make your heroes out to believe what you want them to believe. You have to accept them for who they were."

Daniel gave Christopher a sidelong glance and smiled. Where did that come from? Christopher would never have said something so profound six months ago. "Neither can you judge them based on modern standards."

"I guess they were just men. They made mistakes," Christopher said.

"And now we are paying the price of those mistakes," Daniel responded.

Ezra joined them at the rail. He glimpsed Mount Vernon before it passed out of sight and said, "Those Virginians sure make big houses, don't they."

Christopher spit over the rail. "I seen bigger in Washington City."

Daniel laughed. There was his little brother.

It was almost July, and Christopher had been back for nearly two months. Most of that time had been spent marching up and down the Shenandoah Valley, skirmishing with Stonewall Jackson's rear guard. It had been tiring and frustrating, but they'd taken no serious casualties.

The biggest danger had been exposure, not the enemy. The constant movement meant the supply wagons with the tents and baggage were always miles behind. Daniel couldn't recall the last time he'd slept under a roof. He supposed, if they kept moving like they had been, the army would have to find a more practical way to house the troops. The misery of sleeping out in the rain and the mud and the accompanying illness couldn't go on forever.

Daniel smiled as he recalled the "hardship" they all thought they had gone through that first campaign. Now, they constantly marched and slept in the mud, ate an unvaried diet of salt pork and hardtack for weeks on end, burned under the hot sun during the day, and froze at night. Many tried at first to carry everything they thought they needed to stay comfortable on their backs. But, almost everything not required to stay alive or fight the enemy soon ended up abandoned along the roadside.

That first march from Falmouth back to the Shenandoah, Christopher had ridden in a supply wagon most of the way. But he was soon tramping over the hills, obsessed with getting his strength back. Daniel supposed he wanted payback for the harsh treatment he'd endured while a prisoner.

Daniel remembered his first sight of Christopher in that camp at Bell Plains. The sight left him shaken and speechless. Still a teenager, Christopher looked like a man of thirty—an emaciated man of thirty. He looked like a walking skeleton covered with thin parchment. And that was after a month of convalescence. Daniel didn't want to imagine what he looked like upon his release.

Now they were going south to join McClellan's army battling for

Richmond in the Peninsula southeast of that city. Their transport would take them to the mouth of the Potomac, down Chesapeake Bay to the James River, and then up to Harrison's Landing to join the Army of the Potomac.

At first, Daniel hoped they would arrive in time to join the Army of the Potomac as they marched into Richmond as conquerors (he thought it would be particularly satisfying for Christopher). But, McClellan had been outflanked by Robert Lee's Army of Northern Virginia and forced to retreat in a series of losing battles back to the James River. Kimball's brigade, along with another brigade pulled from the Shenandoah, were going down as re-enforcements and rear guard for the beaten and worn troops.

When they passed out onto the Chesapeake, the water became high and choppy. Soon, almost everyone suffered from seasickness. The rails filled with men retching over the side, their faces pale and sweaty despite the cool breeze. There was a chorus of cheers when the ship turned into the bay at Hampton Roads, followed by curses and exclamations when they learned they would have to spend the night on the ship.

The next morning, the transport ship left the bay and turned toward the mouth of the James, a complement of gunboats taking up position on both sides. The squat boats, bristling with cannon, looked as ugly as they did deadly. Daniel tried to imagine what being cooped up inside one of those turrets would be like during a battle and shuddered.

He was thinking about advancements in sea warfare when they passed the *USS Cumberland*. Sunk just a few months ago by the Confederate iron-clad *Virginia*, it now sat on the bottom of the bay with only its masts sticking up out of the water. The majestic old wooden ship, even with her massive Dahlgren cannon, never stood a chance against the squat little warship.

They moved up the James at a snail's pace—the sailors having to take constant soundings to avoid sandbars. New growth pine forest lined the banks, occasionally broken by the sight of an old plantation home. There were few signs of the industrious tobacco plantations that made the area one of the richest in the new world a hundred years ago.

As they reached their destination at Harrison's Landing, a heavy after-noon rainstorm came up, just in time to soak the men as they disembarked and marched inland. The atmosphere was hot and steamy, and the rain offered meager relief.

Everywhere was mud and massive puddles of water. The men they passed were half dressed and unresponsive to anything going on around them. As the brigade marched through camp, they drew little more than indifferent, or even malevolent, stares.

They marched into the pine forests and stopped somewhere out front of the entrenchments. The brigade formed a battle line, and the men tried to dig up enough soil to build up embankments, but they eventually gave up trying to get enough dirt out of the root-filled ground.

That night they slept on the battle line behind the meager entrenchments they'd created.

—◊◊—

Daniel stood in the drawing room of his parents' house. The sun was shining, and a cool breeze blew in off the lake through the open window. Despite the cool air, Daniel was sweating. In the room with him were his parents, Christopher, and Susan Johnston. Susan was across the room clutching a handbag, her eyes darting around, refusing to look at Daniel. His parents stood on either side of him, both talking at once. His mother dabbed her tear-filled eyes with a handkerchief, and his father angrily waved his hands as he spoke. Christopher stood in front of Daniel, smiling.

"What's wrong with you, boy. You had one job to do—and you failed," his father spat, shaking his head in disgust.

"Oh, Danny. My baby, my baby," his mother wailed.

Daniel did not understand why they were so upset. He tried to catch Susan's eye but, seeing him looking her way, she turned her back to him.

He looked at Christopher, who seemed the only one willing to meet his eyes without rancor. Then he realized the front of Christopher's jacket was covered with blood. His younger brother opened his mouth to speak, but only blood came out, pouring down his chin and onto the floor.

Daniel turned to his father in shock and was met with a wagging finger. "Now see what you've done."

Daniel opened his mouth to scream, and the world exploded.

He sat up. The cool breeze was gone, replaced by a humid heat that raised steam off everything—the wet trees, the wet rocks, the muddy ground, even Daniel's wet, muddy uniform. Sweat beaded his face, and droplets ran down his back and chest under his clothes. He gulped in the heavy, damp air.

There were another series of explosions. Iron shrapnel and pine splinters buzzed through the air.

Christopher sat next to him, hunched over with his rifle across his lap. He smiled and said, "Helluva wake-up call, ain't it?"

Daniel nodded. "When did this start?"

"Just now." Christopher snorted a laugh. "Woke you up. You shot up so fast, I thought you were gonna jump into one of those trees." Christopher laughed.

"I'm glad you still have your sense of humor," Daniel said. He let out a harrumph and picked up his rifle. He removed the oil cloth he'd wrapped around the breech, retrieved his toolkit, and ran a pick through the nipple hole a couple times to make sure it was clear.

"My sense of humor is about all I have left," Christopher said.

Daniel paused and looked at his brother. Then returned to inspecting his rifle. He pulled the cork out of the end and was preparing to run a patch down the barrel when the bugle call to assemble blew.

Sergeant Howe came down the line, bellowing as only a first sergeant could. "Up and at it, you lazy jackanapes! It's too hot here, we're headed to cooler climes."

"You mean we're going to Hades, Sergeant?" Ezra asked, smiling.

"I can't speak for everyone, Rouse, but I'm damn sure you are," Howe shot back.

The brigade marched back the way they had come, back behind the defensive position they'd passed the day before. Once out of range of the shelling, they fixed a quick breakfast, then turned around and marched back to the front.

They formed a battle line and entered the forest, this time going farther than they had the night before. Their orders were to push back the rebel skirmishers and pickets that filled the woods.

The men had to constantly move around trees and over bushes, so they couldn't keep a straight battle line in the dense woods. The line rippled as they advanced, and sometimes Daniel found himself far ahead of the men that were supposed to be at his side. In those moments, his chest would tingle as if he could feel the sights of a rebel gun lining up on his heart.

A branch snagged Daniel's rifle and pulled him off balance. As he untangled the rifle and pulled it forward, he cursed the tree, the heat, and Virginia in that order.

Then, as he began to quicken his pace to catch up to the line, he heard the unmistakable buzz of a minié ball, followed by a dull thud. He looked over his shoulder at the tree he'd just cursed and saw a fresh hole, about head height. He decided to remove the trees from the curse list and appreciate them for the cover they provided.

Soon, the buzzing of passing bullets became a frequent occurrence. Daniel strained to see where the shots were coming from, but other than an occasional patch of gray, he couldn't see anything but trees. He assumed it was just skirmishers firing and falling back. If it had been a full battle line standing firm, they would have come upon them by now.

There was a pause in the firing, and Daniel saw unfiltered sunlight ahead. He stepped out of the woods into a field of oats. It was about a hundred yards wide and empty, so he figured the enemy running to the other side of the field explained the pause. Unfortunately, the Federal soldiers would not have that luxury.

They had only gone a few steps out into the sunlight when the harassing fire became full volleys. Daniel tried to make himself as small as possible, hunching over and drawing his head down between his shoulders.

Instead of straightening as it should have, the line buckled and threatened to fall apart. Daniel wanted back in the cover of the trees and was sure everyone else did as well. But, from the way the line was crumbling, it was apparent they had differing ideas on the best way to get there. Some thought going forward as fast as possible would be the best way to go, others didn't want to get any closer to the rebel line than they had to. Sergeants and corporals shouted themselves hoarse trying to get the men to come back into alignment.

Then the artillery fire began.

A deafening boom shook the trees, followed by the shrieking roar of incoming shells and a ragged line of explosions over the field. The smell of black powder and hot iron filled the air. For a moment, the deeper buzz of flying shrapnel drowned out the sound of passing minié balls.

The first couple volleys, the shells went long, and most of the shrapnel hit dirt. But, by the third volley they had their range and several shells exploded directly over the line. Hot shrapnel tore into flesh, and men screamed in horror and pain.

Before them was a line of trees populated with enemy soldiers; behind lay woods they knew to be empty and safe. Between the two lay a field blanketed by cannon and rifle fire.

The pace of the line slowed until it ground to a halt. A wave of panic swept the line. Daniel felt his resolve shattering and looked around for reassurance. It was clear on every face, the men were ready to crack.

"Retreat!"

The relief that washed over Daniel was so overwhelming his knees threatened to buckle.

The entire brigade turned as one and ran back to the tree line. Once in the safety of the trees, they waited for their own artillery to come forward.

As soon as a Federal battery was in place, an artillery duel with the Confederate battery began, which the soldiers appreciated very much. Not only did it draw the enemy fire away from them, but the duel was also an impressive sight, with cannons belching flame six feet or more with every blast, and the exploding shells lighting up the shadows of the forest.

Soon, the Confederate battery retreated, and they advanced once more. By then the enemy skirmishers were long gone, and they crossed the oat field without incident. The brigade stopped and bivouacked deep in the woods. They deployed almost every other man in the brigade on the picket line and dug trenches. Captain Daggett explained to the men that they would try to hold this forward position while the Army of the Potomac finished its retreat to the camp at Harrison's Landing.

—✺—

They stayed in those woods through the Fourth of July, under constant fire from artillery and snipers.

Their supply wagons still hadn't arrived, so they had no spare clothes or tents (except for a few scrounged up for the big bugs). By now the whole brigade put off an odor that rivaled that of the sinks.

Each morning, as the sun rose, so did the heat. Steam rose from the dew on the ground, covering the earth in a thin mist. Daniel hadn't stopped sweating since their transport ship had entered the James River almost a week ago, but it was worse during the day. His shirt was white and crusty from layers of sweat. Sweat trickled down his face and body, and he couldn't get enough water—though it tasted bitter and smelled like Hades.

By the time they were pulled off the front line, almost half the brigade had either swamp fever or diarrhea.

The weeks following, except for the flies and the heat, they could have been in any army camp anywhere. They ate, they slept, they stood guard, they policed the camp, they drilled, and they complained—but not much else. Occasionally, someone on General McClellan's staff would come in from wherever they passed their time, and they would have a grand review for his inspection.

Once in the many weeks they were in the Peninsula, the general himself, George B. McClellan, appeared and inspected his troops. McClellan got his start in the war in West Virginia and singled out the other troops who had been there, including Kimball's brigade and the 8th for particular praise. But he didn't impress Daniel. He'd already decided the man was a pompous windbag.

They were harassed daily by cannon fire that never seemed to do much damage and stopped as soon as the Federal artillery responded. They would regularly go out on patrol, looking (without success) for some rebels someone spotted somewhere.

Daniel hated this part of Virginia. The Shenandoah had been a paradise compared to the Peninsula—with its heat and humidity and bugs and mud. He was always tired and thirsty. And most of the time he suffered with the quick step—the quick step to the sinks.

The lice that had been their constant torment since training camp seemed to thrive in the warm, humid climate and, when they weren't fighting gray-backs in the woods, the men were fighting them in their clothes. Daniel saw one soldier wearing a necklace of lice, strung together on a thread. Some were even still alive. Daniel could see their legs wiggling.

Of equal torment were the flies that flew everywhere and covered everything. They tormented the horses, mules, and beef cattle. They swarmed the sinks and the commissary, and it was common to find dead flies in the rations. The white tent walls were black with flies. And trying to stand motionless at attention was an open invitation for the beasts to fly into your face.

The ground was a thick, sticky mud when it rained, or a dry powder that clung to everything on the rare occasions when it didn't. Even the newspapers back home were questioning the fitness of the Union camp, describing the surrounding swamps, bad water, and how the rate of diarrhea among the soldiers was almost epidemic.

The bad publicity pressured the army to open a constant supply line between Harrison's Landing and Washington City. They got new tents (no more Sibleys—now they had two-man tents that could be divided between the occupants and carried on the march), new clothes, newspapers that weren't weeks old, and fresh fruit and vegetables.

Eventually, even the 8th's supply wagons showed up, and the men were able to retrieve their personal items many thought were long lost.

—〰—

With all the misery they were going through, and the free time they had to kill, Christopher started drinking again.

Daniel suspected it when Christopher and Ezra started disappearing for hours at a time. He prayed it wasn't true, that they were just out exploring the camp as they liked to do. But, he couldn't ignore the glassy eyes and impulsive giggling. When it rained and they were forced into tents, the smell as Christopher slept was unmistakable.

One night, Charlie Locker, sergeant of the guard that night, woke Daniel from a sound sleep.

"Danny, you'd better come quick," Charlie said. "Christopher's done it again."

Daniel shook his head and rubbed his eyes, trying to decipher what Charlie was saying. "Done what?"

"The drinks, Danny. It's getting him in trouble again. I don't know what will happen this time."

Now Daniel was wide awake. He put on his shoes and stood. Charlie turned to go and waved for Daniel to follow.

They walked for several minutes and were well outside of the 8th's territory when Daniel heard angry yelling. He looked at Charlie, who nodded. Then he ran toward the sound as fast as he could.

Guided by the raised voices and, despite the late hour, the light from a large campfire, Daniel came upon a group of seven men. Three men stood together by the fire, yelling insults past two nervous-looking provost guards, toward Christopher and Ezra, who were standing at the edge of the firelight.

Christopher stood with his head bowed and hands held in front of him, palms out. Ezra stood with his head back, chest puffed out, eyes wide and lips pursed in a sneer. His hands were half-clenched claws ready to strike.

"What's going on?" Daniel asked.

Everyone spun toward him as if a reb soldier had snuck up on them.

"What's it to you?" one of the three asked.

"Sergeant Locker came and got me, said my brother was in some kind of trouble."

Christopher had turned his back on Daniel and shook his head. As Charlie joined the group, he spun around and said to him, "Charlie, I told you I didn't want him here."

"I don't care what you want, Christopher Galloway. I am the sergeant, you are the private. You don't tell me what to do. I tell you."

Christopher's shoulders slumped even more.

One of the three stepped toward Daniel. "I'll tell you what's going on. Your brother tried to take my head off, that's what's going on. If the provost hadn't shown, I would've had to kill him."

A jolt of anger clawed up Daniel's back and took root in the base of his skull. "Maybe you were needing a beating."

The crowd contracted as the man took a step forward, fists raised, followed immediately by Ezra and Daniel. The man's two pards followed suit, and the provost guards raised their rifles and stepped into the middle.

"Enough!" Charlie yelled. "I don't think anyone wants to go to the clink tonight. So let's see if we can come to an agreement. I will describe the events as I see them, based on everyone's testimony. When I am finished—and not until I am finished—you can make whatever rebuttal you want. Understood?"

The man cocked his head to one side. Then he squinted his eyes. "What's that you say?"

Charlie sighed. "I talk. You listen."

The man shook his head. "I don't know...Ain't you in the same company as these troublemakers?"

Charlie gave them all a hard stare. "Right now, I am all that stands between you and the stockade."

At the mention of the stockade, a wooden pen located near the sinks and stables, everyone got very quiet. Men had died of the flux after spending time there.

"All right," Charlie began. "The five of you were up after hours, drinking illicit liquor. All in violation of orders. At a certain point, Private Galloway there fell asleep with a bottle of liquor in his hand. Private...I'm sorry, what did you say your name was again?"

The man squirmed but answered, "Wells."

"Yes, Private Wells attempted to take the bottle from Private Galloway. Private Galloway woke with a start and struck Private Wells. From what I understand, Private Galloway was not fully awake and he struck several more times, until Private Rouse and Private Wells's companions pulled him off.

"At that time, Private Galloway appeared disoriented, but Private Wells wanted restitution and struck Private Galloway as he was being restrained. Then a..what do you Irish call it?...a donnybrook broke out involving all participants, which attracted the provost guards' attention.

"Does that sum it up?"

No one responded right away. Wells and his pards talked among themselves for a moment. Ezra and Christopher looked at each other, and Ezra gave Christopher a slight nod. Daniel divided his glares between Christopher and Private Wells.

Then, Wells spoke up. "I guess that about does it, 'ceptin' I didn't mean to hit him when he was restrained. I was just looking for a fair fight."

Charlie cocked his head. "Really, Private Wells. You are aware of the rule against fighting?"

Realizing he'd said too much, Wells stammered until Ezra cut him off.

"That about sums it up, Char—Sergeant. Chris was just startled, is all. He didn't mean nothing by it."

"Of course. And you, Private Wells, did you mean anything by it?"

Wells shook his head.

"Then I think we can chalk this up to one big misunderstanding. We will confiscate the remaining liquor of course. I suggest you all go directly to the sack before I have to haul you all in for disobeying orders and being up after hours. No? Good. Dismissed."

The crowd dispersed, and Daniel walked back to their assigned area with Christopher and Ezra.

He glimpsed the scrape on Christopher's jaw and asked him if he was all right. Christopher nodded in response. They walked the rest of the way in silence.

The next day, Daniel caught Ezra coming back from the sinks and stopped him.

"Tell me what happened?"

Ezra shrugged his shoulders. "Charlie pretty much covered everything."

Daniel poked Ezra in the chest. "Pretty much isn't good enough. What made Christopher go off like that?"

Ezra frowned and rubbed the spot on his chest Daniel had poked. "Like Charlie said, Chris was sleeping. He must have been dreaming about chow time, because when Wells tried to take the bottle, he jumped up, screaming, 'Don't take my rations' over and over. Then he started beating on Wells."

Ezra smiled. "And it was a helluva beating too. You should have seen it. Christopher's—"

"I don't want to hear it. You two need to lay off the joy juice."

Ezra suddenly became uncomfortable. "I try to tell him. He don't listen to nobody since he got back. Something's wrong, Dan."

The last sentence came out as a whisper.

"What do you mean?"

"I can't put my finger on it. He's just not the same. Moody. One minute, he's laughing and carrying on, the next he's looking around like he wants to kill somebody. I don't know what to do." Ezra sighed. "I try to look out for him best I can."

Daniel was speechless for a moment. Then, he put a hand on Ezra's shoulder. "I know you do, Ez. I know I blamed you for what happened before, but I was wrong. You're a good pard, you know that?"

Ezra dropped his eyes and nodded.

"Let's make a pact. You try to figure out what's going on and let me know what you find, and I'll do the same. Deal?"

Ezra nodded.

"Good. Let's get back before Christopher gets himself in trouble again and we're not there to pull his fat out of the fire."

They walked back in silence. Worries were spinning through Daniel's head like a Christmas toy. Christopher was holding something back, but so was Daniel. He had in his pocket the last letter he'd received from Susan, right after Kernstown. In it, she'd broken off their relationship. She tried to explain her decision, and it almost sounded like something her father would have written. They were socially too far apart, their religions couldn't mix, etc. She also said she was going back east to go to school and wouldn't be able to write him as much as he deserved while he fought for the future of the country.

He hadn't told Christopher or anyone else about the letter. He continued to write almost daily, only now all his letters were to his parents.

Now it seemed they both had secrets. But something was particularly dark about Christopher's. Something had happened to him, probably when he was a prisoner. Daniel was going to make it his mission to find out what.

CHAPTER TWENTY-TWO
SECOND BULL RUN

By the middle of August, the army had evacuated all the sick, support staff, equipment, and baggage from the Peninsula. The remaining army mobilized the morning of the sixteenth and headed out cross-country toward Yorktown—except for Second Corps, of which Kimball's brigade was now a part. They marched out to the old picket line to act as rear guard.

After creating a line of dummy troops (old uniforms stuffed with straw and armed with broken rifles or sticks) and placing them in the trenches, Second Corps moved out the next afternoon. It had been dry for several days, and the passing of thousands of men had already pulverized the dirt in the road to a fine powder. They had not even gone a mile before dust covered everything, giving the men a uniform tan appearance from head to toe.

Christopher's mouth felt as if he'd been eating mud pies, and his stinging eyes watered continuously, creating muddy streaks down his cheeks in the path of his tears. He tied a bandana over his face and thought of all the things he'd like to say about the army and its leaders but didn't. That would have required opening his mouth. Instead, he internally cursed out the officers, the South, the politicians, abolitionists, slaveholders, and his own misguided ideal of glory and heroism that had brought him to that hot dusty road on that August day in 1862.

They reached the Chickahominy River after midnight. The men were dirty and tired, ready to drop where they stood or strike out at the slightest provocation. But the big bugs insisted they make camp on the other side of the river, so they had to cross a long, poorly constructed pontoon bridge in the dark.

The crossing was slow, the pontoons bobbing up and down as the men stepped from one to another. Tired, half conscious men stumbled each time they took a step and discovered the plank was not where they expected it to be. By the time Christopher reached the middle of the bridge, he was trembling with anger and fatigue.

Christopher was straggling again. The 8th was somewhere ahead, and he hadn't seen a familiar face for hours. He'd recognized a few men from the Irish Brigade earlier—they were about the only soldiers left that still carried the old buck and ball muskets distributed to many soldiers early in the war. So he assumed he was somewhere with the First Division, surrounded by New Yorkers.

As he was thinking of camp and how far ahead his brother and pards may be, he brought his foot down, only to discover the plank had dropped a foot from where it had been. He pitched forward into the man in front of him.

The man spun around and pushed him back. "Watch your step, bub!"

Christopher's instinctive response to apologize came and went in the time it took for him to regain his balance. Instead, rage blinded him to everything but taking the man down.

Being short didn't have a lot of advantages, but one was the ability to get inside an opponent's defense. And that was all this man was to him—an opponent.

Christopher ducked his head and twisted his body. He stepped forward and drove his shoulder into the man's midsection. At the same time, Christopher put his foot behind the man's heel and pushed until he stumbled back and over the side of the bridge.

At the last second, a hand grabbed the man and stopped his fall. Christopher stepped back in surprise as Daniel said, "Watch it, mister. We almost lost you."

"Like hell!" the man exploded. "That little weasel tried to push me over the side. I'm gonna thrash him."

Daniel tightened his grip and gave the man's arm a little tug. He rocked back on his heels, and his hands shot out to his side as he fought to keep balance.

Daniel leaned in and whispered, "I'd be careful if I was you. You're still awfully close to the side. Wouldn't want you falling in."

The man looked over his shoulder at the black, fast-moving water and gulped. Then he yanked his arm out of Daniel's grasp and glared at the two brothers. "You two are strangers here. These men are my pards. Anything happens to me, you two are going in the drink faster than a sawbones can take an arm."

"And you'll still be dead," Daniel said.

The man looked at the two and spit. "Watch your step, short stuff," he said to Christopher.

Christopher smiled and tapped the base of his sheathed bayonet with his finger. "Don't worry—bub. I'll be right behind you."

The man turned and joined the steady stream of men marching to the other side of the river. Christopher looked around. Other than a few curious looks, the whole incident seemed to have gone unnoticed. He smirked and started to take a step when Daniel grabbed his arm and spun him around.

"What the hell, Danny—"

Daniel gave him a hard shake. "What was that about? You almost killed that man."

Christopher opened his mouth to reply when the truth of what his brother said hit him and drove all the air from his lungs. He'd almost killed a man for pushing him.

He couldn't speak. He looked at Daniel and shook his head. "I don't know…" he finally said.

They resumed their march, both now wide awake.

"I don't know what's come over you, Chrissy—"

"Don't call me that, dammit! My name's not Chrissy. It's Chris, or Christopher, or even Notch. But don't call me that little-girl name."

"All right. All right. But you have to tell me what's going on with you.

This is crazy. You're drinking and fighting all the time now. This isn't like you. You never fought before—not like this."

Christopher shook his head. "I just been on edge is all. And, in case you hadn't noticed, we're in a war. In war, you fight."

"The other side, Chris. Not each other."

"Like I said, I'm just on edge is all. I swear, between you and Ezra I can't get a moment's peace. You're like a couple mother hens always brooding over me.

"And where did you come from, anyways? I didn't see you on the march, then suddenly there you are. You been hiding?"

"I was just a few paces behind you."

"Brooding."

By the time they reached their campsite, the fatigue had returned, and both brothers dropped in Company D's general area and slept without interruption until reveille the next morning.

Two more days of marching brought them to Yorktown, recently captured in a siege one participant described as reminiscent of Washington's siege of Cornwallis during the War of Independence. The way Christopher had heard it, McClellan had been reluctant to attack and dragged the whole affair out until the rebels tired of waiting and just up and left. But he was too tired to contradict the man and let him talk. He figured the truth of the matter was probably somewhere in between.

They only had a day in Yorktown, but the men spent it taking in historic sites, bathing in the York River, and gorging themselves on green corn from the town warehouses and oysters from the riverbed.

Ezra spent the day with Christopher, which wasn't unusual. What was unusual was that Daniel also seemed to be around a lot as well. Daniel normally spent his free time hanging around sergeants and corporals. At one point, Christopher confronted him.

"Why aren't you out boot-licking sergeants or something. Let me be already. Nothing's wrong."

Daniel tried to argue, but left when Ezra suggested he give them some room. That surprised Christopher more than Daniel hanging around. Daniel had never once listened to anything Ezra had to say, let alone acted on it. He suspected the two were up to something.

The next day, they continued their march, turning down the Peninsula toward Newport News in much better spirits. They arrived three days later, again hot, dirty, and tired.

The 8th then left their new corps and sailed for Washington City with the 4th Ohio. Pope's army was drawn out by Lee's forces and beaten at a place called Cedar Mountain. Rumor had it the big bugs feared an attack on Washington was imminent. They sent the Ohio regiments ahead to help protect the city until the rest of the Army of the Potomac could be brought up.

—⁂—

The attack on Washington never happened. By the end of the month, Second Corps was back together and, after camping a short time on the lawn in front of Robert E. Lee's home in Arlington, they moved up the Potomac two miles to make a more permanent camp.

They were digging breastworks for their new camp when Christopher stopped, leaned on his shovel, and took a big breath. "It seems if we ain't marching, we're digging, and if we ain't digging, we're drilling. What we don't seem to do a lot of is fighting."

"You wouldn't say that if you'd been at Kernstown," Daniel said.

Christopher snapped, "Well, I wasn't at Kernstown. I was otherwise occupied."

Daniel stopped digging and looked at Christopher. "I know you were. But a battle is not like skirmishing. It's a lot worse. Compared to that, digging's fine with me."

Christopher threw down his shovel. "Well it ain't fine with me."

Daniel took a tentative step toward his brother. "Calm down. I'm not trying to say what you went through was any easier. Maybe it was worse. I don't know. All I know is when it comes to fighting, I'd rather be doing anything else. You'll think the same first time you're in a battle."

Christopher took a breath and nodded. "I guess none of us have had it easy the last year. I…I just want to do something to make it end. Digging trenches or being the rear guard for a retreat is not doing that."

Christopher paused and looked into the distance, then continued. "I didn't mean to take it out on you."

He was answered by the roar of cannon fire somewhere in the distance.

Everyone stopped what they were doing and looked toward the sound. The fire continued unabated.

Daniel smiled. "Now look what you did. You jinxed us, ya Jonah!"

"I ain't no Jonah!" Christopher yelled back, and Daniel laughed.

"You know I don't go for that superstitious claptrap," he said. "I'm just kidding you is all."

"Well, I ain't no Jonah and I ain't no beat," Christopher mumbled as he resumed digging.

"Better dig faster, boys," Parker said. "If that's coming this way, we don't want to get caught out in the open."

The men took Parker's advice, wondering if they would soon have to put their new breastworks to use.

After several hours of battle sounds, they heard the long roll. Everyone dropped what they were doing and ran for their rifles. As they lined up, several ammunition wagons arrived. They took roll call and distributed rounds. Company officers and sergeants quickly inspected the men's cartridge boxes and rifles.

As Lieutenant Barnes was inspecting his rifle, Christopher looked up at Colonel Sawyer sitting astride his horse next to General Kimball and all the other big bugs and their staffs. *Not that long ago, he was down here with us,* Christopher thought.

Second Corps began its march toward the sound of battle, but it was two hours before the 8th was on the road. They were the Third Brigade of the Third Division of the corps and were last in the line. By then, word had spread that Pope had been outgeneraled yet again and was taking a beating near Manassas.

"Don't worry, General Pope, sir!" someone yelled. "We'll save you!" Everyone laughed and continued making jokes at Pope's expense.

Christopher ignored the joking and fidgeted with the brass plate with OVM stamped across it that adorned his cartridge box strap. It seemed so dull. When he got back, he'd polish all his brass. Ignoring everything around him, he stumbled several times and fell behind in the marching order.

The jocularity lasted until they met the first ambulances. Those coming from the battle were full of screaming, moaning men; those returning were empty except for the puddles of blood soaking through the floorboards, leaving a red trail in their wake.

After that, the jokes stopped, and everyone marched in silence. Soon, supply wagons, messengers, cannons, cavalry, and an occasional rider in civilian dress joined the ambulances on the road. As the traffic increased, the men had to march alongside the road.

"Apparently, we don't rate," Christopher groused, looking at the mud clinging to his shoes.

As they neared the battle, the men had to go around equipment abandoned on the side of the road. The marching over soft, muddy ground and constant dodging of obstacles soon had the men fatigued. The columns lengthened, and the various units mixed as more stragglers fell behind. Christopher was surprised to discover he was surrounded by men he didn't recognize.

Christopher looked around and noted a brass seven on the hats of the surrounding men. He took a guess and asked the man beside him, "Seventh West Virginia?"

The man nodded. At least he was still in Kimball's brigade.

"Any of you boys know a Stephen Cole?" he asked those around him. Everyone shook their heads.

"He's from Western Virginia. He and I were pards in Libby Prison."

"You know everybody in Ohio, bub?" someone asked.

"No, I just thought…"

"You thought because we're from the same country, we all know each other, right?"

"What regiment he with?" someone else asked.

Christopher couldn't remember. It would come back to him. They planned to get together again after the war. "I don't know."

"Well, we ain't with that regiment," the first man responded.

They continued to march through the night. Somehow, Christopher kept putting one foot in front of the other, his world reduced to the small square of earth in front of his feet. Everything else was just shadow and noise.

As the sky lightened in the east, the pace slowed, drawing Christopher out of his myopia. Somewhere up ahead, they'd called a halt. Christopher hoped it would last long enough for him to find Daniel and his messmates, eat something, and get some sleep before they started up again. If not, he'd just drop wherever he could and sleep until the next call for assembly.

After a two-hour rest, they were back on the road. In an effort to keep the formation together, they lined up in three columns by division, followed by their artillery and ammunition wagons. Third Division, with Kimball's brigade and the 8th, was in the right-hand column farthest from the road.

As they neared the town of Centerville, they crested a rise that afforded a good view of the plain before them. What they saw was an army in chaos.

Boards posted along the road listed the names of divisions and brigades with arrows pointing to where they could supposedly be found. But there appeared to be no order to the sea of soldiers spread out before them. Men were clustered in groups, surrounding campfires scattered like stars across the plain. Abandoned equipment and articles of clothing lay everywhere as if the entire army had just dropped their rifles and traps wherever they felt like. Larger flotsam, such as overturned wagons and artillery pieces lay keeled over on broken axels. The only people moving with any sense of purpose were the orderlies delivering messages and the ambulances as they moved through the dejected men, picking up wounded.

"My God," Christopher muttered, crossing himself.

Second Corps crossed the desolate plain and formed a battle line to the left of the road. Once again, the 8th was protecting a beaten and demoralized army.

They stayed in that position for two days while Pope's army continued its retreat. As the army retreated, it burned anything that couldn't be carried or hauled back. Thick, acrid smoke filled the air. At night, the bonfires and burning wagons and limbers lit up the plain, creating deep, long shadows that to Christopher looked like the shades of the dead.

In the middle of the second night, Second Corps moved out. Pope's army had completed its evacuation and was on its way to Washington. Second Corps followed behind, continuing to act as its rear guard.

The march back proved to be even more difficult than the march out. The constant traffic and a heavy but fast-moving, rainstorm had turned the road and surrounding area into a churned-up bog. Despite the efforts to burn everything, abandoned equipment littered the side of the road, some burned and broken, but a lot still intact.

So much mud covered Christopher's shoes each that step was an agonizing effort—as if a ball and chain were attached to each ankle. He cursed the constant obstacles for the extra steps it took to go around them. Sometimes he had to go down into a ditch full of cold, stagnant water to get around a wagon or limber. Trying to then climb back out took everything he had. More than once Christopher thought of quitting. Just lying down and waiting for death or daylight—whichever came first.

Another two-day march followed, with divisions and brigades scattered along the side of the road. The only rest they had in the two days was an afternoon spent in battle line, awaiting a possible attack and taking constant artillery fire.

By the time they arrived at their camp on the Potomac, Christopher's entire body was caked in mud. As he lay down to rest, his muscles ached and quivered. He thought of getting something to eat but was too tired to move.

The only upside, that he could see, was he'd not gotten drunk and had been too tired to dream.

CHAPTER TWENTY-THREE
MARYLAND CAMPAIGN

As summer turned to fall, the 8th moved their camp to Maryland, just across the river from Washington. The new camp, still clean and comfortable, was the best they'd had in a long time. The surrounding populace was enthusiastically pro-Union and supplied the soldiers with fresh vegetables to feed their bellies and good cheer to feed their souls. After weeks in Virginia, where the local citizens treated the Union soldiers with disdain, and sometime open hostility, it was a welcome change.

Their only complaint was that they hadn't seen their baggage since the Peninsula. No one had had a change of clothes or a tent to sleep in for weeks.

Daniel, with Ezra on one side and Christopher on the other, pushed his way through a dense crowd surrounding several matronly women passing out pies and fresh fruit. While the rations they received in camp were better than the salt pork and hardtack they were issued on campaign, most of the fruit and vegetables from the commissary tended to be old and soft. As Daniel made it through the crowd, he found himself standing before a short, plump woman with an infectious smile. He grinned and nodded, suddenly tongue-tied.

It had been so long since he'd spoken to a woman, he wasn't sure what to say. He was embarrassed by the gruff demeanor he'd developed over the last year and was sure it would embarrass and offend the woman as soon as he said something. Not to mention his dirty clothes and ripe smell.

"Goodness, young man, has military life stricken you dumb?" she said, her smile getting even wider.

Daniel shook his head. "No, ma'am. It's just, I'm not sure, that is to say, my concern is that, well…"

Ezra stepped forward. As he did, he removed his hat with one hand while surreptitiously reaching up behind Daniel and nudging the back of his hat. Daniel reached up and yanked it off his head.

"Good day, madam," Ezra said. "What a beautiful day, isn't it?"

"Why yes, young man. Given the warm weather, you would think it was July instead of September. But, I'm guessing you didn't come here to talk about the weather."

As she spoke, she lifted a pie up off the table before her and angled it so the boys could get a good look.

Daniel found himself fixated on the holes cut into the top crust, around which the filling had bubbled out to create a dark red goo that set his mouth to watering. Finding his tongue, he said, "Word has spread of your ladies' baked goods, and we had hoped to procure some. Baked goods, that is."

"Why certainly. We have cakes, pies, apples, peaches, melons of various kinds…What are you hungry for?"

Daniel felt Christopher clutch his arm and whisper, "Everything."

Daniel looked over at his brother and frowned. Christopher's gaze was fixated on the food. Daniel reached up and knocked the hat off his head.

"Ma taught you better than that, you philistine. You take your hat off before a lady."

He looked back at the woman and smiled. "Ma'am. We've been in the field so long, everything looks good. Can we get a variety?"

"Of course. How many are in your mess?" she asked.

Daniel cocked his head at the question.

"You're not the first soldiers we've spoken to today. I personally think it's admirable the way you boys look out for each other in your 'messes.'"

Daniel could hear the quotation marks in her tone as she said the word mess. To her, he thought, a mess was probably something you cleaned.

"Five, ma'am," Daniel said.

Her eyebrows raised. "Five? Most of the boys we've talked to have only had two to four in their messes. You boys must be close."

Daniel nodded. "Since Camp Dennison."

"Yes. Well, we have pies and cakes, ten cents each, or a bag of fruit for a nickel…"

"We'll take three pies, two cakes, and two bags of fruit."

"You're going to buy us out," she laughed, but quickly gathered up the order. Daniel counted out the change and paid the woman sixty cents. They took the goods and headed back to their camp.

"I'm so hungry, I could eat all this right here and now," Christopher said.

"And take a thumping from Parker and Charlie in return," Daniel said. "And I wouldn't lift a finger to help you, either."

"I wouldn't try to humbug my pards," Christopher said with a sniff.

Later that evening, the five young soldiers enjoyed a supper of rice and beans seasoned with salt, onions, and greens, a slice of fresh beef from a cow slaughtered just that morning, and plenty of fresh soft bread. Afterward, they stuffed themselves on cake and pie until they could barely move.

Christopher and Ezra had just started a belching contest when Alex Melville walked up waving a Washington City newspaper.

"You boys seen this?" he asked.

"Do tell, Alex," Daniel said.

"Yes, please. Anything to shut these two up," Parker said, pointing at the two giggling, belching boys.

Alex squatted down and passed the paper to Daniel. As he did, his eyes lit on a half-eaten cherry pie. Charlie noticed, cut off a piece, and scraped it into Alex's outstretched hand.

"Lee's invaded Maryland," Alex said as he shoveled pie into his mouth.

Despite their full bellies, everyone sat up straight. Daniel quickly scanned the newspaper article. "He crossed the Potomac at someplace called the Point of Rocks," he said. "Anyone know where that is?"

"Up around Harpers Ferry," Alex said.

"That puts him north of us," Charlie said. "We'll be marching out soon for sure."

"So now, instead of chasing Jackson around Virginia, we will be chasing Lee around Maryland," Daniel said.

"Maybe," Parker said. "But if we can catch Lee and lick him up here, there won't be anything standing between us and Richmond. We could be home by Christmas."

"Wouldn't that be something," Christopher said with a sigh. Then he belched again.

"We had better divide up our spoils in case we have to march out quick," Charlie said. "Alex, you want another piece?"

"Thank ya, Charlie," Alex said, holding out a red-stained hand. After standing, he wrapped the pie in a piece of cloth and stuck it in his haversack. "You boys take care. I'll be seeing you on the march."

The boys thanked Alex for the information.

"See you, Ish—" Christopher began.

Alex pointed a finger at him. "Don't say it."

"Ishmeel!" Ezra screeched, spitting crumbs.

"It's Ishmael, you ignoramus, and don't call me that," Alex said and stalked off.

Daniel shook his head. "You two just can't leave well enough alone, can you?"

—⁂—

The next day, Second Corps marched to Rockville, Maryland, where McClellan had his headquarters. Almost the entire Army of the Potomac was at Rockville, and the camp spread out for miles in all directions. It looked even bigger than the camp in Harrison's Landing.

The army went on the march in search of Lee, covering only about five miles a day. Daniel hoped the slow pace would allow their baggage to catch up to them. The gray-backs were so bad, the constant itching and rashes had become unbearable. And the smell! The men couldn't stand their own odor, let alone anyone else's.

Western Maryland was beautiful country. Patchwork fields of corn and barley interspersed with fields of clover, surrounded by rolling hills covered with hardwood forests. Daniel thought of the carnage around Manassas and hated to think of the same thing happening here.

On the tenth of September, they camped near Clarksburg, MD, where the baggage train finally found them. Daniel ran for the wagons and found himself in a mad crush of men trying to claim their belongings. As the crowd approached, a provost detail appeared and surrounded the wagons, their rifles held at the ready position, bayonets fixed.

Daniel saw Jonathon, the wagon master for the 8th, climb off the lead wagon. He caught Daniel's eye, held his hand out, palm facing the ground, and gently pushed it down. Daniel stopped and put his arms straight out, trying to slow the rush of men surrounding him. "Hold up, boys. We won't get our belongings this way."

"Out of the way, Galloway!" someone cried. "If I have to wear these same clothes another day, I may go insane."

"You sure you aren't already, Billy?" someone else responded.

The provost sergeant stepped forward and addressed the crowd. "You boys line up right here. We keep this orderly, you'll have your belongings in no time."

There was a lot of grumbling in answer, but no one seemed eager to take on a squad with fixed bayonets pointed at them. Several in the crowd, like Daniel, tried to calm their comrades.

Next to Daniel stood Will Mountain. Born in Ireland, Will was a real "son of the sod," and he fascinated Daniel with his stories of the old country. But, Will had come to America at a very early age, and Daniel wasn't sure how much of his stories were actual memories and how much were imaginative embellishments.

Will was also trying to establish order, and between them and several corporals and sergeants, they soon had Company D calmed down and lined up. Jonathon rewarded them by having their knapsacks unloaded first. It also helped that Jonathon was a Norwalk man and not afraid to show a little favoritism with the boys from his home town.

Given the slow pace of the army's movements, the boys had plenty of time to change and clean the clothes they had been wearing for the past several weeks. The feeling of clean clothes was glorious on Daniel's skin, and he'd rid himself of most of the lice that had been tormenting him—at least for a little while.

Daniel felt pretty good the next day. The army stopped and made camp after only marching three miles. His clothes were clean, his feet didn't hurt, and he still felt fat and satisfied after all the good eats they'd enjoyed around Washington City. Then, before they got a fire going, the 8th's musician sounded out the call to assembly. Once lined up, Captain Reid (promoted after Captain Daggett resigned during the Peninsula campaign) stepped forward and addressed the company.

"Boys, there is a large rebel cavalry force blocking the road before us. The 8th has been ordered to run them off."

"Shouldn't be hard—they're cavalry," someone sniped.

Captain Reid gave a small smile, though he tried to hide it. "That they are. But their bullets kill just as readily as anyone else's.

"Once outside camp, Company D, along with B, will go ahead as skirmishers. I need not say this, but I expect you boys to comport yourselves bravely and professionally. But try to stay alive." He turned to Sergeant Howe and nodded. "First Sergeant."

Sergeant Howe stepped forward and turned on the men. "All right, maggots! Listen up!" He quickly ran through roll call and inspection and had the men marching within a half hour.

The road passed through a patch of woods, and the skirmish lines soon found themselves in trees and undergrowth that had not yet shed any of its fall foliage. Daniel could only see glimpses of his skirmish partner, Alex Melville, through the trees, though they were only five paces apart. By now, everyone knew to use the trees and underbrush for cover and move as slowly and quietly as possible.

As they stepped out of the woods, they saw a large, stately home surrounded by several outbuildings across a recently harvested field. With the clear view in front of them and the sounds of the rest of the regiment coming up behind, they moved a little quicker through the field. Once they reached the buildings, they slowed down again. They used the buildings as cover and hopscotched forward until they reached a road on the other side of the property.

There, they halted, and everyone took a knee, staring intently into the trees on the other side of the road, looking for signs of the enemy. When the rest of the regiment came up, the skirmishers deployed as pickets on the edge of the property. The whole regiment maintained a battle line and rested on arms.

After a couple hours of inactivity, Daniel decided the whole exercise had been a waste of time. The cavalry force, if they had existed at all, were long gone.

From his position on the picket line, he could see the whole regiment, still deployed in battle line, just outside the perimeter of the house and surrounding buildings. Most of the men sat at their place on the line, resting or playing cards, their rifles next to them on the ground, breech side up.

A shrill bugle call brought everyone to attention. As Daniel watched, a big bug—a really big bug—came riding up with his staff. Daniel recognized General French, commander of Third Division, Second Corps, to which the 8th had been assigned. As General French dismounted, Colonel Sawyer and Major Winslow approached and saluted. The men stood and chatted for a few minutes, then climbed the stairs onto the front porch of the large farmhouse.

Before anyone could knock, the front door opened and everyone entered the house, leaving French's staff outside with the horses. The 8th's company officers descended on French's staff, looking for news.

Daniel returned to watching for an enemy he was now sure had never existed. After a couple hours inside, General French left, and the 8th stayed and made camp where they were. As the sun set, Company C relieved Company D of picket duty, and Daniel was able to sleep through the night.

—◊—

The 8th rejoined its division and continued its snail-like pace across the Maryland countryside. They reached Frederick, MD on September thirteenth. The town had been occupied by Lee's army, and Burnside's Ninth Corps had just retaken it.

As they marched into Frederick, the townspeople cheered them as conquering heroes. Daniel couldn't recall such an outpouring of support and appreciation since their train ride through Ohio on the way to western Virginia over a year ago. American flags lined the main road and red, white, and blue bunting adorned all the buildings. The men of the town removed their hats as the soldiers marched past, and the women waved their handkerchiefs and smiled merrily at the men.

On the other side of town, Second Corps struck camp. After dinner, the 8th was assigned picket duty for their corps for the evening. Daniel didn't mind—his belly was full, he felt rested, and he was proud of what they were doing.

The next morning, the sound of cannon fire was their call to reveille. Daniel rubbed the sleep out of his eyes and looked out the end of the dog tent he shared with Christopher. The eastern sky was awash with reds and yellows, but the sun hadn't yet crested the horizon.

Both he and Christopher had been up late on picket. Daniel's eyes burned, and his head felt like it was stuffed with cotton. He lay back down and draped his arm over his eyes. The battle sounds intensified, and soon the popping of rifle fire joined the deep-throated boom of the cannons.

Daniel knew that as tired as he was, he would not get back to sleep. He looked over at his brother, but all he could see in the dim light was his outline. He knew by Christopher's steady, deep breathing and occasional snores that he was still asleep. How, he didn't know.

Daniel rolled over to rise, careful not to wake Christopher. His brother had gotten so few peaceful nights of rest lately, he didn't want to cut short this one. He was halfway out the tent when the bugle call for assembly cut through the sounds of battle. Daniel reached out and shook his brother's leg.

"Come on, Chris. It's time to rise."

Christopher didn't respond, so Daniel shook his leg a little harder.

Christopher sat up and threw his hands around Daniel's throat. Daniel managed a squeak of surprise before Christopher's fingers closed off his airway. His brother's eyes were wide open, but unfocused.

Daniel pulled on Christopher's arms, but they were like iron. He got his feet under him and pushed off, out the tent and onto his back, pulling

Christopher with him.

Then Christopher screamed, "You can't have 'em! You can't have 'em!"

Daniel was getting no air and nearing panic. He slapped his brother as hard as he could.

Christopher let go and fell back. His eyes were still wide, but now focused. He looked around, scared and confused.

Daniel sucked in air and coughed. He reached out and put his hand on Christopher's shoulder.

"You were dreaming, little brother. What about?"

Christopher shook his head. "I thought you were Sp—" He looked away. "Nothing. I don't remember. How did I get out here?"

Daniel heard running feet. Ezra, Parker, and Charlie came up beside them.

"Good Lord, you boys need to save some of that for the rebs," Parker said.

Ezra and Charlie looked on nervously, their eyes boring into Daniel.

Daniel waved his hand. "It wasn't nothing. I startled Christopher is all."

"Well, you better get up. We got roll call," Parker responded and walked away.

Ezra and Charlie helped the brothers to stand.

"This isn't over," Daniel said to Christopher. "After this campaign, you and me are going to sit down and discuss what's going on with these dreams and bursts of anger."

Company D lined up in front of their rifle stacks. Captain Reid addressed the men.

"Burnside has once again engaged the enemy. You need to eat and break camp as quick as you can. Leave the tents and your knapsacks for the quartermaster. We will be under light marching orders and trying to make good time. If we're plucky enough, we may arrive at our destination in time to take part in the battle this time!"

If Captain Reid had been hoping to rouse the men, he was disappointed. They gave him a halfhearted "huzzah" accompanied by several yawns. The men tried their best to keep a disciplined demeanor, but the short night's rest left them listless and grumpy.

After breakfast, they lined up, and Captain Reid addressed his men again. "That, boys," he said, pointing to a high mountain ridge in the distance, "is our destination. That line of hills is the Catoctin range, and we're headed to the other side. I hope you all had a good breakfast because we're in for a helluva march."

Second Corps marched out by regiment across the field to the right of the pike they'd been following. When they reached the hills, they had to funnel their line of march down to columns of four, then two as the woods got thicker and the ground steeper. Soon, they were marching single file up a steep incline on a narrow, rocky road cut into the hillside in a zigzag pattern, their line stretched out all the way to the valley floor.

Only halfway up the hill, Daniel gave thanks to the person who had called for light marching order. His thighs were on fire, his rifle growing heavier with each step, and he couldn't catch his breath. Despite the cool shade of the woods they passed through, he had already sweated through his shirt and jacket and drank half the water in his canteen.

His legs were getting heavy, and he was starting to stumble when a patch of blue sky among the trees ahead told him the summit was near. He pushed on and soon stepped out onto a large, open plateau with a stunning view of the valley before them and the hills and mountains beyond.

At the top of the summit, Second Corps's commanding general, Major General Sumner, looking like someone's grumpy grandfather with his white hair and beard and angry scowl, sat atop his horse, cursing under his breath and ordering the boys to close up.

Daniel hurried to where the 8th was reforming. He took a last look back and saw a long line of infantry still stretching back down the hill. After that, the artillery would have to come up. Daniel didn't know how they'd be able to pull those heavy cannons up that steep hill.

As the 8th fell out to rest, Daniel and Christopher, along with several others, went forward to get a view of the battle.

A Ninth Corps battery was on the valley floor, firing as fast as their crews could load. Around them stood their support infantry, lined up in battle formation across the valley floor, their colors flying out on a wind created by the battle itself. They all seemed impervious to the incoming shells that were exploding in the air above their heads. On the ridge before them was another cloud of white smoke, continually refreshed by the explosions of enemy artillery fire.

As Daniel watched the battle, he realized that, except for a rumbling that seemed to roll off the hills, there wasn't any noise. All morning long, they'd marched toward the sound of cannon fire as if it were pulling them forward. Now, at the summit of the ridge within full view of the battle, there was no sound.

He froze in place and listened. There was the rhythmic tramp of marching feet, accompanied by curses and calls of encouragement as the troops continued coming up the hill. Behind that, a steady breeze produced an almost imperceptible whistle as it blew through the trees. And the trees themselves creaked as they swayed, their leaves rustling like whispers. Beneath it all was the steady rumble that, to Daniel's fervent imagination, now sounded like angry mumbling.

But from the valley floor—nothing. Silence.

"Do you hear that?" he asked Christopher.

Christopher listened and shrugged. "The marching?"

"Anything else?"

Christopher shrugged again and frowned. "I don't hear nothing. What are you getting at?"

Daniel pointed to the artillery firing non-stop on the valley floor. "What about that?"

Christopher looked down at the valley floor for a minute, then his eyes widened. "What? Why?"

"I don't know," Daniel said.

They both stood mesmerized by the phenomena, leaning forward, their mouths agape.

Daniel thought the battle looked like a moving painting—the images in constant motion but with no accompanying sound.

As they watched, more batteries came up the valley floor at a gallop, moved into position, and added their smoke and fire to the tableau. Behind them, more infantry appeared, carpeting the valley floor in blue. In the trees, along the opposite ridge, lines of soldiers appeared and disappeared as they moved through the woods. Occasionally, a cloud of smoke would rise from the trees to tell them that the enemy had been engaged. Throughout it all, silence.

Bugles and drums sounded, accompanied by calls to line up.

Daniel and Christopher looked at each other and shrugged. They left the view and mysterious silence behind as they joined the ranks and moved out.

They followed the ridgeline for the next couple hours. As they marched, the ridge grew wider and the trees fewer, until it became wide enough for them to shift into battle lines by brigade. Skirmish lines were sent forward, and they continued on, ready to engage the enemy.

The wider ridgeline prevented the men from being able to see the battle, but the sound returned with a vengeance. Even from a distance, it hurt the ears. Daniel didn't think he'd ever heard anything like it, not even at Kernstown. The cannons blasted non-stop, accompanied by the staccato rattle of rifle fire. Once, there was a large explosion, and the screams of men and horses pierced the roar of battle.

Instead of descending into the valley and entering the battle, Second Corps stopped on the ridge and went into camp the rest of the day. Then they moved down into the valley as the sun set and the sounds of the battle died away.

"Why we rushed all this way, if we weren't going to fight, is beyond me," Daniel mumbled to Parker as they made their way down into the valley.

"I guess we was reserve," Parker said. "And they didn't need us."

Though the sun still hadn't set, the valley floor was already dark from the long shadows cast by the surrounding mountains. They marched across the valley to the other side before stopping to make camp. The grass they walked over was wet with dew and blood, the ground covered with the debris of battle.

The grass before the cannon had been burned away and the earth blackened. A cannon sat broken and askew, its barrel pointing up to the sky. Next to it lay a headless corpse. Pieces of wood and iron lay strewn about, mixed with unidentifiable pieces of gore.

There were other bodies scattered across the ground, some still alive, their moans eerie and ethereal in the fading light. Many were mangled, like the poor artilleryman next to his broken cannon. There were severed arms and legs and torsos split in two, the halves separated by yards of reddish black goo.

Nor had the horses been spared. Their bloated bodies, torn open and dismembered, lay scattered behind the former battery line.

The air smelled of gunpowder and blood, mingled with the stench of dead flesh and burst intestines. Several men had to fall out and empty their stomachs before they could continue.

Amid this carnage, they made camp. The first few brigades at the front of the marching order managed to find clean places to make camp under the trees along the edge of the valley. But, as those places filled up, the less fortunate found themselves having to clear away dead bodies and cast off equipment to make a place to rest. Daniel looked around, listening to the cries of the wounded and the steady traffic of the ambulances and wondered if an army could be any more cruel and indifferent.

It was a long, sleepless night for Daniel and most of the men of Second Corps. The moans of the wounded continued unabated until almost dawn, by which time most had either died or been carried off the field. Many screamed in agony as they were lifted into the back of wagons, their screams continuing as the wagons bounced over rocks and ruts on their way to the field hospital.

—⁂—

The next day, Second Corps's First Division, under Brigadier General Richardson, marched out in pursuit of the enemy. Second Division and Third Division (which now included Kimball's brigade) stayed back in reserve.

The macabre post-battle activities continued throughout the day. Gangs of escaped slaves, called contraband by the army, roamed the field, collecting the dead. The soldiers ignored the whole process as much as possible, afraid of being jinxed. That mangled corpse being tossed into a wagon could be any of them before the day was out.

If the Lord saw fit to see him killed or injured in battle, Daniel hoped that it was the former. The only thing more terrifying than the thought of bleeding out on a field alone, dying after hours of agony, was being sent to a field hospital to have a limb cut off and dying anyway after days or weeks of agony from infection. Or to live the rest of his days a disfigured cripple.

Then he looked at Christopher. How could he have been so ignorant as to promise Da he would protect Christopher? A person had no control over their own fate in this slaughter, let alone anyone else's.

Word came that afternoon that Richardson had routed the rebels at Boonsboro, and they were falling back toward Sharpsburg. The rest of Second Corps moved out to join him.

As Daniel stepped out away from the battlefield, he let out a sigh of relief. The constant reminder of his mortality had him on edge and, though he'd grown used to the sight of dead bodies, the smell was becoming unbearable.

The enemy was in full retreat by the time Second and Third Divisions joined the First outside Boonsboro. As the three divisions came together and advanced, they took harassing fire from the enemy rear guard, but it was nothing more than light skirmishing.

By the time they stopped to make camp, just past Keedysville, Daniel was feeling more relaxed. It was turning out like almost every other campaign in which he'd taken part. They would engage in a few skirmishes with the rear guard while they chased the rebels back to Virginia, and that would be that for this campaign.

That night, they slept on their arms, but for Daniel, confident that there would not be a major battle, it was a deep, restful sleep.

—⋙—

The next morning, cannon fire was again Daniel's wake-up call. This time, they were the target. Daniel opened his eyes as a shell exploded just a few yards away. He covered his face with his arm and cried out as dirt and debris rained down around him and Christopher.

Christopher rolled over and came up on his hands and knees. "What in the devil was that!" he cried, shaking his head.

"That would be Bobby Lee's way of telling us we're not welcome," Daniel said, trying to sound lighthearted. At least Christopher hadn't tried to strangle him.

Shells and solid shot now rained down upon them. The shells were more dangerous as they scattered chunks of hot iron when they exploded. But there was something unnerving about the large cannonballs that shrieked and roared like a speeding freight train as they passed, destroying anything in their path.

Despite the incoming cannonade, nature had its demands, and Daniel got up to go to the edge of the camp to relieve himself. As he made his way toward a slit trench dug the night before, he saw Bill Farmer standing guard by the regimental colors. Farmer had just been promoted to corporal and assigned to the color guard. He looked proud of his new assignment and his responsibility in guarding the regimental flags. Farmer was older than most of the boys, with a wife and two children back home. That made Daniel think of Elijah Rust, and he said a quick prayer for Farmer's safety.

As Daniel passed the colors, he made a quick salute to the flag and nodded to Farmer. He'd only gone a few feet when he heard the loud shrieking rumble of an incoming cannonball. A vibration rolled up through the bottom of Daniel's feet as the ball ricocheted off the ground. He spun around, head darting back and forth, and spotted the ball barreling through camp at waist height. Men were running and throwing themselves to the ground along its path.

Bill Farmer, also startled by the closeness of the incoming projectile, swiveled his head around while trying to maintain his stance. He didn't see the ball until it was too late. Daniel saw Farmer's face contort in horror, then pain as the cannonball hit him below his rib cage, tearing his body in two. The ball kept going without slowing down, and the two parts of Bill Farmer flew end over end, spurting blood and gore in two large arcs, finally coming to rest twenty feet from each other.

Daniel stood, frozen in shock. A small amount of bile came up from his empty stomach, burning the back of his throat, and he gagged.

Daniel shook and gagged for almost a minute before he was able to relax enough to think. He turned to continue on to the sinks, took two steps, and stopped. He no longer needed to go. Daniel looked down and saw a wet patch on the front his pants. He felt the warm urine dripping down the inside of his leg. "Not again," he quietly moaned. He looked around to see if anyone was watching, the incoming shells and cannonballs momentarily forgotten.

Daniel headed back to their campsite, the image of Farmer's mangled body spinning through the air playing over and over in his head. He was halfway there when he was suddenly overcome with emotion and collapsed to his knees. He put his hands on his thighs and leaned forward, squeezing his eyes shut in an effort to hold back the tears that threatened to overwhelm him. *This isn't war*, he thought. *This is hell.*

CHAPTER TWENTY-FOUR
ANTIETAM

Despite the heavy shelling, Christopher tried to go back to sleep. He figured he was as safe as he could get already. If a shell were to land right on top of him, he couldn't do anything about it anyway. Instead of relaxing though, his body remained tense, locked in a fetal position. A tremor caused his right index finger to steadily tap the ground. Then, his forced nonchalance was shattered as a cannonball ricocheted off the ground only a few feet from where he lay, showering him with dirt and debris.

Christopher scrambled to his feet, shaking the dirt off his clothes. When he stopped, he was trembling. "Jesus, Mary, and Joseph..." he said, unconsciously mimicking his father.

Christopher looked around. There was a commotion going on over by the colors. Other than that, everyone went about their regular morning routines. The officers were talking—always talking—amongst themselves, the enlisted men were hunched over cook fires, cleaning weapons, or going to and from the sinks. There didn't seem to be any urgency to move out soon.

Christopher sighed, made two fists, and squeezed his hands tight until the trembling stopped. Then he figured, since they weren't going anywhere, it was time to find the rest of his messmates and get breakfast going.

As Christopher dug up the sod with his bayonet to make a fire pit,

Daniel walked up and sat down.

"You could help with some firewood, ya know," Christopher said, not looking up from his task.

"Not right now," Daniel replied.

Christopher looked up. "What's the matter? Ain't you hungry?"

Daniel's face was pale, and he was sweating. His head hung down, but Christopher could see his eyes darting back and forth.

"What is it? You look like you've seen a ghost."

"Did you see what happened to Bill Farmer?" Daniel asked, not looking up.

"What happened?" Christopher thought of the shelling still going on around them.

"Damn cannonball cut him in half." Daniel spat the words with a hatred bolstered by fear.

"Good Lord. You mean…all the way through?"

Daniel nodded.

A volley from a Union battery, deployed on the ridge next to the camp, drowned out the sound as Ezra walked up and deposited an armload of firewood by the half-finished pit. As the wood clattered beside him, Christopher jumped back and landed on his rump. Daniel had seen Ezra at the last minute, but still flinched at the sound.

"Dammit, Ezra! What are you doing sneaking up on a body like that?"

Ezra looked at Christopher in confusion and said, "I ain't sneaking."

"Well, I didn't fall on my ass for the fun of it," Christopher replied as he returned to his digging. "Is someone going to help me here or not!"

Daniel retrieved his bayonet and started to dig. Christopher noticed the wet spot on the front of his brother's pants but didn't say anything.

—ↀↀↀ—

Soon, they moved to a low swale that offered more protection from the incoming ordinance and stayed there for the rest of the day. The Federal artillery never silenced the Confederate artillery, but it drew their fire, and for that Christopher was thankful.

At dusk, both sides started an artillery duel that seemed to include every cannon in both armies. The blasts filled the darkening sky with pulsing flashes of light that lit up the surrounding hills and trees like daylight. The five messmates, Daniel, Christopher, Ezra, Parker, and Charlie, climbed to the top of a ridge and lay down on their bellies to watch the show. From their new vantage point, they saw the line of fire stretching out for miles on either side as the two armies exchanged volley after volley.

Christopher lay his hand flat on the ground and felt it tremble. A shiver of excitement and fear coursed through him at the cannons' destructive power.

"You know what this makes me think of?" he said loudly so he could be heard over the noise.

Daniel shook his head.

"That song, 'Star Spangled Banner.'"

Daniel cocked his head and looked at the explosions lighting the night sky. Christopher could practically see the song playing in his head.

"They're not rockets, but I see your point," Daniel said.

They continued to watch the artillery duel in silence.

Christopher thought of the song, and what it meant about the country's survival. Then he considered the possibility of a big battle looming before them, and a feeling of acceptance and contentment overcame him. He'd seen plenty of death over the last year, some of it by his hand, but he'd not done his part. He'd wasted his time drinking and skirting his duties, and it had gotten him captured. Four months in a Confederate prison and a lot of minor skirmishing, but what had he done? What could he look back on and say, I did my part to end the war and save the country? He'd missed the only real battle the regiment had taken part in. It was time.

It looked like there would be a big battle here, maybe even bigger than Bull Run or Shiloh. The entire Army of the Potomac against the entire Army of Northern Virginia. And the 8th would be a part of it.

But, underlying all that eagerness lay a fear that sapped his strength and made his stomach churn. So much skirmishing had made him almost indifferent to flying bullets and exploding shells. But this would be different. If the numbers out of Shiloh were any indication, they wouldn't come away with a handful of casualties—more likely hundreds. The whole regiment could be wiped out.

"There'll be a battle tomorrow," he said to Daniel.

Daniel shrugged. "Maybe. More likely Lee will skedaddle in the night and leave us looking like fools again."

Chris shook his head. "I think there'll be a battle. A big one. And this time we won't be in reserve, or come up after the fighting's done. This time we'll be in it."

Daniel shook his head. "I don't know. Could be. I stopped trying to figure out what will happen next awhile ago."

"I hope I don't let the boys down," Christopher said.

Daniel bowed his head. His response was lost in the sound of explosions.

"Come on, boys," Parker said, rising to a crouch and moving down the ridge. "The morning'll come early, and we have a big day ahead of us. We need to get some sleep."

One by one, they left the ridge and started back. Christopher was last. He took one last look at the explosions still covering the landscape and thought, *I hope the star spangled banner is waving in triumph tomorrow night. And we're there to see it.*

—✦—

Sometime after midnight, a light rain started to fall. Few men had tents, so they huddled around sputtering fires, trying to stay warm.

Reveille came at 3:00 AM. Not that anyone was sleeping. Christopher wasn't, and he was sure few others were—given the speed at which the company assembled. As ammunition was being distributed, Captain Reid addressed the company.

"Boys, we will be in reserve to the initial attacking force."

Some responded with groans of dissatisfaction, but they seemed half hearted to Christopher.

"That don't mean we won't get a chance to fight though. It just means we'll be a little late to the ball is all."

"Well, I hope it ain't over before they throw us in. I'm tired of being the too-late regiment. Too late for the Peninsula, too late for Bull Run, now too late for wherever this is."

Christopher looked around, but he didn't see who'd spoken.

Captain Reid scowled at the interruption, but chose not to address it directly. "The rebs seem pretty well dug in over there by Sharpsburg, so I don't think they'll budge until McClellan's given them everything he's got—including us."

Before anyone else could grouse, Reid ordered an inspection, then dismissed the company to get something to eat. "It might be the only meal you get today," he said just before First Sergeant Howe called the dismissal.

Christopher soaked a piece of hardtack in coffee and nibbled on it but had no appetite for anything more. His stomach churned, and he was suddenly overcome with a melancholy that forced tears to his eyes. He was so tired. He missed his home, and his bed, and his parents. As he nibbled his hardtack and contemplated crying, the light rain turned to a steady downpour.

At sunrise, the rain stopped, and the artillery began.

"Good Lord, don't those boys ever shut up," Ezra said.

"At least they aren't aimed at us this time," Daniel said.

As Christopher listened, he heard the rattle of rifle fire between the deeper booming sounds of the cannons.

"Sounds like infantry already engaged," he said.

Daniel turned his head to listen, then nodded. "Maybe the captain was right. We'll be in the fight before the day is through."

Not long after the sounds of battle began, the Second Division moved out, back down the road toward Keedysville.

"That didn't take long," Daniel said. "I bet we're next."

Watching the soldiers of the other division move out, Christopher needed to run to the sinks, but before he could, the long roll commenced, calling the Third Division to fall in. Christopher's stomach churned, and he thought he would throw up. His legs were like rubber, but he stood and lurched toward the assembly area.

They lined up and fell in behind Second Division.

Before reaching Keedysville, the column turned left and cut across country toward a large creek. There they marched down a short but steep bluff and into the water.

A bottleneck formed at the top of the bluff, caused by the men having to slow down to navigate the steep bank and deep, fast-running water. From that higher position, the men got their first glimpse of the battle they were about to join. Soon a crowd formed as men pushed their way forward to look.

When Christopher reached the top of the bluff, he saw a swath of farmland, covered with a patchwork of corn and clover. There were farmhouses and outbuildings scattered around, their barnyards full of hay, but thankfully, no farm animals. A rebel battery was set up in a field beyond a farmstead that lay just before them. It had tried to fire on the men gathered at the top of the bluff, but a fierce response from a Union battery on the outskirts of the woods to their right forced it into a duel. Already, several of the hay mounds and outbuildings were burning, and dead and dying men lay scattered about the fields.

As he dropped back down the bluff, Christopher lost sight of the battle. The creek was running high because of the rain, so it came up to about waist height on most of the men. Christopher had to remove all his traps and hold them over his head along with his rifle.

As the water reached his belly, he remembered their crossing of the Potomac the year before on their first attempt to take Romney. That crossing had been a lark, the men laughing and splashing one another, boasting of what they would do when they met the enemy. This crossing, the men remained silent and reserved. If anyone talked, it was to complain.

Many complained because they didn't pause on the far bank for the men to change their socks. They marched up the other side, their shoes making squishing, squeaky noises as they walked. The sound of thousands of squeaking shoes, punctuated by the creak of leather and the rattle of bayonets, canteens and rifles, pierced Christopher's melancholy and started to irritate him. After a while, the noise seemed to drown out the battle sounds.

As the battle sounds fell away, Christopher forgot about where he was going and became fixated on where he was. The trees they passed through seemed to be leaning right over his head, blotting out the sky and threatening to fall and crush him. A hint of fall colors sprinkled the leaves, and he marveled at their vibrancy. He looked at the strap crossing the back of the man in front of him and was sure he could see every dimple and imperfection in the leather, no matter how small.

Then the world came crashing back as Christopher stepped out of the trees. Cannons roared, men shouted, horses whinnied in fright, and caissons and cannons rattled as they raced into position. Second Division had formed into battle lines and was moving out straight across the fields toward a small building in the distance. Already men were dropping from enemy artillery fire. Soon they would be in range of the gray-clad infantry lined up on a road in the distance.

Third Division veered left and formed battle lines by brigade. Christopher was relieved when he realized Kimball's brigade was last. Maybe the first two brigades would take most of the fighting and they would just finish the task on an already weakened opponent. As soon as the thought crossed his mind, he felt ashamed. Who was he to ask others to do what he wasn't willing to do himself?

As the battle lines moved through a tree lot, they came under intense artillery fire. Christopher watched as huge limbs, shattered by exploding shells, fell on the heads of the soldiers in front of him. First Brigade, in front, wavered and stalled. Officers rode up and down behind their men, shouting encouragement. Even General French himself came riding up, yelling encouragement and threats in equal measure.

A captain Christopher didn't recognize rode by and shouted, "If any of those men turn tail and run, you shoot them, by God!" Then he rode off. Christopher noted he wasn't heading toward the front.

As Christopher exited the tree lot, he saw a farm ahead. First Brigade was exchanging fire with rebel soldiers ensconced in some outbuildings. As Second Brigade came up, the enemy soldiers spilled out of the buildings and ran.

The battle lines continued on. As they moved through an apple orchard, many of the soldiers plucked apples from the trees as they passed.

Christopher felt emboldened by the sight. If it would be that easy, this wouldn't be so bad. He looked down the line and caught Daniel's eye. He smiled and nodded ahead as they approached the farm buildings. Daniel nodded in return, but he didn't smile.

The men ahead began smashing down fences. A group ran up to a fence, smashed it with their rifle butts, then began flailing their arms and dancing about. Knowing they were green troops, Christopher feared that they'd mistaken the sound of passing minié balls for bees. Then he saw several overturned honeybee houses on the other side of the fence and laughed. They really were bees.

A group of soldiers ran past them on the right, going the other direction. They ran as fast as they could, mouths hanging open, their eyes wide and unfocused. Some were splattered with blood. Many no longer had their rifles. Whoever they were, they were done for the day.

Christopher looked to his left and wondered how the new regiment would do. The 4th Ohio was convalescing from an illness that had laid low most of the regiment. It had been replaced by the 132nd Pennsylvania, who had never been in so much as a skirmish. Christopher watched as several soldiers from the 132nd fell back, dropped to their knees in the corn, and vomited.

Christopher shook his head. *Worthless*, he thought. The 8th would just have to carry them through.

The tremendous roar of a volley fired by a large force thundered somewhere ahead. *First Brigade must have found the enemy*, Christopher thought.

Christopher watched a huge whitish-gray cloud of gun smoke rise up into the sky before them. Its size gave him chills. Just how big a force was it?

No matter; by the time the first two brigades were done with them, there would be a lot less.

Second Brigade stopped right before them. Though visibility was limited, at least one regiment fired a volley into the smoke. Afterward, panic-stricken men in blue uniforms ran out of the smoke and into their lines.

A moment of panic seized Christopher as the whole line started to break apart. The file closers came up, their rifles held horizontal before them, and pushed the men back into line. Officers rode back and forth, screaming at the men and threatening to strike them with their sabers.

Eventually, the officers and file closers restored order, and the line reformed and moved forward.

Second Brigade had resumed their march.

Christopher recognized many of the men coming out of the smoke ahead and wondered, *Had First Brigade broken already? How bad was it?* Of course, being shot at from behind couldn't have helped.

He looked down the line again to Daniel, this time seeking encouragement, not offering it.

Daniel didn't respond. His vision was fixed straight ahead.

The rifle fire before them intensified. Second Brigade had come up beside what remained of First Brigade, and both were now engaged with an enemy Christopher had not yet seen.

Other brigade-size forces were coming from somewhere on their left. At a point on the field, it was as if they hit an invisible barrier. Their lines stopped and broke apart, some men falling, some running, many standing to fight.

There seemed no coherence to the action at all. The larger groups broke down into smaller units, regiments, or even companies—the men seeking solace amongst those they knew. Some men dropped to the ground and fired from a prone position; others stood upright and went through the motions of loading and firing as if they were at drill. Many were clerks or students before the war. For them it was the only way they knew how to fire a gun.

Most disturbing though, was the rate at which men were dropping and not moving. They weren't just dropping in ones or twos—dozens were going down at a time. Many times, those still standing would turn and run.

By this time the forward motion of the 8th and Third Brigade had slowed to a crawl, the men continuing forward, but with short, slow steps, as if fighting a powerful wind.

The sight of the carnage and chaos before them had everyone rattled, even the officers. General Kimball rode up before them, raised up in his saddle, and pointed his saber toward the front. "Now, boys!" he yelled. "We're going, and we'll stay with them all day if they want us to!"

The men gave a halfhearted huzzah and, at the order, brought their rifles up to their right shoulders. They attempted to overcome their fear and move out at the quick step. The line wavered and buckled as some men moved faster than others. They all assumed they were running to their deaths, and some were less anxious to get there than others.

No one was trying to keep the line straight any longer.

The green troops in the 132nd on the 8th's left still had fences to contend with and managed to turn over the remaining honeybee houses. Their officers and file closers had their hands full trying to rally the soldiers as they scattered to avoid the bees. Soon, they were back in line and running to catch up with the rest of the brigade.

As the brigade trotted toward the fight, they met large groups of soldiers running the other way, trying to push their way through the lines. The lines fragmented, and the regiments separated. Christopher lost track of the green troops of the 132nd Pennsylvania and all the others they'd marched with the last several months. His world was once again the 8th Ohio. The men he'd marched with, fought with, argued and laughed with, the men who had been his world for most of the last year and a half.

Christopher no longer heard the cannon and rifle fire, he only heard the breathing of those around him; he no longer saw the buildings and the surrounding landscape, he only saw what lay ahead.

And what he saw made his breath hitch and his muscles weaken.

Confederate soldiers lay beyond the ridge line. Mostly hidden, but they were there. Individually, or in groups, they would rise and fire into the approaching Federal soldiers, then drop back down out of sight.

Christopher now heard the buzzing whine of passing minié balls. He felt men in the line falling or dropping back. Sometimes he would hear the wet thud of a ball striking flesh.

With each incoming volley, Christopher hunched down a little more, until he was leaning forward like an old man in the face of a mighty wind.

He couldn't breathe. He would try to suck in air, but it felt as if nothing was happening. Christopher's head seemed to be floating atop his body, and he stumbled over the slightest ripple in the ground. His hands shook, and he feared he would drop his rifle. His sight had contracted until it was like looking down a long tunnel.

The ground before them was littered with dead and wounded. He'd seen worse carnage, even in the field they'd slept in just a couple nights before. But that had been after a whole day of fighting. This was only a few minutes, and already a regiment's worth of men littered the field.

They had come down into the bottom of a swale earlier and now were running up the other side. Most of the bodies lay clustered at the top of the ridgeline they were approaching. As they crested the hill, Christopher had to look down at his feet to avoid stepping on someone.

He looked up and saw, only a few dozen yards ahead, a makeshift fortification of fence posts and planking. It was thrown up along a farm lane, sunken from years of use until it made a natural trench. Behind that fortification crouched thousands of Confederate soldiers. As the 8th stopped and made ready to fire, they rose up as one and fired a volley that shattered the regiment.

—⚊—

The bullets came in so thick, it was like an invisible hand slapping the regiment the entire length of the line. The buzz of passing minié balls turned to a roar. Men dropped by the dozens.

Christopher cringed and squeezed his eyes shut.

"Hail Mary, full of grace. Our Lord…Our Lord…Hail Mary, full of grace…" Christopher mumbled over and over.

On Christopher's right, the man who stood next to him, and whose shoulder touched his, jerked back his head and then pitched forward as the man behind pushed off the now dead body. Christopher tried to remember his name but couldn't. Later it would come to him. Later, he would remember all their names.

Sergeants were screaming at the men to close ranks. An officer behind them was yelling to take aim. Christopher raised his rifle to his shoulder and pulled the hammer back to full cock. At the command to fire, he pulled the trigger and felt the satisfying punch as the rifle butt pushed into his shoulder.

Christopher didn't wait for the command to reload before reaching into his cartridge box and pulling out another round. He brought the cartridge fold to his mouth and bit off too much paper. Gunpowder filled his mouth, and he tried to spit, but his mouth was dry. The powder had a salty taste and smelled like animal pee. Christopher's nose wrinkled. He tried to spit again before giving up and pouring the remaining powder down the barrel. He hoped it was enough.

As Christopher brought the rifle up to place the percussion cap, he looked around. Officers and sergeants were shuffling men around to fill the vacancies left by falling men, but they couldn't keep up.

A panic-inducing thought almost made him gasp. Christopher leaned forward and looked down the line. There was Daniel, his face and lips blackened by powder, his eyes wild and desperate as he loaded his rifle.

Everyone was firing at will, so Christopher didn't wait. He fired his rifle, noting with satisfaction there was enough powder to expel the bullet, and reloaded. After that, he shut down. The fear and panic, the smell of blood, powder, and excrement—it all drifted away. All that remained was his rifle and rounds, and the tunnel before him, at the end of which lay the hated enemy, killing and maiming his friends.

Christopher continued going through the motions of loading and firing his rifle until someone behind him grabbed his haversack strap and pulled him back off the ridge line.

"Down!" someone yelled in his ear, and Christopher dropped on his belly among the dead and dying. The sight of the enemy in the sunken road before them disappeared behind the crest of the hill.

It was as if someone had lifted an anvil off Christopher's chest. He sucked in a chestful of air and gloried in its richness, full of life-sustaining properties and the scent of grass and clover.

Christopher rolled over onto his back and retrieved another round from his cartridge box. It was a lot harder to load lying down, but it was worth it. After spilling more powder in his mouth, and on the ground, Christopher got the rifle loaded and rolled back over. He tensed to rise and fire, but froze.

Christopher couldn't move. He took a big breath and tried again. Nothing. His brain said move, but his body didn't respond.

He rested his forehead on the ground and stared at the clover before his eyes. He wiggled his fingers and toes. Then, he looked up.

The sky over the sunken lane was a light dirty gray that seemed to swirl around in intricate patterns independent of the morning breeze.

Embarrassed, Christopher looked to either side to see if anyone noticed he'd not shot yet. The sight of Ezra on his left surprised him. He wasn't there a moment ago.

"Howdy, pard!" Ezra said with a huge grin that didn't reach beyond his blackened lips. Ezra rolled onto his side and retrieved a round. As he reloaded, he talked, his words breathless and choppy.

"You know, when I woke up this morning, I said to myself, 'Ezra,' I said, 'Ezra, it feels peculiar hot today,' I did. Little did I know, some secesh general had gone and died and forgot to shut the door to hell behind him as he passed." His grin got wider, but still only on the lips.

"Ha!" Christopher barked out a laugh. Dropping and shaking his head he said, "That wasn't even funny."

"Get it," Ezra said. "Cuz now we got hell spilling out all around us."

Christopher nodded. "I got it. It just wasn't funny."

"Well, you laughed."

"That I did." After a pause, Christopher asked, "So, how do you know it was a secesh general?"

Ezra's smile disappeared. "Cuz all those black bastards are going to hell for what they done."

Ezra rose and fired. Before he dropped back down, there was a tearing sound, and his right jacket sleeve ripped open, spouting blood. The warm liquid spattered Christopher's face.

"Ah, dammit!" Ezra dropped his rifle and rolled over, grasping his right arm with the opposite hand. "We're all gonna die," he said to the sky.

Christopher crawled over. "Here, let me look."

Christopher moved Ezra's hand out of the way and saw a long ragged tear in the jacket sleeve oozing blood. He reached his fingers into the gap and tore open Ezra's shirt and jacket. A long ragged tear in his arm matched the tears in the cloth.

"Doesn't look like it got your bone. So, as long as infection doesn't set in, you won't lose your arm. And it's bleeding, but not spurting, so you probably won't bleed to death. You're lucky, pard. Let me tie a bandana around it and you can head back to the field hospital."

Ezra raised his right arm and wiggled the fingers. He then looked at Christopher. "Tie it off, bub. I ain't goin' anywhere."

"What are you saying? You got a ticket out of this hell. Take it," Christopher said, pointing to his arm.

"You boys need me," Ezra said. "As long as I can stand, I'm standing with my pards."

As he wrapped Ezra's arm, Christopher mumbled, half in jest, "We ain't standing."

Ezra barked a laugh. "That ain't funny."

"No it ain't," Christopher agreed.

Once his wound was tightly bound and the blood flow slowed to a trickle, Ezra finished loading his rifle, rose, and fired again.

Christopher's cheeks burnt with shame. He grabbed his rifle, rose to his knees, and raised the rifle to his shoulder. As he pulled the trigger, a face appeared in his sites, only to disappear in a blast of flame and smoke.

As Christopher dropped back down, Daniel appeared on his right. "You okay, little brother?"

Christopher looked Daniel over for wounds before nodding. "Still alive. You?"

"Peachy."

"Would you look at that," Ezra said.

Christopher looked up at the hilltop. The grass seemed to ripple as if alive. *This truly is hell*, Christopher thought. Now we're plagued with locusts. As he watched, a dark gray sphere came out of the grass and rolled to a stop before them. It was a spent minié ball.

The fighting continued. Shells exploded over their heads. minié balls flew past with such regularity that a steady buzz filled the air. The sun continued to rise, and men continued to fall as the morning went on and on.

The sight of officers riding their horses back and forth behind the lines amazed Christopher. Granted, they made sure not to get too close to the top of the ridge line, but Christopher couldn't imagine how vulnerable they must be alone and up high like that. They made it easy for sharpshooters and artillery, who couldn't resist a man in officer's bars.

The 132nd Pennsylvania on their left had crept back, exposing their left flank. "I knew we couldn't rely on those fresh fish," Christopher said.

Ezra looked over at the number of bodies lying on the ground before the 132nd. "I'd say they've done pretty well for themselves. Helluva way to see the elephant, you ask me."

"And look over there!" Christopher cried, pointing farther down the field to a column of men marching away. "Those boys are leaving already."

"Why don't you focus on the task at hand and quit worrying about everyone else," Daniel said.

"We don't want to get flanked," Christopher said.

"Don't worry, those gray-backs aren't going anywhere."

The Irish Brigade from the First Division marched onto the field and took the place of the regiment that had just left. Christopher's fear turned to wonder as the Irish marched past the previous line and didn't stop until they were within fifty yards of the sunken road. From there, they poured lead into the enemy with their old buck and ball muskets. They paid a terrible price for their audacity though as they began dropping at an alarming rate.

"Crazy Micks," Ezra said. "No offense boys but those Paddies are nuts."

Christopher was trying to seat a minié ball that seemed stuck halfway down the barrel of his rifle when Ezra said, "I'm out."

Christopher and Daniel both looked at him. "What?"

"I'm out of rounds."

Both brothers looked in their cartridge boxes.

"I've got three left," Daniel said.

Christopher didn't want to tell them he still had seven rounds left. "I'm almost out, too," he said. "But I don't know if they'll do me any good anyway, I can't get this one down the barrel."

"My rifle's fouled too," Daniel said. "They need to pull us back."

Christopher looked toward the rear. A steady stream of wounded were making their way to the back, some with help, some stumbling along on their own. There appeared to be a lot of healthy-looking soldiers in the mix. Farther back, to their left, there appeared to be a whole regiment hiding in the trees.

"No one seems too eager to take our place," he said.

"That's the big bugs' problem," Ezra said. "We can't shoot what we don't have."

"The 69th is out here, someone from First Division could take our place," Daniel said.

The fire from the 8th slackened as men took their time reloading and aiming before firing—trying to stretch their remaining ammunition.

Lieutenant Barnes came walking behind the men at a crouch. "If you're running low on ammunition, take it from the dead. Same if your rifle's fouled. Take one that hasn't had much use. There's plenty to be had."

Men down the line rose to their knees and rifled the cartridge boxes of the surrounding corpses. Soon, Ezra, Daniel, and Christopher's boxes were full again. Some boxes they opened were only missing one or two rounds. Those they removed from the corpse and passed the whole box down the line.

All three replaced their fouled rifles with clean 1853 Enfields.

They were loaded and ready to fire when someone yelled, "The lieutenant's down."

Christopher turned his head and saw Lieutenant Barnes on his back, the front of his uniform covered with blood. As he watched, two men dropped their rifles, scooped up the lieutenant, and headed for the rear.

As Christopher turned back around to fire, he saw Will Mountain lying on his side on the other side of Daniel. Will seemed to be staring intently at Daniel, and Christopher opened his mouth to say something when he realized the man was dead. Christopher nudged Daniel and jerked his chin toward the dead man. "No more stories of the old country."

Daniel dropped his head. Christopher thought he was praying, but then he rose, fired, and dropped back down again, reaching for another round. "A lot of good Irishmen dying today," he said.

Christopher took aim and was just starting to apply pressure to the trigger when a white flag appeared behind the enemy breastworks. Then, several more.

"Hallelujah!"

"Praise Jesus, they're surrendering."

Several men stood up on the Federal side and strode down the hill. *Probably thinking of the glory and praise they'll receive for capturing an enemy battle flag,* Christopher thought. They were almost within reach of the enemy works, some with their hands outstretched, reaching for the enemy colors, when the Confederate forces opened fire, mowing them down.

An angry roar rose from the Federal lines, followed by a volley that was so perfectly timed, it was as if they were firing from command instead of from anger. Christopher aimed for a color-bearer who had dangled his flag out before one of the men they had lured out.

He estimated they had been on the field for several hours and marveled at his change in disposition during that time. At first, he'd been paralyzed with fear. Now everything seemed so casual, as if they were out shooting ducks instead of men. Fighting had just become a repetitious task: load, rise up, shoot, drop down, repeat…

Then he had a disturbing thought: maybe he wasn't afraid because he was dead already. Maybe this was his penance—spending eternity shooting and killing. He cast a sidelong glance at Ezra. He knew he should not have done all that drinking. Now he would pay the price for his sins.

He looked up in the sky. The sun was high, almost straight above them. It was only about noon. They first came on the field at about nine. That would mean they would have been on the line by nine thirty or ten. They'd been on the field for at least two hours. How many men had died or been maimed in that time?

Regiments had come up and then retreated all around them, but the 8th and its sister regiments in Kimball's brigade stayed. Christopher saw that the 132nd was still in the fight. They had also replenished their ammunition. Ezra was right—for fresh fish, they were good soldiers.

What remained of the Irish Brigade marched off the field. They now looked like a small regiment instead of a whole brigade. Other New Yorkers from the First Division came forward and took their place. Just not as close.

Even most of the regiment that had been hiding in the trees had finally come forward.

The 8th was positioned at a bend in the sunken road. From there, Christopher could see the entire length of the Federal battle line, and it looked like it was now long enough to envelope the enemy on their right. An artillery battery had set up on a road at the left end of the Federal line and was pouring canister shot into the Confederates from a position that allowed them to sweep the lane at an angle. As he looked down at the dead piling up behind the makeshift breastworks, Christopher almost felt sorry for them.

Re-enforcements for the enemy appeared, marching across the cornfield on the other side of the sunken lane, led by an officer on a white horse. Christopher thought it a splendid sight, with all the pomp and glory he'd imagined war being before joining the army.

Then Federal officers screamed for them to direct their fire at the approaching re-enforcements. All down the line, they gave the men in the sunken lane a reprieve and shot at the newcomers. Almost immediately, the officer and his white horse went down. Shortly after that, the line broke and ran back the way they'd come.

The artillery fire was taking its toll. Return fire from the lane had ceased completely. Colonel Sawyer yelled for the men of the 8th to rise. The incoming fire was now little more than what they had experienced in some minor skirmishes.

"Fix—BAYONETS!"

Christopher felt a thrill flutter down his spine. This was it. Soon it would be over.

The Confederate line broke first on their right, then all down the line men scrambled up the far side of the lane and ran into the cornfield beyond. The Federal soldiers on the left were first into the lane. Christopher watched as they leapt down, bayonet-tipped rifles raised to thrust. Then, instead of striking, they stopped, set down their rifles, and reached for their canteens—offering succor to the wounded.

It's really over, Christopher thought.

"At the quick step! Forward—MARCH!"

Those of the 8th Ohio still able to stand ran down the hill and into the lane, ready for anything. What they found was a charnel house. Bodies piled up like cordwood. Some had been stacked along the edge of the road for cover from the bullets the 8th had been raining down upon them for the last few hours. Blood flowed so thick, the muddy ground beneath them was red and sticky.

The smell of death was overpowering. Christopher felt nauseous, and his stomach churned. If there had been anything in it, he was sure it would have come up.

"Oh my God, what have we done?" Daniel said as he knelt beside a soldier with one cheek blown off. Christopher saw teeth sticking out from the blood and gore, but the poor man lived. His tear-filled eyes looked at them with equal measures of hope and fear.

Most had died from head wounds. Some had neat little holes with little blood, the body appearing to be in a peaceful sleep. Others had ragged, gaping holes from which blood and gray gore had spilt all over the bodies—what remained of their faces frozen in shock and horror.

Against the opposite embankment, an officer leaned back in a sitting position, his head and upper body covered in blood. Across his lap lay a saber he still clutched with both hands.

Slowly, his fingers trembling, Christopher reached out and grasped the saber. As he pulled on the sword, the fingers of the officer flexed. The blood-covered man let out a sigh that sounded full of sorrow and regret. Then he keeled over and fell face first on top of his men.

Forgetting the sword and everything else, Christopher scrambled out of the lane and, falling to his knees, dry-heaved until a trickle of bile burned his throat. He clutched his gut and let out a single sob before rising back to his feet.

"Christopher, give me a hand!"

Christopher turned and looked at Daniel, who was trying to lift the wounded man up. Christopher climbed back into the lane, careful to avoid stepping on any bodies, and grabbed the other man's arm. Together, they lifted him out of the lane and lay him on the embankment.

At once, the man started struggling as blood clogged his airway. He choked and gagged until Christopher and Daniel sat him back up. They looked around in vain for something to prop him up against, but finally had to lower him back into the lane and lean him against a pile of bodies.

"Don't worry, friend," Daniel said. "We'll make sure you get help."

Christopher looked at the bodies littering the fields in front of the lane. "Friend?" He looked at Daniel askance.

Daniel just shrugged and climbed out of the lane. Christopher followed.

By now, most of the 8th had left the lane. They had taken a few prisoners, but Christopher saw that the regiments that had gone in first were herding out hundreds of enemy soldiers and carrying captured flags. *They just got here*, Christopher thought bitterly. *Why do they get all the glory?*

Turning back to the lane, Christopher considered going back for a flag, or even that officer's sword. *The 8th deserves some recognition for what they've done this day.*

Gunfire erupted from the direction of the fields they had crossed that morning. Christopher heard the buzz of passing projectiles and knew it wasn't Federals shooting. A massive line of Confederate soldiers marched through the fields formerly occupied by the Federal troops who were now gathered around the lane, trying to take prisoners.

Officers rode up, calling for men to line up. Colonel Sawyer called out, "Eighth Ohio! Line up! Here!" He swept a line before him with his saber.

Christopher and the others ran to join their colonel.

"Guide on me!"

As he listened, it registered in the back of Christopher's mind that the colonel was addressing the entire regiment, now so small everyone who was left was close enough to hear.

"In two columns! At the quick step! Left—FACE! Forward—MARCH!"

In their haste, the normal assembly order had been ignored. Everyone had fallen in where they could. Christopher and Daniel had lined up together in the front rank, Ezra behind Christopher.

Christopher noted with relief that Charlie and Parker were still with them.

They ran onto the lane leading up to the farm they had passed earlier and turned right, following the 14th Indiana and one of the new Pennsylvania regiments.

By now, the enemy had gotten close enough to shoot with some accuracy, and they fired into the three regiments running up the lane. Several men dropped as they ran, tripping those behind.

Soon though, they stopped and turned left into a battle line that matched the width of the Confederate line that had taken them by surprise.

Colonel Sawyer called the commands for the 8th.

"LOAD!"

The enemy was right in front of them; only a single fallow field separated the two opposing forces. Yet Christopher was calm as he went through the motions of loading his rifle.

"Firing by regiment! By rank! Front rank! READY!"

Christopher brought his rifle up to a forty-five degree angle just above his cap box. He pulled the rifle hammer back to half cock and deftly flicked the old cap off the nipple with his thumb nail. He then retrieved a new cap and replaced it.

"AIM!"

Christopher raised the rifle up to his shoulder and sighted it on the man in front of him, pulling the hammer back to full cock. The enemy line disappeared in a cloud of flame and smoke as the rebels fired a volley into the Federal soldiers.

Christopher's sight wavered as his body shook. Angrily, he forced the sights back to the place where he thought the enemy soldier was behind the dissipating smoke.

"FIRE!"

Christopher fired. His rifle kicked. Not his rifle, he thought. A dead man's. His rifle lay on the slope behind them, fouled with black powder.

"LOAD! Rear rank!"

As Christopher reloaded his rifle, Colonel Sawyer took the rear rank through the same commands. Christopher was relieved when Ezra's rifle came over his shoulder to fire. It meant he still lived. It was reassuring, like the touch of Daniel's shoulder to his as they loaded their rifles.

The Federal soldiers could only fire at the enemy a few times before they were once again out of ammunition. Their lines dissolved as men rifled the cartridge boxes of the dead and wounded for rounds.

Christopher was sure it was time for the 8th to retreat. He didn't know why they hadn't already—too stubborn or too stupid, he supposed. Then, a line of fresh Federal soldiers appeared, marching across the field on the left rear of the enemy line.

Christopher pulled off his forage cap and waved it at the approaching soldiers.

Soon, the whole line was cheering the newcomers to the field. The Confederates turned to face the new threat, but as they did so, more Federal regiments appeared on the field. The Confederates broke and ran.

As the 8th stood cheering the collapse of this latest threat, a volley of artillery shells exploded over their heads. A shell exploded so close over the Galloway brothers it lifted them both off their feet and sent them tumbling along with several others.

Christopher opened his eyes to the sight of dirt and trampled clover. He sat up and swayed back and forth. The earth was bucking and heaving as if it were trying to throw him off. Around him were several other men, either sitting up or lying prone. He couldn't hear anything but a loud, high-pitched hum that made his ears and head hurt. He tried covering his ears, but that just made it worse.

His mouth was full of dirt, and he tried to spit but couldn't. He reached for his canteen but it was gone. Christopher looked down; his uniform was in shreds and he was bleeding from several places, but none of them seemed that bad. He looked around for his brother.

Daniel lay on his back five feet away. Christopher crawled toward him on his hands and knees. As he did, he saw Daniel's hand come up and cover his eyes.

"Danny! Are you all right?" Christopher cried when he reached his brother. Christopher couldn't hear himself, and apparently neither could Daniel, who just looked at him in confusion.

Christopher helped Daniel sit up, and the two brothers inspected each other for injuries. The worst they could find was a gash to Daniel's scalp that was bleeding heavily. Christopher reached for his bandanna and then remembered he'd used it to bandage Ezra's arm. Daniel retrieved his, and Christopher wrapped it around his head. Slowly, like two decrepit old men, they helped each other to their feet.

Others were being helped to their feet and escorted up the hill toward the farmstead. Miraculously, no one had been killed.

The two brothers clutched each other and straightened. Then Daniel started laughing. Christopher didn't know why his brother was laughing, but it was so infectious he joined in. Soon, tears were streaming down their blackened faces, and they clutched their sides. Pain stabbed between Christopher's ribs with each breath. He wasn't sure if he was still laughing or crying. Daniel continued to laugh, and his eyes appeared glassy and unfocused.

Eventually, after they regained control of themselves, they looked at one another and smiled.

Then Daniel's chest spouted blood, and he fell backward out of Christopher's grasp.

Christopher stood looking down at his brother, unable to move. Daniel looked up at him with pleading eyes. The pool of blood on his chest was quickly spreading.

As Christopher knelt, Daniel coughed, and blood spewed out, covering his lower face. Christopher grabbed his brother's arm and pulled Daniel's upper body onto his lap. He put his hand over Daniel's chest wound and pressed down, trying to staunch the flow of blood. He knew he was crying out for help, but he still couldn't hear anything.

He cradled Daniel's head in his left arm, his right hand still pressed down over the wound. His brother's blood flowed around his hand and soaked his sleeve. Blood from Daniel's nose and mouth soaked his other arm. There was so much blood, it flowed down and pooled in Christopher's lap.

By the time anyone answered Christopher's cries for help, Daniel was dead.

CHAPTER TWENTY-FIVE
AFTER ANTIETAM

Christopher, Parker, and Charlie lay in the meager shade of a fence in the yard outside the barn. Next to them lay Daniel's blanket-draped body. Despite the awful smell and screams coming from the barn, Ezra had gone in to have a surgeon look at his arm. He was sure they wouldn't try to amputate but, just in case, he took his bayonet with him.

Christopher's tears had stopped for the moment, and he was physically and emotionally spent. From the sun, he estimated it to be mid-afternoon. How long since they'd joined the battle that morning? Five, six hours? Two hours since they left the field. Since… And still the fighting raged all around them. The yard was full of exhausted and shell-shocked men. Most of the members of the 8th who had survived the day were there. Maybe about two hundred men. Many were inside the barn or already transported to the field hospital in Boonsboro. More than a few still lay out in the field before the sunken lane.

There were members of just about every regiment in Second Corps scattered about the yard and fields surrounding the farm buildings. All of them lying about in dirty, tattered clothes, faces and hands blackened from powder, eyes empty—seeing but not registering what was going on around them.

Shortly after retiring from the field, General French rode up on his fine steed, his uniform wrinkled from hours in the saddle but otherwise unblemished, his hands and face clean. Not bothering to dismount, he made a passionate speech from the saddle. As he spoke, his eyes glistened and his voice caught in his throat. His division, he said, was the best damn division in the whole army. For four hours they held on, unwavering. A rock against which the Confederate Army had shattered itself and around which other divisions ebbed and flowed. He was proud to lead such men and blessed them all.

As Christopher listened, hearing only every other word, he wished he could care. He wished he could take pride in what the general was saying. Four hours they endured hell—not for the general, or the army, or even the country, but for each other. Few gave in to the impulse to run because it would have left their comrades exposed and unprotected. Sure, there was more than a little fear of being branded a coward, but that only got you so far when shells exploded over your head and bullets zipped by all around. When faced with that your body would scream: better a live coward than a dead hero. But then there would be your brother, your friend and mess-mate, enduring the same as you, feeling the same as you, and as long as they didn't run, neither did you.

Four hours. They had almost made it. Christopher moaned and curled into a fetal position.

As General French spoke, Colonel Sawyer approached. His horse, someone said, had been wounded early in the battle. Sawyer didn't have the blackened face and hands of someone who had spent hours firing a rifle, but his appearance mirrored more his men's than the general's. His uniform was rumpled and dirty, with dozens of small holes and tears, and several blackened stains that Christopher took to be blood.

Sawyer didn't speak. He let the general do all the talking. But, as he surveyed what remained of his command, Christopher could see the pain in his eyes. As his eyes passed over the men, Sawyer would occasionally nod or display a small, humorless smile.

Then he saw Christopher, and the blanket-shrouded body next to him, and he stopped. For a moment, Christopher thought he would say something. For a moment, he wanted him to say something. To be his da and tell him everything would be all right. The colonel took a breath, but then paused. The breath blew out, and his whole body seemed to crumble. Without a word, Colonel Sawyer turned and walked away, head down and shoulders slumped. His adjutant followed on his heels.

An orderly came out of the barn with a bucket of limbs and added its contents to the pile by the door. He looked around and spotted Christopher and his messmates. He walked over and pointed to Daniel's corpse. "Bodies go over there," he said, pointing to a line of corpses piling up on the edge of the orchard.

"What?" Christopher said.

The orderly spotted the blood caked in Christopher's left ear and repeated himself a little louder.

Christopher shook his head. "I ain't putting my brother in no pile."

The orderly looked at Christopher with what sympathy he could still muster after the hundreds of deaths he'd seen already that day. "There's a lot of brothers over there, boy. That's where we're going to bury them for now."

Christopher's eyes narrowed. "What do you mean, 'for now'?" he asked.

"Well, I don't think Mr. Roulette would take kindly to us turning his farm into a graveyard. They'll be properly interred later. For now, we just have to get them in the ground to avoid disease."

Christopher sighed. "He stays with me."

"Listen! You can't keep him here! He needs to be buried," the orderly yelled in frustration.

He took a breath and continued. "Look at you. You're covered in blood and I bet you have a busted eardrum. If you try to stand, you'll probably wobble all over the place. Is that blood all your brother's? Or are you injured too?"

"I'm fine," Christopher said, looking at the ground. "Fine enough to bury my own flesh and blood." He looked up and met the orderly's eyes.

Parker stood up, making sure the orderly saw his sergeant stripes. "We'll help make sure he gets buried in the proper place. Are they going to make sure the graves are marked for identification later?"

"Where we can," the orderly said defensively. "If you're going to bury him, there are planks from a busted-up fence over there you can use for a marker. There probably won't be any shovels available 'till tomorrow though."

Parker nodded. "Thanks. We'll find something."

A shell exploded in a tree under which several wounded soldiers were lying. The men screamed in fear and pain as they were peppered with shrapnel and large, jagged splinters from the mangled tree. The orderly ran over to help.

Shortly after that, Ezra appeared. The right sleeve of his jacket and shirt had been cut off at the shoulder and his arm wrapped in a clean bandage. He raised his hand and wiggled his fingers. "Still attached," he said, smiling.

"Good," Parker said. "You need to put your foraging skills to work and go find us a couple shovels."

Ezra looked from Christopher to Daniel's body, nodded once, turned around and went back to the barn.

An hour later, Ezra returned with two shovels and a pickax. By this time, the fighting seemed to have shifted away from them and to the west, though the barnyard still continued to receive its share of incoming artillery fire.

Parker took a shovel, slapped Ezra on his good shoulder, and said, "Rouse, you're a miracle worker."

Ezra beamed. "It's just a matter of knowing where to look."

"And not having the scruples to care who you're taking it from," Charlie added.

Christopher looked at the digging tools with a cold fear in the pit of his stomach.

Parker knelt beside him and put a hand on his shoulder. "Christopher, we have to do this. You don't want to see what time will do to Daniel's body after he's been out in the sun for a few more hours. And we have to be the ones to do it so we can make sure the grave is properly marked."

Christopher stared back at him but made no sign he'd heard or understood. Somewhere deep inside, he knew Parker was right, but he wasn't ready to face it. He wanted to sit with his brother for awhile longer and enjoy the sunshine—despite the battle noise going on around them.

Finally, he nodded and tried to rise. His pants and jacket were coated with Daniel's blood, which had dried and hardened as he'd sat. He discovered that the blood that had soaked through his pants was mixed with shit that ran down his legs. Everything stuck to his body. As he moved, his clothing crackled and ripped from his body, taking much of his body hair with it.

Christopher stood and moved around, grimacing and wincing at the pain until he was free. Ezra took a pair of pants he'd had draped over one shoulder and handed them to Christopher. "Here, put these on."

Christopher looked at the pants and asked, "Where'd those come from?" Ezra shook his head. "Don't ask."

Ezra carried the tools, and the other three carried Daniel to the shade of an apple tree. There, they waited while Christopher took his brother's haversack and went through his pockets. He found some change and a letter from Susan Richardson. Christopher assumed everything else was in his knapsack, wherever the regiment supply wagons were. *Jonathan will be sorry to hear Daniel is dead*, Christopher thought.

As Parker loosened the earth with the pickax, and Ezra and Charlie dug, Christopher sat down to read the letter. One edge was covered with dried blood, but he was able to open the letter and read most of it. As he read the letter, Christopher discovered Susan had dumped his brother.

He felt a growing fury at the woman. She was everything to Daniel. How could she toss him off like that?

And why hadn't he said anything? Christopher looked at the postmark and realized that the letter had come while he was still in a Southern prison. Daniel had carried the burden alone all this time.

They finished digging, and the four of them together lowered Daniel's body into the grave. As his friends shoveled dirt over his brother's corpse, Christopher crumpled the bloody letter in his fist and wept.

Afterward, Parker retrieved a length of fence planking and carved Daniel's name and regiment into the wood. Then he shoved it deep into the upturned earth at the head of the grave.

Men were lighting fires all around them. The regimental officers had fresh horses and wagonloads of rations brought up. The officers sat under a shade tree, smoking cigars or pipes and sipping coffee. Kimball's brigade wasn't going anywhere that night.

The four messmates moved a little ways from the grave and dug a fire pit. Charlie built a fire while Ezra and Parker retrieved rations from the wagons. Soon, they were boiling coffee in their cups and frying salt pork and hardtack in their tin plates. Christopher didn't think he could eat, but he went through the motions.

As the sun set, the constant sound of rifle and artillery fire died down and eventually stopped. All that remained was the moans and cries of thousands of wounded men—many of them still lying in the fields amongst the corpses. Christopher slept only a few hours; he spent the rest of the night watching the glow of hurricane lamps coming from the barn and listened to the constant coming and going of stretcher-bearers.

The wails from the field haunted him like banshees in the night.

—◊—

Dear Ma and Da,

It is with a heavy heart I sit down to write you this letter. We fought a big battle the other day, the 17th of September, near Sharpsburg, Md. It is a day that will haunt me till I die. We marched onto the field, thick with bullets and shell, at nine o'clock in the morning and didn't leave until one o'clock in the afternoon. In that time, many brave men were killed.

Our regiment had just routed a rebel attack where they tried to outflank us (that means get behind us). Danny and I stood side by side during that attack, as we had most of the day, and were almost felled by an exploding shell. Miracle of miracles though, we were spared, though we both should have been pierced many times by flying pieces.

It was at that moment that my brother, my guiding light throughout my life, was snuffed out by a dastardly sniper. Yes, your beloved son, Daniel, is dead. I held him as he expired, and me and some of the boys buried him under an old apple tree on a farm outside Sharpsburg owned by a man named William Roullet.

There are quite a few boys buried there, as our regiment lost near half its number. But we marked Danny's grave well, and I am assured by

Colonel Sawyer that it will stay that way so they can all be properly interred when the time comes.

—⁕—

Christopher stopped writing and looked through the trees toward the battlefield. Though he couldn't see anything, he knew it wasn't far. Two days they had sat, doing nothing, and let the Confederate army retreat back to Virginia. He had no wish to go through another battle like the one they had just fought, but he wanted retribution and an end to the slaughter. Many of the boys were saying one big push, and Lee's entire army would fold. Then they could march to Richmond unopposed.

But instead they did nothing while the rebels slipped away in the night. Now there would be more big battles, and more men would fall by the thousands. Christopher sighed. Danny was right, McClellan was all talk.

He looked back down at the letter. There didn't seem much he could say after that. How are you? How are the girls? It didn't matter. *We're all better off than Danny.* He supposed he should make sure and tell them he was fine and not writing them from some field hospital missing a limb or two.

Later. He stood up, put the pencil in his pocket, and folded the letter in two. He was thankful Colonel Sawyer had been thoughtful enough to make sure there were paper and pencils available to whoever wanted them so they could write loved ones to let them know they were all right. Christopher appreciated it almost as much as the rations and tarps that were distributed so they would have protection from the rain.

Christopher thought about slipping away to go see the battlefield. Technically, they were still bivouacked under arms, so no one was supposed to leave, but everyone knew that was just for show. The enemy was gone, and the big bugs seemed content to let them go. There would be no more fighting around here.

Those that had seen it said the battlefield was still covered with corpses—mostly Confederates. The grave details had been working from sun up to sun down since even before there was an official ceasefire, but they kept being interrupted by photographers wanting them to pose bodies to "more accurately capture the horror of the battle."

Christopher snorted a laugh. As if a picture could capture that kind of horror.

He wondered how he would feel looking upon the enemy dead. Would he feel anger? Sorrow? Would he feel anything at all? After the initial shock and heartache, he'd felt a burning hatred for the enemy and wanted to strike back. That had made the last two days a hellish frustration that had eventually burned out to nothing. Now, he tried his best not to feel anything. It made no difference.

There would be a long and bloody war. Like it or not, he would be a part of that war. This was just the beginning. There would be more battles and more deaths.

He looked around at the couple hundred men who now comprised the 8th Ohio regiment. Only a year and a half ago, they had arrived at Camp Dennison almost one thousand men strong. But, even before the last battle, through deaths (mostly from illness) and discharges, their number had dwindled significantly. Only about half the original number had marched onto the field that day. Only half of that marched off. Some would be back once they recovered, but how many more battles like that could they survive before the 8th ceased to exist?

—⁓—

That night, the dream returned. As Christopher leaned over the bowl of gruel, he felt his ribs press against his empty belly. Before him was an enormous bulldog with Spaulding's face, its fangs dripping saliva as it growled, "What's yours is mine. Give it to me."

This time, Daniel appeared. He smiled down at his little brother and stepped between him and the dog.

"BE GONE!" Daniel cried in a booming voice.

The dog leapt, its jaws locked on Daniel's throat, and blood splashed Christopher's face.

He woke beating the air above him, shouting incoherently in rage and futility.

Once he was fully awake, Christopher reached over in the dark and put his hand on the space next to him. But it was empty.

In a camp of thousands, he was alone.

ABOUT THE AUTHOR

Tom Hicklin was born and raised in Colorado, and has had a strong interest in American history and the Civil War for as long as he can remember. After studying writing in college, he spent most of his adult life working in accounting or IT. He has since retired from the business world and, when not playing his guitar, is now concentrating on his two great passions—history and writing. He currently lives in Cincinnati with his girlfriend and partner and their two dogs. He can be contacted via Twitter (TomEHicklin) and Facebook (TomEHicklin), and for more information, visit his website at https://tomehicklin.com.